ECHOES OF A FALLEN KINGDOM

By B.T. Narro

Book 1

The Stalwart Link Series

CHAPTER ONE

Supper was ready, yet Leo's brother still wasn't home. Leo was only nine—still too young to be out alone at night. But Andar was older, thirteen and nearly a man. Father didn't seem too concerned as he sat before his plate. Perhaps Leo was wrong to be worried. Or perhaps Father was just hiding his worry again.

"He'll be here soon," Darren said and pointed at Leo's chair. "Let's eat."

Obediently, Leo sat and stared at Andar's empty chair. There used to be four places at this table, but they'd sold their fourth chair soon after Leo's mother died. He couldn't help but fear that one day they might have to sell Andar's chair as well.

Leo's brother was a thief, though Andar despised that word. "Thieves steal for money," he would say. "They don't care who they take from so long as they can sell it, but I only take food or clothes from those who don't need them as much as we do."

This was true, Leo knew. But there was no better word than "thief" for what Andar did, and unfortunately it came up more often than either of them liked.

Leo and his father ate silently for a while. Without Andar bringing anything home, their meal tonight consisted only of a watery barley soup.

Darren stood so suddenly his chair fell over, hitting the floor with a loud thunk. "I'm going out to look for him."

Was that concern Leo saw on his father's face? The lines across Darren's forehead always seemed to be there when Leo looked for them, as he did now. It was Rygen, Leo's friend, who noticed something about Darren's face that Leo hadn't been able to forget.

"Does he have bigger bones in his face?" Rygen had wondered aloud one day.

Leo had asked, "What do you mean?"

"Bigger bones than the rest of us," Rygen had specified. "And his face seems to be made out of rock. All of him seems to be made out of rock. How did he get so strong?"

Leo remembered the fear he'd heard in Rygen's voice, as if Leo's father was capable of great destruction.

There were many possible answers to her question, but Leo didn't know which one was right. His father never talked about his past, never even mentioned their mother unless Leo asked. Instead, Leo directed his questions about her to Andar, who always spoke freely about her.

Leo did not fear anything happening to his father. He just hoped Father would find Andar quickly and bring him home. Most streets were very dark during the night. It was easy to become lost.

Leo stayed at the empty table and finished his soup, though his appetite was gone. He cleaned up afterward, leaving his father's half-eaten bowl for when he returned, as well as a full one for Andar. Leo's brother and father always finished everything they could scrape off their plates or bowls. Leo sometimes left some of his helping for his brother to eat, for Andar was growing tall and would probably one day be the size of their father. Leo hoped the same for himself, but he was still small for now.

He looked at the front door, which had no lock. There were similarities to many of the houses in the city of Jatn, Leo's included. Most people who lived around here could not afford locks for their doors. The only lock in the house was the one that came with a small lockbox Andar had taken from the market years ago. It was where their father kept their money, which Darren never showed to Leo or Andar.

They could've purchased a wooden beam and built their own holders behind the door so they could bar it from the inside, but the three of them were away from the house each day. Any intruder who wanted to get in could always break through one of the weak wooden shutters that covered the windows.

There was no safe place in the house. Leo knew this. The only way to keep himself safe if his father wasn't here was by hiding or finding something to use as a weapon.

He finished cleaning up, then decided to fetch the largest knife they owned. It was nearly as long as his forearm, feeling akin to a sword. He set it on their table in the center of the small kitchen, the closest surface to the door.

Leo waited by the window. By order of those who ran the large city, no one was supposed to be out when it was dark. He could faintly make out the street in front of him. Each passerby was nothing more than a shadow. They all turned to look at Leo as they crossed by his window, making Leo wonder if he should put out the lamp on the table behind him. But he didn't want Andar or his father to have trouble finding the house. They all looked the same at night. They *were* nearly the same.

The Farmers' Guild owned all houses of this kind. Leo had lived here his whole life, but he knew enough about the world to understand that farmers were only powerful here in Jatn, and not farmer workers like him or his brother. It was the farmers who didn't actually lift a finger around the farm—the guild master, the overseers, and other men of high rank—who took the income made by the many farms within the city.

Leo palmed his thumb, pressing into the coarseness of his hand. He'd started his work at the farms four years ago, at five, an age when many other boys and girls started the same work. The harder he slid his thumb against his resistant palm, the more he tried to repress his worries. *Andar was never this late. What if Father never finds him?*

Leo jumped, startled, as he heard a crash on the roof above him. Suddenly, he was at the table with the knife in hand. He didn't recall shutting and latching the window, but it was so. He heard no movement from whatever was on his roof, but he could feel that something was still there.

It could be Andar, he realized, but why would his brother climb up onto the roof? And wouldn't Leo have heard him climbing? Instead, it sounded as if he'd landed on the roof after an impossible leap.

Perhaps it's a thief. Leo was painfully aware that he was the only one here to defend their meager belongings. Losing their robes and coin could be the end of them. He wouldn't hide. His father had taught only Andar how to use a knife, telling Leo he needed to be older. Leo would curse the thought right now if he was allowed!

At least Andar had promised he would teach Leo how to use a blade if Father didn't by the time Leo was ten. So much would change in Leo's life upon his birthday, and it was soon. Perhaps he should hide after all...no, he wouldn't.

The door opened, startling Leo again. Weapon at the ready, he spun to face his attacker but let out a relieved breath when he recognized his brother. Andar didn't notice Leo as he quickly shut the door behind him and pressed his palms against it. He struggled for breath, his wide shoulders lifting with each inhale. One hand went to his pocket with speed. He seemed about to pull something out when he looked over his shoulder and spotted Leo. Andar removed his hand from his pocket to reach for the knife.

"Give me that."

Leo handed it over. His brother kept a tight hold as he walked to the window and opened it with his other hand. He peered out silently for a moment, glancing in each direction, then closed the window and gave the same two looks to the kitchen.

"Where's Father?" Andar whispered.

"Out looking for you."

"Keep your voice down." With the knife still in hand, Andar blew out the lamp on the table. It put them in complete darkness.

Leo stood in silence, wondering why his brother didn't seem to be moving or speaking. He was too afraid to say something, for whoever was on the roof might hear it. Perhaps Andar had seen the thief and was devising a plan. He did seem to be listening for something.

There was a scream in the distance, a woman. Leo's heart trilled as a gasp came out.

"That's too far to be from Rygen's house," Andar said as if reading Leo's thoughts.

Suddenly, Leo felt something in the room with him and Andar. Leo focused his mind on it. This thing was unfamiliar, yet he welcomed its presence like a new aroma.

But something told Leo it didn't belong here, in their house. A suffocating fear came over him, stopping him from speaking. This was the only safe place for Leo's family, and Andar had just made it unsafe.

Leo knew he couldn't wrestle it from his brother, whatever it was. Andar was too strong. But he had always been honest with Leo, even when their father had not. He would answer Leo's question.

"What did you bring here?" It might've been the only time Leo had asked that question with dread rather than excitement.

It was also the only time Andar had come home with worry after having taken something. Usually his smug expression put Leo at ease. Leo wished he could light the lamp again and see that same smile, but everything was different about tonight. He knew Andar would lie.

"Andar," Leo tried again. "I know you brought something here that you shouldn't have. What is it?"

Andar still didn't answer. It was too dark for Leo to see anything, but he could hear his brother moving away from the front door and toward their shared bedroom. Leo followed.

He usually wanted to be more like Andar in every way, strong and confident, with sharp eyes and quick hands. But now all Leo felt was anger toward his brother. Andar was keeping this from Leo, which only made him more drawn to it. What *was* it? Nothing had given Leo this feeling before, as if he were a dog and his brother was teasing him with a meaty bone.

Leo needed to see it, to touch it. He followed Andar into their room. Did his brother still have the knife?

"Andar!" Leo whispered with anger.

There was another shout from outside, closer this time. It was from a man. *Not Rygen or her mother.* The scream sounded as if was out of fear or shock.

"Little brother," Andar said as he put his hand on Leo's shoulder. "I need you to be completely quiet and crawl beneath the bed."

Fear took hold of Leo's body, putting him on his hands and knees. Andar had addressed him as if desperate for Leo to obey. Neither of them had actually hidden under their beds before. It was something their father said to do when he left the house, more so when they were younger: *"If someone comes in while I'm gone, hide under your beds."*

It finally had happened, and it was Andar who had brought the danger to their house.

"Are you going to hide with me?" Leo asked.

"Yes, in a moment. Go." With his shin, he pushed Leo toward his bed. Leo crawled the rest of the way. His eyes had adjusted to the dark enough to make out his bed frame. Dust stuck to his palms as he scampered beneath it. He turned around to face outward, the stirred-up filth beneath the bed making his tongue feel dry.

Andar went to open the one window in their bedroom. He took something from his pocket and cocked his arm as if to throw it out, but he hesitated. Leo understood his brother's internal struggle, for Leo felt the same way. He knew Andar should get rid of whatever this was. And yet, Leo couldn't bring himself to urge his brother to do what he needed to do. Leo's will was weak. Hopefully Andar was stronger in this moment, as he was in everything else.

Andar grunted as he finally threw the object. Then he shut and latched the window shutters. Leo felt at ease for just a moment before worrying that now it would be close to Rygen's house.

Andar got under Leo's bed with him. Leo expected his brother to say something, but Andar was silent.

"What was that?" Leo asked.

"A gem, large." Andar whispered the words slowly, with great care. Clearly this thing was of great value. "It was weightless, as if it should float."

Leo was jealous that he'd never had the chance to touch it. But it was close, still. Although Leo could no longer feel it, Andar couldn't have thrown it too far. Perhaps they should go out to retrieve it.

No, that would put them in danger again. But if they were safe, Andar wouldn't be hiding.

"I didn't feel its weight when I lifted it," Andar said. "I felt what was within it." He paused.

"What does it have within it?" Leo asked.

Andar ignored his question.

"Andar?" Leo prodded.

"All I know is that I felt something. I don't know what."

It was the same for Leo, and he hadn't even touched it.

Another question slipped out before Leo could stop it. "Did you see where it landed?"

"No. It disappeared as soon as I threw it."

Because of the dark or because it actually disappeared? Another scream rang out from a woman who was close this time, from the sound of it. Close enough to have come from Rygen's house. Perhaps it was her mother.

Andar hurried out from under the bed and opened the window. Leo followed him and tried to see what he could. There was nothing but the night. Rygen's house was not close enough for them to see its walls.

"Should we go—?"

Andar interrupted, "Father shouldn't have gone out after me."

"Why?"

Andar gave no response. This had to be the most times in their lives that Leo had asked his brother a question that went unanswered. It was maddening. Leo pulled on Andar's shoulder to make him turn.

"What is out there?" Leo demanded.

"What—you mean who. I have no idea, but I think they want what I took."

If it was a *who* instead of a *what*, Leo doubted he would hear screaming. There were creatures that could enter this realm, summoned beasts. Andar knew this as well as Leo, but Andar chose to ignore it. They were common in stories but Leo had never encountered one. He knew it was unlikely for one to be here, but he couldn't think of anything else that would explain the screams.

Leo suddenly remembered he'd heard something land on their roof. He asked, "Did you see something on the house when you were outside?"

"What do you mean on the house?" Andar replied.

"On top. I heard something land there."

Andar sucked in a breath as he went still. He quickly closed the window. "No, I didn't. But I didn't look." Andar walked away from the window, toward the kitchen.

"What about Rygen?" Leo asked. He was too young to defend her from any danger, but he would try anyway if his brother didn't.

Andar stopped. He turned back and opened the window. "Rygen!" he shouted into the darkness. "Are you all right?"

"Yes," she called back. "What about you and Leo?"

"We are!" Andar shut the window. "See, Leo. Everyone's safe."

For now.

"Whatever was on our roof probably jumped off," Andar said.

"Or it's still there."

"*Or* it's still there," Andar agreed, clearly perturbed. "But there's nothing we can do about that right now. We'll wait for Father."

Andar walked into the kitchen and lit the lamp on the table. He still had the knife in hand as he sat, cradling it. Leo sat in the chair across from him. The light played off his brother's face, creating sinister shadows.

"Where did you get the stone?" Leo asked him.

"From the market."

Andar said no more. It was strange for him to be coy. He was rarely at a loss for words, particularly if he was trying to talk himself out of trouble. When he lied to Father, Andar usually provided a convincing story. He was the one who'd taught Leo how to lie, telling many details in a confident tone. Still, Leo had not made use of that skill as frequently as his older brother.

Andar didn't visit the market often. Because whenever he did, he came back with something that wasn't food—something of value. Father had rightfully told him that taking something beyond the price of bread was more likely to get him caught. He might escape immediately, but all it would take to be caught was for someone to see him again. *"They'll remember you better the more valuable an item you take,"* Darren had said.

"Where in the market did you see it?" Leo asked his brother.

"Just at a gemcrafter's table."

"What kind of gemcrafter?" Leo figured he knew the answer, though he wanted to hear Andar say it.

"The only type that comes to this city."

Leo stood up and glared. "Stop lying to me."

"It's true. The only kind of gemcrafter who ever comes to Jatn sells rocks that look like emeralds or rubies but everyone knows are not. No one here has money for the expensive stones, so there's certainly no reason someone with rift gems would ever come here, as you are implying."

Leo realized that Andar wasn't just lying to him. He was lying to himself.

Andar left the knife on the table as he stood. "I don't know why we're scared. No one saw me take it. No one followed me." He moved toward the window as if to open it, then stopped.

It had to be a rift gem. Or at least Andar had to think it was. He wouldn't have been so afraid otherwise. He wouldn't have thrown it out the window, nor would he have hidden under the bed.

But if it was in fact a rift stone that Andar took, then the likelihood of a summoned creature lurking on their roof was far too real. Summoned creatures were from the same place as rift stones—somewhere other than this world. Leo didn't know much about the other realm connected to this one, or whether it was just one realm or many. He'd learned most of what he knew from a book that he'd read with Rygen, but it was written as fiction: *A Summoner's Life*. Nothing from it could be taken as absolute fact.

"Are you sure no one followed you?" Leo asked. "You acted as if someone did."

"I was just being cautious."

"You don't have to lie to me, Andar. There's no reason to."

Andar eyed Leo. He opened his mouth as if he was about to speak but said nothing.

The front door opened, startling Leo once again. Anger bubbled up. He couldn't tell if it was from all the startles, from his brother's lies, or from the unending desire to retrieve the rift stone Andar had thrown out the window. Whatever it was, it made him go for the knife on the table rather than run.

But Andar was there first, grabbing it and stepping in front of Leo as if to protect him. The man entering held his bright lamp high, the glare obscuring his face.

He lowered the lamp, revealing Father's stern expression. "Expecting someone else, Andar?" he asked.

The knife reflected a yellow light as Andar lowered it. Leo stepped out from around him and spoke first. "Did you see anything on the roof?"

Worry twisted Darren's mouth about his square jaw. He stepped back through the front door and turned to gaze up at the roof. He walked out of sight, presumably to get a better angle. Andar had just started after him when Darren called out, "Bring me the knife."

Andar ran, Leo behind him.

Their father returned to their doorway and put his hand out for the knife. "Stay back," he ordered as Andar handed it over. "And shut the door."

Andar did so, then both he and Leo ran to the kitchen window. "Back up," Andar said as he got there first. "We can only open it a little."

Leo waited behind as his brother peered through the small opening he'd made in the wooden shutters.

"What can you see?" Leo asked.

"Nothing."

Someone whistled to the right—the same direction that Andar had thrown the stone. There was a scampering sound across the roof from what had to be something with more than two legs. A small crash sounded close to their bedroom. Andar ran to the bedroom window as if he was crazy enough to open it and look. Leo was going to grab his shirt to stop him, but a moment of hesitation made it too late. He followed his brother into their bedroom as Andar opened the window slightly for a look in the same direction where they'd heard the creature land—the same direction as Rygen's house.

"I still can't see anything," Andar said before Leo could ask.

Their father called out from the front, "Come here, both of you!"

Andar shut and latched the window. He was right behind Leo as they met their father in the kitchen of their small home.

"What was it?" Leo asked.

"I couldn't tell. It's too dark."

"But there *was* something?"

"Nothing for you to worry about."

It was the same thing Darren always said when Leo brought up concerns about money. He was beginning to understand this phrase better. These were things he wasn't old enough to worry about, but someone needed to.

Leo wished his brother and father would sit down and that Darren would exchange the knife for a spoon, but neither made any motion toward the table where their soup was now cold.

"What did you take?" Father questioned.

"I got rid of it," Andar said.

"When?"

Andar's gaze fell.

"Tell me everything," Darren said, his tone leaving no room for argument.

"I finished my work on the farm by the afternoon, which gave me time to go to the market."

"You were just there yesterday," Father complained. "Don't you know better than to visit the same place in a week? Especially the market, where someone is likely to see you take something."

"I know."

"Then why did you do it?"

Their father always scolded through logic. It made it impossible for Leo to argue with him, but Andar sometimes found a way.

But he apparently knew better than to do so today, when they were actually in danger.

"It was stupid," Andar admitted.

"Then why did you do it? You're not stupid."

Andar sighed. "We all know I have moments."

Leo laughed, glad to release some of his tension. With their father back, there was no reason to be afraid any longer.

Darren stopped hunching over his older son. Though he did not laugh or smile, he did seem to let out his breath as if partially relieved. He gestured at the table. "Sit and eat. It's late."

The three of them sat in their seats. No one had a designated chair, but they always sat at the same places, Leo between his brother and father. Leo watched as they looked around and apparently noticed that everything was clean.

"Thank you, Leo," his father said. "It was very helpful for you to tidy up."

"Thank you, Leo," Andar echoed in what sounded to be a genuine tone.

He and Darren ate quietly for a moment. It bothered Leo that no one seemed interested in continuing the conversation, but he was happy nonetheless. They were together. Everything would be fine.

Eventually their father asked, "Do I want to know what you took from the market today?"

"No, because it won't matter."

"Good."

No one spoke again until they had finished their soup. "Now tell me about the screams I heard from around here while I was out looking for you, Andar," Darren said.

It seemed as if everything had returned to normal—Andar would no longer be lying—so Leo let his brother answer their father's questions.

"We know nothing about them," Andar said. "Just that they came from the east, but Rygen and her mother are fine."

"East is the same direction as the market," Darren pointed out.

"A coincidence," Andar said.

"Are you sure?"

"Completely."

Leo was wrong. Andar still chose to lie. But perhaps he was right about one thing that would make his lies unimportant. Perhaps what he took wouldn't matter tomorrow, the next day, or any day after that. Perhaps tonight was the beginning and the end of all contact with that stone.

Leo no longer felt its pull. He was somewhat sad at the idea that he would never find out what the stone did or what kind of creature was on their roof, but he was more relieved.

There had been other things Andar had stolen that he'd hidden, knowing he wouldn't be able to sell them for a while. But he hadn't had to get rid of anything else that

Leo knew of, and he'd certainly never needed to lie to their father.

He still doesn't. It frustrated Leo that Andar chose to do so now, but Leo couldn't betray his brother. Andar had their family's interests in mind after all. At least Leo thought so.

"You won't go to the market for a few days," Darren demanded.

"It'll be weeks, Father."

Darren squinted at him.

"It's true," Andar said. "I have no plans to go back anytime soon."

Father seemed disappointed. "The more you lie to me, the harder it is for me to help our family."

"All right," Andar said in defeat, to Leo's surprise. He had no idea Andar had lied just then. "I'm sorry. But I'm only planning to look around. I will keep my hood on and see what I need to see. I will not take anything."

"You're still growing, Andar. Because of your size, you're recognizable even with a hood. It's the same reason I'm recognizable no matter what I do."

Why has Father ever needed to cloak himself?

"You don't want me to lie," Andar said. "This is the truth. I will go one last time, and it's only to observe. I will be safe."

"When?"

"Tomorrow morning, before the farm."

"Then you must get to bed so you have enough sleep."

Andar stood. "All right."

No one in their small house spoke until Leo and Andar were under the covers of their beds. Leo whispered across the room to him, "Are you going to bury the gem somewhere tonight?"

Andar quickly got up. He walked to the door frame and peered out toward their father's bedroom. After a quick glance, he came back and closed the door.

He whispered to Leo, "We need to forget about that gem. I never had it."

Earlier it was just a stone—a solid, which was a term for anything natural to this world. But Andar had described it now as a gem, a word more commonly used for rift gems.

"You said it was a solid earlier."

"I never said that exactly," Andar argued.

"You said it never could be a rift gem because no one would sell rift gems in Jatn."

"It wouldn't make sense for someone to come to the market with one."

"Unless they found it near the city," Leo said.

Andar didn't reply. Perhaps he had figured the same thing.

"Leo, it's too late for us to speak about this any longer," Andar finally said.

"You agree, don't you?"

"No, you're quite wrong."

"How?"

Andar sighed. "I don't have it in me to explain, but rift gems are not found. They are made."

"They *are* found," Leo argued. "They come from rifts."

"They don't come through rifts whole." Andar grumbled. "You're not going to let me sleep until I explain, are you?"

Actually, Leo would. But when his brother phrased it like that, he didn't see a reason to disagree. He was silent as he waited for Andar to continue.

"Most rift gems are made from stones that summoners relocate to our realm using a rift, but many of these stones can't do anything yet. It's only after a master gemcrafter infuses the gem with Artistry that it becomes what we call a rift gem."

"And then the gem can be used by a mage to make links?"

"Yes. That's another reason I don't think I was holding a rift gem. You seem to have felt what I felt. It was almost alive. I don't see how someone could use it. All I can imagine is *it* using someone." He sighed again. "I guess I don't think it's a solid after all. But it's not a rift gem, either. Perhaps it's a summoner's stone. Eh, I'm just torturing myself wondering. I'm never going to find out."

Leo had read about a summoner's stone in *A Summoner's Life*. Andar had read the same book, but there wasn't much to go on. Not only was the book fiction, it focused more on the strife between a good and evil summoner, not on Artistry and gems. The stone, in the book, was just something each summoner held while summoning. It seemed to help, but Leo didn't know why.

"So you're not going to bury the gem somewhere tonight?"

"No. I'm leaving it alone. It's too dangerous to be near again."

"Then what are you doing at the market tomorrow?"

"I have to get another look at the seller."

"Why? What did he look like?"

"It was a woman. She was hooded, and her shop was in the shadows. I didn't think much of it at first because I was too focused on the gem. But now I'm realizing she was probably hiding herself, as if she was selling stolen goods."

"Then she won't be there tomorrow," Leo said.

"Which would prove my theory." Andar turned in bed to face the other way as if he was done speaking.

"And what would that do?" Leo wondered aloud.

"Satisfy a curiosity."

When Andar offered no other words, Leo grunted in annoyance and turned to face the opposite wall. "Stop lying to me, Andar," he mumbled.

He knew his comment had been loud enough for Andar to hear, but his brother didn't reply.

CHAPTER TWO

Rygen didn't usually return home this early, but she had made sure to finish her work at the Bookbinding Guild quickly. She wanted as much time as she could get for her and Leo to read the newest book she'd acquired. It had taken a lot of pleading and a few promises, but it was now hers, at least for a little while.

The guild master of the Bookbinding Guild would ask for it back after a few days, most likely, but she figured she could read it through at least a few times before then. She just had to invite Leo over here for the first read.

It wasn't so much that they read together. It was more that they read *against* one another. They would sit side by side on Rygen's bed with her brightest lamp at the bedside table. Each of them would read the two visible pages as fast as they could. The first one to finish would say they were done. They were still allowed to look at the pages. When the other person had finished, that person closed the book and would ask the first question. It had to be about something they'd just read. Usually Leo was second to finish reading, so he would ask the first question. If Rygen answered correctly, she received a point. It was her turn to ask a question next. The first person to two points would win, then they would go on to the next two pages.

The competition started only last year, when Rygen was allowed to begin working at the Bookbinding Guild at nine years old, a year earlier than the requirement for most children. Gartel, the guild master, was friends with Rygen's mother, though they didn't seem to be friends much anymore. He used to come by their house quite often, sometimes even stay overnight, but now they didn't seem to speak much. Rygen didn't mind. Gartel was still nice to her so long as she treated his books and his shop with care, as she always did.

The book in her hands was a true tale of history, her favorite kind of story. She read the title aloud to practice her dramatic voice for Leo, for it was always his first question about the book, and she could sometimes earn an excited laugh from him.

"Quim and Kin: Crowns and Betrayal."

Ever since Rygen's mother and Gartel had been teaching Rygen history, they'd enticed her with this story—a recent event that everyone already knew except for her. It was only a little over ten years ago when the story began, just after she was born. Everyone the age of her mother was alive at the time, and it was all they could speak about when the drama was real. Rygen's mother had given her hints as to what the story was about: kings and powerful families, and the most monumental betrayal in history. All it did was make Rygen want to find out more.

She was so eager to begin that she pretended not to notice the pile of clothing her mother had gathered together and stacked in the corner of Rygen's room. No, not today. Was it really her turn? She ignored the thought as she went into her mother's room, which had the only mirror in their home. Tiny and circular, the mirror on the wall was just bigger than Rygen's palm. She and her mother had saved up for months to purchase one. It was clean and beautiful glass, and it would always remain that way so long as no one took it.

Rygen's face and hair were still clean from her bath that morning, a perquisite of working at the Bookbinding

Guild. Her blonde hair was long and messy, in need of a cut. It sometimes tangled near her arms as she put meticulous care into folding parchments and attaching the gatherings. She wished her hair covered more of her large forehead, but she wouldn't be able to see unless she parted it to frame her face instead, as she always did.

She always expected people to stare at the top of her head, but they looked into her gray eyes instead. She sometimes wondered whether they saw her face the same way that she did. Or perhaps it was just this tiny mirror that made her forehead seem so large. She'd asked her mother what she thought, but Verona hardly even glanced at Rygen before saying she was as cute as a puppy and shouldn't worry.

Most children, like Leo and Andar, worked on farms here in Jatn. She used to do the same until last year. Just like the boys, she used to always return home looking as if she'd wrestled in the dirt. The boys didn't seem to mind the dried mud on their clothes or the smudges on their cheeks as much as Rygen did. She saw Leo often, and there were even times that she'd notice stains of blood on his pants or sleeves. But he never complained about any of it, at least not to her.

It used to make her wonder if he actually enjoyed his work on the farm, but she stifled that silly curiosity long ago. Leo had since made it very clear that books would be his future, as they would for Rygen.

It was no use for Rygen to try to see how clean her clothes were using the tiny mirror. She glanced down instead at her dress and took it in her hands, twisting to see each side. It was the last clean item in her wardrobe. The rest of her garments were sitting in a pile on the floor, her mother's mixed in.

"Dammit," she said. She only cursed when her mother wasn't around and when there was no better word to describe her torment. Try as she might, Rygen couldn't ignore her mother's silent request to clean their robes. She went over to her bed and hid the book under her pillow. Perhaps if she hurried to finish her task, she and Leo still might have time to read tonight.

*****

It was late when Rygen returned from the river. She had rolled back a heavy barrel filled with their wet clothing. Her mother was preparing supper but stopped to help Rygen hang the heavy garments. It was warm enough that night that the clothing could dry indoors, where it would be safe from thieves. They opened the two windows on opposite walls and hung their robes over the string that ran across their small kitchen, then they sat and ate.

Rygen was tempted to rush, as there still might be a few moments she could steal that night to read with Leo. But the few times she had tried, her mother had scolded her and explained that it was rude.

"Thank you for washing today," Verona said. "I'll make sure I have enough time to do it next."

"Gartel finally let me borrow *Quim and Kin: Crowns and Betrayal*."

"Oh he did?" her mother replied with a gasp and an overenthusiastic drop of her mouth. It was these responses that made Rygen most feel like a child, but she could never be angry at her mother. "I hope you thanked him."

"I did, many times." *As well as promise to complete extra work for a week as soon as he asks for it back.* "I know it's late, but can I read with Leo tonight?"

"You can read it with him tomorrow after you come back from the binders' guild."

"I don't have long with the book."

"When does Gartel want it back?"

"Soon, he said. It could be after two days."

"Gartel will give you longer than that," Verona said. "It's too late to read with Leo tonight." She looked back at her supper as if not expecting a reply.

Rygen knew there was no point of arguing. She had only one other book besides the one she'd just received. It was a gift from Gartel for her tenth birthday, not long ago. *"A Summoner's Life,"* it was called, a fictional tale about a woman who was not human but Analyte. Like most people, Rygen knew little about the Analytes and the summoners. She figured at first that a book on this subject would be highly valuable, even if it was fiction. It was well-written and at least as long as most of the books she binded at twenty pages. It had no illustrations like some of the others, but that shouldn't stop someone from buying it.

She'd seen Gartel trying to sell it for months before he wrapped it and gave it to her on her birthday. While she still appreciated the gift, for she did enjoy the book, the gesture was dampened by his inability to sell it. But more than anything, it made her curious. Why didn't anyone want to buy that book? The title caught many eyes in Gartel's shop, but whenever those people asked what the story was about, they became disinterested after Gartel told them.

Mother seemed to know the answers to many questions, so Rygen had asked her recently why this was.

Verona let her gaze fall, no doubt revealing she knew the answer, but she stayed silent. It took Rygen some prodding to finally get the answer. The fathers in most families took charge of the coin, and most of them were uninterested in a story about a woman, especially one who was an Analyte.

"Why?" Rygen had asked, for it made no sense to her.

"You have to remember that those who have the coin to buy books lead different lives than we do," her mother had said. "They believe their difference in class is because they are better than us, even though they are not. The men especially are not like Leo's father. Gartel has some of what I'm describing. Have you noticed how he acts toward people who cannot read?"

"Yes. Like they are beneath him." Rygen knew that it was extremely rare that anyone living in houses belonging to the Farmers' Guild, like hers and Leo's, would be able to read. She and Leo had only learned because his father had taught them. Mother learned later, from Gartel, but she was slow and didn't have the same interest in books as Rygen did. Rygen could never think illiterate people were beneath her. She could have been one of them had Darren chosen another house for his boys.

As Rygen went to her room to fetch her book about the Analyte summoner, she heard someone screaming in the distance. It came from the east. The one window in her bedroom didn't point that way, so she hurried to the kitchen. Her mother was already looking out, but it was too dark to see anything.

Rygen heard someone running toward her house. They seemed to be on the only road that ran between many of these identical buildings, but she couldn't see anyone. Hoping to see who it was as he or she passed by,

Rygen held the brightest lamp she and her mother owned up to the windowsill.

Suddenly something landed on their roof. Rygen didn't realize she should be scared until she noticed the fear in her mother's face. Verona took the lamp with one hand and closed and latched the window with her other. She ushered Rygen away and into the doorway of Verona's bedroom, looking up all the while as if expecting something to break through the shoddy roof.

There was movement from whatever was above them, quick little steps as if it had four feet. Rygen figured it was a rift creature, though she didn't know how she'd arrived at that conclusion. She had never seen or heard one before, but she'd read about them in the book Gartel had given her. She was curious to see it, not afraid like her mother.

"Rygen! Do you hear me?" Verona asked in a panic.

Realizing she'd been removed from herself, Rygen suddenly became aware that her mother was pulling her into her room.

"Keep your window closed and hide under your bed." Verona said. She remained in the kitchen, checking the roof.

There was a holder for one wooden plank for the front door. Mother had bought the nails and the metal holders from the market and installed them herself. They'd never had to use them to set the wooded beam across the door until now.

Rygen felt an intense need to glimpse the creature. She might never have another chance. She started toward the front door. Her mother grabbed her.

"What are you doing?" Verona shrieked. "Why aren't you listening?" Her eyes glistened.

Terror gripped Rygen, seizing her voice as she tried to reply. Something had taken hold of Rygen. It had pushed away all emotion except curiosity to meet this creature, almost making her set foot outside their home. Fearful she would lose herself again, she ran back into her bedroom and finally found her voice.

"I'm getting beneath my bed," she told her mother.

She ducked low near her bed but stopped herself, her teeth on her lip. Her curiosity won out over her dwindling fear. She went to her window and opened it. During the day she could see Leo's house from here. Now the earth between them was all she could make out, the land in shadow. She knew she should be hiding with the window closed, but she couldn't help it.

Rygen listened for other screams, but there were none. She crouched low to look up as high as she could, wondering if she might see the face of this creature peering down at her. She didn't know how close it was. It hadn't moved for a little while.

Then she heard its steps as it went from the center of the roof toward the edge above her. The shadowed shape of a large catlike beast jumped down and landed on the black ground. It started toward the darkness and leapt marvelously high before she lost sight of it.

"I think it's gone," Mother called from the kitchen.

"I saw it," she told her mother.

Her mother noticed the window and quickly ran over to close it. "Rygen, I told you—"

"It's going toward Leo's house. We have to warn them."

There was another scream, this one closer, but it didn't seem to be from Leo's house.

"We are not leaving this house," Verona said.

"They might need our help."

"Darren can handle whatever it is." She shut the window and stared at Rygen for a moment. "What did you see?"

"Just a cat," she lied after some thought. Perhaps this way Mother would let them go after it.

Her mother folded her arms. "A cat cannot jump high enough to land on our roof, and that sounded much heavier than a cat."

"It looked more like the size of a dog." Though it was too different for it to be one. The creature didn't seem to have a tail and it was larger than any dog Rygen had ever seen. It probably wasn't much taller than a dog, though its legs were thicker and stronger.

They heard another women's scream, the closest one yet. Rygen figured she would be able to see the woman if she went to one of the kitchen windows, but she knew her mother would never let her.

Fear came out from wherever it was hidden before. Rygen was not going to see this creature again, she realized, and it was time to worry. *Something really is happening out there, something that might find its way in here.*

She and her mother had no means to defend themselves. Mother might've been realizing the same thing, for she looked around as if at a loss about what to do.

Mother grumbled what might've been a curse. "I suppose we do have to see what's happening if we can. It went this way right?" She carefully opened the window Rygen had looked out of earlier.

"Yes."

Rygen's heart pounded. She supposed she had always figured her mother would protect her against any danger, but Verona was not at all like Leo's father.

Rygen had never known her own father, but for the first time in her life she yearned for his strong presence. Her mother was not large, not strong physically. It had never mattered before, but as Rygen had learned from stories, all it took was one moment—one failure—for the hero's life to change forever.

Rygen strained her eyes to look out her window. She heard her loud breathing, but it wasn't as loud as her mother's, who stood with her arm around Rygen.

Eventually, the tense moment passed without incident. Perhaps it was over. Still, she and her mother couldn't tear their eyes away from the shadowed land. Rygen might've been able to make out the outside wall of Leo's bedroom by then unless her eyes were tricking her.

She heard something land in the dirt not far from her window. It was too soft a sound to startle her, as if it was a small stone. But it did send her and her mother away from the window.

"What was that?" Rygen asked.

"I don't know." Mother went back to close and latch the window. She took Rygen's hand and led her to the kitchen. "We'll wait here until we don't hear anything else."

There was another shriek, this one right outside their house. It was on the other side of Rygen's bedroom window, though, on the street side.

She knew there was nothing she could do to keep them safe, but if she at least knew what it was they were afraid of, perhaps she and her mother could formulate a plan.

They were quiet again, listening. Rygen heard something scamper across the dirt outside. It sounded like a heavy beast. *The summoned.*

It darted past Rygen's house and soon could no longer be heard. For whatever reason, she wasn't afraid of the beast, though she knew she should be. It didn't seem interested in getting into any of these houses, only on top of them as if to scout for something. It was the master of this creature that Rygen feared. Who was he or she and what were they doing here?

Why was she so sure it was a summoned? It was more likely to be an unfamiliar animal. But it was something she felt that told her otherwise. She couldn't explain it, even in her own thoughts.

"Rygen!" shouted someone. "Are you all right?"

She recognized the voice as Andar's. It seemed to be coming from his home.

Rygen ran to open her bedroom window. "Yes," she called into the darkness. "What about you and Leo?"

"We are!" Andar shouted back.

She waited for more, but it was all he said. Perhaps he was the one who'd thrown whatever had landed near the outer wall of Rygen's bedroom. If Andar and Leo were concerned for her, then whatever that item was must have something to do with this. But were the boys too afraid to come over and check on her? They only shouted. She couldn't help but feel disappointed, especially because Darren had not come. He shouldn't be afraid of anything, given his size.

"We must keep this closed," Rygen's mother told her as she shut the window once again. "Get in bed, Ry, and go to sleep. I will stay up to ensure you're safe."

Rygen wanted to ask how her mother intended to do that with no weapons, but questions with no answers were better left unasked. Her mother stayed in her bedroom as she shut the door. Rygen got into bed and clutched her new book against her chest. Her mother sat at the foot of her bed and stared at the window. Rygen promised herself that as soon as she was old enough to do so, she would find a way to protect their family, for she couldn't bear this feeling a moment longer.

CHAPTER THREE

It was the time of year for pruning the fruit trees to ensure they grew and produced more fruit. This was not a job for Leo. He was too young, though his brother was old enough to take on the difficult task. Leo spent his days wishing he could climb the trees with shears in hand instead of weeding the ground with no tools, no gloves. He hadn't "earned" either of them yet, for he hadn't been working at the farm long enough. Having labored on this farm since he was six years old, he didn't understand what else he needed to do.

Leo had not mentioned anything about last night to his brother. They usually didn't speak much during their walk to the farm anyway, as both were often too tired, but last night had been unusual. It had been exciting, and not in a good way.

Leo figured this morning might have the same dark excitement, for whatever had happened last night didn't feel resolved. Andar had left the house before Leo, probably to visit the market as he had told their father he would. He had just gotten back when it was time for Leo to leave for the farm, but Andar didn't say one word.

At the farm, a few of the sheep looked ready to be sheared. It was something Rygen used to do when she spent her days here with Leo and Andar. Rygen had received an early acceptance to the Bookbinding Guild a year ago, after proving her care for books and ability to bind them together. Leo would have his turn to prove himself in a week. The meeting with Gartel, the bookbinding guild master, was already scheduled for the day of Leo's tenth birthday.

Leo had never met Gartel, but he knew much about the guild master from Rygen. Gartel used to be friends with Rygen's mother. *Well, not friends exactly,* Leo thought as he plucked out a weed. But that was the word Rygen tended to use. Gartel had refused to meet with Leo when he'd turned nine, as Gartel had done with Rygen. She promised Leo that she'd told Gartel just how much Leo loved and cared for books. He was good with his hands as well, she'd relayed to Gartel, but it was still no use. Gartel said Leo would have to wait until he was ten before they would meet.

Ever since Rygen left the farm, the only fun Leo had there was with his brother. But Andar had been more reserved ever since their farm master had assigned a reeve, a six-year-old girl, to watch for anyone who was slow in fulfilling their duties.

The little reeve, named Chay, wanted to catch Andar stealing. She had made the mistake of telling him, and that the farm master had offered her a reward if she did. She wasn't the smartest child, but it wouldn't matter even if she was precocious. Andar never stole anything from the farm. He was smart enough not to risk his hand being cut off at his wrist.

Leo didn't see why the farm master suspected Andar. Nothing had gone missing, that Leo was aware of, and the farm master had no way of knowing that Andar thieved when he left the farm.

They were given bread for lunch that day. Leo found his brother in one of the barns, where they could eat in shade and privacy. The smell of animal waste kept most others out, but lunch was never anything delicious anyway, so it didn't matter much to them.

They ate quietly until the large barn door started to open outward. It got stuck after just a few inches as a girl grunted in strain from the other side. The door tended to drag on the ground, making it more difficult to open the more dirt it gathered at its base. The girl didn't seem to realize this, struggling to pull it open rather than kicking the dirt free.

She squeezed her body into the small opening but soon got herself stuck. She wiggled and groaned until she fell into the barn.

"So sly," Andar teased. "You'll be a spy for the king one day, no doubt."

She didn't seem to understand his sarcasm, squinting at him with confusion as she got herself up and dusted off. "You steal anything yet, Andar?"

"Shut the door and come over here, and I'll tell you a secret."

Chay turned and tried to pull the door by its rusted handle, but she couldn't free it from the dirt. Eventually it broke free and slammed shut. She fell backward and rolled over. Seemingly without shame, she got up and even ran to Andar and Leo as they sat on bales of hay. Chay huffed, her cheeks red.

"What's the secret?" she asked.

"First you have to promise not to tell anyone."

"I promise."

"Even if it's about something I stole."

"I promise."

"But you promised the farm master you would tell him if I stole something," Andar pointed out.

"I..." No other words came out of her mouth, which hung wide open.

Andar laughed. "Relax, Chay, it's not about something I stole."

"Then you can tell me?"

He nodded. "It's about you."

"Me?"

"About why the farm master really has you watching me."

"To catch you stealing."

Andar shook his head. "That's what he will continue to tell you, so you must not mention this, but the truth isn't that he expects you to catch me stealing. It's that he expects you to *keep* me from stealing."

She thought about his words for a moment, but her confused expression never changed. "What do you mean?"

"He knows I'm not going to steal anything if you're watching me," Andar explained. "Which is true. I never will. So you will never get your reward. He knows this—he's using you."

She let out a raspy breath.

"The only way you're going to get your reward is if you trick the both of us. You have to stop watching me for a while, make me forget that you're trying to catch me stealing. Once I have forgotten, you can start watching me again, but you have to make sure I don't see you doing it. You especially must not speak to me. Only then might you catch me stealing something. You understand?"

"Yes."

Andar stared at her for a moment. "Well, then why are you still here?"

Chay turned and sped toward the door. She had the same trouble with it as before, getting stuck halfway out and eventually tumbling out of sight. The door closed with her grunting from the other side, and soon it was quiet again.

"That should buy me a few days of peace," Andar said.

"Do you know what her reward is for catching you?"

"I'm sure the only thing offered to her is a lie. You know how the farm master is." Andar finished the last of his bread and got up. "Come on," he said. "Perhaps we can convince the farm master to send us off early if we start work again now."

Andar had just finished reminding Leo of how the farm master was. Leaving early was extremely unlikely, no matter how hard they worked during their break. But Leo didn't bring it up. He knew Andar was trying to avoid a conversation about last night, and Leo gladly remained silent. He didn't want to have to lie to his brother about what he had done after Andar had fallen asleep.

Andar returned to climbing and trimming the trees while Leo plucked weeds. Leo spent the afternoon bored, with many questions from last night. What was that stone, really? What creature was on their roof? Did anyone fetch the stone, or was it still out there? It didn't seem as if Leo would ever find out the answers to his questions, except for the last one. He had gone out to search for the stone sometime during the night, after a brief sleep.

He shuddered as he remembered leaving his house without a lantern. It was so quiet that his footsteps seemed thunderous. He moved slowly across the dirt between his home and Rygen's. The stone had to be there unless someone had come to get it already.

He knew he had to be lucky to find it without light, but he couldn't bring a lamp. He didn't want to risk being seen by his brother and especially not by anyone else looking for the gem. There were men besides the guards of the city that he feared, men with great powers.

He searched for an hour, often close enough to Rygen's house to see the wall of her bedroom. Perhaps she had caught sight of something that would help him find the gem again.

When he thought he heard someone coming, it scared him into returning to his bed. Andar was still asleep when Leo got himself under his blanket.

The reeve was nowhere in sight the rest of the day, but the farm master, Rhenol Gale, approached Andar in the evening.

"Get down here," Rhenol demanded. "Hurry."

Leo clenched his teeth as he watched. Andar was at least high enough in an apple tree to possibly break something if he fell, though he *had* surprised Leo many times before, leaping out of trees with shears in hand and landing uninjured.

He threw the shears onto the ground, close enough to Rhenol's feet for Leo to let out a squeak of fear. Andar froze with wide eyes, perched on a limb, as he watched the shears bounce just past the farm master.

"You're very lucky those didn't touch me," Rhenol called up to him.

It was true. If they had, Rhenol could've accused Andar of striking his farm master. The punishment was jail or a whipping, depending on what the farm master wanted. It was an amazement to Leo that Andar hadn't been whipped yet.

Andar jumped down, rolling as he landed. He looked toward Leo as he came to a stop. Was Andar showing off for him? Leo shook his head at his brother.

Leo lowered his head as the farm master turned for a glance his way. He didn't look back up until he heard the farm master speaking to Andar again.

"Birds are gathering." Rhenol pointed up at a small flock circling the sky above the farm. "Some have already tried poaching my seeds. You will run to the western section of the farm and scare off any in that area."

"What about a drum?" Andar asked.

"All are already in use." The farm master put his hand on his hips. "Don't stand there staring at me like a fool. Go!"

Andar still didn't move. Leo found himself running over to break up the inevitable argument. The farm master angered Leo every time he spoke to any of his workers, but it was Andar's replies that infuriated Leo the most. His brother never did what he was told without talking back or at least making it difficult for the farm master. He had been cuffed by Rhenol a few times because of this, but it never seemed to affect Andar's attitude. If anything, it made him disobey even more.

"I could scare off the birds," Leo offered. He stopped before the farm master and bowed his head. "Sir," he added.

Leo didn't get annoyed or embarrassed chasing after the birds, shouting and clapping his hands. It was much better than plucking weeds, and it didn't leave his back sore at the end of the day. Most of those who were tasked with an easy assignment like scaring birds were younger children, usually even younger than Leo. Andar was the only one older than ten who had to do it.

Leo noticed how the workers looked at Andar as he made noise to scare off the birds. They figured he was there out of punishment, but Leo knew the farm master better than they did. He just enjoyed embarrassing Andar, as he did anyone. The difference between Andar and most of these workers was that it actually worked on him.

Leo had asked his brother why he was ashamed of some of the tasks he had to do around the farm. All Andar would say was that he was too old to do them, as if Leo was supposed to understand that. There were plenty of workers—most of them, in fact—who were older than Andar.

"No, Leo," Rhenol replied, his tone as if Leo was dimwitted. "I want your brother scaring off the birds until day's end."

Andar started to jog off.

"Wait!" Rhenol called after him. "What are you forgetting?"

Andar turned around and immediately went for the shears. He didn't look up to meet the farm master's eyes as he handed them off, blades first. As soon as they were taken from him, Andar ran west again.

Leo quickly returned to his patch of weeds without a glance at the farm master. He was glad when Rhenol didn't follow him over.

There were many farms like this one in the city of Jatn, often surrounded by dirt roads and shabby homes. The farmland seeped into the city life, where the walls of nearly identical homes built practically on top of each other acted as fences in some areas to keep the livestock from getting out. There was no privacy for these people, and the smells they had to put up with were the same that all farmers got used to over the years.

Rhenol controlled this farm, but only that. There were many farms throughout the city. Leo didn't think that the other farm masters could be like Rhenol, but his father had told him otherwise. There was nothing even Leo's father could do about this. The Farmers' Guild controlled too much here in Jatn.

"Why don't we move to another city?" Leo had asked. He regretted the question when his father couldn't seem to answer.

"We will one day," Darren had finally replied.

It was later that Andar had revealed something to Leo that their father had kept from him.

"Father wasn't born in the city."

"He was," Leo had argued. "He told me."

"It's a lie, but don't bother yourself wondering why he would lie about it. I tried to get him to tell the truth. He won't."

"When did you speak about that with him?"

"When you were a baby, and several times throughout the years. He wanted to wait until you were older to tell you, but you're old enough now."

It was this year that his brother had told him this. Leo agreed that he was old enough. *Both* of them were old enough to know the truth, no matter what it may be. At first Leo had thought that Andar might be the one lying, not their father, but it was this event that made him realize later that he trusted his brother more than anyone else. Even more than their father, although it didn't feel right to admit it.

It wasn't like Father to lie, but one question kept coming back to Leo's mind—and it wasn't why Father would lie about being born in Jatn. It was why anyone would move to Jatn. Most of the people here were trying to leave but didn't have the means to make it to another city.

It was one of many questions that went through Leo's bored mind during the days he spent on the farm. One could be answered, though, by his brother. One day, Leo had asked it.

"How did you find out Father had lied?"

"Because I wasn't born here, either. I have some memories of traveling. I remember Mother being there. I think I was three or four. We had to be headed to Jatn, because I would've remembered if we ever left the city later, but it never happened."

Leo had been tempted to bring it up with their father, thinking that maybe Darren would tell him the truth even if he hadn't told Andar, but why would that be the case? Besides, Leo could never betray Andar's trust like that. He'd promised his brother he wouldn't bring it up, because Andar was not supposed to have told him.

At the end of yet another hard day, Leo waited in line behind dozens of dirty workers for the day's wage. He didn't see his brother until he was nearing the front of the line, when Andar joined him rather than taking his spot at the back. Leo looked back, worried to find scowls upon the faces of the older men behind him. Their expressions were exactly what he figured he would see, but none of them spoke up.

It was the farm master's wife who paid the wages at the end of the day. This was the only interaction Leo had ever had with her, and he never heard her speak a word. She was an overweight woman at least twenty years younger than the wizened farm master. She looked at each worker with a heavy gaze as she handed off dirty little coins, as if she thought the hard-working folk were taking what she had earned with *her* knees in the dirt.

Leo pocketed his coins and walked out of the farm with his brother. Andar revealed his plan for the evening. "I'm going to the baker's because I'm very hungry, and we don't have enough to pay for what I want to eat."

Leo knew Andar would also buy what he could with their measly coins, so Leo handed over his earnings without complaint. He then walked home on his own, his many questions running through his head.

Father was already home when he arrived, with some cooked carrots in a pot on the table. They were one of the few sweet things they could afford to eat. Leo salivated at the sight.

His father would tell him to change out of his dirty clothing first if Leo sat at the table, as he had attempted on so many evenings, so Leo went to his room and put on his loose yet clean pants and shirt. He always did feel better after he changed, just as he would if they had enough water to spare for him to wash his hands.

It wasn't long before Andar showed up with a loaf of bread. Leo already had bread for lunch, but at least this one looked warm. Andar must not have taken anything, though, for their coin was enough to buy this loaf. But after Andar set it on the table, he reached into his pockets and pulled out three greasy chicken legs, already cooked and even seasoned with salt, it appeared.

Leo was too excited to care that his brother had taken this, knowing it was not from the hands of someone as hungry as they were.

"You're going to wash that coat tomorrow," Darren said as he set one chicken leg on each of their three plates.

"Yes, sir."

They ate quickly. It only took a few moments for their father to finish first. "What did you find out about last night, Andar?" he asked.

"Nothing. The woman was not at the market this morning, and I heard no one talking about it."

"I asked our neighbors this morning," Darren said. "They heard the screams but nothing else."

"Did you speak to Rygen's mother?" Leo asked.

"Yes. They are fine, and Rygen will knock as soon as she is done with supper. She has a new book."

At hearing that, Leo finished quickly. He wanted as much time as he could with Rygen. Hopefully, she would come soon.

CHAPTER FOUR

Rygen knocked on the door as Leo was cleaning up with his family. Leo opened the door. Rygen always had an expression as if there was so much she wanted to say, with keen eyes as if these words would enlighten Leo.

"Hello—!" Leo looked over his shoulder and frowned as he saw his father watching. He turned back to Rygen and bowed stiffly. "Madam."

She curtsied. "Sir."

Leo hated how his father made them *both* do this. Sure, Leo had seen men and women greeting each other in the streets and in shops the same way, but these people were not him and Rygen. Darren wouldn't stop referencing how Leo was a boy and Rygen was a girl when giving instructions on how to behave. Leo was sick of it. She was his friend. Besides, he followed none of his father's advice whenever they were out of sight, and Rygen was more comfortable because of it.

"I invite you to join me at my home so that we may read together," Rygen said in her formal voice that made Leo want to roll his eyes.

Leo asked his father, "May I go?"

"Yes."

He told Rygen, "I accept your invitation."

But before Leo could step outside, his father asked, "What's the name of this one, Rygen?"

"*Quim and Kin: Crowns and Betrayal*," she told him flatly, as if the title of this book wasn't the best one Leo had heard yet. Rygen looked disappointed, though Leo didn't understand why.

"May we go?" Leo asked again. But as he turned to his father, Leo found a look that made him pause. Darren stared at Rygen with his head cocked.

"Can you repeat that title?" he asked her.

She told him again, this time with uneasiness in her voice.

"Did you get this from Gartel?"

She nodded fearfully.

"Why do you care about this book, Father?" Andar asked. He squinted as if suspecting something.

Leo felt the same suspicion. Their father usually only feigned interest in the stories that Rygen brought from the Bookbinding Guild. It was something more than the alluring title that caused this reaction, something about the words themselves.

"Do you know who Quim is?" Leo asked, for his father still hadn't answered his brother's question.

"That's why I'm interested, Andar," he said as he shot looks back and forth between him and Leo. "The Quims—they are a family, Leo, who everyone old enough has heard of because of their past involvement with the king. But I didn't know a story had been written about them." Darren suddenly seemed less interested as he busied himself with kitchen work. "The two of you may leave, but don't stay late, Leo."

"Thank you." He escorted Rygen out before they could be stopped by any other delays. After seeing his father's interest in the book, Leo couldn't help but take Rygen's hand and run with her. "Let's go!"

She giggled as they rushed down the street. "I haven't started reading it yet. I hope you know how difficult that's been!"

"How long have you had the book?"

"Since yesterday."

"Oh, gods!"

Leo didn't know how Rygen could've waited that long, but then he suddenly recalled everything that had happened last night. Perhaps it hadn't been so hard after all. He glanced at the open field of dry dirt between their homes. It wasn't that large an area in the light, but trying to search across it for a small stone in the dark made it seem like it stretched for miles.

They entered Rygen's home. It was nearly identical to Leo's, three small rooms. Her mother was cleaning up in the kitchen. Leo didn't want to disappoint his father, so he bowed to Verona and greeted her. "Thank you for allowing me to come over, madam."

"You're welcome, Leo." She grinned as if stifling a laugh. She had the same prominent cheeks and sharp jawline as Rygen, but her eyes always appeared more distant than her daughter's, which seemed to draw Leo in whenever Ry revealed her thoughts.

Rygen's room was already prepared for their reading competition, with her bedside table positioned near the middle of her bed, a bright lamp atop it. The book sat on the bed, waiting to be opened. Leo ran and jumped onto Rygen's bed. He grabbed the book as she lunged for it.

"No!" she said with a laugh.

He opened it and ran his fingers across the lines of text as if reading with inhuman speed. He turned to keep the book away from Rygen's reaching hand.

"Aha, interesting," Leo teased. "So it's about a family with the name Quim!"

"You only know that because of what your father told you!" She got up on her knees and grabbed his shoulders.

He stiffened his back and stomach to keep himself upright as she tried to pull him down. She groaned in effort, then fell back and gave up. "You're too strong!" she complained.

With a sudden feeling of guilt, he closed the book. Then he turned and set it between them.

"I'm ready," he announced.

She sat up and crossed her legs. He mimicked her position so they could balance the book on their touching legs.

"Go!" she said as she flipped over the hardcover.

Leo's eyes were immediately drawn to the illustration at the bottom of the first page. He didn't spend more than a moment glancing over it, as it only appeared to be a king sitting on his throne. There would be time to appreciate the illustrations when the competition was over. For now he had better read quick.

Leo would only beat Rygen in this game when he focused his hardest to read with speed and attention. Rygen never seemed to put in all of her effort like he did, her shoulders relaxed. Her voice was always calm as well whenever she tested him, as if she didn't feel any fear that he might answer correctly even though he often did.

The story began with the introduction of DFaren Quim, an odd name. The book said that he would one day be more powerful than the king, which made Leo pause. No one was more powerful than the king.

He tried to keep reading, but the subject of power distracted him. There were great powers of this world. Even if he didn't know what they were, he knew they *had* to exist. Leo would one day discover one and it would make Rhenol seem like a peasant. This had to be the case, or there would never be a way for Leo to give people like the farm master what they deserved.

If Rygen's books had taught him anything, it was this lesson. He had always figured this power would come from magic. It was known as Artistry, used by master gemcrafters, summoners, and Ascendants. Books of all kinds talked about these people. There were differences between how the books described magic, but all spoke of its existence as if it were fact. Even Leo's father had told him Artistry was real, though it was all he would say on the matter. Father never had any experience with it himself.

Did Leo have a small taste of Artistry last night? That stone was unlike anything he'd felt before, a calling to become something. What, exactly, he had no idea.

He realized he'd been reading without paying attention to any of the words. Panicked, he started over and pushed himself to his utmost speed. But it was only a moment later that Rygen announced, "I'm done."

He had let her score the first point. The more time he took, now, to finish, the more time he gave Rygen to go over what she had read. She was already quite good at remembering every word, so he didn't know how he would ask her something about the text that she wouldn't be able to answer.

Now a little upset at himself, he pushed himself to finish without distraction. But he didn't have the same interest in the story as when he'd first heard the title. All he could think about was that stone his brother had brought home.

"Is something wrong?" Rygen asked.

How was he supposed to tell her any of this?

It's Rygen, he reminded himself, and was about to reveal his thoughts when she spoke again.

"Is it what we heard last night? The screams..." She looked toward her latched window.

"Yes," he admitted. *But there was much more than screams last night*. "What else did you hear?"

"There was a creature on my roof."

"Mine, too!"

"It must've jumped off mine and then later onto yours. I saw it head toward your house."

"You saw it?" Leo asked in shock. How had they not spoken about this already? They had spent more than a few moments together. The sight of this creature should've been the first thing out of her mouth. "How did you see it?"

"I was watching out my window. Wait." She got up and walked to her window. After a short breath, she opened it slowly and peered out cautiously.

She closed it again, then returned to sit beside Leo. "I just wanted to make sure there's still nothing out there."

"What did the creature look like?"

"I didn't see much in the dark. I think it had four strong legs. Other than that, its shape was like a dog. I spoke with my mother about it today, but she says she doesn't know what it is."

"It sounds like it could be a summoned."

"I was thinking the same! The creature made me feel something that animals of our world don't."

Leo's heart skipped. "Like what?"

"Strangely fearless. I wanted to meet the creature. Did you feel the same?"

"No. Not at all." He did with the stone, though. "But I think I understand what you mean. Did you feel the same with anything else?"

Her brow furrowed. "What do you mean?"

"Not a creature," he specified. "A stone."

She shook her head. But then her mouth dropped open. "Is that what was thrown from your window?"

"You saw?"

"No, I just heard it land. It *was* a stone?"

"A rift gem, I believe."

She gasped. "I knew they were true! How did you get one?"

"Andar took it from a woman in the market. She had it for sale along with other gems."

"Who would ever bring a rift gem here?"

"We wondered the same thing. He went back to the market today to look for her, but she wasn't there. He got rid of the gem last night. That's what you heard, but then did you hear anything else during the night?"

"Yes. I'm certain I heard people looking for it."

"People?" Leo asked.

"Yes, or one person three different times, but that's unlikely."

"Three?" Leo was one of them, but who were the other two? His brother counted for one, probably, even if Leo never heard him get up from his bed. Andar probably had awoken later in the night to search. Perhaps he had gone back another time during the night and there was no third person.

"When did you hear these people?" Leo asked.

"One was soon after the stone was thrown, before I could fall asleep."

This was the person Leo didn't know. He and his brother had been in their room for a while. He felt a chill. Whoever it was searching for the stone first probably had found it, but how did they know where to look? *The creature,* Leo realized. *It saw.*

Rygen clenched her teeth as she grabbed Leo's arm. "Argh, you have to stop doing that. Tell me your thoughts!"

"I think the woman from the market is a summoner. I believe she sent her summoned creature after Andar. Some people probably saw this beast running by, which is why they screamed. Andar must not have seen it, though. Perhaps it followed him by smell, or it has better eyesight than we do."

"And this creature saw where he threw the stone," Rygen added. "It told the summoner."

"Can they speak?" Leo took the opportunity to ask.

"I don't know, but I think the bond between a summoned and a summoner can be strong enough that they don't need words to communicate."

The two of them fell silent. There were still a number of questions that bothered Leo. What was this stone? Why did a summoner have one? And why was someone selling it? Was the seller actually the summoner or someone else?

"Was that you I heard first outside my window last night?" Rygen asked with hope in her small voice.

Leo couldn't lie to her. "No. I went out later."

Rygen was silent a breath.

"Why later?"

"I wanted to move the stone farther from your house. I thought it might bring danger." He couldn't explain himself further. He was too ashamed.

It didn't seem to matter, as Rygen must've understood why it was that Leo hadn't immediately gone for the stone.

"Oh," she replied as her head sank.

He was a coward.

"I should've gone out immediately," he said. "I'm sorry."

It was even worse when she didn't look up. "I understand," she said with disappointment.

It felt as if a rip was making its way through his heart.

Leo promised himself that the next time he needed to be brave, he would, no matter the danger. What was the point of reading all those stories about heroes if they didn't teach him the right way to behave? He imagined Rygen terrified last night as she heard people outside her window. Leo could've fixed that if he'd come over as soon as they'd gotten rid of the stone and explained everything. He could've brought the knife and offered to stay with her for protection.

He had thought of these things last night, but they all seemed impossible as he would've had to climb over his mountain of fear first. He was ashamed that he'd never even tried.

"Why don't we keep reading?" Rygen asked.

Leo nodded as they put their attention back into the book.

They tried to, at least. But Leo couldn't focus on anything else besides the cold feeling he was sensing from Rygen as she refused to look at him. Eventually he gave up and stood from the bed.

"I should head back."

"Already?" Her disappointment sounded insincere.

He nodded. She didn't get off her bed to escort him out. He walked away but stopped in her doorway.

"I promise I will be here for you if you ever need help."

She got off her bed and walked over to him. "Leo, there are some things in this world that are too strong for you to make such promises."

"There aren't," he said with confidence as he felt something stir in his chest. He didn't know where these words were coming from, but he couldn't stop them from coming out even if he wanted to. "I don't know how long it will take, but eventually I will be strong enough to help you no matter what the danger is."

The words themselves were nothing, he realized, if it wasn't for the way he spoke them, the way he meant them. Rygen lifted her eyebrows as if surprised by his speech.

"What do you plan to do?"

Leo didn't let himself falter, even though he was clueless to the answer. He thought quickly as to what the heroes of his stories always did.

"I will learn what I can, and I will train."

She took on a stern look. "I want to as well."

"You will?" Leo felt as small as a bug. If Rygen was to train to protect herself, then she wouldn't need him, and his promise would be nothing.

"I did not like the feeling I had last night," Rygen said. "Why don't we work together?"

His hopes rose. "How?"

"I will learn as much as I can for both of us, and you will train."

She was right. It was better this way. Neither of them had time to do both. Besides, Rygen was always learning things and then teaching him. Leo didn't know what it was they had to learn to be powerful, but he had confidence that she would figure it out.

"Then it's settled," Leo said.

"It's settled," Rygen agreed. "But I still want to read this book!"

"Well of course, there has to be time for reading."

She laughed as she took his hand and led him back to their reading spot. "Come on, it's not that late yet."

He sat beside her again, their knees caressing. Her warmth dissolved his worries and finally allowed him to focus on the text.

*****

When Leo returned home, the rest of his family was in bed with the lamps off. He navigated through the dark kitchen and into the bedroom, where he slid into his bed. During the walk back in the black of night, his hairs had stood. But his body calmed soon after he pulled the covers up over his head.

"What's the book about?" his brother asked, surprisingly not asleep.

Leo had the book with him, tucked between his arm. It seemed to offer some sort of protection, as he still felt that something was not quite right since last night. Rygen preferred that each book she borrowed stay at Leo's house, for Darren would put it in their lockbox in the morning.

Leo and Rygen had finished the book, reading long into the night to do so. They would both be tired for their work tomorrow, but Leo figured that this would be much worse for him than it was for Rygen, so he didn't feel too guilty about it. Any sort of discomfort—thirst, hunger, or fatigue—amplified the agony of his farm work.

"The book's about a man called DFaren Quim."

"Da-faren?" Andar asked. "How is it spelled?"

Leo spelled it out for him, specifying the two capital letters in the beginning.

"A high-born," Andar said.

"A *very* high-born," Leo corrected. "At one point, he was more powerful than the king."

"No. Which king?"

"Our king. Mavrim Orello."

Andar was silent for a moment. "How can anyone be more powerful than the king?"

"Through wealth and followers. There was a war between him and the king eventually, and DFaren would've won except he was betrayed."

"Rygen says this is all true?"

"Yes."

"How does she know?" Andar asked.

"Gartel told her. Remember what Father said? Everyone older than us knows this story."

"Then why don't they speak about it? Why hasn't father told us about it? He's told us many other stories, many tales of heroes and monsters that aren't true. If this story was true, he would've told us because it's more important than all the others."

Leo had had this discussion with Rygen many times. They had figured out that there were different forms of truth in stories of fiction. They could be just as important as true tales.

"Because the stories Father told us let us see what life is like in other places. We'll never see a castle, yet I feel like I've already been to one. We'll never witness a royal wedding, but we can imagine what it would be like. We'll never fight in a war, but we understand what those in battle see and feel. I know all of this from stories that aren't true to every detail, but they are true in other ways."

"I suppose so, except for what you think you know about war. Haven't you heard what people say?"

"No." All Leo knew about war was from the stories his father had told him and what he'd read with Rygen.

"The only people who know what battle is really like are those who have fought and those who have killed."

Leo was silent as he pondered this. He had learned through many failed arguments with Andar that if he wasn't sure of something, the smartest thing he could do was admit it.

"You're probably right."

"It's late," Andar said with a yawn. "Will you tell me about DFaren tomorrow?"

"Yes."

Leo tried to sleep afterward, but a nagging thought kept him awake. Unable to sleep, Leo waited until he heard Andar rustle.

"You awake?" Leo asked.

"Why?"

"Rygen heard more than just one person looking for the gem last night."

Andar was silent for a breath. His voice was a whisper. "How many?"

"Three, and I was one of them."

Leo knew he didn't need to explain his reasoning for going after the gem. They'd both felt the same longing for it. Andar needed to admit he had gone out there before they could move on.

"You went out as well, didn't you?" Leo accused when his brother was too guarded to say so himself.

"Yes," he answered confidently and quickly. "I wanted to move it farther from Rygen's house so it wouldn't bring harm to her and her mother."

Leo was too tired to be angry at his brother for lying. He was sad instead.

"That's not true," Andar corrected himself to Leo's surprise. He sighed. "I wanted to hold it again, maybe keep it, even though I knew I shouldn't. I'm glad I didn't find it. I don't know why I lied to you."

Leo couldn't tell, either, why it seemed so hard for Andar to be honest with him recently.

Leo hardly ever lied to anyone, so he certainly couldn't empathize with his brother. It was easy to be honest, easier than lying. Andar just had to stop behaving in a way that made him want to keep secrets. But that meant no more theft, no more salted chicken legs. Leo wasn't sure he could ever bring himself to lecture his brother about that. He could still taste that greasy flavor from when he'd finished and licked his fingers clean.

"Just stop lying to me," Leo said. He'd learned from their father how to direct his anger into a stern yet commanding voice. Leo used it so infrequently that it always worked. "I'll never be against you."

"I know," Andar said.

"So you will stop lying to me?"

"It's only because of the gem. I never have before, and I won't again."

"Thank you."

"So both of us only went out for the gem once," Andar said. "That means someone else was out there besides us if Rygen heard correctly."

"Did you find the gem?" Leo asked, still worried his brother might lie.

"No. I didn't feel it, either."

"Neither did I," Leo said. "Whatever else was there probably found it."

"How could they in the dark? There's a lot of dirt to search between our house and Rygen's."

"That creature on our roof probably told them somehow. Rygen and I think it's a rift pet of a summoner."

Andar chuckled. "It doesn't surprise me that you two would assume that."

Leo didn't reply. He had no interest in debating something unknown to both of them, for whatever he said wouldn't matter. Andar would eventually prove that neither of them knew enough to speak on the matter, and they'd be right back where they started.

"Are you going to take anything else from the gem seller if you see her?" Leo asked.

Andar took quite a lot of time before answering. "I honestly don't know yet, but I need to see her again. I know I'll recognize her."

"But will she recognize you?"

"No."

Even if Andar wasn't lying, he could still be wrong.

CHAPTER FIVE

The next day brought rain so heavy that there was no way around some puddles on the path to the farm. All Leo and Andar could do was hold up their pants as they waded through. Leo remembered the first time it had rained this hard. He had thought there would be no work for him to do, but there was always something to do on the farm. Always.

Leo and Andar wouldn't be working outside, thankfully, but their indoor tasks weren't always better than the hard labor they usually did. The farm master used to have them mend his torn clothing, but he stopped when a flap opened at the rear of his pants and no one told him for the whole day. He blamed Andar for sabotaging his pants, and rightfully so, but Rhenol couldn't prove it because he hadn't paid close attention as to who worked on which article of clothing.

Other farmworkers would get to clean the root vegetables when it rained, like the turnips or onions. Others churned butter, kept tools oiled and sharpened, and tended to the animals. All were indoor tasks. The outdoor tasks were reserved for those who the farm master didn't like as much, like Leo and Andar. In the rain, they'd cut wood and lug it inside. They'd patch a leak in a roof. They'd even repair fences. It was more than frustrating to spend hours fixing one part of a fence, then move on to another, only to watch the one they'd fixed fall apart from a single gust of strong wind.

It was quite a trek to the farm that morning. Leo's pants were somehow soaked by the time they arrived, even though he'd lifted them as he crossed over every puddle. The storm raged too loudly for the brothers to talk on the way there, so they didn't have a chance to speak about the book.

There was a line of people waiting for directions from the farm master, who stood under the awning of his mansion's entrance. He shouted orders and directed with his hands. Leo couldn't make out any of it over the wind until he and his brother came closer.

Rhenol's face was twisted up in a scowl, obviously made worse by this weather. He gestured at the couple in front of Leo and Andar. "I need people fishing who I trust. There won't be eyes on you at the lake. Do I have your word you'll bring me everything you catch until evening?"

"Yessir," the man replied.

Leo had seen this couple countless times around the farm. They seemed to be about his father's age, barely thirty. They were probably married and had children old enough to work on their own, as many husbands and wives did in this city. It was the only explanation for their good behavior toward the farm master. They couldn't fail. They couldn't leave this place, or they would lose their home.

The income of Leo's family would increase soon once Leo started his work at the Bookbinding Guild, and what an exciting day that would be. Andar kept track of the days better, so he should know exactly how long it would be until Leo's tenth birthday. He would ask as soon as they found out what they would be doing today. Hopefully, whatever it was would be indoors.

Rhenol folded his arms as Leo and Andar stepped up to him. The farm master was a tall, thin man, with wrinkly cheeks and a sharp chin that was always clean-shaven. He gave Leo and Andar a disappointed shake of his head as if they'd misbehaved this morning already.

"There isn't enough work for everyone, so only my best workers will be paid today. Leave," he demanded. "Only come back once the rain stops. This should give you time to think better about your behavior."

Leo knew this was meant as punishment, but it certainly didn't feel that way. He couldn't remember the last time he had the day free, the entire day. It was a struggle not to grin before he and Andar turned away. They walked across the soggy ground of the farm and through the gate that separated it from the other farm land around it. Only when no one could see their faces did they smile at one another. Andar even gave a laugh.

"Rhenol's about as smart as a potato if he thinks sending us off is a punishment."

Leo laughed with his brother. "What should we do when we are home?" he asked Andar. There were many chores that could still be done in the rain. A storm like this could cause damage to the roof of their house. If a hole opened, it might have to be repaired while the storm raged on.

"I'm going to read that book about DFaren Quim before I even think about what else we have to do," Andar proclaimed.

"Oh." Leo was too shocked to reply. His brother seemed to enjoy causing mischief, but he always did what needed to be done in the end. *We do have a lot of time,* Leo realized.

"You can read it with me," Andar said. "You usually read each book many times with Rygen. Might as well do it once with me."

Was that jealousy he heard in his brother's voice?

"Of course." Leo wasn't used to Andar choosing Leo's company over being alone, but he could certainly get used to it.

When they arrived home, they hurried to change into dry garments. They hung a rope across the kitchen and tossed their wet pants and shirts over it. Leo didn't understand why the rope couldn't always be strung from wall to wall, as it was much easier than taking it down and putting it back up every time they washed their clothes, but Darren refused to allow it. Apparently, he didn't like the way it made their kitchen look, but there wasn't much to look at anyway. The walls were unpainted, an odd set of brown and beige tones of natural wood, much of it chipped and some of it rotting in one corner. How was one rope really going to matter? Leo had tried to change Darren's mind about keeping it up, Andar on his side, but there was no point in trying anymore.

Andar had just taken out the book when they heard someone open the front door. They ran into the kitchen from their bedroom in alarm. Thieves were common in this part of the city. They might even be neighbors. But it was only their father stepping in and taking off his heavy coat. Water puddled on the floor around him, creating a new mess where Andar and Leo had already mopped up the puddles they had made.

Darren appeared confused for a moment as he stared at them, then he let out his breath with a frown. "Rhenol sent you home without work?" he assumed.

"Yes," Andar confirmed.

"And the two of you were going to read rather than look for work elsewhere today?" their father asked, his gaze on the book in Andar's hands.

"Why are *you* home, Father?" Andar asked pointedly.

"Yeah," Leo echoed, wishing he was a smart as his brother so he could add something besides one simple word.

"The cave is flooded. There's no point in trying to remove the water until the rain stops."

"So are *you* going to look for work elsewhere?" Andar asked.

"Yeah," Leo said again, really feeling like a dolt. The support for Andar was worth it, though.

"Eventually," Darren said with a hint of a smile. "I wanted to look at that book of Rygen's first. What did you say it was called?"

"*Quim and Kin: Crowns and Betrayal,*" Leo said.

A drop of water splattered against the table. Everyone looked up at the leak in the center of the roof over their kitchen. Darren hurried to fetch a bucket and put it on the table. Leo expected their father to order them to do something, anything. They might not be able to patch the leak until the rain stopped, but problems like this always seemed to spark Darren into action. If there were any tasks to be done, he and his sons were to do them now, not later.

But instead, Darren removed his wet clothing and hung it over the rope. The garments dripped on the wet floor. In only has undergarments, Father strolled into his bedroom. He almost never changed in front of Leo and Andar, making it shocking now to be reminded of his physique. He had strong muscles wherever Leo looked, almost as if they were sculpted out of rock. He was frightening, in a way, even though Leo had never known his father to hurt anyone. He was just so big, like a giant.

There was a quiet moment as Andar stared with Leo, waiting for their father to tell them what they needed to do that would keep them from reading. But he said nothing as they heard him change. Eventually he came out in dry clothing and stopped in front of them as they waited nervously for instruction from the doorway of their bedroom.

"Let me have the book," Father said.

Andar handed it over with a sad look.

"Excuse me," Darren said, gesturing between them. Something about this seemed entertaining to him as he held a smile.

The brothers parted for him. He entered their room and went to sit on Andar's bed.

"I know the two of you would like to read with me," Darren said. "I just hope you can keep up because I'm starting now." He opened the book and looked down at it with a face of concentration.

Leo and Andar jumped onto the bed on either side of their father.

"Wait!" Andar said.

"Stop!" said Leo.

Darren set the book on his lap and put his arms around the shoulders of his sons.

Leo had already read this book, but that didn't stop him from beaming. He relaxed and enjoyed the company of his father and brother. The last time they had read, all of them together, was when Father was teaching Leo so long ago.

"One moment," Darren said as he took his arm off Leo to flip the book over. "Where's the author's name listed?"

"At the end," Leo said. "After the final words."

"That's strange." Darren started to move the delicate parchments to get to the end.

"Wait, you'll spoil it." Leo grabbed his hand.

"I know the story already, Leo," his father assured him. "I just need to see the author's name for a moment."

Leo reached over and put his hand in front of his brother's face. "Don't read anything at the end!"

"My eyes are closed!"

Leo saw that they were. He let down his arm. There was more than one big surprise in the story.

"Who's the author?" Andar asked.

"Miqu Yenu," Darren pronounced slowly, as if unfamiliar. "Sounds like an Analyte woman…"

It seemed as if there was a "but" coming, but Darren didn't follow up with anything else. He stared at the name as if trying to figure out a puzzle. Suddenly he let out a gasp.

"What?" Andar asked.

Darren didn't seem to hear Andar until he glanced over. "It's nothing. I thought I knew the name, but I don't. Leo, tell Rygen to request from her guild master everything he knows about this woman. I'm curious to find out who she is. She's probably in the city. If he knows where she is, I'd like to…" He stopped himself, no doubt aware of how strange he sounded. "I suppose I'd like to meet her. You can tell Rygen that."

"Why?" Leo asked. Darren had showed no interest in any of the other authors or books that Leo had brought home.

"Because she's an Analyte, Father?" Andar assumed.

"I don't know if she is or not." He waved his hand. "Never mind. Don't ask Rygen anything. It's not important." He quickly moved the parchments back to the first two pages again.

This was even more unusual, Darren changing his mind about something. Leo had felt something from the story when he'd read it last night with Rygen, a small flame as it were the start of a discovery. At seeing how this book changed his father, Leo knew not to ignore this feeling. There was more than just a story here, more than just history.

He started reading again, concentrating harder this time. There had to be something hidden in the text. His father knew what it was, but there was no point in prying. It never got Leo anywhere.

The story was not just about one man. Nor was it about just one family. It was about what was once the most powerful guild in the world. The Traders' Guild in the city of Halin made the Farmers' Guild in Jatn look like distant cousins of the king attempting to lord over the people of their small town the same way the king controlled the kingdom.

The Traders' Guild didn't just control all the food that went in and out of the city, like the Farmers' Guild did in Jatn. The traders oversaw all the goods that came into the city, left the city, were produced in the city, and even those that were sold in the city. In other words, all the guilds had to follow the Traders' Guild rules.

Upon reading this for the first time, Leo had wondered why the other guilds would allow this, but the author explained in the first two pages that the Traders' Guild was good, not evil. A tax was paid to the group that went into the upkeep of the city's streets and walls, but that wasn't all.

DFaren Quim was the leader of this guild, a man said to be wealthier than the king at the time. Much of that wealth went to pay armed men who were far more honorable than the guards here in Jatn, some of whom could accurately be called thieves.

"Is all of this true?" Leo asked his father when he was done reading the second page. Andar and Darren had waited for Leo to finish, but they didn't have to wait long.

"Yes, so far," his father said.

"How do you know?" Andar asked.

"From the stories I've heard."

"From who?" Andar prodded. "I never see you speak with anyone. No one ever comes here," he teased.

"I speak with the men I work with, and the people I interact with around the city." He lifted an eyebrow and grinned at Andar. "You don't believe me?"

"It's just hard to imagine you speaking with anyone at leisure, especially listening to stories."

"It makes the days go by faster in the cave," he said in a dark tone, his gaze falling back to the pages open on his lap. "Let's keep reading."

Remembering how sad the story was, Leo decided he would rather hear more about his father. But he kept his mouth shut and read the next two pages in front of him for the second time.

The human king, Mavrim Orello, who was still king to this day, had allowed the city of Halin to remain under the control of the Quim family for quite some time. The citizens of Halin did not pay taxes to the kingdom but to the Traders' Guild instead. The Traders' Guild then paid a stipend to the king.

"Those who know the king," the author wrote, "might be surprised to find this out. But the only reason the king put up with this system was because war against Halin was the only other option. The king knew he might win against DFaren Quim's army, and all the people who might rise up in support of the Traders' Guild, but it was not worth the risk. Not until the cavern diggers just outside the city discovered the greatest rift known in the world."

This time, Leo announced he was done with these two pages while Andar still needed a moment. When he was done, he complained to Leo, "You get to read so much more than I do that you're getting to be faster."

Andar's light tone was as if he was joking, but the jealous spark in his eyes made Leo unsure whether to laugh or apologize. He went with the latter.

"I'm sorry. I'll make sure you get to read each book I do from now on."

Andar smiled. "Thank you."

DFaren Quim had two children who were seventeen and fifteen at the time of the rift discovery. The story shifted to the Quim family, telling much about these siblings. By the time these pages were done, Leo was more interested in one of them, the older brother, DVend Quim. Even at seventeen, he was regarded as one of the strongest swordsmen in the human kingdom. His younger sister, Yune Quim, did not receive the double capital letters at the start of her name.

"It's unfair," Leo asserted. "Why does she not get the same honorable name as her brother and father?" He already knew the first part of the answer, for he and Rygen had figured it out. It was the second part that they didn't understand. "I know it's because she's a woman," Leo added. "But why does that matter? Her father could've given her any name he wanted, including an honorable one."

"Aye, he could have," Darren agreed with a distant look as he glanced up. "I don't know if anyone has the answer to that besides DFaren, but he passed away."

"Father!" Leo complained. "You're spoiling it for Andar."

"I don't mind if I know what happens," Andar said, as he always did. But Leo did mind. He knew the story was better for everyone, no matter what they claimed, if what came next was a surprise. "How did he die? Did one of his children kill him? The girl, because he didn't respect her?" Andar pressed.

"No, no," Darren said. "She wouldn't do that...from what I've heard about her."

"You have to read it," Leo interrupted.

"Fine," Andar said. "It's not a long book, anyway."

Most were about this length, twenty large pages of small written words. Leo could speed through books in a few hours. His father could probably finish them in half the time.

Yune Quim was not known for anything like her brother was. Her father had tried to get her involved in the guild like her brother, who was a captain of the Traders' Guild army and was on the way to one day being the commander. But Yune had no skill with weaponry, nor with number calculations. She enjoyed reading and writing her own books, as well as purchasing paintings and sculptures so she could attempt her own art. Her father did not approve.

Leo didn't pay much attention to these pages about the Quim family the second time through. There was no sword fighting, no progress of the story. The only details were about the siblings and their father. The mother of the family eventually died from an illness. The father, still handsome and virile in his advanced age, married a much younger woman by the name of Karlinda, who was said to be the most beautiful woman in the world. The author focused too much on this woman for Leo's taste, describing how the marriage disrupted the relationships in the family, but Darren read these pages slower than the rest. Leo had to wait each time for his father to finish. Even Andar finished before Darren. Perhaps he was skipping words here and there like Leo was. Leo paid more attention when the story returned to the strife between DFaren and King Orello.

There were many people throughout the human kingdom, like Leo's father, whose job involved digging to search for rifts. As far as Leo knew, a rift was a place where this world and the other were close to each other. Rifts opened and closed quite infrequently, but they'd been known to stay open for years.

When the rift was discovered just outside Halin, DFaren Quim kept it guarded by his army until he could extend the city wall around it. By then, the king had found out about the fresh rift pouring out immense amounts of Artistry, but it was too late for Mavrim Orello to claim it, for it was already within the city. At least that was what DFaren had begun telling all the other powerful guilds in each city.

It was this decision that the author said led to his death. It wasn't a foolish decision, though. It was actually brilliant. He predicted accurately that Mavrim would arrive with an army sometime later and say that the cavern with the rift belonged to him. DFaren had previously explained to the guild masters across the kingdom that their king would become an enemy as soon as any of them had something he wanted, which DFaren did now.

"Wait and watch, but be prepared to support me when I'm right," wrote the author in the words of DFaren. "Stand with me against Mavrim Orello, and we will prove to him and his army that we can stand against any injustice. Everything in this kingdom is changing, starting with each city. Feudalism will be gone a decade from now. The people will have power over their monarch. But we must support each other, or we will be forced to grovel before our king. Make your choice now."

Andar asked their father, "How does the writer know exactly what DFaren said?"

"Because DFaren wrote the message himself, then copied it once for each city for it to be delivered. His family—his son, his daughter, his brother, his cousins—all took the messages to the cities. It was a famous message. Many of the citizens made copies to share with each other, while others memorized it. Most people were, and still are, tired of feudalism. That's why so many like us live in cities controlled by guilds."

How do guilds still control the cities even though DFaren lost? Leo wondered. He didn't want to spoil the ending for Andar, though.

DFaren would've won, Leo remembered reading last night, had one thing been different. There was a declaration of war and one great battle. He read through the details again with his father and brother. He seethed once more at the tale of how the Analytes got involved; how they'd ruined everything.

The betrayal was hard for Leo to stomach the second time, especially knowing it was coming. But it seemed even harder for Darren to read this part, Leo's father cringing as each page led closer and closer to the battle.

Besides small gasps here and there from Andar, no one said a word until the book was done. Darren let out a raspy breath as he closed the volume.

"All of that is true?" Andar asked.

"Yes," Darren said.

Leo's previous question seemed unimportant now. There were much bigger issues that needed to be resolved. "How could thousands of Analytes come all the way to our kingdom just to do that?"

"Their king needed farmers for their land," Father explained. "Joining the war was the method he thought of to get so many of them."

"To take humans as slaves?" Andar asked in disbelief. "There must be a better way."

Darren nodded. "That's what I thought as well. They showed no care for humankind. Killing and capturing men was a decision thousands of Analytes made. It doesn't make sense."

"Why not?" Leo asked, for his father seemed to be hinting.

"Analytes are not that different from us," Darren said.

"Have you met one, Father?" Leo asked.

He thought for a moment. "Yes."

"You're right, it doesn't make sense," Andar agreed. "Why would so many of them risk their lives in battle just to bring back human slaves to farm land that will benefit their king?"

"They didn't risk their lives," Darren corrected. "Their betrayal ensured their safety. It's why they first convinced DFaren to make an alliance with them. It's their lack of regard for humankind that confuses me."

Now Leo understood. When he'd read this with Rygen, the two of them had assumed Analytes were evil. Perhaps that wasn't true. They were, however, certainly dishonorable. This was not known before the famous betrayal, the author had written. In fact, Analytes had a reputation of telling the truth when they first came to DFaren Quim and offered him an alliance. They wanted him to be king when this was over, they had told him. They had tried working with Mavrim Orello and failed. DFaren had to promise that he would trade with them, and they would help each other's kingdoms with any threatening issues.

DFaren had been reluctant to agree, fearful of a betrayal, but it was his young new wife who had eventually convinced him that the Analytes were to be trusted. His children argued against it, however all were in agreement that the battle could be lost without help. The king's army was massive. If the Analytes were turned away, they were likely to join with Mavrim anyway. So eventually the entire family was convinced that it was their only option.

It wasn't until the start of the battle that the Analytes turned on their sworn allies. DFaren was killed, his young wife captured. She was later forcibly married to the king's son. They even had a child together. Leo wondered if this woman who was supposedly the most beautiful in the world, Karlinda, had been part of the betrayal, but the author seemed sure that Karlinda was not. Karlinda was simply wrong.

All of the Quim family who fought were killed, except for the son of DFaren, DVend. His sister had not fought in the battle, but she was imprisoned in the capital like DVend and all the other supporters who had not fought.

Andar seemed shocked by something as he put his hands on the book. "If all of this is true, then could we be taken to the dungeons as well for reading it?"

"No," Darren said. "I wouldn't let that happen."

"But..." Andar paused for a moment, glancing at Leo. "But you can't fight off the entire army of the king."

Darren chuckled. "He would not send his entire army over a book, especially one that tells the same tale that so many people have shared since this occurred."

Leo asked, "How long ago was it?"

Darren's eyes lifted to the ceiling. "It's been eleven years since the battle."

"I wish there was more about the battle," Leo admitted. "How old was DVend at the time? How many people did he kill before it was over? How did he fight that made him so good with his sword? Do you know, Father?"

"People say he was twenty years old at the time of the battle. I don't know how many he killed, but you shouldn't speak about him like he was a hero. He was probably just a talented swordsman born into the right family."

"But he's still in prison?" Leo asked.

"Yes. He will probably spend his life there."

"Only for fighting on his father's side!" Andar said angrily. "It isn't fair."

"Well his sister didn't even fight, and she's in there with him," Darren added. "This is what power gets you." He stood up from the bed. "It has been hours." Father didn't need to open the window for them to hear that the rain had not relented. He put his hands on his hips as he stared at the closed wooden shutters and seemed to be in thought.

"Do we have enough money, Father?" Leo asked. Darren never told him anything about how much they had, but the story seemed to open Father in ways Leo had never witnessed before. Perhaps this was the right time.

"Of course we do," Darren said. It was an answer Leo had heard many times before.

"But what if the storm continues for days?" Leo added.

"That's why we save as much of our earned coin as we can. We will be fine. We are prepared."

Thunder shook the walls, silencing them for a few breaths.

Feeling as though he couldn't be any more vulnerable, Leo blurted out something he'd been holding in for a while. "I think the farm master is going to do something to Andar."

Both of them looked at Leo in confusion.

He mustered up his courage and said the words. "I think he's going to hurt Andar one day."

"What?" Darren said in shock.

"Leo!" Andar scolded, then looked up at Darren. "He's not, Father."

"How do you know?" Leo challenged. "He treats you worse and worse. Father, can you hurt him back if he does something?"

"No," Darren answered quickly and forcefully. "The law prevents it." He seemed to be in thought for a moment as he stared at Andar, looking at him in a way Leo had not seen before. Father's eyes traveled up and down Andar's body as if judging his height and girth.

"What?" Andar asked.

"There's going to be a change starting today," Darren announced. "I'm going to teach the two of you how to defend yourselves."

Was Father a good fighter? He was certainly big and strong.

"Is there time for that?" Andar asked, seemingly worried.

"You don't want to learn?" Darren asked in surprise.

"I do, I do! I was only concerned about having time to train."

"I found time to teach you how to read, didn't I? It will be harder to teach you how to fight, but I will do it. We will start today, after we eat. Can I trust the two of you to take care of procuring our next meal, while I fetch a few things?"

"Absolutely," Andar answered for them.

CHAPTER SIX

It became clear just how good a fighter Leo's father was shortly after their lessons began. He wasn't just large. He was quick. Leo soon asked him where he learned how to sword fight.

"I used to spar with my friends when I was about Andar's age."

"Here in Jatn?" Andar asked.

"Yes."

"Have you kept any of these friends?"

Leo didn't know why every time Andar asked their father something about himself, it sounded as if Andar was trying to catch him in a lie.

"One of them," Father replied. "Franklin digs in the caverns with me."

"What about the others?" Andar asked.

"I don't know where they are now."

"Why not?"

"I stopped seeing most of them when we were older."

"Why?"

Leo gave his brother a whack in the knee with his shoddy wooden sword.

"Ow, Leo!"

He reminded his brother of one of their lessons. "You must pay close attention at all times if there's even a chance someone might strike you."

"I know that, but the rules should be different between brothers." He made a quick swipe at Leo with his wooden sword, tagging Leo on the arm.

"Ow!"

Leo tried to retaliate, but their father put himself between him and Andar. Leo's sword bounced off his father's forearm, not even causing Darren to wince.

"Andar's right," Darren lectured. "Family should not strike each other under any circumstance unless it's to help one another practice. Apologize, Leo."

"He hit me back!"

"But you struck first. Apologize."

I was only trying to stop him from interrogating you. "Fine. I'm sorry, Andar."

"I forgive you. Now let's fight!"

With a grin on his face, Andar came at Leo from around their father. He opened with a jab of his blunt sword. Leo remembered to swipe downward so as to deflect the blow, but Andar was just too strong. He had his weapon back up again before Leo could lift his, gently poking Leo in the shoulder.

The storm continued for three days. It gave them the chance to spar all day in their small house, however Leo and Andar could only swing the sword for so long. Their arms tired quickly, especially Leo's. His wooden sword was smaller than Andar's, but that didn't seem to help much. He held in his frustration no matter how many times he lost, but he would've at least had one outburst if it wasn't for his father's advice.

"You're not expected to win until you're much stronger," Darren would say, sometimes giving Leo a hearty pat on his back. "This is the best way to gain muscle. One day you'll look at that sword and laugh at how small it is, amazed that you once thought it was heavy."

Father not only taught them how to use a sword. He showed them how to punch, block, grapple, and even what to do if they found themselves on the ground during a bout. It was a lot to remember, but although Leo wasn't nearly as strong as his father or even his brother, the strength of his memory competed with theirs evenly.

Leo thought to ask his father if the swords were too much coin, but their chipped condition made the answer obvious. These were not training swords for real swordsmen. They were toys for children made from wood and were probably older than Andar.

Leo was eager to make his father proud as he and Andar showed great improvement over only three days. The storm became a blessing. The one curse was Leo's sore muscles. They only allowed him to do so much each day, but there was plenty for them to do in between lessons. The rain would abate just long enough for them to patch a leak or two in their roof. When they weren't doing that, or sparring, they were out looking for a quick job or two.

The market was empty, but shops around the city were still open. With many people unable to work at the farms these days, the shops were more crowded than usual. Some owners didn't have time to repair or even prevent storm damage, which was how Leo and Andar made a few coins from them.

Leo wanted to stop at the Bookbinding Guild to see if there was anything they could do there, but Andar refused. He despised Gartel and would not see him until he acknowledged that he had been wrong about Andar.

Andar's relationship with Gartel made it difficult for Leo to be excited about his tenth birthday, in which he would finally have the chance to speak to Gartel about working at the Bookbinding Guild. But his excitement was too strong to quell completely. He just had enough willpower to suppress it around his brother for the most part.

Leo had returned the book to Rygen the day after he and his family had read it. He read it a third time with Rygen that night, though they skipped through the slow parts.

When the storm ended, working at the farm was even worse than before. It wasn't just because Leo was sore. It wasn't even that he had enjoyed his time with his father and brother, and this was a sad contrast. It was that the fields where Leo spent the days were pretty much all mud. Leo had to pull out and plant the seeds of the crops that were ruined, which wasn't as bad as trying to support the plants that were damaged. He had to tie them to small wooden rods to keep them upright. He wasn't sure this would help them grow healthy again, but it was what the farm master demanded, so it had to be done.

There were only brief occasions when the watchful little reeve didn't have eyes on Andar. It was at this time that the two brothers would steal fleeting moments of practice with whatever they could grab that most resembled a sword.

Leo hoped for more rain each day, dejected his wish hadn't come true each evening he returned home. But Darren kept up his promise to train them. Leo still sometimes worried that coin for food had gone into these shoddy training swords, but when he voiced his worries his father told him that he had money saved. The training swords were important, well worth the small amount of coins it cost to purchase them.

They always sparred after supper, Leo hoping for a lingering sunset. But this wish never came true, either. There seemed to be mere minutes of light left after each supper. They placed the few lamps they had on the kitchen table and fought around it as they had during the storm, but it did not compare to the freedom of facing each other outside, where there was no chance of backing into a wall while fending off an attack.

Leo still found himself wondering about that stone Andar had brought to their home and the creature that came after it. But his longing for the stone was gone. It was behind him now. Sparring was in his present, and books were in his future—his tenth birthday approaching.

During one morning on the way to the farm, Andar kept stealing glances over his shoulder. When Leo stopped and started to turn for his own look, Andar pushed his shoulder to keep him straight.

"Don't," he said. "They can't know that we know."

"What?" Leo asked, confused.

"You didn't notice that we're being followed?"

"No." Leo resisted the urge to look behind him. "Who is it?"

"Someone with a hood. I haven't gotten a good look."

"Why would they follow us?" It seemed more likely that Andar was imagining it.

"I don't know."

"They could just be walking in the same direction."

"That's what we need to find out," Andar said. "Make a quick turn at this alley and then run with me." He pointed ahead, where the dirt road forked. Just beyond that was their farm, still hidden behind the packed houses and shops. They took the turn onto an empty street. Leo followed his brother's lead as they ran to the end of the short road and turned around.

"What are we doing?" Leo asked after they stopped.

"I want to see who it is. Then we'll run again if they seem to be a threat."

They waited and waited, but no one turned to walk down the same alley. Many people passed by, none with a hood, none even glancing their way.

Eventually Andar said, "Come on. We're taking a different route to the farm."

A different route meant a longer route. "Is that really necessary?" Leo complained. They already might be late.

"We can't risk this person finding out where we are stuck spending each day."

"Why not?"

"They might want to do us harm."

"Why?" Andar asked suspiciously. "Did you do something to someone?" He figured his brother had taken something precious, even though he had promised their father he wouldn't. Or were they followed because of the stone?

"No," Andar said as he gave another look over his shoulder, upward this time as if expecting to find someone on a roof.

There were moments Andar spent alone each day, usually after their work was done on the farm. Leo would go straight home while his brother procured food. He was starting to wonder what else Andar might be doing during this time to be so fearful of someone following them.

"I'm sure you're safe no matter who it is," Andar said when they were just about to the farm.

Leo knew his brother was trying to comfort him, but it only made him more worried.

I don't fear something happening to me.

CHAPTER SEVEN

Darren never cared for digging, but everything had changed after his wife passed. He had reaffirmed his role as a father above all. If digging was the easiest and safest way to make coin for his family, then digging is what he would continue to do.

It wasn't safe in the same way farming was, where risk of injury was low. It was safe in another way.

He was part of a team of men, most of them younger than him, who dug deep through caverns to look for rifts. It was easier to dig into a discovered cavern than to start on the surface, but sections of caverns could still collapse at any point. It was especially more likely after a storm, when much of the dirt was wet. However, it was easier to dig through the mud than hard dirt, and the overseer knew this.

The only reason the job was safer for Darren compared to another was because the overseer of the Digging Guild didn't care who dug, so long as they were strong and didn't complain about the dangers.

Darren had never planned to let anyone in Jatn know, not even his sons, who he really was. He had come here with his wife when Andar was only three, too young to remember the long trip from Halin. Darren had wanted to take the first job he could that would ensure his identity would be kept safe. But even Clancey, the cavern overseer, followed the law that said all overseers must at least glimpse the identification papers of their workers. That meant at least one person had to find out who Darren used to be.

Darren would be a fool to assume he and his boys were safe in Jatn, but it was even less wise to think they could be better off elsewhere. Jatn was well known to be the easiest city for poor children and criminals to survive. The Farmers' Guild was the only guild that provided housing to families so long as one member was employed on one of their farms. With no coin between him and his wife when they'd escaped from Halin, there had been no better place to go than Jatn.

Darren had planned to live like this until both boys were old enough to handle the truth in the careful way they must, but something had changed when Rygen brought that book over.

He had already given up everything that defined who he was, for the safety of his boys, but they would be men soon. They could handle the truth soon enough. Or perhaps these were just excuses because Darren couldn't keep in the truth much longer.

He had a plan. First, he wanted them to make the coin they required to leave the city if they must. The best way to do that was to keep working hard every day, all of them, and stay out of trouble...all of them.

"You never told me what you did during the storm," said Franklin. Darren was glad for his friend's company, even if Franklin always had a lot to say. There was no better way to distract himself than to talk. But Darren couldn't bring up the subjects actually on his mind, only those he forced himself to think of to make conversation. Usually he just waited for Franklin to start.

"I started training my boys to fight," Darren replied.

"Psh, and who trained you?"

"No one, but that doesn't mean I don't know how." Darren swung his pickax into the sloped wall. Mud splashed against his face, but so long as it wasn't close to his eyes, he didn't care to wipe it until the end of the day.

They had spent years in this single cavern. No one knew how or when the cavern formed, but it was Darren's digging team that fell into it while digging down from the surface one day. One man had broken his leg. He wouldn't be able to work for quite a while, and no payment was sent to him or his family for his service. Darren wondered what had become of that man. There was a good chance he and his family had starved to death.

It had been days since the storm, but Franklin probably hadn't thought to ask what Darren had done until now. He'd made sure to tell Darren everything he had done, though. His wife had fallen ill, her condition made worse by the cold. Franklin had run around town looking for any work he could find, shivering to his bones.

"I'm just glad that storm's over," Franklin said for possibly the tenth time.

His size was smaller than Darren's, normal for any man. Franklin had been digging through this cavern for as many years as Darren, and Darren remembered how he'd looked when they began. Franklin, probably in his mid-thirties and one of the oldest of the group, was just as thin now as when they'd met. Perhaps he just didn't eat enough. He probably didn't have a son like Andar who helped keep his family fed, and if his wife didn't work, as many women did not, then it would be even harder for Franklin to eat as much as anyone deserved to eat.

The constant hunger was one of the things hardest for Darren to get used to when he first came to Jatn. Now it just helped him tell the time. When he wanted to keel over from the pain in his empty belly, he knew work was just about done for the day.

Darren wished he could show his boys this cavern. It did nothing for him anymore, but when they'd first discovered it, Darren had felt as though he'd stumbled into a different world. Nothing was familiar about it. The roof in some places was layered like mashed potatoes gone hard. In other places, it looked like a great white blanket with many small piles of sand above, weighing it down. The most fascinating had to be the icicles, except they were not made of ice. No one knew what they were. Some were long enough to reach the ground and form a thin pillar. They were beige and gray like everything else in the cavern, and hard and slick, like used candlesticks with dried wax on the sides.

There were enormous mounds of more of the same nameless substance. It wasn't dirt. It looked more like wet and hardened sand, solid with little white spots here and there, as well as a few deep grooves where water collected. All of that remained untouched. The walls of the cavern were the victims of Darren's pickax. They were mostly rock, but that was only because countless tunnels had been made in the parts of the walls that were dirt already. The rest of the walls were solid and looked like painted wood, marred with grooves both shallow and deep.

Franklin cursed loudly hours after he and Darren had separated that day. "There's a whole other cave here!" Franklin announced.

Darren rushed with the others to gather around the small opening Franklin had made in one of the walls. Franklin stared into the head-sized hole at eye level. He stepped back. "Have a look," he told Darren.

The other twenty workers let Darren glance first. He held up his lantern as he peered through. The caverns were always dark and always warm, no matter what the weather was like above ground. But this cavern seemed to be different. It was dark, yet there were fragments of light that danced along the walls, as if from a source behind a distorted window in the distance.

It wasn't just regular warmth on Darren's face. The heat was heavy, as if Franklin had opened an oven door by making this hole.

Darren stepped away to let the other men fight over who would look next. "Get the overseer," he told Franklin.

"Why me?" Franklin complained.

"So no one else can claim it was them who found it. There might be an Artisary in there."

"Eh, someone always says that."

"Yes, but how often has that someone been me?"

This drew the attention of many of the other men. The colloquial word "Tisary" was thrown around a lot, but no one claimed to know anything. The men questioned Darren as to how he knew.

"I don't," he said. "All I know is that we've spent years in this cavern, and I've never felt heat or seen light like that."

Everyone speculated aloud. They all knew enough about Artistry to understand that this likely meant that a rift was open somewhere in the other cavern. There was no way to know how long it had been open or how long it would last. But that didn't matter. The most important detail to these men was when they would be paid their "discovery coin" for being part of the team that found this place.

Darren let himself be excited for just a moment about the idea of a year's worth of wages. It should mean that he would have enough to take his boys elsewhere. He had thought much about where to go, but now that it might actually happen, he couldn't decide.

He suppressed his excitement. How likely was it that the overseer would even fulfill this promise? There was nothing that twenty diggers could do against the Digging Guild itself. The Farmers' Guild would receive coin from the Digging Guild for this discovery—the two guilds had other agreements as well. The Farmers' paid the salary of all the guards in the city. Hundreds of armed men would slaughter Darren and the rest of the diggers if they tried to use force to get their promised coin.

Without any extra coin, Darren would be forced to keep his boys in this city. However, it could be dangerous to stay in Jatn if this really was a Tisary they had discovered. The men had already begun clearing away more of the wall so there was enough room for any of them to squeeze through. They all looked at Darren to go first.

"Seems safe enough," said one of them as he stepped aside. Darren knew all of their names, but it usually became hard to tell them apart in the dark, especially when dirt masked their faces and clothes.

He got his knees up into the hole. Darren adjusted to a squat, then waddled a few steps to get through the hole. He looked carefully at the ground of this new cavern while holding out his lantern. It seemed just like the dirt from the previous cavern, but something was different about this place.

It wasn't just the heat and the subtle flares of light that rang warning bells in Darren's mind. It felt as if something was living here.

He eased his feet down one at a time until he was standing completely on the other side. The light of his lantern didn't reach far in this wide cavern. He heard water dripping somewhere, which was normal in places like these. He turned for a look at the high walls behind him, finding a ceiling with rock icicles seemingly the same as those he was used to. The walls looked the same as well, their composition still unknown to everyone. It wasn't rock or dirt. It sometimes made him think of mold, as if it had grown here unchallenged over hundreds of years until it became harder than dirt but softer than rock. It was smooth in most parts, mostly white with hues of yellows and oranges. Something was different about it on this side, though.

He put his hand on one of the rocky icicles. *Warmer than the other side,* he thought. *Why?*

Movement caught his eye, spinning him around. He saw nothing.

"Anything?" one man called from the other side.

"Something indeed," Darren replied. "One moment."

He wished he could tell these men that it was animals that made this place feel alive. Animals could be easily controlled, removed, or exterminated, if necessary. But a creeping feeling was getting stronger and stronger that it was no animal that dwelled here.

He saw movement again, but it was not something skittering across the ground, as would be a blessing at this point. It was the ground itself. It pulsed as if a giant heart beat beneath it, yet the movement was so subtle that Darren wasn't sure if the ground was actually moving or if there was something more to the ground—something that ruled the ground like a law of nature—and if it was this that moved the ground.

Darren felt that he shouldn't be here; that it was his presence, or perhaps the hole behind him, that was about to cause something irreversible.

He had to explain this to his men, but he wasn't even sure he could explain it to himself.

The walls began to tremble in the same way as the ground. Darren practically dove into the hole.

"Grab the lantern!" he ordered to whoever was closest. "Hurry!"

He scrambled through after someone got the lantern out of his way, scraping his legs and arms against the rough surface. His limbs stung by the time he was through to the other side.

"Patch it up!"

"It could be a Tisary!" complained a few of them.

"It is," he confirmed. "But if you want your payment for discovering it, then you will help me patch it up. It could all collapse if we don't."

A few helped him move armfuls of the crumbled substance from piles on the ground into the hole. The others gave mutterings of confusion.

"Make way, make way!" said the overseer from behind the men. "What in KRenn's mind are you doing, Darren? Unblock this hole. I want to see the new cavern."

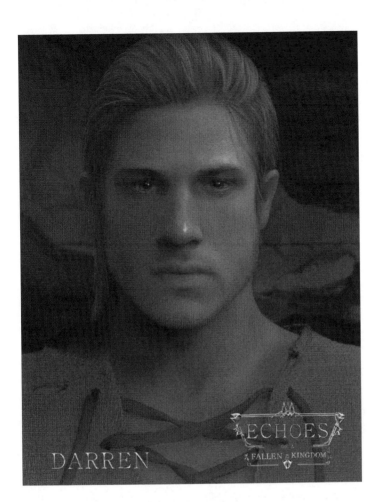

CHAPTER EIGHT

The men spoke the word "Tisary" in excitement in front of the overseer, some already bringing up the bonus coin. The overseer ignored all of them, pushing through to put himself right in front of Darren.

Clancey was somewhat short for a grown man. Darren stepped back so he didn't have to stare down upon him to meet his large, white eyes set in his round face.

"It's dangerous," Darren told him. "I think it will collapse if we enter."

"One small hole isn't going to make the wall collapse."

"Not just this wall," Darren said. "All of it might come down."

"Open it up," Clancey told the others, turning his back on Darren.

"Did you bring the Ascendant?" Darren asked.

"He's here with me," Franklin announced.

They all looked the same, holding their lanterns up near their chests, shadows hanging across their cheeks. Franklin came through with an older man who Darren saw every morning before entering the cavern and every evening upon leaving. The man was an Ascendant, a perpetually bored mage who was paid each day he waited and more whenever he had to enter the cavern to feel for Artistry. Clancey never used the Ascendant unless a new area was discovered, such as it was now.

Artistry normally was in the air and the ground, but its most dense form came from rifts, which only existed in open spaces, usually below the earth.

Darren told the two men re-clearing the hole that they needed to stop this moment. He was glad when they listened without complaint. He took over their task, carefully removing the blockage to keep the hole as small as possible. He asked the Ascendant, "Can you feel Artistry yet?"

"No, the opening needs to be bigger."

Because he is a weak Ascendant, Darren reminded himself. Had he been more powerful, he would've spent his days doing something more important than sitting by the opening of a cave.

Darren was not supposed to know anything about Artistry. In reality, he probably knew more than this Ascendant, who could only feel Artistry when it was rushing around him like an invisible hurricane. It was important not to disrupt the bonds made by Artistry on the other side of this wall because a sudden break might cause a collapse, Darren was certain of it. But how was he supposed to explain this when he was a mere digger? He could only hope that the Ascendant would know.

Darren finished clearing out the hole. It was only the size of his fist. *Should be small enough not to break the bonds.*

The Ascendant stuck his arm inside and let down his head, closing his eyes. Everyone fell silent.

"I do feel Artistry!" he announced. "A *lot* of it."

The men cheered, but the overseer quieted them with an order. "Make the opening large enough to fit the lot of you through."

"It could all collapse on top of us," Darren warned him.

"It won't," Clancey said with confidence, but Darren knew what this confidence was based on. The overseer didn't care whether there was a cave-in. In fact, it would be better for him if all of them died getting to this Tisary, because then he wouldn't have to pay them the promised bonus coin.

"It will collapse," Darren announced loud enough for the men to hear.

No one had decided that he would lead them. He certainly wasn't paid more for the responsibility. But he knew caves well from the one that was discovered in Halin. He had spent much time in the Tisary getting to know the diggers, gemcrafters, and Ascendants who passed their days there. Darren had even met a summoner who his father had learned to trust. The same summoner fought with Darren against the king's army and so many Analytes who had betrayed them. He died in battle, as did his otherworldly pet. So many had perished.

Darren wasn't about to let any more innocent lives be lost, no matter the risk of going against his overseer. But an inner voice reminded him how a risk to him could be a danger to his boys. He needed to keep his mouth shut, although he wasn't sure he could do that.

"How can you tell it's going to collapse?" Franklin asked Darren.

"I felt something when I went to the other side. Everything's connected there. I don't know how," he lied. "But the more rock we break, the more likely that the rest will topple."

Clancey was already sending the Ascendant off to avoid more payment. Darren knew that the overseer had heard Franklin's question as well as Darren's answer, but forcing Clancey to listen was like trying to lecture Andar about always behaving for his farm master.

"Wait, Ascendant," Darren commanded. He had a deep voice that, when used with the right amount of force, would cause even a king to pause. He used it sparingly, for it was a weapon that could come back to hurt him.

Clancey looked up at Darren with eyes of hatred. Only foolish men such as the overseer were never afraid. "You do not give orders to my Ascendant."

But the Ascendant had already stopped where the light was dim, looking back with a face covered by shadow. All Darren could make out was lifted eyebrows and the whites of his eyes.

"Can you feel when a connection has been made because of Artistry?" Darren asked. He already knew the answer, but he had to make a point.

"Yes," said the Ascendant with a liar's confidence.

"Then you would've mentioned such a connection when you felt the Artistry just now." Darren continued to announce his point before the Ascendant or the overseer could argue. "I know what I felt in there. It was all about to come down if we didn't repair the wall. It's the same way I know when it's time to eat or sleep, or when it's time to fight…"

He gave Clancey a quick glare. "It's an undeniable feeling that we disturbed something in there. If this Ascendant was any good, he would've picked up on the same feeling, but he did not. He would be elsewhere if he could. I don't mean any offense," he told the angry Ascendant. "I'm only concerned about the safety of everyone here. We are not disrupting the Tisary until an Ascendant arrives who can alter the bonds of Artistry. They must be powerful to do this, strong and confident enough that they would be willing to enter first once the bonds are broken safely."

"Nonsense and more nonsense!" Clancey spat. "You are a *digger*," he reminded Darren. "What could you possibly know about Artistry? Make an opening, or I will find men who gladly will do so and take the coin I'm sure the lot of you have dreamed about for years."

No one moved, so Clancey raised his voice. "Do it now, or I'm leaving to find a new team."

Eyes—so many pitiful eyes—were upon Darren. Death was the only thing worse than missing out on enough coin to leave this city for good. If he told them they would die, they would believe him. But even he didn't know the answer to this with complete confidence. He knew about Artistry, but he was not an Ascendant. He could not feel the actual strength of the bonds. He could not tell just how much damage would occur.

He could see, however, how desperately these men wanted to break through. They were so close to their dream. Every one of them had spoken about the coin they would receive upon discovering a Tisary as if it would change their lives completely.

And it would. Darren could not exclude himself from this, no matter the risk. He was just like the rest of them now, no matter where he'd been born or under what name.

But he had to try one last time. "It can't take more than a day to get the right Ascendant here. There must be at least one employed by the Farmers' Guild if the Diggers do not have one."

"It doesn't matter how quick it takes to get them here," Clancey said. "They are paid handsomely for their time and effort. You know nothing of Artistry. They must use a stone if they are to cast any spells, and each stone is worth more than all of your lives. You can't even fathom how much the Ascendant herself is worth."

Clancey was wrong about them always needing the stone. But he obviously had someone in mind, and this woman was probably easy to fetch. Darren tried to suppress his anger toward the overseer.

If Darren simply gave his body the order to attack, he knew his instincts would do the rest. It had been a long while since Darren had killed. He could easily slay Clancey before these twenty men could stop him. All it would take was one strike to the overseer's head with the pickax.

Darren grumbled out his frustration. "We wait for a strong Ascendant to break the bonds."

Clancey let out a bitter laugh. "Who are you to order these men to wait for their bonus coin?" He lifted his arms as he looked side to side. "Do the lot of you really want to wait?"

"Yes," Franklin replied, and many others chimed in with the same answer.

Clancey grimaced and lowered his arms, then mumbled something about their stupidity. "Just make the damn opening," he said. "Large. Or I'm leaving to get others who will replace you."

The men looked toward Darren. Although their faces were dark, he could feel that their desire to open up this Tisary had diminished out of fear.

Darren wanted to refuse the overseer again, but even he wasn't completely sure of the outcome. Perhaps they would be safe.

Or perhaps all of them would die here.

"Go slow," he instructed Franklin, as the two of them started scooping away the loose chunks of solid earth. "Everyone else, get back. Clancey, get an Ascendant who can actually do something. You will need her to verify the power of the Tisary anyway. Might as well have her here to save our lives if we need it."

"I will fetch her if the opening is done by the time we get back. If not, no bonus for any of you."

"The opening will be complete," Darren promised.

He was relieved when the overseer finally left with the weak Ascendant, both shooting looks like daggers over their shoulders.

Darren did not expect the sudden uproar from all twenty men that followed. They told him they must get their promised coin. He would be blamed if they didn't. Even Franklin joined in.

"My sick wife needs a doctor, Darren. This Tisary is a blessing," he said. "The gods have blessed all of us."

"Aye," agreed many.

Darren didn't believe in the gods. But even if he did, they had already cursed these men, not blessed them. For years, they dug and chipped away at the earth under the risk they would die down here with their bodies broken and mangled. Darren would not let that happen.

"Clancey doesn't pay dead men," he said. Fortunately, he didn't need to add anything else. It shut all of them up.

He and Franklin continued to clear the hole. No one urged them to go faster. He and Franklin made sure that the opening was at least a little bigger by the time the overseer returned.

"What in KRenn's mind is this?" Clancey complained as he walked up to inspect the hole. "A rat could barely fit through there."

Darren ignored him, eyeing the robed woman accompanying the overseer. It was strange to see a woman down here, pleasantly strange. It made the hot, dank environment seem just a little more bearable. Darren had felt no attraction toward any woman since his wife had passed, and this beautiful wizard was no different. All she did was remind Darren of what he had lost, what his boys had lost.

"Is this opening large enough for you to make sure it's safe on the inside?" Darren asked her.

"Let me see." She seemed partially deterred by the twenty staring men in her path as she made her way through.

She was clearly uneasy as she put her hand into the opening, looking back as if to ensure she had space.

"Give her room," Darren ordered as he pushed everyone back. He couldn't, however, stop all the eyes from drifting down toward her backside as she leaned forward to get a better angle for her arm.

"There is a great amount of Artistry in there," she said, her head turned and eyes closed. "There are strong bonds as well."

"What does that mean?" Franklin asked.

"How do I explain?" She pulled her arm out and faced the men. "Do all of you know that Ascendants can create links?"

"Yes," Franklin said. It was something everyone knew, though he didn't sound insulted by the obvious question.

"Do you know how these links are created?" she asked.

Franklin looked around to see if anyone had the answer. Darren kept his mouth shut.

"The Artistry," the wizard continued, "naturally forms a connection between two things that are similar. The more similar they are, the stronger the bond can be. An Ascendant is able to strengthen or weaken these bonds. Some Ascendants can even create their own bonds, when nature itself does not. The more Artistry is in an area, the stronger the bonds."

"Get to the point," Clancey urged. "There is a Tisary just past this wall, isn't there?"

"Yes, but getting to it will be difficult."

Clancey groaned. "No, it won't. My men will break down this wall."

"There's no telling what might happen if they do that," she said to Darren's relief. "This whole cavern could collapse in on itself."

"That's absurd," Clancey argued. "We're only talking about a hole big enough to fit a man."

"I realize that," she said with evident irritation. "But the bonds on the other side are strong. Everything is linked together; the ground, the walls, and the roof. Even a small hole in the wall could cause one reaction that will start another. You're lucky it hasn't started already."

"So Darren was right," Franklin announced. "He said it was dangerous, made us wait for you."

"Yes, all of you are lucky he did that," she said with her eyes on Clancey.

"Just get on with it, Lane," the overseer told the woman. "Do what you need to."

"It could take days."

"Days!? Do you honestly expect me to tell the digging guild master that, after all these years, we discovered a Tisary but have to wait days to get to it?"

"You can also tell him that this might be the densest Tisary in the world. I recommend you tell no one else, though. I'm obligated to tell the farmers' guild master about what I found here, but I will instruct him not to tell anyone else. He will talk to your guild master, and I'm sure they will create a plan going forward."

"They already have a plan," the overseer insisted. "They will collect the Ascendants and gemcrafters needed to turn this Artistry into coin."

"If they're smart, they will be more careful than that."

"*If* they're smart?" Clancey was incredulous. "I know you think you're important because you have some talent with Artistry, but your talents won't matter, woman, if you speak about the guild masters like that. Now break the bonds or do whatever you need to for my diggers to get into that Tisary *today*, or you will have to answer for disobeying me and insulting the guild masters."

Darren stepped in. "Then you will stay here with us as we make this opening," he told Clancey.

The overseer opened his mouth as if to argue, but Darren continued.

"Who knows what we might discover in there? No doubt it will be more valuable than all of our lives, but there's a good chance it will be more valuable than yours as well. Imagine if the guild masters heard that we diggers had first access to this Tisary because you were too afraid to be near the opening."

Clancey stared up at Darren, arms folded. Then he glared at Lane. "I'll give you today only. Tomorrow morning, we enter." He started to storm off.

Franklin called after him, "When do we get our promised coin?"

"Tomorrow, dolt. When we can step foot in the Tisary."

Franklin ignored the insult, cheering with the other men. Lane quickly got to work pressing herself against the wet wall, her arm jammed into the opening. She was so focused on her task, she didn't seem to mind dirtying her robe.

Darren didn't want to disturb her, but he couldn't go without at least expressing his gratitude.

"Thank you," he told her.

She opened her eyes, then looked up to meet his face. "You're Darren Litxer, I assume?"

Had someone mentioned his surname to her?

"Yes, and you are, Lane...?"

"Lane Writhe. I've never heard of a digger convincing his overseer to do anything, especially not waiting to get into a Tisary. I don't know how you convinced him, but I'm glad you did. These men might be dead if you hadn't. How did you know about the bonds?"

He was more interested in asking her questions of his own. What kind of employed Ascendant would risk everything to comment on the intelligence of her guild masters? Clancey wasn't far above her in rank, though he was above her nonetheless.

"I stepped foot in there before we closed the hole up again," Darren said. "I felt something that seemed to be alive."

She looked curious but said nothing of it. Instead she smiled. "I hope these men realize what you've done for them."

The diggers had stepped back and formed little circles, all of them chatting away about what they were going to do with their coin.

"It's you we have to thank," Darren said. He offered his hand.

She took her arm out of the wall to shake his hand. He was surprised at the coarseness of her palm. What kind of Ascendant was this?

He felt something from the smile she gave him that he'd figured he was incapable of feeling anymore. He was suddenly aware of there being so much more to her. She was tall for a woman, like his late wife. She seemed to be a few years younger than Darren, not a wrinkle on her face. Her hair was light, though he couldn't quite tell the color, for everything was darker in the cavern. He wondered about her past.

Is she married? asked a timid inner voice that Darren hadn't heard since he was a shy boy.

"I'm going to be working all night," she told him, "so I'd better get back to it. But I should warn you about something before you leave with the rest of the men."

Darren looked behind him. He hadn't noticed everyone walking off.

"What is it?" he asked her.

"This Tisary could change everything, and not for the better. It was the discovery of a Tisary like this one that led to the war between the Quims and the King."

There was no one who knew this better than Darren. "I will be leaving this place as soon as I get the coin promised to me."

"Good," she said. "Though I do hope we'll see each other again under better circumstances."

He was flustered as he searched for words. Her voice was smooth and confident, even when standing up to Clancey.

All Darren thought to do was nod his head like a fool. Then he made it even worse by bowing before her. It was the only way he knew how to greet and depart from women.

"Oh," Lane said with a small chuckle. She curtsied exaggeratedly. "Goodbye, sir," she said in a mock formal voice.

"Goodbye," he said in his normal tone.

He stood there for a moment as she closed her eyes and got back to weakening the bonds on the other side of the wall. Embarrassed, he turned and walked off.

The thought of the coin that he would receive tomorrow erased his shame. He had hoped for this day for years. It would soon be time to take his family out of this wretched city.

CHAPTER NINE

It was a long walk out of the cavern. When Darren and the other diggers had originally discovered this underground opening, getting in and out was easy. But now, years later, the cavern was two miles in length, depending on which tunnels Darren took. The longest tunnel was one that led to solid rock, a waste of months of digging. But the Tisary that Franklin had broken into was just about a mile from the only opening.

Darren found Franklin waiting for him when he surfaced. "Stayed to chat with the pretty wizard, did you?" Franklin asked with a grin.

"She needed to be thanked for what she did."

"I'm sure gratitude is not the only thing you want to give her." He laughed. Darren did not. "Why is it that you've never spoken about women? I know you lost your wife." Franklin's tone had softened. "But that was long ago. Don't your boys need a mother?"

Franklin's wife was sick. It would not be appropriate to ask him how long it would take for him to be interested in another woman if she passed, though the question did come to Darren's mind. He gave his friend a sour look and opened his mouth to express his displeasure. But before he could say anything, Franklin threw up his hands.

"Whoa, whoa, whoa," he repeated. "I don't know what I'm saying. That was completely wrong. My head's not on my neck straight after hearing about this coin we'll be getting tomorrow. Of course Andar and Leo don't need a mother. I was just thinking a woman might help you, was all."

Darren silently forgave his friend. "It would, so long as she was the right woman. I can't afford to feed another person no matter how pretty she may be."

"You can after you get your coin," Franklin said with a smirk.

"I wanted to talk to you about that. I'm going to be leaving this city, and I suggest you do the same."

Franklin cocked his head. "Why?"

"There will be strife here. It might not be for a day or a week, but it will come to Jatn."

"It shouldn't," Franklin said. "The Farmers' Guild governs this city. It's their laws that say the Tisary goes to the discoverer, in this case the Digging Guild. They are paid bonus coin, like we will be tomorrow. Everyone's happy with that."

"Not everyone. The opportunity of great wealth that comes with the Tisary not only attracts the powerful, it will turn them aggressive. The farmers' and the diggers' guilds aren't the ones we need to worry about. The city will become dangerous from the others who come here."

"What others? The king? Again?" Franklin laughed.

"Why not?" Darren posed. "And if not him, then someone else."

"You always worry too much. Just take your coin and buy yourself a small house somewhere far from this place. I will."

Darren supposed Franklin should be safe, but Darren's family might not. Word was bound to get around of the digger who knew too much about Artistry. Powerful people *would* be coming here. All it took was one of them to be suspicious enough to search for him. Armies could form, like before. Recruitment would be quick and drastic. Anyone with skill or knowledge might be absorbed into the strife.

A boy approached Darren and Franklin, stopping in front of Darren to look up nervously as if afraid. "Are you Darren Litxer?"

"I am."

"I have a note for you."

Darren had a feeling that he knew exactly what this was. It was unfortunate that Franklin was beside him as he took the note.

"Oh, a letter for a digger?" Franklin teased. "Who do *you* know who's fancy?"

The boy ran off when Darren took the note. "It must be a mistake," Darren lied as he opened it. As expected, the note was blank. "See," he said to Franklin. "Someone just made an error."

"Now that's strange. The boy knew your surname. How could the note be blank? It was sealed."

Darren pocketed it, hoping to end the conversation. "Just be careful from now on, especially with the coin you're going to get."

"Yeah, yeah. Last I checked I was older than you. I know a few things. I keep my family safe." Franklin sounded offended.

"I apologize. I'm just worried."

"Yeah...always worried." Franklin tossed a hand in the air as he walked off. "See you tomorrow when we collect our coin. Don't be late!"

Darren wouldn't. Clancey would use any excuse he could not to pay.

Letting out a sigh, Darren patted his pocket. He had received many notes like this one, blank yet sealed. They always meant one thing. He had to visit Raenik immediately.

There were too many men that Darren despised. Hatred wasn't good for anyone to hold onto for so long, but Darren had no way of getting rid of Raenik, or any of the others who bothered him deeply. The only peace would be when Darren brought his family out of the city.

That might be soon, Darren reminded himself, which would mean that this could be the last time he saw Raenik.

Raenik's shop was in the north, where most of the buildings had a second story to them. The man was a tailor, though Darren assumed he probably wasn't very good at it. The only people who were good at their work were those who depended on it for coin. Raenik had another service, one that Darren had unfortunately needed when he first came here with his healthy wife, Leo in her womb, and a three-year-old Andar.

Some of the streets in the north were riddled with disgusting puddles of human waste, the smell as putrid as in most of the southern side of the city. No dumping was allowed in the north, but Darren saw plenty of people tossing out buckets of different kinds of waste all the time. No one was any different here than they were elsewhere. Some people just had coin and education, while others didn't. There were only a few who were different, like Lane. He had just met her, and yet he somehow knew that no matter the power or wealth she accumulated, she would always care about the lesser man.

The lesser man. Darren wanted to spit. The phrase was used by overseers and guild masters to describe people like him, diggers and farmworkers. He was disgusted that their words had permeated into his thoughts.

Raenik's shop was one of few with a link active. When Darren opened the door, a bell rang on the other side of the shop. Darren had seen people's reactions upon entering for the first time—confusion and amazement. Many would shut the door just to open it again, confirming that the bell rang each time. They would always ask the same thing. "How?"

"Magic," Raenik would reply. "My shop is practically made of it."

No, his shop was made of deceit and crime. The only reason he had enough coin to pay a powerful Ascendant to link the door to the bell was because of the business he conducted in the back of his shop, where no tailoring was ever done.

The laws of Jatn were lenient regarding identification papers. There wasn't much effort put into finding those with false papers or those falsifying the papers themselves. So the city was known across the kingdom as a place full of runaway criminals with false identities.

Upon entering the city ten years ago, however, Darren had found it to be nearly impossible to locate someone like Raenik. He didn't know where to look. Of course there were no signs on shops advertising paper falsification. There was no one in the market selling the parchments with new names or with the necessary seal of the king at the bottom. There was, however, Raenik at the market one day.

Darren didn't know how Raenik identified Darren as someone who needed false papers, but then again Raenik was skilled at his true work. It took him less than a few minutes to convince Darren that he could not only be trusted, but that he had exactly what Darren needed.

The issue wasn't just the amount of coin it cost him to get papers for himself, his wife, and Andar. It was that Darren had to give Raenik his old papers. The only reason Darren hadn't destroyed them before then was because he had heard that counterfeiters like Raenik kept them after the exchange was over. It was the only way patron and supplier could trust each other. Raenik couldn't go to the guards because he would incriminate himself. And Darren couldn't go to the guards because Raenik had possession of his old identity.

Darren had realized his mistake when he finally showed Raenik his true identity papers. The tailor's eyes bulged with opportunity. He even gave a laugh. "*The DVend Quim?*" he'd asked as if in disbelief.

All Darren could do was nod and glance at the closed door over his shoulder. They had been in the back of Raenik's shop, first through a locked door and then through a hidden opening that was only revealed once Raenik had stuck his arm under his desk and moved something. *More Artistry*, Darren had realized. *Another link, this one far more powerful than the link between the bell and the door.*

It had not taken long for Raenik's plans with Darren to become clear. Even after Darren had paid nearly all the coin his family had, the longer form of payment had just begun.

Darren now waited for Raenik to appear, the bell chiming as Darren shut the door behind him. He knew they would both desire privacy for whatever Raenik wanted to discuss.

Raenik appeared at the top of the stairs and motioned for Darren to come to him. Darren obeyed. Neither of them spoke nor bowed. Their relationship had begun without a greeting. They'd never had one since, and Darren was certain it would end without a goodbye one day. Soon.

More garments were on display on the second floor, just like the first. But the long dresses here had lines of dust clinging to their bottoms.

"Were you going to tell me?" Raenik asked. He wasn't an ugly man, always clean-shaven with his hair combed back. His eyebrows were thick, a bit messy, but that just did more to frame his bright blue eyes. There was no denying that he was smart, capable. It was his lack of regard for others that twisted Darren's insides. How Raenik could go about his life without caring what he did to people was a mystery.

"Tell you what?" Darren asked in return.

"You're going to pretend you have no idea why you're here?"

"To threaten someone again, I assume." It was the same request he received every time. Darren didn't know who these people were in Jatn who weren't doing what Raenik asked of them, but the guilt Darren felt every time he threatened them was sickening. All seemed innocent, most of them ready to run at any sign of conflict. All that was required was for Darren to take on a certain look and posture. He had gotten good at it over the years. The fear in their eyes was immediate. He would tell them to do as Raenik had told them to do, and then he'd leave. Darren was often kept awake at night worrying that one day someone would not obey. He had to make sure he got his posture just right so he could avoid that, the threatening look in his eyes equally important.

Raenik sighed in clear frustration. "You always make this more difficult than it needs to be, and for what? The result is the same. You do as I ask."

"Get on with it," Darren said.

"The Tisary, *DVend*. You claimed you would tell me if one was ever discovered."

Darren was too shocked to reply. How had Raenik already found out? He'd always seemed like a lone criminal, practically incapable of working with others, but perhaps he was more involved in the powerful guilds than Darren knew. *There could be someone above him*, Darren realized with dismay, *someone even smarter and richer than he is who knows what I used to be.*

Yes, Darren had made the promise to tell Raenik if a Tisary was discovered, not that Darren had any idea how Raenik was supposed to use it for himself. But if there was someone else involved with Raenik, someone of high rank in the powerful guilds, then all of it would make sense.

Darren had to get out of this city.

"It was *just* discovered," he said. "I had just left the cavern when I received your summons."

"I'm disappointed with you. We have to trust each other."

"No, we don't. That's what blackmail is for. Now what do you want with me?"

Raenik folded his arms as if he might scold Darren, but Darren reminded the older man just who Raenik was scowling at by stepping closer. Raenik only tightened the fold of his arms.

"You will stay in the cavern and continue to dig," he demanded.

"I will not."

"You will work the Tisary with the others who are selected."

"No."

"And you will continue to create more tunnels to look for other Tisaries when your job is done."

"I will do none of those things."

Raenik looked dumbfounded, as if actually surprised by Darren's refusals.

"Have you forgotten that I can expose you?"

"You won't. Use me for something else. I'm not staying there." Darren couldn't purchase the horse, carriage, and other supplies he needed to get his family out of here if he was underground during all the daylight. He considered lying to Raenik, but Raenik would find out Darren wasn't there by tomorrow morning.

"Did you know there's a reward for anything that leads to your capture, DVend?"

"I told you not to call me that." But no, he had not heard of a reward. One must've been issued as soon as Karlinda helped him and his sister escape prison, but news of this reward did not reach Jatn before he did.

There was certainly one for his sister as well, then. Darren hoped she was safe.

"Yes, a *handsome* reward," Raenik added. "So handsome that I sometimes wonder if it's worth the risk of turning you in. The only reason I'm not considering it at the moment is because you're useful to me."

Darren stepped even closer, forcing Raenik back. "What you should consider is what will happen if you make me desperate."

"You have been desperate since I've met you."

"Test me, and you will find that to be wrong. I will go back to the cavern tomorrow, but only to receive the discovery coin I was promised. I will not have anything to do with that Tisary." *And soon I will be gone.*

Raenik stared back at Darren, but only for a moment. His eyes drifted down to the corner of the small room as if trying to think of something. Darren wouldn't give Raenik's twisted mind time to scheme. He turned to leave, but Raenik didn't let him go without a warning.

"There are other things precious to you besides keeping your identity hidden. You don't want to play the game of threats with me."

My children. Darren had to stop himself from turning with a swing of his fist. He refrained from speaking for the moment so as to keep control over himself, a scream of rage suppressed. He chose to let his eyes do the work, but Raenik surprisingly showed no fear.

"I know what I said," Raenik told him. "I wouldn't want to take action against you, but it's *that* important you stay in the Tisary. I need to know everything that happens in there, and I promise it will be the last favor I ask."

"You will give me my old papers back?"

"After two months, I will. I shouldn't need you anymore after that."

"Fine," Darren lied. "Just give me a day to myself tomorrow. There are matters I must take care of."

"No, the team will be chosen by then. You must speak to Clancey in the morning and join them."

Darren knew he wasn't a good liar. There was too much to consider if he stretched the lie farther, such as how long it would take Raenik to punish Darren when he did not show up for work in the Tisary, and what that punishment would be. He would rather converse with Raenik through fists, or better yet, blades, but that would land Darren in prison faster than if he disobeyed Raenik.

He had his boys to consider foremost. Their safety wasn't at risk here, but Darren's was. He couldn't get involved in the Tisary, and he couldn't leave the city without at least one day to prepare once he had the coin. He wasn't even sure how easy it would be to convince his sons to go. Andar should be fine with leaving, but Leo's tenth birthday was nearly here. Soon he would be an apprentice at the Bookbinding Guild. Darren didn't know what he could tell Leo to make him want to give that up, but he was sure he could force his boys to leave if it came to that. He hoped it wouldn't.

Raenik still needed an answer. Darren couldn't manipulate men like this with deceit. He didn't know why he had even tried.

"I'm not returning to the Tisary, and you will do nothing to me or my boys, or you will regret it."

There was no point to stay any longer. Darren held his glare for one last moment before leaving Raenik red-faced in obvious fury.

It was late, the sun setting quickly. Darren had to get home before nightfall, or it would be difficult to navigate through these windy streets, many without names. He looked forward to seeing his sons. They would probably already have supper ready, Andar having nabbed something delicious for them to add to the meal. Darren still feared the boy would be caught one day, but he had tried to stop Andar from stealing countless times over the years. It was no use, and Andar had certainly proven he was capable. Darren's biggest fear now was not that Andar would be arrested. It was that he would find out about the Thieves' Guild here in Jatn.

His sons smiled at him when he arrived home. "Father," Leo said. "You're late. Is everything all right?"

"Yes, everything's fine." Darren would find a way to tell them about the Tisary, the money, and leaving eventually. But for now he couldn't think past the hunger in his stomach as he glanced at the meal waiting for him. The boys had already eaten, he saw, but they sat down anyway and glanced at one another as if there was a secret between them.

"What is it?" Darren asked his eldest son after swallowing his first mouthful of buttery rice with chunks of seared pork. He didn't know where the pork came from, though he was almost certain it had been transported here in Andar's filthy pocket. No matter.

"We were followed this morning," Andar answered. "Someone with a hood. We never got a good look. I think they wanted to see where we work, but we lost them. They must know where we live, though. I noticed them right after leaving."

Darren's appetite was gone. He was so angry he couldn't sit, nearly knocking the table over as he rose up. He started toward the door, prepared to march all the way to Raenik's shop and beat the life out of the man, but it was a rash thought. Raenik wouldn't even be there by the time Darren arrived.

Who had Raenik sent to watch the boys?

Wait a moment, Darren thought. *The Tisary wasn't discovered until the afternoon. Raenik wouldn't have sent someone to follow my children this morning. He didn't know about the Tisary until later.*

"Father...?" Leo asked, his eyes large. He and Andar were motionless.

"Everything's fine," Darren repeated. "I will figure out who's following you..." Darren was about to say that he would take care of this tomorrow, but he *had* to get to the cavern early. If he wasn't there with the rest of the men, Clancey could take advantage of them without worry of an uprising. Darren wouldn't get all the coin he'd earned, all the coin his family needed. The others wouldn't either.

"How can you figure it out?" Andar asked.

"You must leave early tomorrow," Darren said. "Which means you'll have to get to bed as soon as we finish this conversation. No training tonight. I will follow both of you in the morning and keep myself hidden. Try not to make it obvious that you know anyone is following you. I will locate them."

"And what will you do to them?" Leo asked nervously.

"Only find out who they are," was all Darren would say. He sat down to finish his food while it was still warm.

"If we leave early," Andar said, "it might be before the follower is ready."

"We have to leave early tomorrow so I can get to my work on time," Darren explained. "If no one follows you, all the better."

The boys looked at one another as if this wasn't all they had to tell him. Darren gave them a few moments as he devoured his dinner.

Eventually Leo blurted, "Andar took a magic stone from someone and they came back here to get it."

"Leo!" Andar complained.

"We *have* to tell him. Father, I think it's why we were followed."

He suppressed his frustration. "What magic stone, Andar?"

"We don't *know* it's magic."

"It was," Leo said with so much confidence that it confused Darren. How could the lad be certain of this?

"Did the stone glow?" Darren asked. There were only a few stones of the other realm that glowed, but that was not a requirement for any of them to be "magic."

"No," Leo said. "But it doesn't need to, right?"

Darren had too many questions, unable to decide which one to ask first. Did Leo learn this from reading books with Rygen? Was there really enough information in *any* book for him to be certain when a stone was magic, even if it did not glow? Unless Leo had an affinity toward Artistry, there was no way for him to be certain... Darren felt a chill. He looked closer at both of his sons. There was no doubt in their eyes that the stone was magic. They had felt something from it, and there was only one thing Darren knew of that they could feel from such a stone.

"You're right, Leo," Darren said when he composed himself. "It does not need to glow. What happened to the stone?"

"I threw it out the window," Andar said.

"Which window?" Darren asked.

"Our bedroom."

"*Toward* Verona's house?"

Andar let down his gaze as he nodded. "But not on purpose. I wanted it to land between our homes."

"What happened?"

"Leo and I went out later in the night to move it, but it wasn't there."

"Why did you wait until later?"

"You weren't home yet," Andar said, but then he paused.

"So why didn't you tell me to get it when I came home?"

"I...don't know."

"Then at least answer why you waited to move it." Darren couldn't rid his voice of the disappointment he felt.

"We should've moved it right away, but there were screams...and the creature on the roof."

They were afraid, of course. Guilt quickly dissolved his frustration with his boys.

Darren reminded himself that nothing had happened to Verona or Rygen. Perhaps the boys were right not to go after the stone right away.

"You should've told me all of this as soon as I came home," Darren said. "I had asked you if I should know what it was you took from the market that day."

"I know." Andar kept his head bowed.

There was a silence as Andar shifted in his seat. Eventually he looked up again. "Actually, you asked if you wanted to know what I took."

Darren ignored the comment. "Who did you take the stone from?"

"A woman wearing a hood at the market. She had many stones on her table, but this was the only one that I..." Andar stopped.

"What?" Darren asked.

"I don't know how to explain it."

"I taught you that you always can explain. The right words exist for everything."

"Not this," Andar said, lifting his head. His eyes glistened. "There's nothing like what I felt from the stone. No words for it."

Darren grumbled a curse. He knew what this meant.

It doesn't have to change everything, he reminded himself.

But perhaps it already had. The boys had been followed this morning. A Tisary had been discovered. Jatn was changing, even if they were not. The city would become much more dangerous for all of them now.

The plan to leave was now the only plan. It had to be soon.

"It's going to be all right," Darren said. "Neither of you are in danger," he lied. "And if you ever are, I will protect you." The last statement was true, and he was certain his boys knew this from the way they gazed at him and seemed to finally relax.

*****

Darren couldn't get to sleep that night. He saw more similarities between his sister and his children the older they got, especially Andar. Yune had been on Darren's mind a lot since he'd read the book that he figured she'd written. It was probably one of the only ways for her to make coin, for bookbinders did not ask for authors' papers when reading their book. They only cared about the contents on each page. Authors could use any name they wanted. It did not need to match their birth name.

But the book had made DVend Quim seem so much more of a hero than he really was. He bested everyone he fought, yes, but to claim that he was the best swordsmen in the world was wrong. The best wouldn't have nearly lost his life in battle. The best would've been able to protect his sister. Yune couldn't possibly think this about him.

The hero described in the book she'd written would've saved his wife from a simple illness, and he wouldn't be living in a house that he did not own, with rotted walls that would one day collapse.

He wanted to tell his sons the truth. They were Quims, like him, but that name meant nothing but a prison sentence now. They would find out from him eventually, when they were older and the truth had no chance of slipping from their mouths. Leo was so innocent still. He trusted people too much.

However, Andar didn't trust enough. Darren didn't know how he could fix this, but he would try. The boy deserved companionship one day, and at least a friend until then. All he had now was a brother and a father.

On their way to bed, Andar stopped to ask, "So what was the stone that I took, Father?"

"It sounds to me like a rift stone, like you said. I don't know what type." Darren did, but the true answer would provoke more questions that his sons were too young to worry about. "You were good to get rid of it."

"That's all?" Andar asked.

He was getting too smart, often seeing through Darren's...withholdings of the truth. They were not lies. He refused to think of them like that.

"We shouldn't assume more than we know," he said, now recalling that he often gave them this same line when he wanted them to cease their questions. At least the statement was true, though there was always more Darren knew than he would bring to light. They would understand when they were older. For now, however, the half-worried and half-disgusted looks Andar sent his father's way were as if Darren planned to abandon them any day now. He never would.

"And who do you think is following us?" Leo asked before Darren could shut the door to their bedroom. The boys were in bed by then, sitting up in the dark.

Darren was thankful for Andar's vigilant eyes, for Leo never would've noticed someone following. But there was a reason Andar had to be so vigilant, a reason Darren couldn't be proud of. Andar perpetually feared being caught for one of his past crimes.

Darren had looked over his shoulder the same way for years after arriving in Jatn. He got used to it. Andar probably had as well, but Darren didn't want Andar to have to get used to something like that. It was as much Darren's fault as Andar's. He couldn't provide everything they needed.

"I won't know who it is until I find them," Darren said. "In the meantime, do what your brother tells you. Good night, boys."

"Good night," they answered together."

Darren let out his breath when he got into bed. He was exhausted, and yet he found no comfort in shutting his eyes. His body was alert, as if detecting danger. He felt as though he needed to get up right now to look for his sister. Leo was supposed to have asked Rygen about the author of that book, but he hadn't mentioned anything.

No, Darren had told him to never mind. Darren was becoming more forgetful. It was the...withholdings of truth. This was why he couldn't lie. He was bad at it.

The boys were already suspicious that Darren was keeping things from them, especially Andar. He clearly didn't want to pry, and Darren didn't know why, though he was thankful for it.

His thoughts drifted to his sister. Yune could take care of herself, as she always had. Their father had put too much focus on Darren when he and his sister were younger, though Yune had never seemed jealous. She enjoyed the freedom and privacy, two luxuries DVend never had.

His late wife came to mind. His heart twisted. If only they'd had the coin for a healer, she would still be alive. He had begged up and down the streets long after all his pride was gone. Not a single person even seemed to consider helping.

He didn't cry when his father was hung, because he had known after the war was lost that his father would die, and Darren never saw it with his own eyes. But when his wife, Farinda, had died and turned so cold and pale, Darren couldn't stop weeping. There were only moments in the next few weeks where his eyes were dry. Andar was hopefully too young to remember. He had known his mother by another name, Larena.

Darren was glad that the Tisary would provide enough coin for Franklin to ensure his wife recovered. But there were too many others dying around the city when they could live. Everything that the people of Jatn needed was within reach; it was just in greedy hands.

Darren's father had put many measures into place in Halin to ensure that no one died who could've lived with the proper care. No one, no matter how poor. It was surprisingly easy. Medicine was cheap for the wealthy.

Darren had almost forgotten about Lane Writhe, but the moment she came to his thoughts he couldn't seem to think of anything else. She was young to be a powerful Ascendant, probably a few years younger than Darren. He didn't feel young himself, though he knew he was. At thirty-one, he had so much life left to live. He would see that his boys were not entrapped in poverty, as so many families were. He still had a year before Andar was considered an adult, four for Leo. Even after, Darren had time. He felt even stronger than he had during the war, the years of digging seeing to that. He couldn't remember the last time he held a real sword, though training the boys made him realize that everything he knew was still part of him. His body wouldn't forget.

The loss of Larena had torn his heart, but the rapid thumping in his chest sparked by Lane made him recall what love felt like.

There's still time, he told himself. *There's still time for everything, but it all starts with tomorrow.*

CHAPTER TEN

Darren let his boys walk ahead of him for a while before he started to follow them. Both of them had been told not to look behind them. If the woman from the market was indeed following, she would take less care to hide herself if the boys never seemed to suspect she was there.

They followed his instructions to use their normal route to the farm. Darren saw no one. He let there be more and more distance between him and the boys as he became more comfortable. He kept track in his mind where they were on which street as he took side roads and even climbed onto buildings that looked secure enough to hold his weight. He stayed as hidden as he could while he watched everyone who was going in the same direction as his children.

If there was someone following them that day, Darren didn't see them.

He would have to try again tomorrow, leaving at the normal time. Darren circled around to put himself behind his boys again. They stopped just before the long fence of the farm and finally looked back. Leo ran to him, setting Andar into a jog.

"Did you see anyone?" Leo asked.

"There was no one today, but I will follow again tomorrow."

"Ah, and now we're here too early with nothing to show for it," Andar complained. "Rhenol probably isn't even up yet."

"I'm sorry for that, Andar, but I had to make sure I am not late to the cavern today especially. Tomorrow will be different. I have to go." Darren knelt down and opened his arms for both of his boys to come close. Andar was much taller than his father at this position. He would probably match Darren's height by the time he was fully grown. Leo was still small, able to press his cheek against Darren's as they hugged. There was no telling what height he was going to be.

Darren ran across the city to get to the cavern by the time the sun had risen clear over the horizon, the start of the day. The entrance to the cavern was past the western edge of Jatn. There was no wall to designate the end of the city, like there was in Halin. The sporadic homes eventually came to a stop. Darren didn't know how the Farmers' Guild could defend the Tisary from anyone coming to take it. His father had built a wall around the other cavern, keeping that Tisary's existence hidden from nearly everyone until the wall was done. But even Raenik had heard of this latest Tisary already. The Farmers' Guild did not have the same ability to control an entire city, like Darren's father had. The big difference was that hardly anyone in the city wanted to listen to them.

All nineteen of the other diggers were standing in a cluster, watching Darren come toward them. Darren must've been late. Their stormy expressions made him struggle for breath.

"It's the coin, isn't it?" Darren predicted when he was close.

"Aye," said Franklin.

Darren noticed that Clancey was standing far behind them on top of the tunnel that led into the cavern. Beside him were two groups of armored men, about twenty strong in total.

"How much did he pay each of you so far?" Darren asked.

Again, Franklin answered for everyone. "Ten gold coins." He spat. "Would rather pay all them guards to keep us from fighting than give us the rest."

They had been promised fifty gold coins each upon the discovery of a Tisary. Not only had they found a Tisary, they had found one that might have more Artistry than any other discovered, at least in human land. There was not a lot of news from the east, where the Analytes lived.

Diggers were paid one silver and three copper coins per day. Ten coppers were equal to a silver coin, and ten silvers were equal to a gold. Darren and these men were promised fifty gold coins—a little more than a year's worth of work. Ten gold coins was certainly significant, but horses were expensive in Jatn. So a horse *and* carriage were too expensive for most diggers to ever purchase. Darren had spoken to merchants over the years to get a better idea of how much he would have to save. The cheapest horse and carriage that could take his family more than a few miles without breaking down would cost ten gold coins. That didn't leave enough to start their life in another city.

"I'm going to talk to Clancey," Darren said as he marched past the diggers.

He heard them wondering aloud if there was really anything he could do. Franklin told them, "If there's some law, Darren will know of it."

The laws here were against them, though. Darren could not strike his overseer without losing his hand. These guards were likely to be city guards, paid by the Farmers' Guild, which meant that the guild that controlled the city had already decided what was of the law. They would do nothing to Clancey for breaking his promise to Darren and the other diggers.

He found little reason to approach Clancey other than to collect his ten gold coins. He would prefer receiving his payment without having to get close to the gnarled face of the overseer. Clancey was uglier than any of the diggers, looking as if he'd grown up swinging a pickax in a dark cavern just like many of the men he now lorded over. But unlike these men, his face was scratched and pocked as if he'd fallen more than a few times while at work.

"How dare you?" Darren yelled as he started to walk through the guards. He didn't know what came over him, but there was no stopping now as the men in boiled leather armor held him back. He didn't fight them, but he didn't lower his voice, either. "Just because you have the coin to hire these guards, you think there will be no repercussions for cheating everyone?"

"Keep it to yourself, Darren," Clancey said as he approached. "If you calm down, I will explain."

Explain? Darren was so shocked at Clancey's calm reply that he lost all his aggression. Had Clancey ever offered to explain anything? Every word he'd spoken to the diggers was an order.

He gestured with a nod of his head for Darren to follow him away from the guards. They walked above the cavern, upon grass a healthy shade of green. The world was so different on this side, the sky a fresh blue sprinkled with clouds. But there was so much more to the world, to Aathon, than any one man could hope to see. For years, Darren and the diggers had spent their days in the dark. They deserved so much more than ten gold coins. But it seemed as if Clancey knew this, grimacing as if pained by something.

"Your coins," he said as he handed Darren a small pouch.

Darren looked inside. He hadn't touched a gold coin since he was in Halin. They were bright and smooth, nothing like the worn down coins of copper he usually handled.

"And the rest?" Darren asked.

"Listen to me—I didn't know this would happen. I thought all of you would be paid what you were promised."

"You make it sound as if you want us to be paid what we deserve. If that's true, then make it happen."

"You think these are my coins I'm handing over? I don't have that much money! They belong to the diggers' and farmers' guilds. It was the men above my rank who made this decision. It was their coin they didn't want to part with."

"And what did you do about it?"

"What can I do?" Clancey turned his pockets inside out, showing they were empty. "It's all the coin they gave me. The rest went to the guards."

Darren felt as though he had to believe Clancey. He had known the overseer for many years, and he was never one to soften any order, to pass blame to anyone else. He commanded the men, then took everything they threw back at him, never deferring, never sympathizing.

So why would he sympathize today? Then Darren realized what it was.

"You were promised a bonus as well."

"Yes, and I received a fifth of it just like the lot of you."

Darren knew that truly meant there was nothing either of them could do at this point. These guards were loyal to the guild, not to any man here. One even came over and told Clancey, "Give him his coin and get this over with."

"It's done," Clancey replied, showing Darren a sad look. "The diggers are leaving now. Darren, make sure of it."

Yes, they would have to leave. The only alternative was to stay and fight, but their pickaxes were elsewhere. They had no weapons, no armor, and none of them probably had any training. They would be slaughtered.

Even if through some miracle they killed these guards, what would it accomplish? They would be executed all the same. Even if they marched upon the governing building of the Diggers' Guild and demanded their payment, they would be killed.

Fortunately, the diggers didn't take long to be convinced that it was over. It was a surprise to Darren when they left so quickly, but then Franklin explained.

"We knew if there was anything that could be done, you would've thought of it."

"At least ten gold coins are more than enough to treat your wife."

"Aye, but it's not enough to buy us a house without a roof that leaks. She could get sick all over again. Ah, at least it's better than nothing. What work will you do now?"

"I don't know," Darren admitted.

"Well, I hope we see each other again. I can't imagine what digging would've been like if Darren Litxer was not down there with us."

Darren shook his friend's hand. "And your company added light to a very dark place."

Franklin grinned wide. He was missing a couple of teeth but never seemed to care. He smiled whenever he wanted, just as he spoke whatever came to mind.

Darren had better see Raenik to ensure he didn't have a powerful enemy to worry about, now that Darren would stay in the city for a while longer. He headed over there.

He was angry at the diggers' and the farmers' guilds, but that was just it. He was only angry. He wasn't enraged. This anger wouldn't cause him to take action against them. He strived for revenge, yes, but he was not willing to sacrifice anything to achieve it.

It was the ten gold coins, Darren realized. Had there been nothing, he and most of the diggers would've sacrificed a lot to show that they could not be treated this way. It wouldn't be a choice but an instinct—a mistake, as well, no doubt. But none of them would be able to help it. There would be injuries, possibly even casualties. The scene would spread the news of what the guilds had done across the city. Everyone would find out about the Tisary, and they would know the true nature of the promise that the Diggers' Guild issued to anyone working for them.

Still, the damage would be worse to the diggers themselves, and there would be no coin to show for it. Darren did the math in his head on the way to Raenik's shop. Ten gold coins was the same as a hundred silver coins, and Darren made one silver and three copper per day. That meant that ten gold coins were worth about seventy-seven days of work. It was certainly not nothing.

If he had a chance for revenge without sacrificing much, he would still take it, however. The people with power and wealth in this city clearly needed to be taught a lesson. But Darren remembered then how his father used to say the same about the king. Mavrim Orello had decided to take the Tisary in Halin by force simply because he wanted it. So many died because of this decision, and DFaren knew that they would.

"The king needs to pay for this choice," Darren's father would say. Their whole family had agreed that it was a battle worth fighting.

But now that it was over and they had lost, Darren would be a fool to still believe they had made the right choice. He thought about the life he could've given his children had the short war been avoided. He thought about the medical treatment he could've given his wife had they still owned enough coin in Halin.

Darren would have to find work again. Perhaps he could not only make peace with Raenik but find a way for the rich "tailor" to employ him. The tasks would be dastardly, no doubt, but Darren would always have a choice on how to handle whatever Raenik wanted him to do.

What was he thinking? This was Raenik. When had Darren become so desperate? He would find other work. It might take months or even years, but he would save enough in the end. Besides, Leo probably wanted to stay here longer. His birthday was tomorrow. He already had a meeting set with the bookbinding guild master, thanks to Rygen's mother. Darren was certain Leo would excel at that work.

After figuring out what to do with Raenik, Darren wouldn't let the day go to waste. Farms always employed men like him, but their wages were only a silver coin a day. Leo and Andar had already given their family the biggest benefit from the Farmers' Guild: If one member of a family worked on a farm, the rest could live in the provided house as long as the guardian resided there as well.

Darren couldn't be a guard, even though the payment was better. The Farmers' Guild looked into a person's history before employing a guard. He was glad for this fact, for he wasn't sure he could swallow his pride and work for the very guilds that had cheated and disrespected him and the other diggers.

He was too old to be an apprentice of any kind. No one would accept him. He did do accounting for his father when he was younger, though. He was quite good with numbers. Could he find work related to that?

His father, DFaren, had always wanted Yune to be more involved with the family's work. He'd tried many times to push the book of numbers and a quill in front of her. She'd tried. She'd tried with all her heart. Darren wound up feeling sorry for her. She kept making small errors, punishing herself for it with anguish and tears. Eventually, DFaren didn't have the heart to keep pushing her. She was no good with a weapon, either, and certainly had no mind for battle strategy.

She enjoyed the art of writing and painting, dabbling in both as she got older. Plays, she absolutely adored. She wrote and performed in a short one that was her gift for Darren's sixteenth birthday, a year before the Tisary was discovered and everything changed. Darren let out a laugh as he remembered a piece of her play. She was superb as an evil witch, her cackle unlike any sound Darren had heard her make before. It was so loud that it echoed down the halls of their mansion. It had even made their father laugh. The rest of the small audience joined in after. Each line that Yune delivered from then on was more and more exaggerated. Her monologues about how she would take revenge on the hero divulged plans that were silly and childish, like tickling him until he couldn't breathe or setting a plate of cake out in front of him that he could not eat!

Darren laughed harder as he remembered. She was quite talented, at least in this role. Her delivery was impeccable. He remembered nothing else from the play, only her character. It was one of the better gifts Darren had received for any of his birthdays, but none could compare to the sword of fine steel that his father had given him on his tenth birthday when his true training began.

Darren had to get a gift for Leo tomorrow. The poor people of Jatn did not give gifts on every birthday, only when children turned five and ten. The last gift children received was when they turned fourteen, when they were considered adults and probably all thought themselves to be as well, though they still looked like children to the rest of the world.

Not to some men, Darren realized as he remembered some of the disgusting marriages even in Halin between fourteen-year-old girls and older men.

His concentration broke as he came to Raenik's shop. A crowd had formed so dense that it took a bit of pushing to get through. One of the larger men pushed back as if looking for any opportunity to fight someone, but he froze when he looked at Darren and had to lean his head back to meet Darren's gaze.

He made it through to the front, only to find an armored guard standing before the entrance to Raenik's shop. The door lay on the floor in the shop as if it had been broken off its hinges and flung forward by a charging horse. But there wasn't enough space in the street for a horse or even a man to reach their full speed before ramming into the door.

The door had been sturdy, made of thick wood and fastened with a strong lock that could've kept even a team of guards from breaking in if they did not possess an ax.

Darren didn't know what else besides Artistry could've broken such a door off its hinges. There were two men inside the building, both glancing around as they spoke softly to one another. One was armored like a guard, resembling the one blocking people from entering, but the other had no armor or weapons. He wore a cloak and a cap that made him seem like some sort of official.

A detective, most likely. *So even the ranking guilds don't know what happened here.* The inside of the shop was a mess. Garments of all kinds covered the floor. Most racks had toppled. One shelf on the wall was split in half, the middle ends dangling.

"Is Raenik here?" Darren asked the guard before him.

"No, who are you?"

Darren showed him his false papers. The guard gave one look, then glanced over Darren's shoulder as if he was done with Darren.

"Raenik is a friend," he lied. "Do you know where he is?"

"No."

"Was he in the shop when it was found like this?"

"No," the guard said again. "You have anything to do with this?"

"No," Darren answered.

"Then leave it alone."

Darren wasn't going to figure out anything else by staying here, so he took his leave. The secret opening in the back wall seemed to be safe for now, but it just took someone finding the crank under Raenik's desk to open it. There was a good chance that many of the real identification papers were still back there, including Darren's. He would have to come back at night and hope there was some way for him to get inside.

He started to wonder about Raenik, but it almost seemed pointless. There were infinite possibilities of who Raenik could be involved with. Anyone could've come here and done this. *Well, anyone who has skill with Artistry.*

The only person he knew in the city who matched that description was Lane Writhe, but it wasn't as if he knew enough about her to tell if she was really capable of this kind of destruction. There had to be other Ascendants in the city. *But how many have no involvement with the high-ranking guilds?* A detective would not have been there if anyone in the powerful guilds already knew what happened.

It would be a relief to find out that Raenik had been killed, but that was unlikely. Darren had seen what kind of damage needed to be done to a person before they died. There were no signs of blood in Raenik's shop. He was alive somewhere, probably wishing he had done something differently. *Good. Let him squirm.*

Darren might not have to worry about the man anymore. He just needed to get his papers. If he destroyed them, he could finally relax.

At least it seemed clear that Raenik was not responsible for whoever was following Leo and Andar yesterday. But Darren found himself wishing it was Raenik, for then he would at least know who his enemy was. He wouldn't be able to sleep not knowing who was following his boys and why.

CHAPTER ELEVEN

Mornings were usually difficult for Leo. It was hard to get out of bed when he knew he had to spend his day at the farm. Usually, the thought of breakfast was the only thing that motivated him to grit his teeth, brace himself against the cold, and slip out of bed. However, today was different. He would not have to go back to the farm ever again, for today was his tenth birthday.

His excitement gave him energy. The cold felt like nothing. He even guessed he could go the whole day without eating because there was something beside his bowl of oatmeal that captured his interest. A book he had not seen before sat on the table. His father stood beside it wearing a grin.

"You bought me this?" Leo asked.

"I did, for your birthday."

But the book was big, probably expensive. "How much was it?"

"We have enough, don't worry."

"Are you sure?"

"Yes, Leo." Father gave a laugh. "We have enough coin."

"Now that I'm ten, will you tell me how much we have?"

"Enough."

Andar walked out of the bedroom and gave his brother's back a hearty pat. "It's your birthday, finally! And you're standing here bothering Father about how much coin we have? Don't you have to get ready to go to the Bookbinding Guild?"

"That leaves very little time for reading," Darren added. He scooped up the book. "I'll hold onto this until you're done with your breakfast."

Leo sat down and ate as quickly as he could, not even giving the oatmeal time to cool. He burned his tongue, but he didn't care. Before he was finished, he asked, "May I bring the book over to Rygen's house?"

"Finish your breakfast before we discuss anything, but don't burn yourself."

Too late for that. Steam wafted up from his bowl as he winced and gingerly touched his blistered tongue.

"Eh, this is my fault," Darren murmured. "I should've let it cool first." He handed Leo the book as Leo got up from the table. "Just make sure you reach the Bookbinding Guild before the sun is completely over the horizon."

"I know," Leo said. It was the time when nearly all jobs began. Almost everyone had to be somewhere before the sun was completely over the horizon, or someone else might be there to take their work. He wouldn't let that happen.

Leo opened the front door, about to rush out, but he jumped back in surprise as Rygen stood there with her hand poised to knock. She became startled as well, tossing the pie she held into the air. It flipped over once before Leo caught it with his free hand. It wobbled, but Leo managed to balance it. Good thing it wasn't very large.

"Great catch!" Rygen said as she took back the pie carefully with both hands, only to present it back to him. "Your birthday gift from me and my mother."

It was no doubt from the bakery where Rygen's mother worked, but it was still warm and appeared fresh.

It didn't seem to be days old like the other items Verona was allowed to take home. Perhaps she had purchased it?

"Thank you!" Leo said, wondering what delicious flavor awaited under the crust. He moved his hand toward his mouth, remembering his burned tongue. Where was the time he needed! Normally he couldn't wait for it to pass, but now every second was precious.

"Are you going to share?" Andar asked as he stood in the kitchen with their father. His tone was hinting, as if he already knew Leo would provide the right answer.

"Of course!" Leo put the pie on the center of the table. "And you can have some as well, Rygen."

"Thank you." But she seemed more interested in the book that Leo had tucked between his arm and his side.

"It's a gift from my father," he explained.

"What is it about?" Rygen asked.

"I don't know yet."

They all filled their mouths with pie and the delightful sweet flavor of apple.

After Darren swallowed, he answered, "It's the tale of the swordsman who was actually the best in the world."

"Better than DVend Quim?" Rygen asked skeptically.

"Yes. The swordsman is a greater legend. The book has many details of his bouts and battles."

These details were what the last book lacked. Leo ran for a look outside his house. He couldn't see the horizon well enough from here, so he climbed onto the roof. He put his hand over his eyes and squinted. The sun appeared to be rising quickly, already halfway over the horizon. There was hardly time to finish the pie, for he should be early on his first day.

He jumped down, falling onto his side from the impact. He quickly got himself up and ran back in the house, announcing that there was just enough time to finish the pie. As soon as it was gone, he handed the book to his father.

"Please put it in the safe box," Leo said.

"I will."

Leo grabbed Rygen's hand and nearly dragged her out the door. She chuckled. He had been to the Bookbinding Guild before. It was on the northern side of the city, a farther walk than the farm.

"There's time," Rygen tried to tell him. She seemed to be moving her little legs as quickly as she could to keep up.

"We should be early."

"Leo, there's time," she repeated. "It would be better to prepare you for your interview, don't you think?"

He slowed to a jog. "What should I know?"

"Gartel doesn't know much about you. Whenever I tried to tell him how interested you are in books and how excited you are to turn ten, he said he'll learn about you then. Well, then is now, so you should be prepared to talk about yourself."

Worry filled Leo's stomach, making him regret eating so quickly. "You told me he's nice to you."

"Yes, but I have seen him be mean to others."

Leo must've shown his fear, for she put up her hands. "But I'm sure he'll be nice to you. You love books, after all. He only speaks ill about people who cannot read or who don't respect books."

Leo frowned. "But there are so many people who cannot read because they have never been taught, yet they work hard."

"I know. He...he's not easy to describe." Rygen slowed to a walk and seemed to be thinking. "He's really nice sometimes. It's because of him that my mother and I can still live in the housing provided by the Farmers' Guild. He told me he has a deal with them. I think he pays them rather than has a deal, but that doesn't matter right now. Gartel *does* have bad feelings toward some people, and not all of them deserve it. You shouldn't worry, though."

"I think I know what kind of man he is, then." Leo imagined the overseer at the farm being nice to the people he actually cared about.

Leo had already heard of Gartel's "deal" with the farmers' guild master. His father had told him and Andar about it when they'd asked how Rygen and her mother could stay in that house despite neither of them working on a farm for more than a year. It hadn't come up between him and Rygen, and Leo was too jealous to want to think about it much anyway.

He had never before been allowed to enter the Bookbinding Guild. He arrived at its door knowing this time that he would step inside…a chill ran down his back.

The door itself was enormous, made of thick, dark wood that seemed as if it belonged in front of a castle. It must've cost a fortune. Beads of brass ran across its surface, seemingly serving no purpose other than to decorate the entranceway. A title was engraved into the top of the door, fancy letters with all kinds of loops and swirls. *The Bookbinding Guild.*

Unlike other guilds, this guild hall was also a shop. If anyone wanted anything to do with creating, selling, or buying a book, they came here. It was likely that the author of *Quim and Kin: Crowns and Betrayal* had met with the bookbinding guild master several times during the process of creating the book. Rygen had not seen the author, and when she asked Gartel about the woman, he said that the woman preferred that nothing be known about her.

Leo had recently told this to his father, who seemed disappointed at the news. Darren never offered a reply, though, even when Leo had asked why he cared about this author and not about others.

Leo put that out of his mind for now. Rygen knocked on the door with two hard swings of her fist. She shook her hand. "Ow, it always hurts me. But it's the only way he can hear. He'll keep the door open later in the day to make it easier for patrons to enter, but only we are allowed in right now." She took Leo by the shoulders and gave him a little shake. "I'm excited for you to be here, finally!"

All he had leading up to this moment was excitement as well, until this morning. Now it was as if he had a tenuous hold on this opportunity and any wrong movement would cause it to slip through his fingers.

He had chosen to ignore everything else in his life but this appointment, but he was quickly remembering that there was much more than just working at the Bookbinding Guild. If this went poorly, Leo would be forced to return to the farm. Rhenol would punish him for missing part of the day. Even worse, there was still someone out there who had followed him and his brother. They could've followed him and Rygen today, or trailed Andar while he was alone.

Was Father walking behind Andar today? The three of them had discussed this earlier, but no one seemed to plan for the busy morning that led to Leo running to the Bookbinding Guild with Rygen.

Would Andar be safe without him? *Of course*, Leo realized. He had never done anything to protect Andar. It was always the other way around.

Was Leo selfish to be here? He'd wanted this job so badly that he'd never wondered before. His family had always supported his decision, but could it be wrong?

No, he would make more money for them than if he stayed a farmer. He just hoped they would be safe.

Leo was wrong earlier—he had protected Andar. It happened every day on the farm. He always talked Andar down from disobeying the farm master. He talked Andar down from a lot of things. Andar had wanted to tease the little reeve as well, as if doing so would stop her from bothering him. In fact, Leo could imagine Andar slacking in his work if Leo wasn't there to urge him on.

He heard the sound of a bolt striking metal on the other side. The door was pulled open. Leo had heard enough about Gartel from Rygen to recognize the bookbinding guild master. Andar had also worked here, though never at the same time as Rygen. He hadn't spoken about Gartel much, like she had, even before Andar had been removed from the guild. Leo figured that the two of them had never gotten along in the same way that Gartel and Rygen did.

With his short gray beard, Gartel Lusitan looked older than Leo's father. The guild master stood tall, though, looking down at Leo with brown eyes that seemed uninterested in what they saw. His gaze bounced over to Rygen. "Who is this?" he asked.

"This is Leo, who I told you about. It's his tenth birthday today. He wants to be a bookbinder."

Gartel squinted at Leo and crossed his arms. "What's the last book you read?"

"*Quim and Kin: Crowns and Betrayal*, sir. I read it several times with Rygen."

"Hmm. Rygen, you'd better present the book to me in the exact shape it was in when I lent it to you."

"Leo and I would never harm a page." She set down her leather bag. It was old and marred with dirt stains that she'd tried unsuccessfully to remove, but she always took good care of the contents it held. She carefully pulled out the book and handed it to Gartel.

It was painstaking watching him flip through the pages to scan for damage. He didn't quite seem satisfied when he closed the book and stared at Leo, but at least he didn't appear bothered anymore.

"And what did you think of the book?" Gartel asked him.

"The story was sad but engrossing. I realize that 'betrayal' was in the title, but even that did not prepare me for what the Analytes did to the Quim family and to all those who fought for them. The story left me with many thoughts, as any good book should do." Leo paused, for he'd elicited no reaction from Gartel. "Shall I go on, sir?"

"Tell me what you thought of the book, not the story."

"Oh." He looked at the cover as best he could while Gartel had it wrapped in his arm. "Whoever put the book together did an excellent job. Sometimes the binds and parchments stand out more than the story, which makes the words lose power, but not with this book. It was bound beautifully. I didn't notice the binds and parchments, and I didn't think about how someone had written each of the words I read. All I thought about was the story until you asked me about the book itself just now. That must be the sign of a well-made book, a craft I hope to learn one day."

Gartel's mouth quirked, putting Leo's heart at ease. Gartel glanced at Rygen, "You never told him it was you who bound this book?"

"I didn't want to brag."

"You put this together by yourself?" Leo asked in shock.

She nodded, glancing down. "But I only did that," she said as she looked to Gartel. "I could never copy the words as well as how they were written originally."

"You will one day," Gartel assured her. "You just haven't been trained to scribe yet. Now the two of you can come in, but Leo you mustn't touch anything unless I give you permission." Gartel made room for them to enter.

"Yes, sir."

Gartel closed the door after them and bolted it. Leo could smell something familiar. It was like leather but mixed with something dense, as if dust had a smell.

"I hope you brought your identification paper," Gartel said as he stood in front of Leo, blocking his view from pretty much everything on the first floor.

No one called it just an identification paper, although that's what it was. Everyone always said "papers" as if there was so much more information than just Leo's name, birth place and date, and his family members' names. Perhaps there were some people who required more than one sheet to verify their identity, but Leo did not and probably never would.

Leo's identification papers were old and wrinkled. His father kept the single sheet rolled up and in the safe box most of the time. Unrolling it felt like touching his toes without bending his knees. He was eager to let it roll back to how it wanted.

But Gartel stared at it with a wrinkled nose as if something on it was bothering him. He looked at Leo again, but there was something different in his gaze this time. Leo had not yet felt welcomed by Gartel, but that was expected from what Rygen had told him. This look, however, left Leo feeling the need to check his face for remnants of pie.

Leo suddenly felt aware of his ragged clothing. His garments were clean, but they were probably still not good enough for someone like Gartel. There were a few small holes down by the wrists of his sleeves. Leo had rolled them up so the holes wouldn't be as noticeable, but he saw now that the loose fabric was dangling from his elbow and revealed another hole in the material.

It had been too hot that morning for him to wear his leather jerkin. It was his finest piece of clothing, something Andar had stolen for him years ago. The buttons no longer closed, but at least it would have hid the various stains that had bled into his shirt and slightly faded over the years. He would no doubt be sweating, but that seemed a hundred times better than squirming in front of Gartel as the bookbinding guild master's look changed to one of disappointment.

"There will be no test," Gartel announced, then tried to hand Leo back his rolled up paper. Leo did not accept it or the statement.

"Why not?" Leo asked. He was too shocked to feel anything. There had to be a mistake.

"Rygen, you never should've brought him here," Gartel told her. "Now I have to disappoint him."

"Why?" Rygen asked with a shaky voice, as if already accepting what Leo refused to believe.

"Leo *Litxer*." Gartel smacked Leo's paper with the back of his hand. "You must've known that this boy is the younger brother of Andar Litxer."

Andar...Leo's heart dropped. Could this really be why his chance was ruined?

"Yes, I know they are brothers," Rygen said, "but I didn't think it would—"

"It does. I trusted Andar by allowing him to work here, despite his reputation. But it was a mistake. Not only did he steal from me, but he has refused to admit it and return what he took. How can I possibly employ his younger brother when Andar Litxer still has something of mine?"

Rygen's eyes glistened. Her face tightened as if she might cry. She looked to Leo as if hoping he had an answer.

"Andar says he didn't take anything," Leo told Gartel in a small voice.

"You don't sound very confident about that because you're probably smart, as Rygen says." Gartel lectured him with a finger. "You know your brother is a thief and can't be trusted. Isn't that right?"

Leo had been ready to do *anything* for a chance to work here rather than go back to the farm. He felt tears pooling in his eyes now at the thought of having to beg Rhenol to let him work there again. He would certainly be punished, but laboring there for the rest of his life was worse than anything else Rhenol could make him do.

"Give me an answer," Gartel demanded. "Not just for me, but for you as well. Isn't your brother a thief?"

"He only steals what others do not need." Leo swallowed to keep his voice strong. "He cherished his job here. He respects books and your work. He would not steal anything from you."

Gartel leaned down and nearly whispered, "Is that what he told you, or is that what you believe?"

Leo couldn't be sure what he believed. All he knew in that moment was that there might still be a chance to change his fate. He had been prepared to do anything to work here, but he wasn't sure he could do what Gartel was asking.

"Well?" the guild master prodded.

Leo swallowed again. His voice shook. "It's what he told me, and it's what I believe."

Gartel sighed as he stood up straight. "Well, I do not believe it. Tell him he's to return the gold ink before I will even consider testing you, Leo." Gartel turned sharply as if not wanting to see Leo again.

"Gartel," Rygen said with more confidence than Leo had been able to muster since meeting the guild master. Her eyes were red, but there were no tears. "No matter what Andar did, Leo will not steal from you."

"I won't," Leo said. "Never. I haven't stolen anything in my life."

Gartel half turned, looking at Leo with one eye. "Because you have an older brother who does it for you." He straightened and let down his folded arms. "Perhaps you're right—perhaps you won't steal anything. But Andar obviously has influence over you. He might convince you one day to let him in here while I am gone. He could trick you, tell you he just wants to see my shop again. He's good with words. He will call this place beautiful. He might describe the smell as one he misses. All it takes is a moment of weakness, and he'll be in here again stealing something of even more value. Imagine what people would think of me if they found out I had another Litxer working here after what the first one did. They would lose their respect, and I would lose their business. No, it cannot be done. I'm sorry, Leo. I know this is what you wanted, but it's not what I can give you until the matter of theft is resolved. Now I have much to do, and I'm sure you have other work to get to. Go, and do not come back here asking for another chance unless you bring Andar and the golden ink with you."

Neither Leo nor Rygen moved. Gartel started to shut the door. He shooed Leo. "Go."

"Can you give us a moment?" Rygen asked.

The look Gartel gave her was disapproving, but it softened when she turned to face him squarely. "Fine, a moment. Knock when you're done, Rygen. An author with a new story came to me last night and work must start today." He shut the door.

It took all of Leo's strength not to cry. A new story, perhaps by an old author or a new one—it could be about anything. But all Leo would have to do with it was read it when the book was all finished and bound. His back already ached at the prospect of returning to the farm.

"Is there any chance you can get Andar to bring the golden ink back here?"

"It was at least a year ago. If he did take it, he would've sold it."

Rygen looked at the cobblestone at their feet. "Then I don't know what to do." She glanced up with tears running down her cheeks. "I'm so sorry, Leo."

He had to leave before he cried in front of her. He tried to say that he would be all right, but nothing more than a squeak came out from his throat. He swallowed and tried again. "I'm fine."

"That Andar—it's just not fair!"

"I have to go."

Rygen swung her arms around him. It felt like a brick was in his chest and the harder Rygen squeezed, the more impossible it was for Leo to hold back his tears. Finally one slipped out. He leaned out of Rygen's hold and turned to walk away. His legs moved on their own, forcing him to run.

As soon as he burst into a sprint, the dam behind his eyes broke. Tears streamed down his face as he sobbed.

CHAPTER TWELVE

Leo was at least thankful for the long run to the farm. He thought it would give him time to calm down. But sobs still threatened to come out with each of his sharp breaths when he made it to the gated fence. Anger ground his insides. He despised Andar, Gartel, and even Rygen in this moment. Leo hated everyone and everything.

It took all his control to stop crying as he approached the farmhouse, but how was he supposed to get through this day? How was he supposed to get through any day after this?

Rhenol was standing on the porch of his mansion with a smirk on his face. Leo still didn't know what to tell him besides to stop smirking at him, but Leo wouldn't deliver such a comment even in his state of rage.

Rhenol spoke first. "I thought you would be a bookbinding master by now!" He gave a sharp laugh. "Didn't work out, did it?"

Leo made a fist to strike Rhenol, but he knew he would lose that hand as soon as he did. He couldn't look up at Rhenol's ugly face, so he kept his head bowed as he shook his head.

"And now you've come here to beg for more work?"

There wasn't even anyone nearby to see this. Did the farm master really have to make such a point out of this?

"Please let me work here," Leo practically whispered.

"I can't hear you. Louder. And look at me as you speak, boy."

"Please let me work here," Leo said. All the air was gone from his chest. He couldn't breathe unless he did something…unless he struck something. His fist was balled again.

"If you were your brother, I would've thrown you off my farm by now. But I'll give you one more chance because you've behaved. Miss another morning, however, and you *and* your brother will have to find work that isn't on a farm. Do you understand what this means for your family?"

"Yes," Leo mumbled. He didn't want to open his mouth and reveal his grinding teeth.

"You won't be able to stay in the house we provide for you any longer."

I already told you I understand. "I will come every day," he barely got out.

"And what else?"

"Sir?" Leo asked.

"You were late today." He gave a pause to allow Leo to answer.

"I will stay until nightfall."

"Good. Now get to work."

Leo would, but he had to let out this anger first. He had to see his brother. He knew what he had to say would hurt Andar, but Leo couldn't keep it in any longer.

He was surprised to find Andar in the fields, bent over and picking weeds as if taking over Leo's horrible work. He shot up at the sight of Leo.

"What happened?"

"It's your fault!" Leo yelled. "He wouldn't even give me a test because of *you!*"

Andar looked around, making Leo aware that many other farmworkers had stopped to stare at them. But he couldn't stop yelling even if he wanted to. Tears broke through and fell down his cheeks.

"You were so stupid to steal from him. How could you ruin this for *both* of us?"

Andar approached with his hands out. His voice was low. "I didn't steal anything from Gartel, *ever*. I've always told you this, and I don't lie to you, Leo."

Even through his anger, Leo knew to believe his brother. But for some reason, that didn't matter right now. There was no stopping his rage. He opened his mouth and let words come out without planning.

"It's your fault!" he repeated, and realized then why the truth didn't matter. "I'm never going to be able to work anywhere else but on a farm. That was my only chance, and you ruined it."

"But you believe that I didn't take anything, don't you?" Andar sounded desperate to be believed. "I wouldn't, Leo."

It didn't matter. Andar *was* a thief. He had *ruined* Leo's opportunity, no matter if he took the golden ink or not. His reputation was bad enough that Gartel wouldn't believe either of them.

"It's because of you that I can't bind books," Leo yelled. "I have to be here, probably for the rest of my life! You're a thief, Andar. You. Are. A. Thief!"

He knew the word hurt Andar. It was why Leo used it. Thieves were scum. They didn't steal for any purpose but to acquire coin without work. They didn't care about the needs of others. They only thought of themselves.

That wasn't an accurate description of Andar, but striking out was the only way Leo could feel better.

Or so he thought.

Andar only shook his head and walked off, leaving Leo alone in a field of farmers who continued to stare.

"What?" Leo yelled at them. He caught a few bad looks before they glanced away.

Andar didn't look back as he went into the nearby barn and closed the door after him. He would be punished if he was found not working, as would Leo, but he couldn't bring himself to bend over and begin pulling weeds.

Leo's anger was gone; the brick in his chest had been replaced by a hole. None of this was Andar's fault, he knew. But Leo's pride was already so hurt for realizing he had done wrong to his brother that he couldn't bring himself to apologize. He would rather die.

He cried softly to himself as he got to work.

Andar came out of the barn about an hour later. He ignored Leo as he worked the fields with the others. Leo looked over countless times, silently telling Andar he was sorry. But Leo knew it didn't count if he didn't say the words out loud. Andar didn't deserve to be treated this way. He probably hadn't stolen the stupid golden ink.

Leo's anger returned, though it was sharp and pointed this time. Gartel became his focus. The guild master had wanted Leo to speak ill of his brother, and for what? Would he really have allowed Leo to take the test to be a binder if he'd spoken the right words about Andar? No. The only way was for Andar to admit to something he had not done.

During lunch, Leo took his meager meal to the barn hoping his brother would join him in their usual spot. But Andar did not come. Leo felt like crying, but he didn't seem to have any tears left.

Leo didn't see his brother for hours. It was evening when Andar finally approached from behind and startled Leo.

"I'm sorry," Andar said.

Leo's eyes watered. How could his brother be the first one to apologize? "No, I'm sorry. I didn't mean anything I said. I'm just angry at Gartel."

Andar nodded. "I'm sorry for him, is what I meant. He's mean, Leo, but in a different way than Rhenol. I'm sure the work is better in Gartel's guild, but *he's* no better than the rest of them. I worked for him for a year. I always did everything he said. I followed all of his impossible directions to make sure everything was absolutely perfect, even when it didn't need to be. Yet, in the end he still didn't trust me enough to believe that I didn't take that ink. Someone else must've stolen it. They probably knew I would be blamed. He has many people working for him."

"I know."

"He's rich," Andar added. "That ink wasn't made of gold. It was only colored gold. I'm sure he's still a rich man even after losing it, and yet he doesn't care that he has now ruined both of our lives."

"I'm sorry," Leo repeated. "This is his fault, not yours."

His words seemed to do nothing to relieve Andar's growing anger as he started to pace. "There are too many people like him and Rhenol. Something has to be done!"

"Get back to work, Leo and Andar!" screamed Rhenol from past the fruit trees in the distance.

"Nothing can be done," Leo said as he continued to dig up the wet soil.

He was hoping his brother would prove him wrong, but Andar didn't say anything.

"I have to stay until night because I was late," Leo told him. "But I can make it home on my own. You don't have to wait for me."

"Of course I'll wait with you. It's hard to get home at night."

Leo wiped his eyes with his arm. He supposed he wasn't out of tears just yet. "Thank you."

Andar crouched beside him. "One day, we will find a way to take revenge against Gartel. I promise."

Leo knew it wasn't smart to make such promises, but it felt so good to agree.

"Yes, we will."

* * * * *

Leo was thankful for his brother's help getting home, for navigating the streets in the dark was almost like trying to reach their home with their eyes closed. Everything should've been familiar, but nothing was recognizable in the darkness.

However, Andar had walked home at night before today. Perhaps he hadn't taken this exact route back from the farm, but he had been around the city many times after the sun went down, when no others were about. He didn't steal from the people themselves when it was dark, as it was much too dangerous. Many were out for nefarious reasons. It was the shops that Andar usually targeted, he'd told Leo. The owners were less careful in the north about locking up and closing all their windows every night.

The brothers were both in poor spirits when they arrived home. Their father was already there with a grand meal set out for them of golden potatoes and a whole chicken!

"It's late," Darren said. "Are the two of you all right?"

"Yes," Andar answered.

Leo was starving, but the sight of all this food and his father smiling caused him to lose his appetite. He knew what Father would ask him.

But to Leo's surprise, Darren simply frowned. "Oh Leo, I'm sorry." He knelt and opened his arms.

Leo ran in for a hug. He was too exhausted to cry anymore, though his body tried, expelling a couple dry heaves from his chest.

"The test must've been difficult," Darren assumed.

Leo didn't know how he was going to tell his father the truth. Andar had already been through more than he deserved because of this. Leo couldn't stomach the thought of their father blaming him, even for a moment. But it was Andar who answered as Leo tried to think of the right words.

"He didn't let Leo take any test. When he found out he's my brother, Gartel made Leo leave."

Darren finished embracing Leo and stood. "What reason did he give?"

"He still believes I took his golden ink. He says he won't see Leo until I give it back and apologize, but I never took it!" Andar's voice started to quiver. Leo was surprised to see tears pooling in his eyes as he continued. "It was the best work either of us could have, and he took it away from us for *nothing*."

"This isn't right." Darren started to pace. "It isn't right at all." He gestured at the table, though he didn't stop walking around their small kitchen. "Eat, eat," he said.

"And you?" Leo asked.

Darren stopped and gave a long sigh. "Yes, we should all eat. It's late." He took his seat.

"This must've cost a lot," Leo worried aloud.

"Don't you fret about that. We have enough coin. It's Gartel who remains the issue." Darren sat staring up at the discolored wall in front of him. After a while, he said, "You will take this test, Leo. I can't guarantee you will pass it, but I will make sure he at least allows you to take it."

"How?" Andar asked. "There's nothing I took that I can return, and I'm not going to apologize for something I didn't do."

"You won't have to," Darren said.

"What are you going to do to him?" Leo asked with hopefulness. He relished the thought of his father pummeling Gartel. Leo had always hated his farm master, but this pointed anger—this need for revenge against Gartel—was unprecedented, for never had Rhenol taken away something so precious, and for no good reason.

"I'm just going to talk to him," Darren replied.

"But..." Leo started to object before stopping himself. Talking never did anything with men like Gartel. Andar had wasted so much breath trying to talk back to the farm master. All it had gotten him was punishment and a worse attitude from the very person who could make Andar do whatever he wanted. But Leo couldn't worry about it much more with all this food in front of him.

He ate as much as he could. It was the first time in memory that he absolutely had to stop while there was still food on the table. It wasn't exactly that he was completely full. He was just too exhausted to keep chewing. He couldn't even sit up any longer. He had to get to bed.

Apparently, he still wasn't done crying. Many tears slipped out that night, wetting his pillow enough for him to flip it over and wet the other side as well. He knew his father would try his best, but Leo had to accept he would be working at the farm for at least a few more years. One day he might be strong enough to dig in the caverns like his father, but from what Darren had told them, the only thing better was the pay.

Every night for as long as Leo could remember, he had looked forward to this day. He thought everything was going to change when he turned ten. His true life would begin as a bookbinder. He would not only read new stories all the time, but he would have pride in his work. He would be part of putting a book together. He would even be able to hold and enjoy it when he was done.

But that was only going to remain a fantasy. Leo's true life was as a farmworker, and maybe one day a digger. He would never make anything he could be proud of. Would he ever have *anything* he could be proud of? Andar seemed proud of what he stole. But what did Leo have? He thought of the old farmworkers who sometimes had to perform the same jobs as he did, but they were usually quicker. They were paid the same, though. Were they proud of their work? Would he be when he was as old as they were?

A comment from Andar late into the night startled Leo a bit. "Someone in the Bookbinding Guild knew I would be blamed when they took the golden ink. They could very well still be there."

Leo didn't know how to respond.

Andar continued, "It's not just Gartel who deserves our revenge. It's whoever actually took the golden ink."

"Would the guards do anything about this?" Leo asked.

"I went to them when Father did nothing. They said Gartel has every right to force me to leave, no matter the reason. If he says I took something, then all they are going to do is punish me. They're useless."

Leo had been so absorbed in his own despair that he hadn't realized his brother had been awake this whole time as well. Andar had lost hope like Leo had today, but for Andar it had happened years ago. He was in an even worse position.

"Did you cry after it happened?" Leo asked.

"All night."

He had often wondered what it was like to be Andar, the older brother who felt the need to steal. It must be so different than being the younger brother who always did as he was told. But something was different in that moment as Leo empathized with his brother. He felt something deep in his soul, a connection to Andar that he couldn't quite pinpoint.

The stone Andar had brought home had given Leo a heavy sense of power and duty, as if something needed to be done with this gem. That needy feeling was similar to this one, but how?

It had been more of a sense than anything else. *A sense, yes.* Like a reflex to bundle up against a strong gust of wind. It was this same sense that brought up a connection of some sort between Leo and his brother. It went past friendship, past their similarities, and even past blood. It was subtle but with hints of strength that reminded him of the stone, of Artistry, of magic.

He wanted to ask his brother if he felt it, but wouldn't Andar have mentioned it?

How could I even describe it?

Eventually, Leo thought of a way.

"Andar," he whispered. "Do you remember the musicians who came to Jatn last year?"

"I'll never forget them." He hummed an eerie tune that sent a needle down Leo's back.

This group of musicians had performed a song so mesmerizing, it was the only thing that had ever made the people in the market stop moving. Leo had heard lute players strumming away before, but no sound they'd made could compare to the strange and wonderful music these market players produced.

It made him aware that there was more to this world than what he could see, and even what he could hear. It reminded him that magic was real.

This group promised to return the next day so long as they were offered enough coin by those in the market who were lucky enough to hear them. Nearly everyone gave something, Leo even dropping two copper coins into the hat the players had set out.

They did return the next day, but they didn't receive enough coin to come back a third time. Leo had made Andar promise to fetch him if he ever went to the market and found them there again. He'd wondered since that day if Artistry could be used in music somehow and had discussed it with Rygen many times. Neither of them knew enough about Artistry to answer his question, and there was nothing in any of the books they read about magical music.

But magic was everywhere. Every tale that ever discussed it said so. Connections were made with and without the help of living beings, and only a select few—Ascendants—would ever know of these connections.

Part of Leo knew it was silly to think one of these connections had been made between him and his brother, but another part of Leo told him not to ignore it.

"I'm feeling something," Leo told his brother. "It reminds me of what I felt the day we heard the music at the market."

Andar sat up quickly. "Me, too."

"What is it?" Leo asked.

Andar was still and silent. "I don't know." He lay back down. "Maybe it's just a memory."

Even if it was just a memory, that didn't stop Leo from believing there was so much more he would one day discover about himself. *Wait, train, and grow. One day things will change. One day I won't be a simple farmer.*

And neither would his brother. Then, and only then, would everyone who'd wronged them pay.

CHAPTER THIRTEEN

It was difficult for Rygen to walk to the Bookbinding Guild this morning. She had expected Leo to be at her side, but after what happened yesterday she wasn't sure when he would want to see her again. She knew he was hurting. She had spent the night wondering what she could do to help him. She figured Gartel wouldn't change his mind no matter what she told him, but she had to at least try something.

She was nervous as she knocked on the door to start her day of work. Gartel let her inside, greeted her as usual, and started to walk off.

"Can I speak with you a moment?" she asked, a slight tremor in her voice.

He turned and looked down upon her. "Not if this is about Leo Litxer."

"Please, just give him one chance," she pleaded. "You promised my mother you'd give me a chance, and I've proven to be an excellent worker. You tell me that all the time. I'm sure Leo will be as well."

"Well, even Andar was an excellent worker, very good with his hands. In fact, he never made a *single* mistake." Gartel let his comment sit for a moment, reminding Rygen that she had made her share of errors that resulted in damage...which had cost Gartel some coin in the end. She suddenly feared that she might lose her chance to be here.

He's just trying to scare you, she told herself. Rygen straightened her spine and looked him square in the eye.

"But Andar made the worst mistake of all," Gartel continued. "He stole from me."

"How do you know it was him?"

"No one else has the reputation of being a thief!" Gartel yelled, but it seemed as if he regretted doing so as he relaxed his face a bit. "I will not discuss this," he said as he turned away from her. "I don't want you binding any books today while you're upset. You might make a mistake. Speak to Lester for other tasks today."

"Lester will treat me unfairly," she told him. "He doesn't like me."

"He will like you eventually. You just need to spend more time with him."

She would've laughed had she been in a better mood. She avoided Lester more than she would a worker with a wet cough. She'd rather spend more time with Leo on a farm, even if he was sulking.

She hoped he wasn't, but she couldn't exactly picture him with a smile on his face.

The Bookbinding Guild was usually a busy place, especially later in the morning. It was still relatively quiet now, for none of the tools or machines were in use. Not even the soft sound of string rubbing against parchment could be heard yet. The place seemed so big when Rygen came early. She enjoyed watching the enthralled faces of patrons when it was their first time stepping inside this place. To them, it was just a shop, not a guild. But it was unlike any other shop. The machines looked exciting at first, however that was only when it was unclear what they did.

The presser was the biggest and strongest, able to crush bones to dust. There were two of them, always used by men. There were a couple women here, but no other girls like Rygen. She used a sewing frame every time to help her get the first parchments in place, but it didn't look nearly as exciting as a presser.

There were other machines and tools, many of which she had never used because Gartel wouldn't allow her to yet. Her binding work was actually quite boring at times, too repetitive. But boring was a luxury, as her mother always said. There was nowhere better for Rygen to be.

There was a knock at the door. She would gladly take any opportunity to delay speaking to Lester about work, so she unlocked and opened the heavy thing for the next worker to enter. Her eyes went only as high as the enormous muscled chest of this man. She had the reflex to close the door out of fright but made herself at least look up to catch a glimpse of his face first. She relieved her fear with a sharp breath.

"Darren, what are you doing here?"

"I'm going to speak to Gartel. Where is he?"

His harsh tone resembled nothing of the kind father of Leo's. This was a man with a temper, and Rygen had best not get in his way. She pointed a finger across the open hall that made up much of the first floor, at the closed door of Gartel's study in the back.

Darren took a direct route between tables laden with unfinished books, various tools, and small machines. Lester stared at Darren and opened his mouth as if to tell him that patrons were not to enter this area, but Darren shot him a look that silenced Lester before a word came out.

Darren didn't pause as he came to Gartel's study. He turned the doorknob and walked into the room.

"You don't knock?" Gartel said. Fear flooded his face as he looked up from his desk. He quickly stood. "What's the meaning of this?"

Darren shut the door.

Rygen could hear his muffled voice but couldn't make out any of the words. She hurried over and pressed her ear against the door.

"You will give my son a fair chance to prove himself," she heard Darren demand.

"It doesn't matter how well he proves himself when he or his brother could come in and take something at some point," Gartel argued.

"They won't."

"You can't guarantee that."

"I can, and I can also guarantee what will happen to you if you don't allow Leo to come back today and start his test."

It was silent. The moment stretched on too long. Rygen strained her ears and thought she heard a whisper.

"I can take your threat to the guards," Gartel warned.

"What threat? I told you it's a guarantee. Now tell me you understand or I'm going to become angry."

It was silent again.

She heard footsteps. "Wait," Gartel called. Feet shuffled about. There was a crack as if something had fallen over. "All right, I understand!" Gartel shouted.

"Keep your voice down," grumbled Darren.

Rygen jumped as someone grabbed her by her shoulder. "Get to work," Lester told her. He had a long face, with deep wrinkles on his cheeks from the false smile he always put on for patrons. He never showed this smile to Rygen.

It seemed that he hadn't been told by Gartel yet that he would be assigning Rygen her tasks today. He shoved her away from the door and leaned his ear against it.

She knelt to put her ear in a spot he wasn't covering.

"And you will take back Andar as—"

Lester pushed her away again.

"Stop," she whispered with gritted teeth and resumed her position.

He shoved her again. Enraged, she pushed him back. He seemed surprised as he stumbled. She put up her arms to defend herself as she tried again to listen through the door.

"There's only enough work for one of them," Gartel was saying with a soft and nervous tone.

Lester pushed Rygen so hard that her feet left the ground. She fell hard with pain radiating from her back, a small scream slipping out.

"I told you to get to work," Lester said, looking as if he wanted to kick Rygen.

The door swung open from the other side. Darren stepped out. After a glance at Rygen on the floor, he went straight toward Lester, who was quickly backing away.

"Did you just push that little girl?" Darren thundered.

"Who...who are you to tell me...what to do?"

"Do you need someone to tell you not to push little girls, or do you already know?"

"I..." Lester backed into the corner as Darren rounded on him.

"What's your answer?" Darren asked.

"I already know."

"Then why did you do it?"

Rygen had never seen this side of Darren. She hoped she wouldn't witness violence. She had seen some on the street, men fighting each other like animals. It had caused her to scream and look the other way after seeing and hearing the crack of someone being struck in the chin.

"I won't do it again," Lester said.

"Promise that to her, but only after you apologize."

He leaned wide to look around Darren's shoulders. Rygen got herself up.

"I'm sorry. I promise I won't do it again."

Even though it was forced, it did make her feel better.

Darren turned away from Lester and came toward Rygen. She was afraid, but then he showed her a soft look of worry and crouched in front of her.

"Are you all right?"

She nodded.

"Has he done that before?"

She shook her head.

"Tell me if he does."

She nodded again.

Darren stood and glared at Gartel, who watched from the doorway with wide eyes. "You will give Leo a fair chance. That's all I ask."

"Fine. Now leave!" The guild master seemed to have gathered some courage, yelling at Darren as if he were an approaching bear.

But Darren didn't leave just yet. "Do us both a favor and make sure I never have to come back."

Then he finally turned and walked straight out of the shop. No one moved until he'd closed the door after himself.

It was too awkward for Rygen to even meet the gaze of Lester or Gartel. She found herself to be afraid still, though she didn't know why, her heart racing. She wished she had some sort of task she could run off to, but she still had to talk to Lester for her work for the day.

It was a relief when Gartel called her over and the three of them made a small circle. Rygen stood with her head down.

"That man is a brute," Gartel said. "You might meet other men like him one day, so it's best you know how they behave. They are animals."

The statement reminded her of the two men fighting in the street. Now it was easy to picture Darren as one of them, and she couldn't imagine him being the first to fall.

Gartel had paused and looked at her, so she nodded to show she understood. She still couldn't look up from the floor for more than a moment.

"Brutes don't care about laws or morals. They have no respect for anyone. They are scoundrels, but we don't live in a just world. Sometimes we have to do things we know aren't right just to survive. I will be speaking to the guards about this, but in due time." The guild master stopped to fix his shirt, which was askew as if Darren had grabbed it. Rygen finally felt able to look up to him again.

Gartel stood up straight. "For now," he continued, "I will let Leo initiate the Bookbinding Guild test. But I don't approve of the situation, and neither should either of you."

"I don't, sir," Lester said. "And I do understand the situation."

"And you, Rygen?"

She let her gaze drop again as she nodded, though she couldn't tell what she felt yet.

"The boy will be here later," Gartel said as he walked back toward his study. "I'm very busy, so don't disturb me until he arrives."

Rygen didn't believe Gartel, for he was never "very busy" in his study. The busier he was, the more time he spent running about the large building. But she said nothing of it. She was glad when the door closed and Lester walked away from her. She would figure out her own work today.

She felt strange the following hour as she waited for Leo to arrive. She was uncomfortable no matter how she sat or stood. She couldn't focus on anything for more than a few moments at a time, with jolts of fear rising up from her stomach every time she had a flash memory of the mean face Darren had worn throughout most of the ordeal.

He had so much honor in how he'd stood up for her…and so much hatred toward Lester for putting his hands on her. But she didn't know what to feel about how he had convinced Gartel to give Leo another chance. Was Gartel right that Darren was a brute? Was he an animal like the fighting men in the street? He had always been kind to Rygen and her mother, but something about him had always put Rygen on edge. It was as if she knew he was capable of destruction—something about the way he carried himself. And his anger—Rygen had always known it was there. He never needed to yell or pound the table, but something always seemed to be bothering him. The thought of him becoming unhinged scared her more than anything Lester might do to her.

She had to find a way to ignore all this when Leo showed up. She was supposed to be ecstatic that he had another chance. She knew that she was, but she just couldn't feel it yet.

CHAPTER FOURTEEN

Leo had thought he was sick when he first woke up that morning. *I have to go back to the farm again. Back to the farm, forever.* It took him until he finished breakfast to realize that he was not ill after all, at least not physically. But not even being sick would've allowed him to stay home. Everyone in Jatn knew that the only thing to do when they were actually sick was to get to your work on time and find a way to get through the day. It might mean laboring only when the farm master was watching, but missing a day was not an option.

There wouldn't be any options for Leo now. *Every day, back to the farm.* He couldn't seem to get up from his chair even when he was done eating. Eventually, Andar put his hand on Leo's shoulder.

"Let's not be late."

Leo nodded and got up.

Their father had already left to speak with Gartel. Leo had no hope that this would amount to anything. He figured that his father had to try, but he knew better than his father did as to what kind of man Gartel was. It would be like trying to convince the farm master to give Leo the day off and still pay him. It was more likely to elicit laughter than anything else.

But Andar was in the same position as Leo, and he never complained.

Not to me, at least. When Andar has an issue with someone, he tells them. It's why he and the farm master argued all the time. Inspired by the thought, Leo wanted to march over to the Bookbinding Guild and tell Gartel what he deserved to hear.

You claim that it brings dishonor to employ a thief like Andar, but you dishonor yourself. You take away opportunities; no, you take away lives from people who only want to work for you. It's not as if we're asking for free coin. An honest wage for honest work. It was a phrase Darren had repeated many times, often stating that it didn't happen enough in Jatn. He'd use it as an answer to many of Leo's questions, such as why all the guild masters were rich when they did the least amount of work.

Whenever Leo looked over toward his brother, it seemed as if Andar knew how Leo felt already. He would gaze back and smile apologetically with the lift of his eyebrows.

At least Leo felt closer to his brother throughout all of this. He hadn't been sure they could be any closer, for they already did everything together. But there was now a connection past their words and actions, past their blood. He was certain of it, though he had no idea what it was.

They started their work on the farm as if it were any other day.

"I don't believe it! He actually did it!" announced Andar soon after. Leo turned around and saw their father approaching.

He motioned for them to come to him. They ran over as he crouched.

"I spoke with Gartel," he said warmly as he looked into Leo's eyes.

Leo's heart lifted.

"Before you get too excited," Darren told Leo, "You should know that I only got him to agree to test you fairly. But even though he agreed to that, it would be foolish for us to believe it. He *will* test you, but I'm sure the tests he gives you will be more difficult than he gives others. You have to make sure to do everything he says in the exact way that he tells you to do it. Look for hidden meanings, tricks, anything he might use to make you fail. Eventually you will prove yourself, I'm sure, and he will accept you as any other worker. But you may have to work harder than you ever have before because he will want to break your spirit."

Andar grabbed Leo and shook him. "You will be great."

"You should run there now," Darren said. "I'm sure he'll have a lot for you to do before sundown."

"Thank you!" Leo started to run but stopped as he remembered the most important thing. "What about Andar?"

Darren's mouth scrunched.

Andar glanced at their father before looking over at Leo again. "Don't worry about me right now. Get there as quick as you can, Leo. Go!"

"Are you sure?"

"Yes, go go!"

"What about my task at the farm today?"

"I will speak to the farm master," Darren called. "I will take over for you today."

"But the cavern?" Leo asked.

"They can dig without me for one day."

Leo was still too worried to run off. Andar wouldn't come with him? How was that fair?

"Go," Andar said with a laugh that sounded genuine. "We are fine."

He really shouldn't be late. Leo ran off again, looking back all the while. The two of them showed him nothing but smiles. He looked straight ahead to see where he was going, but he did check back once more. Their faces had changed as they spoke to each other. It was hard to tell exactly what expressions they had from here, but Leo was almost certain that Andar had a fiery look about him.

Leo would've turned around if he could have thought of one thing he could do to help the situation. But if he refused to work with Gartel until Andar came with him, then they would both end up stuck at the farm.

*****

Darren had feared delivering this news to Leo. He knew how any boy in Andar's position would react. It was unfair for Leo to be given a chance at something that Andar could never be part of again, no matter how much he deserved it.

Andar looked at Darren as if Darren was his boy, not the other way around. A boy who might've misbehaved, and he would get to the bottom of it right this instant.

"What did you say to Gartel?"

Darren didn't appreciate the way his son spoke to him, as if about to scold. Darren's reflex was to correct Andar, to make him remember that he was always to respect his father. He knew now was not the time, however. Andar was right to be upset. He had done so well to put on a smile for Leo, or Leo never would've left Andar on the farm. Now the responsibility to give Andar what he deserved fell upon Darren, but he had already failed. What else could he do but deliver the news?

"I told him he would give Leo *and* you a fair chance."

Andar's eyes widened.

"But," Darren continued before Andar could get too excited, "Gartel doesn't have enough work for both of you."

The disappointed look returned. "And you chose Leo."

"*He* chose Leo," Darren corrected. "He still believes that you took that golden ink from him."

"And what do you believe, Father?"

"I know you didn't take it."

"Do you really?"

"Of course, Andar! You wouldn't lie to me, would you?"

Andar rested his forehead on his fingers with a fallen gaze. He started to shake his head. "I don't want to be asked anything about the truth right now. I just want you to tell..." He swallowed, looking as if he was about to cry.

A wave of fear flooded Darren. He couldn't remember the last time he'd made Andar cry. It was then that Darren realized how wrong he'd handled the situation— not this one. A situation Andar was no doubt gathering the strength to bring up.

"I just want you to tell the truth now. If you believed that I didn't take that damn golden ink—"

"Without swearing, Andar."

"That damn golden ink!" he repeated. "If you believed that I didn't take it, then why didn't you go threaten Gartel back then? You gave Leo a chance at a better life, but where was my chance? Don't I deserve one?"

"Of course you do."

"Do you even know that I like books just as much as Leo does?"

"I know, Andar."

"And I don't have a friend like Leo does who will share them with me. We're too poor to buy any, except one for Leo's birthday that he'll let me read. How nice of him! Do you have any idea how many times I could've stolen a book? No, don't answer that. Tell me instead, do you know how many times I could've stolen something even more valuable than a book!"

"I'm sure you have the opportunity all the time."

"But I never take anything! Never!" Andar still held back his tears, though Darren didn't know how. The boy was visibly shaking now, his face red. "If I'm going to risk imprisonment, then I will steal only what the family needs. Always what the family needs! But what about me? Do either you or Leo ever care about what I need?"

"Andar—"

"Don't try to lecture me! What good have all of your lectures done? I'm going to be working at this farm for the rest of my life because it's the only way our family will have a house to live in. At least recognize how much I do for you and Leo."

"I do recognize it."

Andar paused for the first time. "And?"

"I'm doing everything I can for the family, like you are. Leo's work at the Bookbinding Guild isn't only for him. He'll make good coin. If the three of us keep working hard, we will one day be able to leave the city. I have earned a lot, Andar, much more than I would if I were farming. But my digging work is over. I'm going to look for better work for *both* of us."

Andar looked disgusted. "You tell us nothing! Now you say all this? How am I supposed to trust anything you tell me if you still haven't answered my question. Didn't you see how embarrassed and angry I was when Gartel tossed me out of his shop like rubbish?"

"I did notice, of course."

"Then why didn't you do anything!" he screamed, drawing looks from the other farmers in the field.

Darren would not lie to his son anymore. He had told Andar at the time that there was nothing he could do, but Darren had just proven that he could've at least tried. He had been threatening people for Raenik for years. He might've even been successful convincing Gartel to keep Andar around.

Darren resigned himself with a sigh. The moment he feared the most was about to come true.

"You were ten," he prefaced. "I still didn't know how closely you followed my advice not to take anything of value. I know now that you didn't steal anything from Gartel, but I wasn't sure at the time."

Andar folded his arms. "When did you become sure?"

Uneasy, Darren squeezed a knot at the back of his neck. "I can't say I remember the exact moment."

"And why would you? It's not as if you spent every moment of every day thinking about how much better my life would be if I was still in the Bookbinding Guild. I loved that work. Gartel and I never got along, but I don't get along with anyone but my brother! All I have is my work, and all that work is now at this farm. This *wretched* farm! Had you really cared, you could've searched our small house and the few pockets of my clothing for any sign that I had taken this golden ink. If I had sold it, you would find coin. But there was none! You didn't even bother to look."

Darren thought back to that day. He had been fearful to search for this stolen ink because he thought he might find it. If he never looked, he could one day convince himself Andar was innocent, as he had now. But it had taken too long. Andar had no longer seemed upset by the incident, and Darren had eventually forgotten about it. What a fool he was. Andar rarely, if ever, complained. Of course he still suffered every day, just as Darren did for the injustices that he had to endure.

How could he make this right? It wasn't as if he could go back to Gartel and force him to take in Andar as well. Any man could only be pushed so far.

I should've made him take Andar back first. He would prove himself as the good worker he was, one who did not take from his guild master. Then Gartel would accept Leo as well eventually.

Darren had always thought he did everything he could for his sons. He worked. He brought them food. He taught them, trained them. He raised them to be young men he was proud of, but through all of this he had neglected Andar's wish for a better life.

"You're right," he admitted. "I should've told Gartel that you would be coming back to work there, not Leo."

Andar looked surprised, silent for a breath. "Well, now it's too late to change that. It's too late to change *anything.*" Andar looked off in the distance as if thinking of something. "Now are you going to help me join a guild? It's the least you can do."

After a moment of thought, Darren realized that there was only one guild to which Andar would not only be accepted at the age of thirteen, he would thrive. However, everyone knew that most who sought entry into the Thieves' Guild were criminals, not young men like Andar. Many were murderers and rapists who needed coin while skulking in the shadows.

Darren would do everything short of accepting death before allowing Andar to give his life to the Thieves' Guild.

"Which guild do you have in mind?" he asked his son. *Has he heard of the Thieves' Guild yet?*

"Any guild that doesn't involve farming! They all have to be better than this."

What is it about the farm work that he despises the most?

Darren thought he figured it out. "It's not often that the overseer at any guild is better than Rhenol."

"That can't be. Most of the people we meet are good, so there should be good overseers as well."

"There aren't, Andar. I will tell you why. The people who are in positions of power are there because of three possible reasons. They earned it out of betrayal and corruption. They earned it because they are friends with the right person. Or they were born into it."

"What about the men who have worked hard enough to be promoted to an overseer? Not all have backstabbed."

"Not all," Darren agreed. "But the honest men who work hard and are promoted because of it do not last. They sympathize with the workers rather than use them to further the riches of those above them."

"The bookbinding guild master is different than that," Andar argued. "He is wealthy and sympathizes with the worker. He's just a fool who doesn't trust me."

"He is the third example of men in power: Those who are born into it. His father was the guild master, as I'm sure you remember. Gartel's life is books. It always has been."

"Then find me a guild master whose work is their life, like Gartel. I will work for them."

"You don't want to," Darren informed his son. This was a lesson he should've taught Andar long ago. "These men are bakers, tailors, and shoemakers. And in this city, they are all controlled by the Farmers' Guild. They are men who must produce. They are not rich. They cannot offer fair work to boys like you. They must use workers as you are being used here."

This was too blunt. Darren could see his cutting words at work. Andar's shoulders slumped as his hope drained from him.

"What about the men who travel for their work? The stonemasons, the woodcutters. Them—I want to be one of them. Help me become an apprentice."

There were all kinds of terrible pains a man could experience, but few compared to the foresight that the son Darren had raised for thirteen long years might soon abandon him as well as Leo, Andar's closest friend.

"They travel, like you said. Their work in Jatn will run dry, and then we might be separated from you for the rest of our lives."

There was an awkward silence as Andar stared up at Darren like the fierce boy he was. Darren had to say something before Andar would speak the words that might change their lives for the worst.

"I will find you work that's better than this. Just give me time."

"Don't bother. I'll find it myself."

"When do you have time to look?" Darren asked, not as a challenge but out of genuine curiosity, for it sounded as if Andar had thought about this for quite some time now.

"Each evening," Andar said. "When I'm usually out looking for something to take for us."

Darren didn't see how he could disagree. He nodded. "Fine, but I will keep looking for you as well."

He had to be a better father to Andar, or soon it might be too late.

"I'm sorry," he told his son. "You deserve more."

"So many of us do," Andar said as he turned his back on Darren and focused intently on the field, as if it was the only thing on his mind. He reminded Darren just how secretive Andar could be with his thoughts. He and Leo were brothers, but there were some aspects to them that were completely opposite.

CHAPTER FIFTEEN

The door to the Bookbinding Guild was open when Leo arrived. He couldn't help but think that it was his father who had unlocked this door. He would make sure to one day be a great bookbinder, as it was the only way he could think of to repay his father.

Leo hadn't gotten a good look at the place before, when Gartel had blocked his view as well as his access. It seemed that most of the first floor was taken up by this one grand room, where Leo assumed much of the making of the books took place. There were many tables and more than a few workers, but he didn't see Rygen. Expecting to run into her, or at least Gartel, all Leo could do was stand awkwardly in the doorway and try to avoid the eyes of the other workers.

There were other bookstores in the city of Jatn, but there was only one guild. This was the sole place where a story was born from parchments and spine. Shop owners sometimes bought books from this place, Rygen had told Leo, in hopes of selling the volumes elsewhere. But none of those shops were as successful as this place. *Gartel must be rich.*

Authors knew to come here with their written work. It was the only place in Jatn where they would be paid, but there were more stories that would never become books than those that would. Rygen sometimes talked about how she wanted to write her own story, but Gartel wouldn't allow her to "waste" the parchments and ink until she was older.

When Leo had asked what she would write, she'd said that she didn't know except that it would have summoners. Leo had always been more fascinated with Ascendants, who were the most powerful mages. Once mages discovered their ability with Artistry, it seemed as if nothing limited what they could do. Summoners, however, were restricted by the creatures they could connect to in the other world. Sure, they could tame more powerful creatures the stronger they became at summoning, but they still depended on these creatures for everything. Meanwhile, Ascendants could do anything from curing sickness to making walls of fire. At least they could according to the stories Leo and Rygen had read. Perhaps Rygen didn't believe in the possibility of these feats as much as he did, and that's why summoning was more interesting to her.

His distraction came to an end when Leo heard footsteps from the stairway nearby. It made him aware of how quiet this place was even with all the people working. It was the size of it, he realized, as well as the soft nature of the work itself. He watched Gartel descend the stairs. Leo's heart thumped. He would do what was asked of him, no matter what.

Gartel looked distracted with his own thoughts as he gestured and spoke to himself, and he didn't seem pleased with whatever conversation was occurring in his head. But he appeared even less happy when he glanced over and saw Leo. The guild master sauntered over with a look as though he was above dealing with Leo right now.

"Thank you for giving me a chance," Leo said. He was a slave to Gartel, in some sense of the word, but it didn't matter. It would still be better than being on the farm.

"The work will be difficult," Gartel warned. "You will not speak back to me."

"I won't."

"Your first task is to make parchments."

"The same parchments that will be used in a book later?" Leo asked with excitement.

"They'd better be good enough to be used in a book, or you will have failed."

Leo's nerves got the better of him, stealing his ability to speak.

"Are you uninterested? I would be happy to find another boy or girl who is."

"I'm very interested, sir. What do I need to do to make these parchments?"

"First you should know that it will take you nine days of work, and that's only if you get it right."

Leo didn't know how parchments could take nine days to make, but he wouldn't speak unless asked a question. He wondered where Rygen was. Wasn't she supposed to be here every day?

"Today you will only begin the process," Gartel said. "Lester will give you the pelt that will become parchments when all is finished." The guild master pointed at the tall and thin man leaning over a table. He seemed to be attaching loose parchments to a spine with the use of some sort of holder. "I'm only going to tell you this once, so pay attention."

Afraid to even blink, Leo stared back at Gartel.

"Take the pelt to the river *outside* the city. Choose a spot where you are unlikely to be disturbed by man or animal. It should be a place where the river runs fast enough to clean the pelt. You will pin the pelt down with rocks on its edges so that the river does not take it away. You will watch the pelt to ensure it is not stolen or lost. Don't bother coming back to me if you lose it. You will not be welcomed here. Understand?"

"Yes, sir."

"It will take two days for the river to clean the pelt. Bring it back here when it is ready, but not before sunrise or after sunset."

How will I know exactly when it's ready? Gartel was already walking the other way. *It takes two days,* Leo reminded himself. *Perhaps it will look different by then.*

He walked over to Lester, who spared Leo one glance before returning his focus to his work.

"I was told you would give me a pelt?"

"Is that a question?" Lester asked. He sounded to be mocking Leo.

"May I have the pelt?" Leo asked.

"It's in the storage." Lester pointed with a lift of his chin. He seemed to be guiding Leo toward a closed door in one corner, but there were other rooms nearby. Leo couldn't be sure which one was right.

"The one in the corner?" Leo asked.

Lester sighed. "Yes."

Leo was glad to leave Lester, though he had wished for some assistance. Would it have been so difficult for the man to fetch the right pelt for Leo? Who knew what else he'd find in the storage.

The door to the storage had a loose doorknob. Leo tried to turn it, but it did nothing to unlatch the door. It took some jiggling and maneuvering, but eventually he got it to work and stepped into a small room packed with various things all unfamiliar to him. The rest of the Bookbinding Guild was obsessively organized compared to this place. Barrels of different heights and girths took up most of the small space. They all had lids hiding their contents. Shelves along the walls were cluttered with containers of different sizes. He wondered if they might have ink in them, perhaps even ink with some kind of value. Was this the place Andar had been accused of stealing from?

There was one common feature among everything in here. It was all brown and blackish. There were no windows, no lamps, very little light. Leo didn't see any pelts until he stumbled over one on the floor. He started to pick it up, but it was quite heavy. He wondered if he'd even be able to carry it once it was wet. *Did Rygen really do this?* The pelt seemed huge, even folded in on itself.

As Leo got his hands underneath it for better leverage, he felt something wet. He set the huge pelt down again for a look at his palms. They were red with what appeared to be blood. He had a sudden need to itch his face, now incapable of using his hands. He rubbed his cheek against his shoulder instead. Then he took a breath and reached down again. He gathered the folded pelt against his chest, for it seemed to be the only way to carry it. He shuffled out of the storage and almost dropped it as it slipped, but he clung tighter.

He somehow made it to the open door of the building and looked back in hopes that someone might at least offer some advice. The workers, including Lester, ignored Leo. Gartel was nowhere in sight. Where was Rygen? Perhaps Gartel had sent her away to ensure Leo had as little help as possible.

Wasn't there at least a wheelbarrow he could use? This pelt was already heavy. He grumbled from the strain and left.

The river twisted through the town of Jatn, most of it running through the northern side. Leo wondered if anyone might steal the pelt if he disobeyed Gartel and took it to that part of the river instead of making the trek outside the city. Leo would watch it the whole time. Even if someone did try to take it, couldn't he scream for a guard? They were supposed to be prevalent in the north.

He reminded himself that he was working his way toward being a bookbinder now. He had to do whatever Gartel told him. He would make it to the part of the river outside the city, though he wasn't sure he could get there before lunch.

What would he do when he was hungry? Gartel had mentioned nothing of eating, and it wasn't as if Leo had time to waste visiting an inn with a kitchen, nor did he have coin.

No matter what happened, he would clean this pelt and return it to Gartel.

*****

Leo's arms burned from strain by the time he made it to a spot by the river that he deemed to be good enough. It was shallow here, allowing him to see the bottom where heavy rocks rested that he could use to pin down the pelt. The water ran fast, threatening to take Leo away as he stepped in hesitantly.

He held his ground and pushed the pelt down. It was a nuisance getting the rocks on top of it while maintaining his balance, but he succeeded in the end. He stood there in the water for a long while, watching the pelt. It seemed to be inching away slowly, but his eyes might've been playing tricks.

Leo stood in front of it, his feet close to it. He waited another good while, watching as the pelt continued to look as if it was sliding downstream. But Leo knew that he was not moving, and the pelt never appeared closer to his feet. It was just an illusion, or perhaps his worries getting the better of him. He stepped up onto the bank and stood there with his pants and sleeves dripping.

He didn't know how long he watched that pelt, scared of losing it every time he so much as blinked, but it had to have been well over an hour. Eventually, the sun had dried his pants and he could sit comfortably with his legs folded. But then hunger started to get the better of him.

He had seen no fish in the river yet. There probably were few to none. Any fish that made their way down this river were probably caught when the water passed through the city.

Well, at least Leo would not go thirsty.

He checked for people many times, but it didn't appear as if anyone came this way. He figured it was because a few hills separated this part of the river from the last houses of Jatn.

There wasn't much to distract Leo from his hunger. Nothing was around him except for a patch of yellow flowers a good walk away. Grass covered the rest of the ground. A few thin clouds appeared to be having a little gathering by the horizon. The sun bombarded them, tinting them silver.

Eventually, Leo got up and walked to the flowers. He had little hope of finding anything to eat, but he couldn't let another moment go by without at least checking to see what was in this patch.

The flowers were small and dusty, certainly inedible. There was nothing else. He hurried back to the river and was relieved to find the pelt still there. *The rocks probably won't ever come loose, unless there's a great change to the current.* He could return to his home, he supposed. By the time he made it there, Andar and Father should have arrived as well. Leo had missed lunch, and the pain in his empty belly was now so intense that he feared the long walk might soon be impossible.

Gartel had told him to watch the pelt until it was done, and that it would take two days. Did he honestly expect Leo to stay here *overnight* without eating? Even the farm master treated him better than that. Leo was fed lunch, albeit a meager one, on the farm. More importantly, he was allowed to go home before sunset.

He wasn't going to be able to stay here much longer without eating. *I at least have to go home once for food. Then I can return.*

His mouth started to salivate as he ran. He hoped Andar had stolen something delicious for supper. It was unfortunate they couldn't save any of the chicken Father had brought home last night. It would be spoiled by today, so Darren had eaten all that Andar and Leo could not finish. Leo wasn't sure he'd ever seen a man eat as much in a single sitting as his father had last night. It had to be four times what Father usually ate for dinner.

It means he never even comes close to filling his belly, Leo realized. Hopefully one day that would change for Darren. Leo's belly was never filled during lunch, but it was full usually during dinner when Andar contributed.

Night was starting to creep over the town as Leo warily stumbled down the last few streets to his home. He was so hungry that he figured he could eat at least half the chicken his father had brought yesterday.

His father and brother were already home, with food on the table! Leo could barely get out a hello before he stumbled over to his seat and picked up his fork. It didn't even matter what he was eating. He hardly noticed it until he finished his first bite. Rice. All there was today was rice. There was a pang of disappointment, but it wasn't going to stop him.

It wasn't until he was done that he noticed the tension between his brother and his father. There was a look in both of their eyes as if they wanted to say something. Darren finally spoke.

"Did Gartel not feed you?" he asked Leo. He seemed ready to get up and march over to the Bookbinding Guild depending on Leo's answer.

"I was too busy to eat." He wasn't sure why he lied to his father. "In fact, I have to go back soon." Even through his hunger, he had never escaped the fear of losing the pelt. Leo figured it was safe out there because no one without a lantern would be able to see it, but he wasn't going to take the risk.

"You must eat something during the day," Darren lectured. "And you will not be going out at night. Whatever Gartel wants you to do, it can wait."

"It can't. I'm washing a pelt in the river. I have to return to it."

"Ah," Andar said. "I remember washing pelts. You made sure it will stay put?"

"Yes."

"What part of the river did you leave it?"

"*At which* part of the river," Darren corrected.

Andar glared at him. Leo felt his eyes widen as he feared their father would react with anger. But surprisingly all he did was put up a hand and say, "Never mind my correction." He turned to Leo. "Which part?"

"Outside Jatn to the east, past the hills."

Andar laughed. "It's that far, and you still plan to watch it all night?"

Leo nodded.

"No one's going out there, Leo," Andar said. "On the rare chance that someone happens across it, they won't even see it."

"There's still a chance it could be taken."

"Not as big of a chance of something happening to you," Darren told Leo. "You're not going to be sleeping outside the city. You're only ten!"

"There are no animals, and I have no money for anyone to take."

"There are worse things someone can do than take your money." Darren took on a dark look. "You're staying here."

Leo suddenly felt nauseous with worry. What if something happened to the pelt? He couldn't go back to the farm. He couldn't.

"If you're that scared of leaving it," Andar said, "then I will help you fetch it. It can stay here with us overnight. Tomorrow you'll put it back in the river, early. It will still be done in two days."

"Are you sure?"

"Completely. Come on, let's go while there's still a little light."

"Clean up and rest, Andar," Darren said as he stood. "I'll go with Leo."

"I want to," Andar argued.

Darren glanced at him. "All right. But wait here a moment." He went into his room. Leo looked at Andar to see if he knew what Father was doing, but his brother had a crease down his forehead as if curious as well.

Darren came back with a dagger he must've purchased recently, for Leo had never seen it before. It was not a fancy weapon, the metal blackened. But the handle seemed sturdy and the point appeared sharp. Leo gladly let Andar take it from their father's hands.

"Don't use it unless *absolutely* necessary," Darren instructed. "And fetch the pelt quickly. I don't want either of you out at night."

They started toward the door.

"Wait," Darren said and hurried after them. He took off his belt. It must've been new as well, for it had a holder for a dagger that Leo had not noticed yet. "Lift up your arms," he told Andar.

He did. Darren tried to put the belt around his son's waist, but it was far too big for even the last hole to be close to reaching the buckle. Darren put it over Andar's shoulder instead, then took the dagger and inserted it into the small sheath. He snapped shut the holder.

"Jump around a bit," Father instructed.

Andar did as Darren watched the handle of the knife jiggle about. Apparently satisfied, Darren put his hand on Andar's shoulder. "All right, be careful."

Andar moved quickly toward the door, as if eager to get away from Darren's hand. Leo followed him outside and looked back at their father. He stood in the doorway and watched them for a moment before closing the door.

"Are you angry at Father?" Leo asked as they ran.

"No, everything's fine."

Leo figured his brother was lying, but it didn't seem right to pry. If Andar wanted to tell him something, he would've.

Andar didn't say a word during the long trek there. He carried the heavy, dripping pelt on his own as he led Leo back through the dark city toward their home. Eventually Leo forced Andar to let him help. Together they made it back and dumped it on the kitchen floor. Exhausted, Leo was barely able to get out of his wet clothing before crashing onto his bed.

CHAPTER SIXTEEN

When Leo got up from bed, Andar and their father were preparing breakfast. The pelt was still wet. A puddle had formed around it as it lay in front of the door.

"Are you able to get it to the river on your own after breakfast?" Andar asked Leo. "I don't have the time to walk to the river and make it to the farm on time."

Leo tried to hide his worry, knowing the pelt was too heavy for him to take on his own.

"I'll help him," Darren said.

"Don't you have to be at the cavern at the same time that Andar has to be at the farm?" Leo asked.

"Not today."

His father didn't explain. Leo took that to mean they would have a quiet breakfast. He was too tired to speak much anyway. The rest of his family appeared the same as they blinked with heavy eyelids and slid spoonfuls of mush into their mouths. It was still early by the time Leo was ready to leave with his father.

Whoever had followed Leo and Andar that one time had not returned. Leo wondered if the person had been in Andar's imagination, because nothing came of it, but he trusted his brother's keen eyes. He didn't know what to think about that anymore. All he could do now was continue his work.

"Can we stop at Rygen's?" Leo asked as they left their house behind. Darren carried the entire pelt with ease. "And I can help you if you want." Leo already knew the answer, but he felt better offering.

"I'm fine. What do you have to speak to Rygen about this morning?"

"I didn't see her yesterday. Gartel told me nothing about her." Leo realized he still hadn't answered the question, probably because he didn't know the answer until right then. "I suppose I just want to make sure she's all right."

"That's kind of you."

"Did you see her yesterday when you went to speak with Gartel?"

"I did. She seemed fine then, but we can still make sure."

Darren halted a few steps away from the door, allowing Leo to take the lead and knock. Rygen's mother answered. "Ah, Leo and Darren, is something wrong?"

"No, I'm just wondering if Rygen is all right?"

"She's fine. She left for Gartel's already."

"Isn't it too early for her to start work?"

"I thought the same, but she insisted."

Leo didn't know what to make of that. Would Gartel even be there to let her in?

"Do you think she could be heading somewhere else?" Leo asked.

Verona looked at Leo sideways. "Well now I do. Did she tell you something?"

Darren stepped forward, putting himself in front of Leo. "He's only speculating. I'm sure this is just another day of work for her."

Verona seemed to think nothing of the wet pelt, hardly giving it a glance. She was probably familiar with them from Rygen's early work at the Bookbinding Guild.

This was another reason Leo really needed to see her. His family offered tremendous help, but only Rygen knew what Gartel might be thinking, what he wanted exactly.

Leo was hoping for some advice. He hated to go another day without anything to eat.

Rygen was always intuitive—she should've assumed he would stop by this morning. But why would she leave early if that was the case? She wasn't at the Bookbinding Guild yesterday, either. It was starting to feel as if she was avoiding him.

Leo thanked Verona and continued his trek toward the river with his father. Ever since yesterday, everyone had been acting differently around Leo. Even now, Darren had no questions or advice. It might've been the longest they'd walked without Darren speaking. Leo had many questions, but he found himself wanting to test how long this would go on. Would his father let them walk the entire way to the river without saying a word?

When the city of Jatn was behind them, Leo couldn't take it anymore. Anger had built up, making him feel as if he was about to burst.

"What happened yesterday!"

Darren looked at him in surprise. "You seem to be accusing me of something. Where is this coming from?"

"Everything's changed since you convinced Gartel to give me a chance."

"The only thing that's changed is that you work for him now. Isn't that what you wanted?"

"Yes, but—"

"Everything else is the same."

But it wasn't. Father was different. Andar was different. Even Rygen was different. Leo knew his father to be lying.

The older Leo got, the more he realized that men lied just as much as boys did. The only difference was that boys lied for themselves. Leo's father lied for some other reason. Was it to protect him and Andar? What did they need to be protected from when their lives were already so difficult? Leo would go another day without eating. Andar could spend years on the farm, the place he hated the most.

Leo almost thought to ask his father to fetch him something for lunch, but Darren was just as busy as the two boys. It was strange for him to have the time to carry the wet pelt for Leo this morning. Something *was* different.

"How is your work?" Leo asked.

"Just fine. I can be late one day."

Leo wanted to scream. When had both his father and his brother started to lie to him? More importantly, why? *Something about the Bookbinding Guild,* Leo assumed. Perhaps Andar was jealous. Would that be such a surprise? Leo would be jealous if he were Andar. In fact, he had been jealous when Andar started working at the Bookbinding Guild. Leo had forgotten that.

Of course, Andar had complained to Father for not giving him an opportunity to redeem himself at the Bookbinding Guild. That's why he's upset with Father. That's why Father is acting different.

It didn't even occur to Leo that Andar could be jealous because he acted as if he was fine. *It's scary how good my liar is at brothering.*

His mind had flipped the sentence, but it almost made sense that way as well, which scared Leo even more.

He was about to ask why Andar wasn't permitted to go back to the Bookbinding Guild, but a couple answers came to mind. Gartel probably hadn't allowed him. He had been adamant that Andar had not only stolen from him but had disrespected him and his business. The other reason was that someone needed to continue working on the farm or the family wouldn't have a house to live in.

If I were Andar, I would ask father to work on the farm so I could work elsewhere. But Andar was different than Leo. He never complained. He was always angry at something, but he usually never showed it, never wanted to speak about it. Leo couldn't hold in his anger that way.

There were many things Andar could do that Leo couldn't, and he wasn't sure three years would change any of that.

They followed the river out of the city. Leo stopped and told his father, "I can carry it the rest of the way."

"It's quite heavy," Darren said as he adjusted the pelt in his arms.

"I want to."

Darren seemed proud as he handed it over. The weight threatened to take Leo back a step, but he held his ground. He continued onward along the river. "Goodbye," he called to his father, unable to look over his shoulder without possibly falling over.

"Goodbye, Leo," Darren said.

Leo wasn't trying to make his father proud. He'd just rather be alone than deal with the uncomfortable feeling any longer.

It didn't take long to set the pelt on the bottom of the shallow river and hold it down with rocks. When he was done, Leo had nothing to distract him from his guilt gnawing away at him. He longed for the feeling of hunger instead, for anything was better than this. What could he do to right this wrong? Perhaps if he and Rygen both spoke to Gartel about Andar one more time, they could convince him that someone else had taken the golden ink.

But Gartel was as stubborn as a mule. He wouldn't believe anything unless there was proof. It didn't matter that Andar had never taken home anything from the Bookbinding Guild. He had no secret spot for his stolen items. There was nowhere in the house for him to hide something from Leo and Darren. They would've seen items appear out of nowhere, or they would've seen the coin he'd received from selling them.

There had to be some other way to prove Andar was innocent. Leo thought on it for a long time. He only came up with one answer. He had to figure out who had done it. Not only that—he had to prove it. Rygen's help would be needed.

He threw the rock he was playing with into the river. Why was she avoiding him! Could he have done something wrong?

When it was late in the day, Leo found himself missing his farm work. At least he would be near his brother and would have eaten a midday meal. It was too late to go back now. He wanted to kick the farm master for how he and Andar were treated there, a nice sharp boot to the shin.

He wouldn't mind the opportunity to give Gartel one of the same. Nothing would be more satisfying than to kick him in his rump and hide behind something before he was able to turn around. But kicking a guild master was bad enough for Leo to lose a hand if he was caught. Still, the thought—along with a few other violent ideas for revenge—kept him entertained.

Eventually he was starving too much to focus on anything but the pain. Fortunately, it was evening by then. The pelt should've been clean enough, for it had nearly been two days. But what if it wasn't? What if he did all of this, losing his work at the farm, for nothing? He could leave it overnight, he supposed, risking everything to ensure the pelt was as clean as it was going to get.

Leo had a better idea. He removed it from the water for a look. It didn't seem as if the day in the river had done much for the pelt at all. Just like yesterday, it was all skin and fur. Wet skin and wet fur. Leo held it so that it wouldn't touch the grass and absorb any dirt, bundling it in his arms. It almost looked like a wet animal cuddled against his chest, but gods it was heavy. He sighed. He really did need help, but he wasn't about to get any. He had better start his trek to the Bookbinding Guild. He had to make sure he got there before Gartel left.

The sun started to set quicker than Leo had predicted. So Leo hurried for a while, but soon it became clear that a speedy walk wouldn't get him there in time. He had to run, pushing his body to the utmost limit as the last of the evening sun went down fast. How far could he go like this, fueled by nothing but a small breakfast? He felt as heavy as stone. His feet were rocks. His legs were tree trunks.

He slowed for what he thought would just be a moment when he was only a few streets away. It was a mistake. He started to lose his balance, the pelt slipping. He lost part of his vision to white spots. He stumbled backward, so he threw himself forward.

It was too much. He seemed to fall slowly, unable to do anything about it except wait for impact. *Protect the pelt*, he thought, but there was nothing he could do. He crashed down on top of it.

He felt no pain, nothing but terror. He scrambled to get himself and the pelt up as soon as he could. Maybe if he was fast, it wouldn't soak up the dirt from the road.

No, it looked to have absorbed all the dirt it possibly could. Still fighting for breath, Leo swiped furiously at the tears welling in his eyes. He cursed himself inwardly. Then he cursed Gartel. Wiping the pelt as much as he could, Leo ordered himself to keep moving. But the damn thing was so heavy. He cursed it next. His arms ached for relief.

He felt like a corpse come to life when he made it to the Bookbinding Guild. The door was still open, thankfully, though there was a city guard standing beside it. Why was he here? Leo didn't have time to stop and wonder as the guard glanced his way. Leo walked past him and was relieved to step inside. Even if the pelt was not good enough, at least his suffering would soon end.

But it wouldn't, he realized, if he couldn't find work elsewhere. As he looked around for Gartel, he spotted Rygen busy at a table. He couldn't give her a single thought. He was too distracted as he pondered how quickly his dream to become a bookbinder was no longer important.

The wish for a better future suddenly burned hot, revitalizing him. He found strength in that single thought. Questions came with it. Had he done a good enough job with the pelt? What was next? Soon even his hunger had abated, dominated by curiosity.

Gartel came down the stairs and eyed him.

Leo gave the pelt another quick inspection. He'd done surprisingly well wiping the dirt off after his tumble. The pelt had dried enough that it no longer left a trail of water behind. All in all, in wasn't too bad.

Gartel walked over. He had a confident stroll with his usual displeased expression, as if sure Leo would disappoint him.

Leo realized he didn't want to say one word to Gartel. He would receive disapproval if he did anything wrong and bitterness even if he accomplished his task. So he held the pelt up with shaky arms, eager for Gartel to stop looking at it and just take it.

I never want to see this pelt again!

"How long did you keep it in the river?"

"From yesterday morning until now." Leo would not tell Gartel it had been removed during the night. Usually guilt came with any lie, but now he took great pleasure in it. The more he could lie to Gartel, the bigger he would feel. And he had been feeling so small as of late.

Gartel finally took it from Leo. There was a clear difference of how the weight affected this man compared to Leo's father, who had made the pelt look as light as paper. Gartel showed strain as he rotated the pelt to look at the skin side. Even as he, a grown man, held it, the damn thing looked huge. What kind of animal died to make it? A damn bear? Leo couldn't stop cursing inwardly, painfully aware that he would remain hungry until he made it home nearly across the city.

"Fine," Gartel said. "Now you will pack it into a barrel of lime and water." He held out the pelt.

Leo knew he should take it, but he couldn't bring himself to reach for it again. He had questions first. How long was it to stay in this barrel? What would Leo have to do during this time? Was he supposed to stay here overnight? What about food? What about *payment*?

"And then what?" Leo asked, taking the pelt into his arms and throwing some of it over his shoulder.

Gartel looked down his nose at Leo. "It will take a week for the lime to loosen the fur enough for the next step. During this time, you will take not one but two pelts to the river. Two days to clean the two of them." The guild master held up two fingers. "Then you will clean more pelts, and more pelts. By then, the one you're holding will be ready for paddling...if you make it that far."

Normally Leo would take that as a challenge he looked forward to beating, but he knew it to be an ominous warning instead. How was he supposed to do this for a week more? And there would be *two* pelts now!

Leo had to ask at least one question. "What about a wage and food, sir? I have eaten nothing today but breakfast."

"A wage and food are only for loyal workers who have proven themselves."

Leo had expected such an answer. He wished Andar was here. He would think of something to tell this man that would make him see reason. Leo didn't know how he was supposed to accomplish that on his own. Tears started to surface. He breathed heavy as he steeled his nerves. He would not cry here in front of Gartel and Rygen.

Rygen, where had she gone? He no longer saw her, at least on this floor. There were a few other workers, so it didn't seem as if the lot of them had been dismissed for the day. She was still avoiding him! But why?

"No complaints?" Gartel seemed surprised.

Leo shook his head.

"Then follow me."

Gartel led Leo to the storage room where Leo had gathered the pelt off the ground. Gartel grabbed something off a tall shelf. It was too dark in the dank room at this time of day to see what. After some fiddling about, he lit a lantern.

Gartel walked a few steps over to a batch of barrels. He took the lid off one in the back, then navigated back through the barrels carefully. He set down the lamp and grabbed the pelt out of Leo's arms.

"Watch how I put it in, making sure not to knock over a barrel." Gartel held the pelt high and walked sideways, checking around him far more than Leo thought necessary.

Leo silently begged for Gartel to actually put the pelt into a barrel rather than bring it back for Leo to finish the task. He was certain he didn't have enough strength in him to lift that pelt over his head.

And tomorrow he would have to bring two to the river. All he wanted to do was get home, eat, and sleep. He couldn't imagine training with his father and brother. That had stopped anyway since yesterday.

Everything was different now, he reminded himself. Everything was worse.

Gartel actually put the pelt into the barrel and secured the lid over it. Leo was too shocked to feel relief.

With despair creeping up on him, Leo told himself that everything would be better one day. He used to believe this firmly, but now he wasn't so sure.

Leo followed Gartel out of the storage room. He still didn't see Rygen. If she was avoiding him, then fine. He would avoid her, too, until she apologized. Never had he needed her more than he did now, and she had abandoned him.

"Come by early tomorrow," Gartel said. "Before sunrise."

It hardly gave Leo enough time for the only two things he needed, eating and sleeping. He would have run home had it even been possible. Instead he walked and held in his tears for no other reason than to prove to himself that he could.

It was dark when he finally arrived. His father frowned at him. "Have you eaten?"

"No." And that was the least of Leo's troubles. His hunger would be resolved shortly. He sat down in front of his plate. "And I have to manage two pelts from now on."

"Two at once?" Andar asked in surprise.

"He never made you do that?"

"No."

"What about Rygen?" Darren asked. "How many pelts did she have to clean at once?"

"I don't know. She's avoiding me."

"What did you do?" Andar asked.

"Nothing!" A tear nearly slipped out. Leo's face was hot from his rage.

"She has not spoken to you?" Darren asked.

"Not since you convinced Gartel to give me a chance." Leo suddenly realized a possibility. "Did something happen to her while you were there?"

Darren sighed. "Nothing that should cause her to avoid you. You should let her explain herself, though. There's no point in us assuming anything. Go over there after you eat."

"Why?" Leo replied angrily. He still had a plan to avoid her.

"Eat," his father said. "You must be famished."

"Rygen can advise you about the pelts," Andar said. "She knows Gartel better than all of us."

Leo wasn't sure why he hadn't touched his bread yet. Perhaps he was too angry and too tired to think about chewing it.

No, he was wrong. As soon as he thought of its taste, his mouth flooded with saliva. He grabbed the warm loaf and bit into it. Some of his tension was gone immediately. Perhaps it was best to speak to Rygen. There had been nothing they couldn't talk about before. Why should that change now?

Leo looked at the bread in a new way as he ate. Starvation was death. Salvation was food. So many destitute people slaved just to eat. So many rich men exploited them for coin. He ripped off another chunk, this time with fury.

"Gartel won't feed or pay me yet!" he said through his full mouth.

"He can't do that," Andar replied. "Even a new apprentice is supposed to be paid for each day of work. It's the law." But he didn't sound as confident as Leo would've hoped.

Darren shook his head. "It should be, but it's not." With a sad look, he told Leo, "Perhaps Rygen can speak some sense into Gartel."

Leo wondered, *why can't you?* The answer not only to that but to what his father had done in the Bookbinding Guild was becoming clearer. Darren didn't seem to want to go back unless he absolutely had to. It was the reason he went in the first place—because he had no other choice. And he had taken away Gartel's choice to ban Leo from the guild. How could Father have done this to such a stubborn man? And now there was a guard at the door, perhaps to stop Father from coming in again.

It was another reason Leo needed to see Rygen, to find out what his father had done. He finished his bread quickly. It was disappointing that another dinner had gone by without Andar adding to the meal, but Leo didn't say anything about it. Leo could sense how his brother suffered. Leo felt it on top of everything else that made him suffer recently.

There was no harmony for Andar, for Darren, and especially not for Leo. It was as if their family had been divided by invisible walls. They could see each other, but their interactions were impeded by something that usually wasn't there.

If Leo knew how to resolve it, he would. But all he could do now was figure out what was going on with Rygen.

He excused himself and walked over to her neighboring home. He knocked on her door, then immediately heard her and her mother discussing who it could be. They sounded close, no doubt in the kitchen. Hopefully, he hadn't interrupted their dinner.

Verona answered, with Rygen glancing at Leo curiously from a table where a meal appeared to be finished. When she saw him, however, she looked away and busied herself with tidying up.

Leo did not bow, which he was certain would make his father displeased if he found out. "I know it's late," Leo said to Verona. "But it's important that Ry and I speak."

"That's fine, Leo," Verona said and moved aside to allow him to enter. "I'll finish up," she told her daughter.

Rygen looked up once more at Leo. Surprisingly, she held his gaze even though it felt as though they were enemies.

"Can we talk in your bedroom?" Leo asked.

She nodded and turned around to lead him there. At least she wasn't pretending nothing was wrong. But what exactly bothered her, Leo still had little idea...unless it had to do with his father. He swallowed a lump when she closed the door behind him. He didn't want to know something that would change how he saw his father, but he couldn't keep going on like this. Whatever bothered Rygen had to come out.

Rygen stood in the center of her small room. Leo knew it was the same size as his, but he shared his with Andar. The second bed took up a quarter of the space that Rygen had open, a clean floorboard almost beckoning for something to be put there.

She did not start, glancing at him as if waiting for him to begin. So he did.

"Should I apologize for something?"

"No." It was a long "no," as if she was saddened he had to ask.

"Then why have you been avoiding me?"

She looked down.

"This has been the hardest two days of my life," Leo admitted. "I have no idea what I'm doing for Gartel. I needed you." *I still do.*

"I'm sorry. I'm truly sorry. I just...I didn't know what to do, so I tried to give myself time to figure it out."

"Is it about my father?"

Rygen looked up with hope. "Did he tell you?"

She was disappointed when Leo shook his head. "No," he said. "What happened?"

"I don't know. He and Gartel were behind a closed door. But I know Gartel wouldn't change his mind...unless he was threatened."

Leo wasn't surprised. He always figured he father could've threatened Gartel, but he trusted his father to do the right thing. "A threat must've been necessary."

"Only brutes threaten people!"

"Are you calling my father a brute?" Leo had heard Rygen use the word about other men, those who'd rather fight than come to an agreement. Those who were angry for no reason. Those who didn't care about anyone but themselves. Leo's father was not a brute, and Leo would scream at Rygen if she insisted he was.

"It's what Gartel called him, and I don't know if he's right."

"He's not."

Rygen glanced up just enough to meet Leo's eyes. "Are you going to tell your father any of this?"

Leo couldn't believe what he was hearing. "Are you *afraid* of him?"

"A little," she said in a tiny voice.

"He would never hurt anyone."

"That's not how he makes it seem."

"Who, Gartel?"

"Well, yes. But I meant your father as well. He can't threaten someone without the promise of violence, and he threatened Gartel."

"He still wouldn't hurt anyone."

"Are you sure about that?"

Only if they deserve it, Leo thought. "He would fight off anyone trying to hurt me, Andar, or even you."

She closed her open mouth, then gave a nod. "That's true. But would he hurt Gartel?"

"If Gartel deserves it." Darren had taught Leo that violence was only the right defense when nothing else would work. With men like Gartel, Leo could easily see how nothing else could work. But did Leo have any hope of explaining to Rygen that a little violence might be necessary? Was this even true? It wasn't exactly a defense, after all.

Rygen didn't speak for a long while, though Leo knew her head was not empty. It never was. Eventually she asked, "Does your father believe Gartel deserves it?"

"No." It was the only answer Leo could give. Fortunately it was the truth. Gartel did not deserve to be hurt, yet. Leo saw that his father did scare Rygen, but Leo would never feel that way. Darren protected him.

"If Gartel did something to you," Leo told her, "then my father would make it right. There's no reason you should be afraid of him, but other men should be. He's not a brute. He only does what's right. It's the real brutes, the men who do wrong, who should be afraid of him. It's why Gartel must be afraid of him."

"I think you're right," she told the floor. "Darren did protect me."

"When?"

She looked up and finally seemed herself. Clearly relaxed and free of tension, she told Leo what had happened from the beginning of Darren's visit to the end. He had threatened Gartel behind a closed door because of what he did to Leo and threatened Lester in front of everyone because of what he did to Rygen. Leo had never heard his father deliver any threat, but he had never thought his father to be gentle, either.

It took a moment to figure out his feelings. He was not surprised, but he was not disappointed. He was proud, in fact. Leo had wished he'd seen this side of his father.

"Lester deserves worse for shoving you to the ground," he told Rygen. "He's a brute, not my father. And Gartel...he's not a brute, but he's mean. Now I have to clean two pelts in the river. I don't know how I'm supposed to carry them back."

"He'll send someone to help you once they are wet, like he did with the first."

"He sent no one."

"He didn't?"

"No. And he isn't paying or feeding me, either."

"He's not?"

"No! I've gone hungry each day."

Her brow furrowed. "He gave me a midday meal. Did you ask about it?"

"Yes, he said payment and food were only for workers who have proven themselves to be loyal."

"How does he expect you to be loyal if he doesn't give you anything in exchange for your work?"

Leo wasn't sure why he laughed, but it was a long and hearty chuckle that made him forget his anger for a moment.

Rygen smiled. "Do you want me to say something to him?"

"Do you think it will help?"

She thought for a moment. "No, he won't like that you've complained to me."

"Then don't say anything. I'll figure something out."

They were silent for a while.

"He wasn't like this at all with you?" Leo asked.

"No."

"Is he nice?"

"Sometimes, when he's in a good mood. I'm sure he'll be nice with you eventually."

Leo laughed again.

CHAPTER SEVENTEEN

The following week was arduous for Leo even though Father gave him enough coin to purchase some bread each morning on the way to the river. With Leo making no coin himself, he feared how purchasing a lunch that was usually free would hurt his family, but his father insisted that Leo eat something between breakfast and supper every day.

Leo was constantly bored. But with energy from the bread, he was able to repeat his father's sword fighting lessons as he waited for the river to clean two pelts at once. It was much better to practice with an opponent, but Leo's imagination was vivid enough for him to put Gartel in front of him and pretend to counter his attacks. It was still boring, but Leo figured his work would become interesting once he could start removing pelts from the barrels.

*****

When a week had passed, it was finally time. But it didn't take long after Leo started working on his first pelt to miss waiting by the river all day. He had to use a wooden paddle to remove all the hair from the pelt, then take it to the river briefly to be rinsed of lime. It was to be set out in the sun to dry before Leo eventually had to spread some sort of dust paste all over it. He thought he heard Gartel speaking about "chalk" to someone one day. Leo figured this was the paste he had to use, but he couldn't be sure.

Gartel took no time to teach Leo anything. He simply told Leo what to do to prepare the pelt, and Leo had to do it without question. When all was done, the nearly finished pelt was to be put in some sort of stretching device and scraped with a blunt knife. It was impossible to do all of this while staying by the river, but Gartel told Leo to leave the new pelts in the river alone. Leo just had to keep track of them and collect them when they were ready to be put into barrels. Leo wanted to ask what would happen if he went to the river and one or more were missing, but he knew such an unfortunate event would not be his fault. Bringing it up would only give Gartel a reason to put blame on Leo, as the guild master seemed to do with everything else.

"If you break, cut, or scratch the pelt too deeply, you will ruin it," Gartel had told Leo. "And you will have shown me that you do not have the ability to be a bookbinder."

Leo spoke with Rygen every day now. He knew much more about what she did at the guild, and it had nothing to do with cleaning pelts. In fact, no one in the guild was cleaning pelts except for Leo. He'd asked Rygen who used to do it before him, but she didn't know.

"The parchments were delivered to us by someone who does not work in the guild," she'd said. "Gartel pays for them."

"So they aren't made here?"

"Not for a long time."

That made Leo curious to ask his brother, who had worked there more than a year before Rygen began.

"I cleaned pelts at first," Andar told Leo. "Then Gartel made Lester do it when he saw how good I was at binding books. But Lester didn't do it for long. I don't know what he told Gartel, but eventually Gartel started paying for parchments."

It made something even more clear to Leo. This was not a job anyone wanted, yet Gartel gave no hints as to how long Leo would have to do it.

His spirits had improved, though, simply because he had begun earning coin. He was paid eleven coppers a day. It was one more than he made per day as a farmer, but it also seemed to thicken the invisible wall between him and Andar, and Leo didn't know why.

He missed his brother. He was happy to see Andar whenever he came home, but they couldn't talk to each other like they used to, not until everyone had gone to bed. It was something about their father that made Andar keep to himself. Leo had asked about the issue between them, but Andar never admitted to anything being wrong. It always felt awkward after that, so Leo stopped bringing it up. He would rather enjoy his time with his brother. They often argued about who was worse, Gartel or Rhenol.

It started as innocent bickering, but eventually the things Andar told Leo that the farm master had been doing to him worried Leo deeply. He knew Rhenol would never hurt Andar unless his brother stole something or struck the man, but Andar's anger was stronger than ever. Leo could sometimes feel it as hot as flames while they talked rather than slept, as if Andar's bed had been set on fire. Rhenol made a point to embarrass Andar whenever he could. It was almost as if he wanted Andar to attack him, so he could legally take one of Andar's hands.

Leo wondered all the time whether his work with the pelts would ever come to an end. He had to start two new ones every time he took the two clean ones out of the river. He began to lose track of the days.

Whenever he had the chance to do anything different than his routine, he jumped at the opportunity. While paddling a pelt, he overheard Gartel speaking with Lester about going to the market. Neither of them seemed willing to go, though both agreed it had to be done. Leo hadn't heard enough to figure out what it was they wanted, but it didn't matter. Eager to prove himself, he tried to get their attention without them realizing he was eavesdropping. He beat the pelt louder, even gave a grunt or two.

They glanced over but said nothing. Leo noticed Rygen working at a table nearby, grinning up to her ears as she watched Leo.

If it's obvious to her that I'm trying to get their attention, then it should be obvious to them.

Leo took a quick break from his paddling. He decided to take a risk, walking over to Gartel and Lester. He hated both of them probably equally, Lester for pushing Rygen down, Gartel for the way he looked down upon Leo. But Leo put on a smile anyway. "I could go to the market."

Lester scoffed and started to say something about how a boy like him could not do this, but Gartel interrupted to ask Leo, "How many times have you been there?"

"Hundreds," he answered truthfully.

"It'll probably be too hard for him," Lester said.

"Harder than taking care of pelts? I think not."

Leo felt as though his pride was strong enough to lift him off his feet. Perhaps Gartel didn't think Leo to be quite as lowly as Leo assumed.

"It's simple enough that not even a boy like him can go wrong," Gartel told Lester.

Leo's pride evaporated in an instant.

"Take this gold coin." Gartel handed it over as if it wasn't anything. Leo had never held so much money, and yet it was a single coin. It was worth ten silvers, a hundred coppers. It was the value of about nine days of work, give or take a few coppers. He was so entranced that he almost missed what he was supposed to do with it.

"You will buy all of the clasps from a metalworker at the market. The man I want you to do business with has blond hair and a small nose. Do not buy from any other metalworker. Do not ask their names or if they know me. All will lie as soon as it's apparent you have coin to spend."

Leo and Andar had already figured this out about people at the market. Everyone was their friend there. Everyone had the best deal. Everyone was prepared to be cheated so that Leo and Andar would be happy.

"He will be expecting someone from my guild," Gartel continued. "Grab a bag from the storage room before you go. Make sure you do not tell him who sent you until you're sure you're standing in front of the right metalworker."

"Blond hair and a small nose."

"Long blond hair," Gartel added snidely, as if Leo had forgotten.

You never said "long" before. But Leo held his tongue.

"I got it," he assured. "All the clasps. Long blond hair and a small nose."

"He will charge you fairly, or he'll have to answer to me," Gartel postured. "You will bring back the silver coins that are left over from that one gold in your hand, and don't even think about taking one. I will speak to him to confirm how much he charged and for how many clasps. I expect you back soon."

Leo hurried to the storage room. He grabbed the first bag he found, a leather pouch big enough for him to curl his arm inside, then headed for the exit of the guild. Rygen waved to him as he left, so he stopped to wave back, but Gartel yelled at him.

"There's no reason for goodbyes. You should be back soon!"

Leo felt his cheeks go red as everyone on the floor stopped their work to stare at him. He hurried out of there.

He was certain that he had at least seen all of the workers of the Bookbinding Guild by then, but he had not been introduced to any of them. Rygen had told him their names, but it was only Lester that he was able to remember. Leo would have to speak to the others at least once before he could find a place in his busy mind to remember them.

The weather was nice, with a breeze that cooled Leo as he ran. He had made sure to put the gold coin in his pocket, but that didn't mean he was about to leave it there and trust it would stay. He had it in a firm grasp. Nothing had been known to jump out of his pocket before, but this was a gold coin! Who knew what force from man or nature might come up this very moment to take it from him.

He had a stifling fear that brought him to a quick stop. If he lost this coin, Gartel could have his hand. He could have both of them! Leo looked at his hands. They were calloused and small compared to his father's, but they were his. He cherished them. He would be nothing without them.

He made it to the market in good time. It wasn't too busy at this hour compared to the mornings. Most of the people here were probably high-ranking men or women who, like Gartel, needed something to help them sell their goods. Or they were workers for those men and women, like Leo was. They certainly looked the part, many dressed with hats and coats that were completely unnecessary in this weather. Leo had realized years ago that the more clothing someone wore, the wealthier they were. He had seen an extraordinarily fancy woman one time who could barely get out of her carriage. Her dress was lavish and layered, but as stiff as a board. She had some sort of close-fitting cloth around her legs so that no skin was showing, along with shiny shoes with a pointed tip. Her hat was the most absurd, with a long feather sticking out from its center that forced her to dip her head low when she emerged from the carriage. She took one look around her, a judging glance at Leo, then murmured something to the man who had helped her out. Soon she was back in and the carriage was off.

At least the wealthier men and women here in the market spent their days working, most likely, not riding around in carriages and holding up their noses at everyone else in the city.

The market itself seemed big, but Leo knew it not to be. He had been here one night with Andar, after all the sellers had gone home. It was nothing more than a circular shaped opening in the center of the city, cobblestone on the ground. Leo and Andar had raced around its diameter. Of course, Andar had won, but even Leo was able to finish without losing his breath.

Now there was just enough room to walk between people without bumping into them. Even without climbing on anything, Leo could see most of the shops, which were usually nothing more than a surface with a mounted sign as high as the seller could get it.

Below the first "metalworker" sign that Leo found was a fair-haired woman. A couple of men leaning against her wooden booth didn't seem too interested in her wares. Leo looked around for another metalworker.

Leo navigated through cloaks and coats, tall boots and shiny belt buckles, but he didn't find the metalworker he had been sent to locate. He grew nervous about being here with a gold coin. He felt a hand slip into his open pocket, and the thief was gone before Leo could turn around to find him. Fortunately, there had been nothing in that pocket. Leo gripped the gold coin even tighter.

He was starting to sweat with tension by the time he realized that he needed a better view after all. Andar had shown him that there was a place to climb up onto one of the nearby buildings. The back wall was lined with wooden planks. He had to be quiet as he scaled it, for Andar had told him that the owner would come out with a broom to smack off anyone he found using his wall.

Leo made it to the roof, where a dirty puddle covered one corner. He stepped around it carefully, the roof creaking beneath him. He could see all the shops from here. Every one of them had a sign with bright paint, although some had fancy writing that made it difficult for Leo to read unless he was closer. He figured metalworkers would use plain letters on their signs, so he looked for that.

Movement caught his eye. It was Andar, he was sure of it, quickly walking into a dark alley to leave the market behind. Leo had recognized his long shirt of gray.

What is he doing here? Shouldn't he be at the farm?

It certainly didn't look like he was here to buy anything, like Leo was. In fact, it looked a lot like he was stealing something...

Leo's heart dropped. Had Andar left his work at the farm? What would it mean for their family? Their father didn't have enough coin to purchase a house. They were expensive, even the small ones on the southern side.

Leo watched for a while, unsure what he would do if he saw his brother again.

Fortunately, he didn't. Eventually he realized that all he could do was finish his task. Gartel would be angry if he was late returning.

He found another metalworker, this one with blond hair. Leo climbed down and hurried across the market until he was in front of the metalworker's shop. His nose was small, hardly there at all. His hair was long, falling past his shoulders. This had to be the one.

Leo looked carefully at his table. He saw no clasps for books.

"Excuse me," Leo spoke up to the man. Andar had taught Leo never to call any merchant "sir" or "madam." It was supposed to be the other way around, and messing that up was like asking to be cheated. "I was sent by Gartel to purchase all of your clasps."

The man leaned down behind his little shop. He hadn't even looked Leo in the eye, making Leo wonder if he had been heard, but the man stood up holding a bag. It clanked as he set it down. He reached into it and pulled out a handful of metal clasps.

A couple appeared ordinary to Leo, but one had been carved into the shape of a tiny fist. Another had a very real looking skull. Could it have been made out of bone? Leo didn't know what else could have that texture. He let out a sound of marvel that brought out a smile from the metalworker.

"A few more good ones in there," the man said as he dropped the clasps into the bag. "You can take a look on your way back. Have the payment?"

Leo was relieved to hand over the gold coin to the right person.

It took the metalworker but a moment to give him back two silver coins. Leo pocketed them as quickly as he could and looked around to see who might've taken notice. No one appeared to be watching him, but you can never tell with thieves.

"Keep one of those for yourself," the metalworker said with a sly grin. "I won't say anything to Gartel."

"I can't do that." Leo was eager to leave, but he couldn't turn his back on the frowning metalworker who appeared ready to lecture him.

"I know boys like you. You work hard and don't get paid enough. I was one. Take a coin. Give it to your father. He'll be happy with you."

"Thank you, but I can't. I must be going."

Leo hurried out of there. Although tempted to take a silver coin from the bag and slip it into his pocket, a temptation was all it was. Everything he had been working toward was worth so much more than a silver coin. Gartel might've put the metalworker up to this.

But Gartel didn't know I would be going to the market today, Leo realized. *That didn't matter. There could've been an agreement made between them that if anyone came to pick up the clasps, their loyalty would be tested.*

It seemed a bit far-fetched, but loyalty was important to Gartel.

That silver coin was still tempting him, the blasted thing. It was worth about a day of work, an entire, difficult day of work.

It made Leo realize that his work at the Bookbinding Guild had been harder on him than what he'd done at the farm. Strange, considering that the farm work was more demanding. So why was this worse?

It was the removal from his brother, the lack of a midday meal provided to him, and the nauseating disrespect that Gartel had displayed.

The farm master was just as disrespectful to Andar as Gartel was to Leo, but that was because Andar gave Rhenol a hard time whenever he thought he could get away with it. Leo had done nothing but obey Gartel.

What was the matter with his brother? Why disobey so often, and why leave work to come to the market? Leo loved his brother, but there were aspects to his personality that Leo would never understand. He just hoped that Andar wasn't thieving for coin. The amount he could make was much greater than his pay at the farm, but it was not as high as the potential for disaster.

Leo distracted himself by looking at the various clasps in the bag. Most were ordinary, small strips of metal carefully crafted. Rygen had taught Leo that these clasps were not just for design. It was important for books to remain shut when they were not in use. Otherwise the pages would expand. This didn't sound so bad, but Leo had seen books that had not been kept shut. The pages were wavy, creating lumps that would not flatten out no matter how hard Leo pushed down on the cover.

Leo knew much about books, but the opportunity to show off had never come up. He couldn't think of a single question Gartel had asked him except, "Do you understand?"

There were some clasps in the bag that were unique, like the skull he had seen earlier. He found one with a dagger and another with a shield. These were probably meant for the more expensive books, the ones Leo would never be able to afford.

*****

When he arrived home later that evening, he expected Andar to say something about the market. There was tension in the silence between the three of them as they ate. Leo was certain that Andar could feel it even though his brother did nothing to show that he was uncomfortable. Their father was a mystery as usual. Leo had always assumed that the same thought cycled through Darren's mind: He would do everything he could to raise Leo and Andar well. But now Leo figured that perhaps there was more to Darren than being a good father. Andar would sometimes ask Darren about his past, as if trying to catch him in a lie, but now his brother no longer seemed interested.

When they went to bed, Andar still hadn't said anything about the market or leaving the farm. Leo couldn't bear the thought of being lied to by his brother anymore, so he couldn't bring himself to ask. He needed to know what was going on with Andar, though. It might not be Leo's business, but they were brothers. They were supposed to tell each other everything and never lie. Andar was the one who had made this rule, and now he was the only one to break it.

Leo stayed up for a while trying to figure out how he could find out what Andar was doing. Eventually he came up with a plan.

Leo didn't sleep much that night, but he got up when his brother did and ate breakfast with him in silence. The rest of their morning was just like usual, getting dressed to leave, discussing the weather, rubbing their eyes. But Leo took care of everything he needed to a bit slower. He had to make sure he left the house at the same time as Andar.

Their father was out before them, thankfully. Leo and Andar left the house together. They split immediately, Andar walking toward the farm and wishing Leo a good day. Leo wished him the same.

Leo went north until he could no longer see his brother. Then he stopped and ran back home. He still had to get to his work by sunrise, so that didn't leave much time. The house was still dark at this hour, but Leo didn't want to use a match to light the lantern. Either Andar or their father might notice one was missing. So Leo searched as well as he could.

Part of him wanted to find nothing, but he couldn't think of a single reason Andar would've gone to the market yesterday and kept that information to himself. Not a single reason that was good, at least.

Another part of Leo did want to find something. He wanted proof that he was right to assume Andar was stealing more than just the minimal food and clothes their family needed. At least then he could present the evidence to Andar, and there was no way his brother could lie to him.

But what Leo ended up finding under Andar's mattress put him in even worse of a dilemma than before.

It was coin, a lot of coin. Leo quickly counted them in groups of fives. They were all coppers, but they were quite valuable because of their quantity. He counted fifty-three of them! How did Andar get all of this money?

The answer was obvious, but it sickened Leo to accept it. Andar had to be stealing valuables to sell—what their father had strictly forbade. Andar could be put in a dungeon if he was caught, and there was nothing Darren or Leo could do to help. Leo didn't know which was worse: the potential punishment or the fact Andar was keeping this coin a secret. He seemed to have no intention of using it for anyone but himself.

Leo put the coins back as they were and ran out of the house so he could arrive at the Bookbinding Guild on time. He racked his mind. What could Andar have planned with this coin? What was worth risking his life?

Only one answer came to mind: the gem Andar had taken from the market so long ago. Nothing had affected his brother in the same way.

Nothing had affected *Leo* in the same way, either.

CHAPTER EIGHTEEN

Finding work would've been easy for Darren, but he strived for a better type of work than digging. He had been right to assume that he couldn't apply for any of the jobs that involved math. Almost all had to do with finance, and everyone in that field told him they would look into his history.

Being a city guard was impossible for the same reason, not that he could live with himself even if it was an option. He always spoke of Andar to the guilds he visited. But all with better work than the Farmers' Guild had no openings for a thirteen-year-old boy with no training. It didn't matter how much praise Darren gave his son, who was excellent at anything requiring the use of his hands or mind. He hadn't received the right training, and now he was too old to start. Darren heard the same two excuses every time, and every time he found himself closer to making a scene. They didn't want a boy who was thirteen because he would be considered to be a man in one year, able to open his own shop where he would no longer be an underpaid apprentice.

Darren still had much of the coin he'd received for discovering the Tisary with his digging team. It was unfortunate he hadn't been paid what he'd been promised. *It was worse than unfortunate*, he often corrected himself, but he didn't have the capacity to remain angry at a group of rich families he'd never met. There was too much else to worry about. Andar had practically stopped speaking to Darren and his brother, closing up. Darren was eager to find work for his oldest son so Darren could take over at the farm. Perhaps in a few more days he would take over anyway and allow Andar to apply himself however he wished, but Darren feared the boy would spend his time thieving instead. At least while Andar worked at the farm he was safe.

Rage came in seemingly random moments as Darren walked about the city. He had trouble believing that there was no honest work for him here that was better than digging or farming. He wasn't a brilliant man, but he knew himself to be skilled at many things. It was his history that hampered him, like an injury that would never go away. Any other city would be better, he told himself, because then he'd have his papers from Jatn, which said he was born there. No one would doubt the truth of his claims. Here, it would be easy for anyone to discover that there were no records of anyone by the name of the mother and father who Darren had made up to hide his true identity.

At least he'd received no messages from Raenik. He'd gone by Raenik's shop a couple of times since his disappearance. Raenik was never there, though someone had come by to replace the door with one that could actually shut and lock. A sign had even been posted saying that his business was temporarily closed. Either he was alive still, and he was the one to do these things, or the people who did this to him were kind enough to ensure his shop wasn't robbed while he was missing or dead. It seemed unlikely. But if Raenik was fine, why wasn't he back in his shop?

Fear, Darren realized. Perhaps he had finally made an enemy of the wrong person. Darren's nerves were on edge every time he thought about who had his true papers now. He'd planned to break into the shop to retrieve them, but someone had barred the windows from the inside. If someone, whether it be Raenik or not, had the ability to do that, they'd probably already removed all the true papers of everyone Raenik had "helped."

An internal warning told Darren he was being followed. He didn't stop or look around. He had dealt with many people following him before in Halin, where he was recognized every time he left his family's mansion. He had tried not to spend much time in the mansion, for usually he would find himself trying to sort out some minor issue between some delegate and a trusted worker of his father's. Yune was always better at handling those issues, but some men didn't want to listen to a woman no matter how correct she was.

Who would be following him here? There had been no sightings of anyone trailing his boys after the one time Andar had spotted someone. That was a while ago.

Darren kept going as he looked for somewhere he could duck into and use to his advantage. He tried to think of a reason he might be followed. He didn't look as if he had money, and he certainly wasn't an easy target to overpower. He had no destination in mind at the moment. All he could think was that Raenik had sent someone to watch him, but Darren couldn't figure out a reason for this.

He had also never figured out why his boys would be followed if it wasn't Raenik's doing. Unable to come to any other conclusion, he figured this *was* Raenik in some form. Perhaps he was in trouble and needed leverage. He would use Darren in any way he could. Or perhaps he wanted revenge for Darren disobeying him by leaving the cavern after the discovery of the Tisary. This could be a hired mercenary with a weapon.

Adrenaline made it difficult for him to keep a steady pace. No day was a good day to kill someone. He made a sharp turn into an alley and sped down it. He could be quick when he wanted to, even now that he was thirty-one. He should be able to lose this mercenary.

Darren turned a corner, then he jumped to get his hands onto a roof and pulled himself up. He got low to keep out of sight, but a thought made him pop his head up. If this was a mercenary sent to kill or punish him, they would only keep trying if he didn't deal with them.

So he watched as someone with a hood made the same turn he just had. There was little time, as they moved fast. Darren acted on instinct, jumping down on top of them.

He flipped his pursuer over and pinned their arms to the ground before they could get out a weapon, but her face had the soft features of a woman. He noticed strands of long hair billowing out around her surprised expression. She wasn't small of stature, but she certainly wasn't strong enough to win a bout against Darren. His knees were across her arms, pain showing through her gritted teeth.

"Who are you!" he demanded.

"Not an enemy, so you can get off."

Something told him to trust her, but he would be a fool to do so. He pulled down her hood. There wasn't much light in this alley, but there was enough for him to see the distinctive color of her hair.

"You're an Analyte," he exclaimed stupidly. Of course, she already knew this.

He was too shocked to figure out what to do with this woman. He hadn't seen an Analyte in many years. Not a single one had shown themselves in Jatn since Darren had come here. Like every Analyte, her hair was a shade of purple. But the hue of this woman's locks was so light that it was almost silver. It was a touch darker toward the middle of her head. The first time Darren had seen an Analyte, he'd thought the hair color seemed unnatural, as if it had been dyed somehow. The same feeling came back again.

He looked closer at her face, staring into her eyes. Her gaze was so oddly piercing that Darren felt as though she was searching his soul. He also saw a reserve of aggression there, but she seemed to be making herself calm for now, especially considering Darren's weight on her arms.

"Don't move," he told her as he took his knees off. He searched her up and down with his hands for a dagger, pushing against her taut flesh in every place a weapon could be hidden. She didn't seem the least bit uncomfortable as she let him search, even as he checked her inner thighs where a dagger could be strapped.

"Take your time," she said sarcastically. "I'm sure if someone sees you, they would assume you are only searching for a dagger."

It was a good point. He was glad to be done, quickly getting off her.

He had a flash memory of Analytes turning on his people in the midst of the battle. They'd slaughtered so many humans, stabbing many in the back with their swords. But this woman seemed too young to have fought that day, although she was certainly an adult. She probably wasn't much younger than Darren, perhaps five or seven years at most. The only reason she couldn't have fought was because Darren was only twenty at the time of the battle.

Other than her pale purple hair, she looked human. She had an appealing unlined face, with a patrician nose and prominent cheekbones that highlighted the harmony of her features. But her dark, cunning eyes told Darren she was not dependent on her looks for anything. She had an easy confidence in the way she looked at Darren that he had seen many times before. Appearing wise beyond her years, she obviously knew something that he didn't. In fact, there was probably much she could teach him.

"Who are you?" he asked again, his question no longer a demand.

"I'm glad to see that you're not the kind of human to hold a grudge against every Analyte because of the actions of a few of us."

A wave of fear passed through him that he did not show. She knew who he was. How was that possible?

"No, but I do protect myself and my family at all costs," he warned her.

"I told you I'm not an enemy. If you didn't trust me, then you would threaten me as you have threatened many others on behalf of Raenik, then you would leave while I was still shaking. This has been your strategy, and I've seen how well it works. But you and I need to forge a basic trust quickly if we are to accomplish anything. You asked me who I am, and I'll tell you. I'm Erisena. Yes, I'm an Analyte, but I had nothing to do with those who betrayed your family."

Her words were too practiced, too smooth. She had prepared this speech, which meant she very well could be lying. He needed to interrogate her further, but she had only paused for a brief moment.

"Your life is about to change," she told him in a hushed tone. "I can warn you about some of these changes or let them surprise you. The choice is yours." Then she whispered into his ear, "DVend."

She still appeared confident and unafraid. Only the best liars would have such a placid demeanor while standing before Darren, especially when there were no witnesses around to protect her.

But there was one attribute Darren noticed that changed his mind. It had to do with her intense gaze into his eyes. She didn't just care whether he believed her or not, she needed him to understand something. She wanted him to do something. Liars only wanted to escape with the truth withheld.

She obviously knew Raenik very well, at least that was clear.

"Are you the one who wrecked Raenik's shop?"

"I won't lie to you, but there are certain answers I cannot give you until I know I can trust you. I can see you believe me, which means I can tell you that I'm both similar and opposite to the Analytes who betrayed your family. Do you understand my meaning?"

"No. Speak clearer."

"I fought and still fight for the same reason they did, but I would never betray your family."

"You're too young to have fought in that battle."

"Yes, but I am not speaking of that battle. And I could tell you the same. I would've thought you were older. You don't appear to have more than thirty years to your name—a name everyone knows. You must have been in your teen years when you fought." She let out something between a scoff and a laugh. "You are known as the best swordsmen in the human kingdom, but I heard little about how young you were. I can only imagine how good you would be now if the outcome of that battle had been different."

She assumed him to be younger than he was. Darren glanced around for anyone listening. He walked to the corner and peered around the building they used for cover. An empty alley. He thought he felt another presence nearby, though. He stopped all movement to listen.

Erisena interrupted. "This is good news, Darren. Good news for both of us."

"Explain." He put himself in front of her, refusing to trust her words, as convincing as her gaze was.

"I've been to every city in the world, but finding you has been the most difficult out of anyone else I've found. I figured you were here, but there had been no tidings of a man of your stature. You've done well to keep your name off the tongues of rumor mongers, but eventually I came into contact with Raenik."

"You mean recently."

"Recently action had to be taken, but I met Raenik a while ago. He's stubborn."

"Is he alive?"

She squinted. "Do you ask out of concern or curiosity?"

"Just answer my questions without one of your own."

"He's alive."

"What did you do to him?"

"Convinced him to help us." She lowered her voice to a whisper. "It's not wise to talk here much longer. I was going to follow you until we came across a better place to meet, but you figured out I was behind you. There are people who should not see us together. Not until it's time." There was a catch in her voice that had him paying even closer attention. "I'm looking for humans and Analytes who want to take back what you fought for. I have already recruited many men and women who would be glad to fight with you."

If women wished to fight, it was likely that they were Ascendants. How many could she really have recruited? Darren had only met maybe a dozen in his lifetime.

There was a more important question. Who would this elite army fight?

There had been much discussed here that could destroy everything he'd work toward. All it took was the wrong person hearing Erisena say the name of her target aloud, a target Darren knew very well. He had dealt with the king personally on occasion. Mavrim Orello was the only man in this world who scared Darren. Fear, he felt often. Fear for his boys, for his identity, and of running out of coin. But those fears were slow, creeping dreads. Only Mavrim gave Darren the acute prick of terror in his chest.

"You don't wish for revenge?" Erisena asked.

"What would revenge get me?" Darren countered.

"Satisfaction."

"There is no satisfaction for me anymore. It was taken after the Analytes betrayed us. Everything else was stripped away after the slaughter. There is only peace and safety left."

"You must be speaking only for your children."

"They are everything."

"And what of your sister?"

He didn't want to show his interest, but it had already slipped out from his widened eyes. Erisena showed him a forgiving smile. "I don't know where she is at the moment, but she is in the city. I'm sure I can find her again with your help."

"How did you find her the first time?"

Erisena cast her gaze downward. "We've done many things to get the information we have, and I'm not proud of all of them." She glanced back with fire in her eyes.

"But it's all for justice. For people like your sister, and Teyro, who are still alive."

Teyro...Darren hadn't heard that name in many years. He was an Analyte Ascendant and an officer of the army of Analytes who'd come to Halin. He had betrayed Darren's family with the rest of them. A flash memory showed fire exploding in the midst of his men, their bodies spiraling out like dolls.

Erisena gasped. "You don't know what Teyro did, do you?"

"What are you talking about?"

"He fought on the side of your family even after the betrayal."

Darren's eyes narrowed. "You can't possibly know that."

"I know it as well as anyone can know something. His wife is with me. She's helping us find him."

Darren supposed it was possible that the fire could have been from another Analyte, but Teyro was known as the strongest mage in both kingdoms. It seemed unlikely for anyone to have cast such a spell besides him.

Perhaps Erisena thought she was telling the truth, but she must have been tricked. She did seem like the kind of person whose eagerness could blind her.

No matter. Darren was not intrigued. Whatever her plan, he wanted nothing to do with it. He considered playing a role to at least learn more about his sister, but Erisena had admitted that she didn't know where Yune was. Darren was just as likely to find her as Erisena was.

Punctuating his point with a menacing jab of his finger, he ordered, "Stay away from my family." Darren walked off, preparing to ignore any argument Erisena might make. But she grabbed his arm with both hands, her grip surprisingly strong.

"Fine, don't believe me about Teyro, but one day you will see."

Darren tried to pull his arm out of her grasp. He was shocked when she still held on; she stumbled a bit but quickly planted her feet.

"You can't leave yet. I haven't told you what's most important. It's about your sons. They will be in danger."

He gave her a threatening look that loosened her grasp. He took his arm out of her light hold and wanted to grab her by the neck. He settled on her shoulder instead.

"Now listen closely—" he began.

Her eyes flashed, but her voice stayed steady. "It's not me who endangers them. Never would I or anyone loyal to me hurt anyone in your family. But they will be in danger soon. You really have no idea what I'm talking about?"

He let go. Even though this might be some trick to keep him here, he had to at least hear her out.

"What do you think you know about them?"

"More than you, apparently. Or you will figure out what I'm speaking about after some thought. When you do, remember that we, together, can protect them much better than you can on your own. We have the same goals, don't you see? I want to spare the lives of innocent people and give them justice for what the king has taken away."

"Spare the lives of what innocent people?"

Her jaw dropped. "Oh Darren, you don't know the truth about the two kings' agreement after the war? I had thought the Quims knew all of this. You *must* join me. There is so much happening in this world that you clearly know nothing about."

He had to admit that she was convincing, but people like her chose just the right words to get their way. This was Erisena's talent. She was the recruiter. She had probably been sent here by someone else, someone who would use Darren in the same way they might be using Erisena. No one fought for the lives of innocent people. No one fought for justice. They all fought for themselves, just as his family had. People might argue otherwise. They would say DVend's father, DFaren, wouldn't have been able to live with himself if the city and the Tisary had been taken over by the king. This was true, but this wasn't a reason for fighting. It was an excuse, and excuses were all Erisena gave as her reasons to fight, to kill.

"I will send someone to find you later today for your answer," she told him. "It should give you enough time to figure out why your sons will soon be in danger and why you need to join us. I will not force you, as I have not forced anyone before. But I have to know your decision soon. You are now a danger to me until I know your allegiance."

She surprised him by starting to walk away.

"You never asked if I still have any skill with the sword," he said.

"Because it doesn't matter," she called over her shoulder. "If you have forgotten, then you will remember."

CHAPTER NINETEEN

Darren thought much about what Erisena had said of his sons. Finding the answer to why they would soon be in danger was like trying to remember something nearly there. He dug through the depths of his mind for information he knew he had within him, but he just couldn't reach it. Andar and Leo were different than most boys, he knew. They would be different than most men, he had always figured. But it was how they would be different that he hadn't predicted.

Erisena must've been the one who had followed them. *She's done more than that,* he realized. She seemed to have figured out something about them that Darren was certain he would figure out soon. He knew his boys too well not to.

He walked around the town aimlessly as he thought through this, checking for followers every time a feeling of warning distracted him. He seemed to be completely on his own again, a notion that had taken quite some time to get used to after his wife passed.

What did Erisena mean about the truth of the two kings' agreement after the war? It was already something dastardly. Why would it be a lie?

After the Analytes had changed sides to join King Orello and won the war in a slaughter, one thousand soldiers loyal to DFaren were sent to Analyte land. They would be farmers for the rest of their lives. Most everyone knew that these humans would be trapped as slaves, but the way they were slaves was different than how most people knew the word. They didn't have a master. They were slaves to the Analyte land, living from the food they grew. It was the same life that many humans led, but these men were not allowed to leave the Analyte kingdom ever. They had to remain on the land they were told to farm.

It didn't make sense for any of this to be false. The Analytes had plenty of fertile land, yet not enough farmers to take full advantage. They had a strong army and had promised to defend any human farmers who came to their land, but no farmers came. There were barbarians all over the continent, this was known, but it was mostly Analyte land that they pillaged. The barbarians stayed out of the Analyte cities, which were protected, and the Analyte king didn't have the means to protect all the farmers across his land. He still didn't to this day, Darren was sure. There was just too much land. It was why humans were enslaved to cultivate it. They no doubt were paying taxes as well, probably with the currency of their crops.

The only reason the human king had agreed to this, everyone knew, was because he had clearly done so prior to the Analytes betraying his enemies. It was the reason for the betrayal. Darren sometimes wished that his father had promised the Analytes something they wanted more, but there was nothing they needed more than farmers, which was why it was so unlikely for this to be false.

Erisena was probably lying. It was a recruitment ploy. The promise of truth and enlightenment had always been a way to make sheep out of the ignorant. Darren let this go from his mind to focus on Andar and Leo.

He stopped as he remembered something. Andar had stolen a stone a while ago from the market...from a hooded woman. Darren felt a chill as everything started to connect. It was a testing stone. Erisena was looking for a certain type of person, and Andar was it. He had inadvertently brought her to their home.

That beast on the roof…Erisena was no normal Analyte. Darren cursed loudly enough to draw a look from a woman passing by. He apologized and hurried off. He turned into an alley where he could have a moment to himself. Sweat ran down his forehead. He knew what she meant now. She was probably right about Andar, perhaps even Leo.

He had to see them, but they were both working. He paced for a moment.

This couldn't wait. He would get Leo first, only because Leo was closer. Neither he nor Andar would understand why Darren was about to interrupt their work. They would ask many questions. How was he supposed to deal with their curiosity without letting them know that they might be in danger?

Whether or not he would figure it out in time was not as important as finding out about their immediate future. He headed to the Bookbinding Guild.

*****

It was the early afternoon by the time Darren arrived. He didn't see his youngest son, but there were walls and doors hiding his view from the entirety of the first floor. Leo was probably back somewhere working on pelts. Darren was glad not to see Gartel. He didn't want to deal with the bookbinding guild master again if he could help it.

He stood just inside, meeting the eyes of the donkey of a man who'd pushed Rygen. He looked away quickly, pretending not to have seen Darren. The slender man fumbled around a desk, clearly trying to busy himself. Darren ignored him, waiting for Rygen to notice him in the doorway.

She looked over when he took a couple of steps toward her. She seemed scared of the sight of him at first, or perhaps just a little surprised. Finally, she stood and smiled, then made her way over.

Darren wanted to ask about his son. He wanted to make sure there was nothing Leo was withholding from him. He needed to know Gartel was treating the boy better these days. But now was not the time. All the issues that had bogged down their family as of recently seemed insignificant. Erisena had made him realize just how narrow his view of the world had been. He was a bit envious of Rygen's mother as he watched her daughter walk over. Could this girl ever be in the same trouble?

"Hello, sir," Rygen said with a curtsy. "Are you looking for Leo?"

"Yes, Rygen. Do you know where he is?"

"I'll get him for you."

"Thank you."

She was too frightened to talk the last time Darren saw her here in the Bookbinding Guild. He had figured that reaction was caused by the man who'd pushed her down, but Darren had seen the same look on her face for a moment when she'd noticed him by the doorway. She had not been startled; Darren didn't often bring that out in people. It was fear he'd seen across her soft features at first.

He didn't know why she would be afraid of him. He would do nothing but protect her. Fortunately, Rygen's look at Darren was now friendly, more than just a polite smile on her face. He wondered if it was gratitude for lecturing the man who'd pushed her.

Darren wished to speak with her mother when there was time. He and Verona used to help each other quite often when their children were young. There was no leaving them alone, so either Leo and Andar were always at Rygen's house or Rygen was at theirs. Verona had often made it clear that she thought Darren to be a fine father and husband. He had caught her meaning throughout the years, but he hadn't been able to summon the same feelings for her.

He didn't know what it was about Lane Writhe that had brought out these emotions from him once again. She had been a bother in his thoughts ever since he'd met her. The dream he'd had of her taking off her mage robe and climbing into his bed did not help, either.

Verona had no longer shown interest after meeting Gartel. The guild master was a blessing for many years. Books came into their lives shortly after Gartel had.

Part of him was relieved Leo had grown to hate Gartel. That would make it easier when it came time for Darren to take his sons out of the city.

Was this still the plan? He hadn't asked himself that question since meeting Erisena.

He felt a spark of adrenaline in his chest that he figured had died out long ago. It reminded him of his training, of fighting for something. Darren fought every day in one sense of the word, but it was a different kind of battle. His was akin to trying to fend off an illness. Poverty was like that. All work and precautions went into prevention rather than aggression. That would change if he actually accepted Erisena's offer.

There was the excitement again. He was still young and foolish, Darren reminded himself. And if he wanted to live long enough to see his children grow up, he would not act on these emotions.

Leo appeared startled when he entered the main room and saw Darren there. The boy walked over as quickly as he could, the way children do when every part of them wants to run, yet they are not allowed to do so.

"What's wrong?" he asked Darren the moment he was close. "Did something happen to Andar?"

"He's fine." *As far as I know.* So Leo had the same worry about Andar that Darren did. One day he might get himself into the kind of trouble that Darren could not get him out of. It was another reason to leave Jatn.

Darren would have to tell Gartel that he was taking Leo for a while, but there was an easier way to do it than walking around the enormous shop looking for him.

"I have to take you from here for three hours," he told his son. "It's very important and must be done. I'm going to wait here. Hurry and inform Gartel."

Leo's face scrunched up. "What are we going to do?"

"We're going to get your brother, then I'm taking you both home. Remember, three hours. I'm sure Gartel will understand when you tell him how important it is for your *father.*"

"Gartel won't let me leave work, and Rhenol will *never* let Andar leave."

"Gartel will let you leave, and Rhenol will let Andar leave. The faster we can begin, the faster you can return. Go find him now. I'll wait here."

"But you haven't told me what we'll be doing."

Because Darren still hadn't figured out how to explain this. "It's an important test that has to be done now. I'll explain later. Go on."

But Leo didn't move. "What kind of test?"

Darren raised his voice. "Leo, go now and I will explain later."

Leo grumbled, but he did turn and head toward the stairs.

Darren couldn't remember the last time he had to speak that way to Leo.

As he waited, he realized that there was no way of telling his sons what they were doing without giving them the complete truth.

Gartel did not show himself, thankfully. Leo returned and said they could leave.

Leo asked many questions that went unanswered on the way to the farm, the place where Andar slaved too much for a boy. Darren had made a decision on the way there. If Erisena was right—if they would be in danger—then it was better that they didn't know until they needed to.

Andar didn't mind at all when Darren said he would be taking him off the farm.

"Let me be the one to tell Rhenol that I'm leaving," Andar said.

"It's better if I do it," Darren informed him.

He waited for Andar to realize why that was before walking off. Andar really was almost a man now. Darren would have to stop making decisions without him soon.

Andar nodded, then told Darren where to find Rhenol. There would be a time that Darren would figure out how to get Andar off this farm for good, but it was not today.

Darren had only dealt with Rhenol a few times, and he vividly recalled each of them. The most memorable was after Rhenol had made Andar cry in shame. When Andar was just a child of six years, he had ripped the back of his pants without realizing it while working. Rhenol had called attention to it in the most immature way, cupping his hands around his mouth and shouting that he wasn't paying Andar to show off his arse. Darren would never know whether the farmers laughed at the embarrassed little boy just to support Rhenol, or if they were just cruel, but Darren had focused his ire afterward on Rhenol.

A new pair of pants had been delivered by some poor messenger boy to their home later that night. To this day, Darren wasn't sure if confronting Rhenol was what started the divide between him and Andar.

And now I've gone and done the same with Leo and Gartel. There just wasn't enough good to grasp onto in the city, and trying to fix the bad seemed to make everything worse.

A change was what they all needed, especially Andar. *Just get them out of the city*, Darren told himself. He didn't know how many times he had repeated that phrase.

He had gone over the plan many times before. Even if new issues came to distract him now, he trusted the plan. It was simple and effective, the best kind of strategy.

Rhenol didn't bother to hide his displeasure upon seeing Darren. Darren kept the conversation quick for both their sakes, and soon he was headed out of there with Leo and Andar whispering to each other behind him.

He could tell by their curious tones they were asking each other what was going on. He let them speculate, speeding up so that he would not eavesdrop.

When he neared their house, though, it was time to start. The first part was easy. He waited for his boys to catch up to him. They ran up to his sides.

He told Andar, "Describe again the woman whose gem you stole."

"I didn't get a good look. She had a hood. I think she was beautiful."

"How do you know if you didn't get a good look?" Leo asked.

"You know how you know a girl is pretty before you *really* see her?"

Leo thought for a moment with a face of confusion. "What?"

"You notice that she's pretty, so *then* you look." Andar paused. "You don't know?"

"I still don't understand how you can notice she's pretty if you haven't looked."

"You've glanced, but you haven't really looked."

"I think Leo's too young to know what you mean," Darren interrupted.

"But you do, right Father?"

Darren's heart warmed. It was a surprise how honored he felt that his son had finally asked him a question that connected the two of them. As of late, everything Andar expressed had been demands.

"I know exactly what you mean," Darren agreed.

"I think girls are pretty," Leo said. "Rygen is very pretty."

"Oh?" Andar exclaimed in a way that made Leo tense up.

"I just said she's pretty. I don't mean I want to marry her. She's only pretty." Leo paused a moment, looking as if he hoped someone would reply. "Isn't she pretty?"

"Who's talking about marriage?" Andar chuckled at his own comment as he looked up toward Darren. But Darren's shock seemed to give Andar the same type of panic as his brother. "I mean...I wasn't talking about Rygen. She's too young. I was thinking of others...never mind what I mean. I was making a joke. I don't have these thoughts."

Darren chuckled and patted his son on his back. The last statement was certainly a lie.

"Certain thoughts are going to go through your head no matter how polite you want to be, but I'm sure you have none of those thoughts for Rygen," Darren assured. "As long as you know the right and wrong way to treat a woman, then that's what matters."

"These thoughts still go through your head...?" Andar swallowed. "After Mother?"

Darren nodded as guilt creased his forehead.

"What thoughts?" Leo asked. "Kissing someone?"

Andar pounced on the opportunity. "Do *you* think about kissing Rygen?"

Leo stared at his brother with wide eyes. "No," he answered as if fearful it was the wrong answer.

"You do. You think about kissing Rygen."

"I don't." There was no confidence to his tone.

"You know, Leo, she might *want* you to kiss her."

He stared at Andar again, this time without moving. "No, she doesn't."

"Really, she might."

They came to the door of their home. Darren didn't want to interrupt the conversation. Andar was teasing Leo a bit, but this was the first time he'd heard them speak up about anything except work since Leo's birthday. Besides, this was a conversation Darren should've had with both of them long ago. Had his sister heard this, she would've shouted with triumph that she had predicted this would happen. Yune had told him that her children would be passionate, artistic, and sophisticated. His would be fighters with palms as rough as dirt. It was not meant to be an insult. Andar certainly was a fighter; it was in his bones and flesh. He seemed to have trouble existing in any environment where someone had authority over him. But Darren wasn't too sure about Leo yet.

Unfortunately, the conversation did not continue. Andar asked Darren, "Why did you bring up the woman with the gem?"

"I'll tell you as much as I can as soon as we're done." He opened the door to their home and let his boys in first. He closed the door after them and hunched a bit to bring himself closer to their eye level. "For now, I need both of you to answer my questions and do what I say. It will not make sense, but something happened today that has led to this...experiment."

"At least tell us what it has to do with," Andar said.

"The woman," Leo answered. "The stone."

"Oh yeah," Andar said an agreement. "You met her today, didn't you?"

Darren cursed to himself. He didn't know why he thought he could keep any of this from them. They were too smart. "I can't be sure it's the same woman because you never got a good look, but I did meet a woman who might've been the same one from the market...and the same one who followed you that one day." He put up his hands as the boys opened their mouths. "I will tell you more when we are done. Remember what I said earlier."

"But what are we doing?" Leo asked.

"We will find out," Andar told his brother. "Let's listen to Father."

Darren showed Andar a look of gratitude.

"Leo, fetch something from your room. Don't let Andar know what it is. Bring it back here and hold it tightly. Andar, turn around."

"Can I let you see it?" Leo asked his father.

"Yes, it doesn't matter if I see it."

"This just sounds like a game," Andar commented snidely.

"Even if it were, it would be better than working," Leo said.

Andar laughed. "That's true."

Leo went into the bedroom he shared with Andar. He didn't come out for a while. Darren didn't want to rush him, though. It was important he select something completely of his own will.

There were a few different tests Darren could use to decipher if his boys would be in danger, but he had none of the right materials. He had to make up his own tests, though he was unsure how well they would work.

Eventually Leo returned with the newer book Darren had bought for his birthday, the heroic tale of the best swordsman in the world, a man who was specifically not DVend. It probably was not a true tale, but Darren had seen Leo reading it over and over nonetheless, so it had done its job. He'd acted out some of the swordfights to show Darren how incredible and detailed they were in the book.

But there had been something lacking in the way Leo spoke about the story. It was just that to him—a story, and nothing more. There were no questions about this swordsman, about the king, or even about the nature of power and betrayal. It seemed to be that Leo let the tale out of his mind as soon as he put the book down, but the story of the Quim family still made Leo bring up questions to this day. The most recent was when he'd asked if it was legal what the king had done: sending away so many humans to Analyte land. It had started a discussion about why the laws do not apply to kings.

Andar had commented that it was the same way with parents. They set rules for their children that the parents themselves did not need to follow. At least he hadn't specified by saying "fathers," though his meaning was almost as blatant.

"Without looking, Andar," Darren asked, "do you know what Leo is holding?"

"Probably his book."

"Aww!" Leo complained.

Darren told Andar, "You can turn around for now."

Andar had a satisfied grin.

"Let me choose something else. This will be *much* harder."

"Wait a moment, Leo," Darren said to stop him as the boy ran back into the room. "Come out here again." He crouched in front of both his sons when they were side by side. "This is not a game to see how well Andar can guess what you're going to pick. You should choose something that you feel a connection toward. And Andar, don't put yourself in Leo's head to try to figure out what he would choose."

"Then how am I supposed to guess?"

"It's not supposed to be a guess. You should try to feel what it is."

"Am I allowed to touch—?"

"No, you will feel it with your mind."

Leo let out a small gasp.

Darren didn't know what to tell his youngest son that could stop his excitement. It was too late.

"That sounds like Artistry."

Andar froze. "It does."

Darren couldn't keep it hidden any longer, being as intent to test them as he was.

Andar's smile flattened as he looked at Darren. "Wait, this *really* is about Artistry?"

Darren sat with a sigh. This would have been much easier had they been born in his father's castle, as he had been, where walls protected them and trusted Ascendants could test them secretly. His children hurried over to him. They both spoke at once, Darren unable to decipher exactly what they were saying, something about them being Ascendants.

"You're too young to have any skill with Artistry," he told them truthfully. "These tests might tell us about your futures, though. Might," he repeated in hopes of squelching their excitement. There was no good news that could come out of this. They would either return to work disappointed, or they would return to work with a set expiration date to their safety.

"You mean we really might be mages?" Andar asked.

"You might have a connection with Artistry. But you shouldn't let that excite you. First, the both of you may not have this connection. Second, even if one or both of you do, it doesn't mean anything on its own. There are probably thousands of people alive right now with some power over Artistry, yet they've never realized it. They've never honed their skills. They've never been taught a single lesson."

"But that could be different with us," Leo said. "You could teach us what we need to know."

"I am no Ascendant."

"If that's true," Andar said with a quizzical expression, "then how do you know how to test us?"

"Because I've learned something about Artistry throughout my life, as I'm sure you will as well, whether or not you have a connection toward it."

"We are old enough to hear the truth about everything," Andar said. "Tell us who you were before we were born. I know you're not just a poor digger!"

"There is no shame in being poor in this world, Andar, and that's what I am. You've seen how hard we work. It is impossible for most people to ever have enough money for their own home. I am not someone else. I am your father, Darren Litxer. Your mother was Larena Litxer. I learned how to fight from my teen years, wrestling and sparring with my friends when we were old enough to buy training swords. I know what I know about Artistry from what I've heard and what I've read. I used to have more time for reading. You know who I am."

Andar's eyes narrowed. "I know you have reason to lie to us," he said. "Yes, I do know who you are. You are a father who cares." He did not speak it like a compliment. "But sometimes you care too much. You worry that we are not ready for things we are obviously ready for."

"Have I not taken you here to test your affinity toward Artistry?" Darren asked rhetorically.

"And it took so much to get that truth out. It always does with you. Aren't you tired of keeping things to yourself? I wouldn't be able to stand it!"

It was Leo's gaze that caught Darren's eyes. He stared at his brother as if he knew something that he was about to bring up, but even with an open mouth, Leo said nothing. Andar apparently had a secret that Leo knew about. But Darren didn't know what to do about it.

Boys were supposed to be easier to raise the older they got. This was something his wife would say after she had fallen ill, when times were at their worst. *It's not as true as you made it sound, Fari.* It was as if she'd known from the beginning of that sickness that it would take her life. Not only that, she knew that Darren would think he couldn't continue on alone. She had tried to prepare him as best she could.

He constantly felt that he had failed her.

"Andar," he told his eldest son calmly, "one day you will be a grown man, and then I can rely on you as heavily as I rely on myself. But until then you will keep in mind that you are a child and I am your father. I know what's best. Now I have taken you and Leo out of work, which may come back as punishment to the two of you. We have to make the most use of this time. We are going to finish what we started."

Andar took a breath. "All right."

"Go fetch something Leo, and don't let your brother see. Make sure it evokes some sort of feeling."

Leo went back and forth a dozen times, but Andar was never able to feel anything. Darren wished he could give the older boy more to go on, but Darren had no connection toward Artistry so he didn't know what it should feel like. All the talented mages he'd met said that they could feel the hidden connections in the world and some could even create their own.

He had been interested in Artistry, but he never had the time to sit down with a mage and question them like his sister did often. Yune had been obsessed with learning everything she could about it. She had tried to become an Ascendant, but she was just like Darren in that no connection could be made between her mind and Artistry.

Leo eventually had run out of items to bring back into the kitchen. He had even gone through both blankets, both pillows, and every article of clothing each of them owned.

Darren switched their roles afterward. Andar seemed to be sulking when he first brought in Leo's extra pair of pants. Clearly Andar had nearly no connection to this piece of clothing. But Darren didn't force him to start with something more likely to elicit a feeling. Andar needed time to get over his disappointment.

Darren was nearly certain that Leo wouldn't be able to feel a connection when his older brother hadn't. Andar was the one who had stolen the rift stone.

Perhaps I'm doing this all wrong. Darren thought he understood Artistry well, but the way that a mage used it was far different than the way it naturally made links. He didn't know what exactly he was testing for here: a natural link between one of his boys and an object, or if one of his boys had an affinity toward Artistry itself. But he did know enough to tell that if one of them felt what it was that the other held out of sight, it would mean that great powers could be in the boy's future. But these were powers that, without proper training, would do nothing but endanger their lives.

Leo was not able to feel anything that Andar brought out. It soon became clear that he was just guessing, eager to get one right, for he took it harder every time he was wrong.

It was a shock to see his youngest act this way. Leo had endured such disrespect at the farm and now at the Bookbinding Guild. Yet it was this that made him stomp his feet and slam his fist on the table as he got another wrong. Andar no longer sulked, wearing a worried expression.

Darren had wanted this result: for them to go through every item they could without getting it right, but he had failed to predict just how hard the two of them would take it. When Andar came back and announced that everything had been used, Leo demanded that he keep going.

"Use the same things again," Leo said. "I know I'll be able to feel something."

"Not without me going again." Andar walked past Leo and turned around. "It's my turn."

Darren didn't have the heart to stop them, so he let each of them go through every item in their room once again. He empathized with their frustration too much to be relieved at their failures.

Many people felt something from rift stones. Even Darren had felt a spark of something here and there from the various stones that had come across his path. Erisena had gone too far to assume so much out of the boys just because Andar had taken a gem from her. Darren would be pleased to tell her honestly that there was nothing about his boys that could benefit her little rebellion. They were more likely to get her and themselves killed.

"Maybe we're just not old enough yet," Andar said after many more failed attempts. "We can still learn."

Leo perked. "That's true. Most people don't learn until they are at least fourteen."

"The two of you should head back to work," Darren said. They wouldn't move, so he added, "We can try another test later if I think of a different one."

"It's to see if we can feel connections, right?" Leo asked.

Darren nodded. "Yes, but there is more to it than that."

"The stronger the connection to the object, the better the chance we should feel something, right?"

"Yes."

"What if it's a bad connection?"

"What do you mean?" Darren asked, knowing Leo couldn't be referring to a weak connection, which was the only meaning he heard.

"If it's a negative connection," Andar specified for his brother. "Like if something elicits hatred or...some other bad feeling. That's what you mean, right, Leo?"

"Yes, a negative connection."

"If the connection is strong," Darren said, "then it shouldn't matter whether it's negative or positive."

Leo stared into the bedroom for a while. "If I bring something out here, can you turn around as well, Father?"

"You don't want me to see?"

Leo shook his head.

All children have secrets, Darren reminded himself. But this had to be a secret that both brothers knew about, so it was only a secret from him. He had better search their room later.

"I will turn around as well."

He turned around and faced Andar's back. Leo's tone made it sound as if he was onto something. *It isn't just that*, Darren realized. There was a strong tension that filled the air of their small kitchen. Some people believed that thoughts and emotions, when they were strong enough, could travel through the air the same way Artistry did. It was a theory Darren had found himself believing the more intuitive his boys became.

Leo took a lot of time before returning. "All right," he said. "Do you feel what I have, Andar?" His tone was jovial, perhaps trying to hide whatever dark emotion had gone along with removing this secret from its hiding place.

"Gods..." Andar whispered to himself. "I feel it. I know what you have."

Leo gasped. "I feel something also, like..."

"Like there's something here," Andar said.

"Where?" Darren asked.

"In this room," Andar answered. "It's like a smell that I can sense...wait...I don't feel it anymore."

"Me neither!" Leo complained.

"Go put that back, Leo," Andar ordered.

"All right."

"Then bring it out again!" Andar called to him.

Leo came back. Both boys were silent for a while.

"I don't feel it anymore," Andar said.

"Same," Leo said.

"Put it away again," Andar told him, then asked Darren, "What does this mean?"

"I don't think it means anything."

"What!" Leo yelled from the bedroom. He hurried back into the kitchen. "But we felt something."

"I'm sure you did, but that might not have been Artistry. If there is a link, you should always be able to feel it." He opened the shutters of the nearby window. "Look, it's late afternoon. The two of you must return quickly. I will think of more tests we can do when there's time." They didn't move. "Come on, we don't want Gartel or Rhenol to become more angry than they already are."

Darren was thankful when they left the house without argument.

"Hurry off," he told them.

"Wait, I forgot something," Andar said and ran into the house before Darren could object.

He went into the bedroom and was there for longer than it would take to grab a forgotten item. Eventually he came out with his hands in his pockets, no doubt hiding whatever "secret" Leo had brought out for the final test. Darren didn't force Andar to show it. He might as well let his boys have their secret. He had a secret of his own.

He shuddered soon after saying goodbye to them. He hoped to be wrong about this. He hoped he didn't understand Artistry well enough to conclude what he thought he might've just concluded. But somewhere deep within him he knew the truth. That final test was more than enough to prove it.

They didn't just have a connection toward Artistry. For them to have *both* felt something that then went away quickly meant it wasn't a connection between Leo and the object. Nor was it a connection between Andar and the object. Those links should be static. There were links made between people sometimes. These links were so rare and could be so powerful that they had their own name.

Most links were light and easy to break. These were ethereal links. But others were strong and embedded so deeply through Artistry that they could not be broken. These were stalwart links, and when such a link presented itself between two brothers, only death could break it.

There were only theories that suggested what made these links, but the most agreed-upon was that it occurred when two objects—or people, in this case— were remarkably similar for years and then something very drastic changed between them. It was as if the link itself was trying to hold together something that would've inevitably broken, as if Artistry was dedicated to similarity, which was nearly a fact in itself.

There was no way Erisena could have picked up on a stalwart link from simply following the boys one day. All she probably thought was that they would be Ascendants when they were older—she would use their power.

Darren would be damned before he let anyone figure out the truth, for people like Erisena might kill to use a stalwart link.

He would tell his boys, though. They deserved to know. But when? What should he do first?

Never had he needed his sister as much as he did now. Darren was completely lost without some guidance.

CHAPTER TWENTY

Darren felt ill. He sat for a moment, alone in his kitchen, and went through his options. It wasn't long before he realized that there was only one worth taking. He had to make coin and get his sons out of Jatn. Because Erisena was in this city, of all places, it was likely that she would want something to do with the recently discovered Tisary. It would be a source of conflict soon enough. But it might also be the only source of income for Darren.

As much as he wanted to trust that Erisena wouldn't endanger his boys if he was mad enough to join her, it would be foolish to rely on her. He had failed to find other work for Andar, not that his eldest would make more coin than Darren would, no matter the job. And someone had to work on the farm so that they wouldn't be thrown out of their house.

One option, Darren told himself again as he stood. He would sleep the rest of the day if he let himself lay on his bed for just a moment, as his body was telling him to do, but he had to get to the cavern. The pay would be better now if work was available. He just had to ignore his pride, for the Diggers' Guild had broken its promise about the amount to be paid to him and the other diggers.

More importantly, Darren had to ignore the danger he would bring upon himself by being there. There was no other place in the city more likely for strife now that a Tisary had been discovered.

He made his way to the edge of the city limits. There were no walls around Jatn, and it didn't seem as if any kind of barrier was in construction around the cavern. The only thing that protected it was a gang of men with swords and bows. They appeared bored. Most sat, some playing cards, others dueling.

Hired swordsmen. It was the lack of armor that gave them away. Neither they nor their employer expected anyone to fight them. They were there to prevent theft and tampering.

Darren found his old overseer sitting in a chair just within the entrance of the cavern, no doubt using it for shade. Darren tried to put on a friendly face as he approached, though a disarming smile wasn't his strong suit. Clancey stood rather abruptly.

"Why are you here?" He looked around for the closest mercenary. Two of them stared down from above. Clancey loosened up a bit when he noticed them.

"I couldn't find better work," Darren admitted. "I'd like to dig."

"I already have enough diggers."

"I'm sure none are as good as I am." He stepped closer. "Besides, you owe me. Need I remind you that I made you avoid a collapse that could've killed you and everyone else. Not to mention that the Tisary would've been damaged, if not destroyed."

Clancey looked bored and not much else. But it was an act, Darren knew.

"I don't think your masters would like to find out the truth," Darren commented.

"I thought you and I understood each other."

"We do. You understand I need work, and I understand that you're going to provide that for me even if you'll have to explain another worker to your masters."

"Stop calling them that. You speak as if I'm a slave, but if anyone is—"

"Then I am," Darren finished the statement. "I see we do understand each other. We are all slaves of someone else. Where's my gear?"

Clancey scratched his cheek. "You will be paid the same that you were before the Tisary discovery."

"I will be paid two more coppers per day. One silver and five coppers."

"That's how much the *Tisary* diggers make," the overseer complained with a shake of his head.

"Good, because that's what I will be." Darren walked past him. "I'll have a look around now to see where I'll be needed most."

"No, stop." Clancey waved petulantly for Darren to return. Darren turned around but did not move toward him, so Clancey took a brave step closer. "I want you out of here, and don't come back."

Darren closed the last distance between them. "You understand that I have nothing else but this work. You understand what I'll do if you take that away from me."

Clancey looked for the mercenaries again, but the only two who could be seen from here had moved.

"I could scream for them," Clancey warned. "Best that you listen to me."

"Did you know that I am very good at fighting?"

Clancey leaned back slightly.

"It's been quite a while," Darren said, "but a good fight might be just what I need if there's no more work for me in the city. We're already on the edge of Jatn. I bet I could escape after it was done. You know mercenaries don't like to run. Most don't even want to fight."

Darren had to mean his words, otherwise they would be worthless. He *would* like a good fight. He silently bet himself he could kill enough of them to make the others run. He probably wouldn't even suffer a single wound.

It was only then that he realized how hopeless he would be if this didn't work. He was risking his life for coin, but it was because this was all that was left. How did this happen?

Clancey stared at him, but Darren saw right through the smaller man. He was an obstacle in that moment, nothing more. Darren already thought of five different maneuvers that would make Clancey submit quickly.

"What in KRenn's mind happened to you?" Clancey tried to step back, but Darren reached out quickly to grab his shoulder.

"Am I to start work today or not?"

Clancey cursed. "Fine. Your digging gear will be brought to you soon enough. It's already evening. You'll only get three coppers today." He squirmed out of Darren's grasp.

"That's fair."

Darren had made an enemy out of someone who had merely disliked him before, but at least he had work again.

The cavern looked just as he'd remembered, at least the part he could see in the light. The ceiling was covered in the usual icicle-shaped material. No one knew what to call whatever it was made out of, clearly not rock or dirt, but hard enough to remain where it hung if no one disturbed it. The whole cavern was like that, completely still except for the drops of water that ran down the hanging points from the ceiling. But many walls had been grazed by men over the years. They had lost their light color, now a faded brown as if the rest of the cavern was alive except for these patches.

Darren passed by workers he didn't recognize, each with their own lamp. It seemed that a few of them were still digging into the natural tunnels to search for another rift. Most other diggers were around the Tisary. They had made good progress since Darren had last been here, having formed a tunnel with rounded curves. A group of people stood in the middle of the Tisary. They didn't appear to be diggers, for none had the right tools.

Darren's heart sputtered as he recognized Lane Writhe standing on the outskirts of the group as if either uninterested or uninvited to the conversation. She wore a mage robe, a dark gray color with the hood hanging down her back. She looked younger than he remembered as she noticed Darren and waved at him. The Tisary was well lit, showing him her expression with clarity, yet the expression did nothing to tell him her thoughts.

She had the kind of face that seemed as if it was easy for her to show annoyance. Perhaps it was the natural downward tilt of her light brown eyebrows, or it might've been the drastic curve of her chin above her thin neck. He noticed a light set of freckles underneath her eyes that trailed down to her cheeks. The angular shape of her eyes was familiar from the last time he had seen her. Now with light he could indeed tell they were dark, a contrast to her light hair.

"Darren?" asked a familiar voice. Franklin laughed when Darren turned to him. "You didn't even see me with Lane here, did you?" He laughed again, then quieted his voice. "I don't think I would've seen you, either, had I been you seeing her." He seemed to confuse himself by his own words. "Had I been...you? I mean..." Franklin paused. "Ah, never mind. It's good to see you!"

Darren had told Franklin not to come back here, for it would be dangerous, and yet here both of them were. It would've embarrassed Darren, but this was Franklin. A simple explanation was all it took for Darren's friend to understand him.

"It's good to see you as well," Darren said and shook the man's hand. "I couldn't find any other work."

"Same, same. But you know others have come to beg Clancey for their work back. He told them all the same thing. We've got enough diggers. Yet, I see you convinced him otherwise." Franklin chuckled. "Back to your old ways. I tried to be mad for a while about being cheated, I did. But they paid us too many gold coins for me to hold a grudge."

"Yeah," Darren agreed.

"It still makes them bastards, though."

"It certainly does."

One day I'd like to give all of them a reason to stop being bastards. It was probably what Erisena planned, but she had not faced opposition like a king before. By the time she had half as many men as would be necessary, her rebellion would be squashed.

"Go say hello to the pretty woman," Franklin teased. "She's not here that often, so you might as well take advantage. Besides, she keeps looking over."

Darren glanced her way and met her gaze again. She left the group of men who appeared interested in something that one of them was holding. Darren met her halfway.

"You shouldn't be here, Darren," she told him. "It's going to be dangerous eventually."

I am danger.

Where had that voice come from? It sounded like his old self.

"I can protect myself."

She looked him up and down. "I suppose you can."

"What about you? Are you immune to danger?"

"I know when to run."

"That shouldn't be too hard to figure out even for me," Darren said. "It'll be when the king's troops arrive."

She laughed. "Yes, exactly. So you have read up on what happened at the last Tisary."

"I have."

"And you still decided to come back?"

"It's the only place I could find work."

She squinted at him.

"Really," he told her. "I've been around the city looking for better pay."

"Oh, you did not say better pay. You said work."

If anyone could help him figure out what to do about his sons' stalwart link, it was Lane. He didn't see how he could even bring it up, though, let alone ask her to advise him. He wasn't supposed to know about this link, and there was no way she could break it that Darren knew of.

"What are you doing here these days? Hasn't the bond of the Tisary to the cavern already been broken?" he asked, though he already knew the answer.

"This air is heavy with Artistry, and everyone who comes here needs something from it. It's my job to assist them."

"You must be quite the mage to assist them while talking with me."

"Eh, one of them is an Artistry gemcrafter. He doesn't need any help from me."

"And the five other men?"

"Various highbrows of different guilds who all have something invested in the work of this gemcrafter. How are your sons?"

He was shocked. "How did you know I have sons?"

"I inquired about you." She said it so plainly, as if it meant nothing. "I'm sorry about your wife." She lowered her head.

"Thank you. And my sons are fine, though I wish I could find better work for my thirteen-year-old. He's far too talented to be stuck at the farm."

"Andar, right?"

Now Darren was even more shocked.

"Who told you his name?" he asked.

The cunning look she gave would've frightened him if anything could penetrate the overwhelming attraction he had been trying to suppress.

"Erisena..." was all she muttered, and the attraction was gone.

He stepped back from her and frantically looked around. Franklin was busy working, while the group of men still spoke amongst themselves.

Lane put her hand on his arm. "I didn't mean to startle you."

"Is she an Ascendant like you?" Darren asked.

"No, she's a summoner."

That confirmed his first thought about her. "You really shouldn't be here," Lane told him. "Erisena will give you everything you need in exchange for your support. She'll provide a house for your family. You won't have to dig. Andar won't have to farm. Leo can remain at the Bookbinding Guild for now if he wants. He's still young."

"All of this will be in exchange for what?"

"You act well, *Darren*. I would not have known who you were if Erisena hadn't told me, but I could tell there was something about you that was different. I was not surprised when I found out the truth. I can see you are not surprised, either. You knew there could be something like this about me when we met. There are many of us who are ready to fight for change. You did before, why not again?"

"Because I have children now."

"Even more reason to give them a better future." She gripped his arm tighter.

"I can't give them anything if I'm dead. You are too young to know the kind of power the king holds, and so is Erisena. You don't see any of it here in this wretched city, but I assure you that you'll regret everything the moment you spot his army."

"His army will come no matter what. I will be used by one side or another *no matter what*. So I might as well pick my own side."

"That's fine. I'm not telling you what you should do."

She let out a sigh and removed her hand.

"Darren!" Franklin called.

Darren turned to see his friend pointing at a boy with a shovel in one hand and a pickax in the other. The boy stood far outside the tunnel leading to the Tisary and made no motion to enter even as Darren walked toward him. There was no doubt that this delivery boy was told he'd lose a hand if he were to even step inside the Tisary.

The notion infuriated Darren. The hands of the poor men of this city already belonged to the powerful. It just was up to the highbrows to decide when they wanted to take them.

CHAPTER TWENTY-ONE

Andar was slow getting back to the farm. He couldn't believe that he still had to finish his work after the day he'd had, but his father was right. The overseer would already be angry with him for leaving. He had better not make it worse.

There had been something almost magical developing between him and Leo recently. Andar had felt fleeting sensations of some sort of connection before today, but none had been like what he'd just felt. He knew without a doubt exactly what Leo held in his hands during the final test. It had been the coins Andar had thought he'd hidden well enough. His brother was not one to snoop, so he wouldn't normally look under Andar's mattress. Why had he thought to look there now? Because something was changing. It was both scary and intriguing.

A link, Andar said to himself. Links were all he knew about Artistry. He didn't know what this link meant, how it had formed, or what he could do with it. But something was there to grasp with his mind. His father had made it seem as if it was nothing, but Father was either wrong or lying again.

Andar tried on the way back to the farm to feel for this link between him and his brother, but it didn't take long to realize that it was impossible. He had no control over it. It was only up to the link itself when it wanted to show up again. At least for now. Who knew how things would change when Andar became stronger.

How would he do that? *Leo must be thinking the same thoughts as he runs back to the Bookbinding Guild.*

Everything would be different now, wouldn't it? Would their father finally start telling the truth about everything? Andar had his doubts, but a new hope had emerged.

"Ugh," Andar muttered as he returned to the farm and met eyes with the overseer. Rhenol didn't seem to be busy with anything as he stood scowling in the middle of a field. *Was he waiting for me?* Andar wouldn't put it past him. There had been many times when Rhenol had taken time out of his day for no other reason than to make Andar's life more miserable. Their relationship had soured years ago, when Andar ripped his pants and ran home crying. He was just a child, mercilessly teased by the overseer. Andar's father had gone to the farm to speak with Rhenol. New pants were delivered shortly after, but they weren't worth the trouble Andar had endured since.

And now father has gone and demanded that I be excused from work. Andar had thought that things couldn't be worse with Rhenol, but the fury on the overseer's face made Andar realize he was wrong.

"I'm sorry," Andar said in hopes of repairing the damage. "My father needed me."

"I don't care. From sunup to sundown, you are to stay on my farm and work. I've warned you that you would be punished if you broke any more of my rules. You will not be paid for today."

"I was only gone a few hours!"

"And you will not be paid for tomorrow, either."

"What? Why not?"

"Say something else and you won't be paid for the day after as well!" Rhenol leaned over Andar with a face that burned red.

The overseer couldn't be serious. Two days of no pay, and three if Andar spoke one more word? Why was there never justice for abusive men like Rhenol?

Andar gritted his teeth. He felt words making their way up his throat. He tried to stop them, but he knew he wouldn't be able to. His anger was too strong.

"My father must've really embarrassed you to treat me so unfairly."

"Three days of no pay!" Rhenol seemed to take great joy in this as he put on a devilish grin. But his mouth straightened as his look of fury returned. "*You* should be embarrassed. How long will it take you to learn to *listen*?"

Spit sprayed out from the overseer's mouth, a drop of it striking Andar just under his eye. He wiped it off on his sleeve. He couldn't speak or move, or he might tackle this old and ugly man.

"What now?" Rhenol asked. When Andar didn't reply, he prodded, "Well? Nothing?"

Andar still didn't speak.

"Then get back to work. My wife and I just finished a feast. I had the servants leave all the dishes for you to wash and dry. Make sure you don't drop or even chip one thing, or your hand is mine."

Andar stomped off. He tried to calm himself on the way to the mansion, but he was only angrier by the time he made it there. He couldn't stop muttering insults about Rhenol, lording his wealth and his fat wife over all his starving workers.

There was a moment of panic as he realized that his emotions were getting the better of him. The overseer would enjoy taking his hand. Andar couldn't let that happen.

But as he started washing these lavish plates, the set of them worth more than Andar could earn in a month, his thoughts took him on a rampage. He should be the one taking Rhenol's hand—a just punishment for all the hardship he'd caused so many people. The man was wealthy. He could easily pay his workers more, but the Farmer's Guild only employed overseers as greedy as Rhenol. It was the only way to keep paying the workers a measly silver a day. If one overseer, just one of them, was kind enough to offer more to his workers, then the rest would have to as well. Otherwise all farmers would work at the only place that paid them a fair wage.

How could there be so much greed among the people who already had everything? Andar would change that one day. He just wished he knew how so he could start working toward it today.

He'd seen more than a few people with a hand missing. One was a servant here who usually worked within the overseer's mansion. She was an older woman who probably had lost her hand many years ago. It was the only way to explain her comfort using her left and how she showed no emotion as she worked. It could've been Rhenol himself who had cut it off after she'd broken something valuable.

The other memorable sight was a beggar Andar had come across in the street. He was just a boy, not much older than Andar, his right arm ending in a stump. It was the only time Andar had given coin to a beggar. It wasn't as if he had any to spare that day. It was just that he couldn't bring himself to walk by without doing something to help the grief-stricken boy who stared at his bowl containing a few measly coins in a way that Andar could not shake from his memory. Unaware of his surroundings, the boy looked as if he was reliving the severing of his hand over and over. Andar would behave the same way if his hand was taken.

There were too many plates, cups, forks, and knives in Rhenol's kitchen to be used by only two people. Some had remnants of food smeared across them in a purposeful way, like one plate which had a streak down its center as if someone had crushed and wiped a berry just to dirty another thing for Andar to wash.

There was one gold plate, however, that Andar was deathly afraid of touching. It already seemed mostly clean. He would save that for the end.

He kept eyeing the gold vase in the corner of the dining room. It sat high upon a tall cabinet. The cabinet itself was finely crafted, dark oak with a glass case that opened on metal hinges. A plethora of silver plates and bowls were neatly positioned inside among forks and spoons. They seemed to be too fancy for use, a single fork worth more than all the wooden kitchenware at Andar's house.

Although he was perturbed by this, the gold vase was what really enraged him. What was the point of it? All Andar could think of was that it was designed for hand-taking. Should a servant drop it while cleaning, Rhenol would take a hand. Should someone be so foolish as to steal it, Rhenol would get a hand.

Then why was Andar so tempted to steal it? What was it about gold that made him forget everything he cared about? He was stupid once before, and it had cost him years of suffering. He'd had a good job at the Bookbinding Guild. He'd known Gartel would notice that the golden ink had gone missing, but Andar had told himself that without proof Gartel couldn't do anything.

Proof was a lost concept to these types of men. Andar knew this now.

If Rhenol wanted, he could bury the golden vase during the night when no one would see him do it. The next day he could claim that Andar had taken it. "He was the only one in my mansion while I wasn't home!" Rhenol would tell the guards. "It has to be him."

The guards would search Andar's home. When they didn't find it or any coins, they would search his pockets. They would find all that he'd made from stealing from the rich. They would say he had sold the vase. Rhenol would take his hand. Andar had to find a better hiding place for his coins.

He might just break something valuable around here out of anger. Taking away pay for three days—it wasn't just done for glee. *It was to provoke me.*

Andar didn't know which hand the overseer would be allowed to take, right or left. Rhenol was never specific with his threats.

Could this be what Rhenol had planned by sending Andar here, alone, to wash dishes? Fear washed over him. He stopped scrubbing and walked to the front door for a look outside. No one was around. He went to every window on the ground floor. There were workers in the fields, but no one was nearby.

I've underestimated the old man.

It was getting late. Andar had to finish his work and leave this place, but what would happen afterward if he was right that Rhenol could bury the golden vase and blame Andar?

He needed a witness, someone he could trust.

It didn't take long before he realized that there was no one. So he settled for someone else—someone who would tell the truth even if she didn't necessarily trust Andar.

After the better part of an hour, he found the little reeve and convinced her to come back to the mansion.

Chay had not bothered Andar much since he'd tricked her into leaving him alone. He'd first thought that his arduous work at the farm would be a little easier without Chay spying on him, but then he'd realized that he actually missed her company now with Leo gone.

It wasn't so much her company, actually, that he missed. It was just company in general.

"What did you need to show me?" she asked after he brought her inside. She walked cautiously as she followed him through the entrance room and toward the kitchen in the back.

"Do you see the gold vase?" He pointed high.

She leaned her head almost all the way back. Her mouth opened as she saw it. "*Ohhh,*" she whispered.

So even children marveled at gold.

"Rhenol is going to claim that I stole it or maybe something else, but I'm not going to take anything. I never would steal from my master." *Never again*, a voice specified in his mind.

"Why is Rhenol going to say you stole something?"

"Because he hates me." Andar lifted his hand. "He wants this, but I'm not going to let him get it. Stay with me until I finish cleaning the dishes in the kitchen. It will only take another moment. Then we can leave together. You can watch me walk to the fence of the farm and let myself out."

"I'm supposed to be watching other workers."

"Chay, he's trying to take my hand! You will have to watch him cut it off. Now, don't you think it's better that you stay here with me for a *little* while longer so that doesn't have to happen?"

She nodded quickly.

Andar got back to finishing his task.

Chay took hold of a stool as she waited. She played with it, shifting its weight onto one leg at a time until Andar told her to stop. Then she started doing the same with a chair until Andar scolded her again.

She really frightened him when she grabbed the end of the table and started to hang by it, holding up her small legs. He screamed, "What are you doing!"

She let go and landed on her feet. "Are you almost done?"

"Stand still so I don't have to worry about you, then I will finish faster." Perhaps the little reeve was not a child from a poor family as Andar had first thought. She likely came from money, or else she would show more fear about damaging furniture.

"How did you start your work here?" he asked.

"What?"

"Does someone in your family know the overseer?"

"My father. They are cousins."

Andar stopped to think. Would she still tell the truth?

But he didn't have another option. He figured that any of the other workers could be convinced by Rhenol to lie. This child's need to tell the truth might make her the only one unable to be swayed.

And if Andar was wrong, there was at least a good chance that she was a terrible liar. Perhaps her false testimony would not be enough.

Soon there was only the gold plate left. Andar looked at it closely before touching it. Was it solid gold? He wiped his finger across the top. It did not feel like metal. Could it be ceramic or even glass? That would explain the gold color. He wished he knew more about how things like this were made...or how *anything* was made. He had read too few books, most about Artistry and swordsmen. He should've read more.

What was he thinking? He'd had no access to books that would answer his questions about what this plate was made from. It might've been glass coated in gold, or perhaps it was just painted. He doubted it was solid gold, but he couldn't know without having been an apprentice of a metalworker.

"What are you doing?" asked the reeve.

Unable to answer, Andar decided it was time to pick up the plate. He still had a feeling that there was more to it than he could see, some sort of trap, but he couldn't just leave it dirty.

He tested it very carefully, lifting it with a pinch of his thumb and forefinger. Something felt strange about its weight. It wasn't just that it was heavier than it should've been. He let one side of it rest on the table as he picked up the other side a little higher. It felt as if it were connected to the table by spider webs, but there was nothing to be seen below or around the plate.

Andar started to let it down, but something was definitely off. The plate didn't want to fall, even when Andar moved his hand completely away from it.

This was not an ordinary plate. The gold disk returned to its resting position in an eerily slow manner, as if it were underwater.

Skyfire and ash! Is this Artistry?

Whenever something happened he couldn't explain, his first thought was it had to be Artistry. Later he would figure out the real solution. He would for this as well.

No, this was different. He could feel it in the same way he knew something had happened between him and Leo.

He looked over to see what Chay made of this, but she was busy staring at the gold vase on the cabinet high above her. She looked over her shoulder at Andar.

"It moved," she said as she pointed back to the vase.

Andar felt a chill as he realized what this meant.

"How did it move?" Andar asked.

"Like this." She tilted her hand in the same way Andar had tilted the plate. "It almost fell," she added.

His heart missed a beat. How close had he come just now to losing his hand?

"It's a link," he informed Chay.

"What's a link?"

He took a moment to think of the simplest way he could explain it.

"When someone moves this plate, the gold vase will move in the same way. They are connected through Artistry."

She gasped. "Because it's gold?"

"No, gold has no magic to it. Rhenol must've paid an Ascendant to make a link for him. He didn't create this situation to blame me for stealing something valuable. He did it to blame me for breaking something—that vase."

Now Andar was even more glad that he had brought Chay here, but he started to have his doubts as she looked back and forth with confusion between him and the vase.

He explained, "When I pick up this plate, the vase will fall over and break against the floor. It must be painted glass and not solid gold, or it probably wouldn't even crack, same as this plate. They have to be the same material for the link to be created." At least that was what Andar figured. He didn't know much about the link itself. Depending on the Ascendant, the link was either strong or weak. It would last either days or seconds. And it was more likely to break the more strain it took.

But he couldn't be certain about any of this. All of this information he had gathered from reading tales that were mostly fantasy.

He did know one thing. He was not going to touch that plate, which he told to Chay.

"So how will you clean it?" she asked.

"I won't."

Rhenol appeared in the doorway. Andar was surprised he hadn't heard the old man come into the mansion. The wood floors should've given away his footsteps. *Ah, he took off his boots,* Andar realized. *He was hiding and listening.*

"I said you will clean every plate, so you will."

Andar started to snicker. "Of course I'm not going to! Didn't you just hear what I said? You paid for a link." He stifled a laugh. "How much did the Ascendant charge you to link a dirty plate to that vase?" Andar grinned as he imagined a mage's surprise at being summoned to this farm for such an expensive and ridiculous task.

But his amusement came to a sudden end when Rhenol spoke. "I'm telling you to clean that last plate. Are you disobeying this order?"

Andar grumbled a curse. It didn't matter that he had figured out the trap. He was still trapped. The feeling was all too familiar—getting out of one problem just to find himself in another. His whole life followed this pattern.

He was sick of being utterly incapable of doing anything but following orders.

"Yes, I'm disobeying this order, because you're ordering me to destroy your vase!"

The old man turned his attention to the pale little reeve staring up at her relative. "What are you doing here?" Rhenol demanded.

It was no wonder that their relation had come as a surprise to Andar. Not once had he seen Rhenol speak to her in a way that was different from the way he spoke to his other *slaves*—as if they were one wrong move away from punishment.

She ran out of the room without a glance back.

Andar usually hated when Rhenol came to speak with him while other workers were around. The overseer always tried to make some show of his power. But now they were completely alone, no witnesses, and never had Andar felt as vulnerable.

"This is the last time I'm going to tell you," Rhenol said. "Clean that plate."

Andar looked at it again, wondering if there was some way he could scrub it clean without knocking over the vase. If his understanding of links was correct, then any pressure applied to the plate would also be applied to the vase. Even if he wiped the plate while it rested on the table, the pressure could cause the vase to fall over.

Andar knew this would be a stupid question, but he couldn't think of anything else to say.

"What happens if I don't?"

The old man's thin lips turned inward as he stepped toward Andar. "You have already disobeyed me so many times. I have tried to correct your behavior. I have tried and tried. If you cannot follow a simple order, then you are no longer to work here or on any farm in Jatn. You do know what that means?"

"You can't take away our house. Someone else in my family will work on a farm if I'm unable to."

"No, Andar. You are wrong. When I tell the guild how you have *continuously* disobeyed me despite my warnings, they will listen to my recommendation that no Litxer be allowed to farm anymore."

Did Rhenol really have the power to do this?

It didn't matter—Andar would not break that vase. Anything was better than losing his hand.

He wanted to ask Rhenol why he hated him so much. Why did he have to make everything this difficult? But Andar knew the answer already. The overseer didn't see the situation the same way that Andar did. *Andar* was the one making everything difficult. It was Andar's father who embarrassed Rhenol, who demanded things of him, and it was Andar who constantly talked back.

But was that really enough justification to pay good coin to create a trap just to take his hand? Andar couldn't contain his rage. He eyed one of the meat knives he had finished cleaning earlier. How satisfying it would be to stick the blade deep into Rhenol's gut.

He shook the thought from his mind before it became too tempting.

"What are you going to tell them after I pick up the plate and the vase falls and breaks?" Andar asked. "Will you say I knocked it over after being told to clean it?"

"It fell while you were trying to steal it, and I caught you in the act."

They would certainly take his hand for that. One thing didn't make sense, though. If that was true, why couldn't Rhenol have knocked the vase over earlier and claimed that Andar had tried to steal it?

Because he hasn't let me into his mansion until today—when I was most upset after being told I had to work without pay. He must've paid the Ascendant after Father took me home. He set this whole thing up just to create a realistic story.

That meant Andar really didn't need to be the one who broke the vase. As long as it broke, and no one else was here to see the truth, then Rhenol could say whatever he wanted. It's why Rhenol didn't fear revealing the plan. There was no way to stop it. Workers would be questioned about whether they heard anything break while Andar was inside the mansion, and they would confirm he was there. The overseer could claim he was upstairs, and nowhere near the vase, when Andar tried to steal it.

"I'm glad you changed your mind and decided to clean the plate," Rhenol announced.

The overseer went for the plate. Andar put himself in front of the larger man.

"This is madness! Skyfire and ash." Andar refrained from doing anything that might leave a bruise or a cut, grabbing his overseer.

The old man's strength surprised Andar when he threw Andar out of the way. Rhenol wasn't really as old as Andar had thought him to be. He was probably only fifty, his ugliness and severity making him appear decades older.

Andar ran toward the cabinet with the gold vase atop it. He positioned himself underneath.

"You should've listened to me!" Rhenol called out, then grabbed the gold plate.

The vase tipped over the opposite way as Andar had expected, rolling along the cabinet top away from him. He ran as it fell.

Something happened that made him gawk. The vase came to a nearly complete stop in the air, although it touched nothing. It then fell with normal speed. Andar caught it with both hands.

He thought it was over until he saw the gold plate launch itself out of Rhenol's loose grip. Andar didn't understand it, though he knew it had something to do with its link to the vase. He tucked the vase under his arm as he dove. He grabbed the falling plate out of the air and brought it in to his chest to ensure it would not strike the hardwood floor.

Rhenol seethed as he stepped toward Andar. He would take one or both of the gold-painted glass items and break them right there. Andar didn't know how he got to his feet so quickly without the use of his hands, but he was up and running for the door with Rhenol right behind him.

"Thief! Thief!" Rhenol yelled. "Andar is stealing!"

"I am not!" he yelled back for anyone who might be within earshot. He was a lot quicker than the overseer, able to make it to the door and set down both expensive items before letting himself out.

Andar was glad to see a small group of farmers had stopped their work and started to come toward the mansion. Andar lifted his arms. He yelled as he made his way toward them.

"I have nothing. He is trying to pin a break or a theft on me, but nothing is missing or broken in his mansion. Listen now, for he might try to break something and claim I did it!"

The gaze of the onlookers shifted to the mansion. Through the open door, Andar could see Rhenol picking up the two devices of his trap with a furious look upon his face.

"He tried to steal these things, but I caught him!" the overseer claimed.

"Lies! You made me enter your mansion to clean your dishes, then you tried to trap me."

"You're a liar and a thief!"

Andar turned to his fellow farmworkers. There were only three of them in front of him, though small groups were coming closer to listen. These impoverished men and women were his only hope. If Andar didn't have their trust, Rhenol could claim anything he wanted.

"All of you have seen that he hates me," Andar argued. "He's trying to set me up so he can take my hand. You must believe I'm telling the truth. I wouldn't be so foolish to steal something as large and valuable as a golden plate or vase. I would never get it off the farm. He chose the most valuable thing he could to ensure my hand would be chopped off. He's vile."

Andar felt that his last words were worth repeating.

"Vile!" he yelled to the overseer. "A disgusting man with no morals."

"Get off my farm, thief!" screamed Rhenol as he made his way over with his golden vase still in hand.

"Gladly."

"If you or anyone from your family tries to come here again, I *will* have your hand, thief. *Thief!*"

Andar hated that word. Every time Rhenol said it, Andar felt insects crawling around inside him.

"And don't try to work on any other farm. The guild will find out about this!"

Andar ran. He would've stopped and hurled every insult he could think of at the hateful man, but he was just hoping to get far enough away before...

"And don't think that you can live in a guild house any longer, thief! You and your family are gone. No home. None!"

Andar turned around. He tried to think of something to say, but tears came to his eyes before he could think of anything. Embarrassed, he turned and ran to get out of there as fast as he could.

CHAPTER TWENTY-TWO

Leo returned to the Bookbinding Guild. There was no guard stationed there anymore. Leo supposed Gartel was no longer afraid of Father or just didn't want to pay the guard anymore. The answer didn't matter to Leo. He'd had a blissful reprieve from work, wondering what the future might hold for him and his brother now that they had discovered something about Artistry. He didn't care what his father had said afterward. Leo had definitively felt something.

But now the reprieve from work was over. The bookbinding guild master stopped his conversation with a worker when he saw Leo return. Leo spotted Rygen. She showed him a nervous look as if Gartel had spoken about him while he was away. The guild master motioned for Leo to follow him and took Leo to an empty corner.

"What did your father want?" Gartel asked in a low enough voice that no one could overhear.

There was no answer Leo could give that would forgive his absence. He could tell this man that his father had helped him and his brother discover that they were Ascendants, that they would one day change the world. Even if it was true, Gartel would just scold Leo for missing work.

"I think it was a test of some kind. He didn't tell us."

"A test for what?"

Leo thought of a plethora of lies he could choose from, none of them good. He had prepared an apology, not an excuse. So he gave it.

"I'm sorry, Guild Master. It was very important to my father to take me and my brother away from work at this time, but he didn't explain why. He had us do a number of tasks that didn't make sense to us. I could guess what they might be, but I wouldn't want to waste your time. I was hoping to finish all the work that I could with the hours left in the day."

Gartel straightened his back, no longer leaning over Leo. "There's no way a brute like your father could have prepared a speech like that for you. You came up with that, didn't you?"

Leo took offense on his father's behalf, but he didn't show it. "Yes, but it's not just a speech. It's true."

Gartel folded his arms and scowled at Leo. "Do you agree with what your father did?" He paused, but Leo wasn't ready to answer. "He took you away from work, and you can't even explain why."

"I trust my father."

"Because he's your father?"

"Because he cares about me and my brother. He would do anything for us."

"Yes, I've seen that. But all it takes is one mistake for a man like your father to be put in prison. He doesn't have the wisdom of a learned man. He behaves as if the rules of society don't apply to him. He might always have intentions to help, but he will cost you something precious one day. It might even be losing him. You shouldn't trust him blindly. Think for yourself. Act on your own. Did you want to leave work today?"

No, but only because you would be angry, Leo dared not say aloud. He'd been excited when he saw his father, after the worry had passed. And now there was a thrill within him. It was the same thrill he felt when his father had convinced Gartel to give Leo a chance to be a bookbinder. That was the last day he'd felt it until now, and it was his father who had brought it back. How could Gartel claim Darren was a brute? He might not have the same education as this bookbinding guild master, and Leo supposed it was true that his father ignored the "rules" of society. But it was because of his father that Leo could make steps toward a better life.

"I didn't want to leave," Leo lied.

"Good, because I was going to let you start learning how to bind today, but after your father came I started to wonder if you are really ready."

Leo doubted this was true. It seemed more likely that Gartel was just using this to turn Leo against his father. Perhaps Darren had embarrassed the man again.

Leo's expression must have revealed his skepticism because Gartel prodded, "I thought you wanted to bind books? Was I wrong?"

Leo buried his aggression and realized that he was excited if this was indeed true. But he would only remain that way if he ignored everything Gartel said about his father. He could do that for the moment at least.

"I want it more than anything." *But not as much as becoming an Ascendant.*

Leo felt his excitement slipping away as a newfound hatred started working its way into his heart. Gartel thought he was better than everyone in Leo's family, than all his workers. He'd even acted as if he was doing Rygen and her mother a service when he'd been involved with Verona.

"I told Rygen to show you what she could today," Gartel said. "I expect you to remember everything she tells you."

Rygen would be teaching him? His bitterness dissolved.

"Thank you," Leo said. "May I begin with her now?"

"Of course."

Rygen stood as Leo approached. She showed a big smile that lifted his heart.

"Congratulations!" she told him in an excited whisper. "No more parchment work."

"Are you sure?" he had to ask before he could let himself feel glee. "Gartel could always change his mind." *If my father embarrasses him again.* Leo would have to speak with his father to ensure that didn't happen.

"Well, let's do everything we can to make sure he doesn't. Are you ready to learn how to bind a book?"

"Are we going to do one before the day ends?"

She laughed. "*Cer-tain-ly not* in a single day. But I can show you some of what I know."

"Yeah, let's begin!"

"All right! I have fresh gatherings waiting for us at the press. There isn't much time left today, so we will do what we can." She stopped in the walkway between tables and turned around. "What did your father want?"

"Oh, I really must tell you later." Leo looked forward to the conversation. Rygen might think of something that he hadn't yet to help explain what he and his brother had felt.

"It's that complex?" Rygen asked.

"In a way." Leo went closer to her and whispered. "It's about Artistry."

She sucked in a breath. "Now you have to tell me."

"I will, but it would take the rest of our time if we start now."

"Does your father know an Ascendant?"

"No, it's not that."

"All right, we'll speak after work on the way home."

That was true—they would finally be able to walk back together. Rygen had been avoiding Leo until recently, and even when she hadn't, he was always forced to stay later than she was, as if Gartel wanted to punish him.

Rygen took Leo to the press. *Gatherings*—a phrase Leo had learned to mean groups of parchments—were neatly stacked already, but Rygen straightened them out again using the table as a hard edge. Then she described to Leo what she was doing as she stuck the gatherings into the opening in the press and turned a crank to squish them together until it was nearly too hard for her to turn the crank anymore. She reached around the nearby stacks of gatherings and produced a small saw that surprised Leo at first. It might've been the only time he'd seen anything sharp in Rygen's hand besides the small dinner knife she had shared with Leo and her mother during a meal.

"Three saw cuts must be made in the back of the gatherings," she said. "And they must be done at equal distances from each other. I've done it enough that I no longer need the measuring board, but we will use it this time."

She sawed into the paper until three grooves were made.

"Now each gathering must be individually held together with linen thread." She brought the gatherings over to a different apparatus. Three sections of thread hung down from a wooden beam that matched the distance of the three grooves she had made with the saw. Rygen sat down without delay and started looping needle and thread through. She tried to explain the pattern she was using, but Leo lost track as her hands moved too quickly.

By the second explanation, he had gotten it. Rygen explained that this process could take quite a while depending on the length of the book. Some days she did nothing but thread individual gatherings together. Those were the most dull, for the parchments were often blank during this process, to be inked later. Much of Gartel's income came from copying and selling existing books rather than binding new ones.

"It's easier this way for the copier at the end," Rygen explained, then focused on Leo's eyes as she often would before discussing Artistry. "The best copiers can control four pens at once if a spell has been cast on them. On the pens, I mean. Not on the copier." She laughed.

"Have you seen this?"

"No, but Gartel says that one day he'll show me. He'll show me a copier with linked pens, I mean. He won't be the one copying."

Leo chuckled this time, bringing out another laugh from Rygen. But he was more amused at the idea of Gartel using Artistry. He seemed to be a man who could handle books and money and not much else.

Rygen started to show Leo the next step of using a plow to prepare the top to be gilded. She was telling him that they called it gilded even if gold was almost never used, but Gartel interrupted them.

"Can Leo sew gatherings now without error?" The guild master's question was obviously rhetorical. It would take many hours of training.

"I thought I would show him the rest of the process first," Rygen said.

"He can see what happens next once he's done a few books. Spend the rest of the day making sure he can."

Gartel left before Leo could ask if sewing the gatherings was what he would be doing tomorrow. He wouldn't complain. It was better than preparing the parchments, and preparing the parchments was better than his farm work.

He felt sorry for Andar.

"Andar was really good at his work here," Leo told Rygen on their way back to the sewing area.

"Yeah," Rygen mumbled. But then she turned and asked, "Why?"

"He has good, quick hands," Leo explained. "And I'm starting to see that you do as well."

Her face went red. "Oh, thank you, but I've had a lot of practice. You will, too."

Leo spent the rest of the late afternoon and evening working closely beside Rygen. She started by showing him what to do each step of the way, but it didn't take long for him to want to try it himself. He seemed to get everything wrong at first, like how to position the gatherings, how to loop the thread so that it didn't twist and tangle, and where to put his free hand so everything would stay in place. It seemed difficult for Rygen to explain how he should correct his errors, for everything was very subtle and needed to be perfect.

Eventually, they switched so she could sit and show him again. He noticed things he hadn't the first time he'd watched her, not just the intricacies about how she worked, but about her. Rygen was different than other children. Leo had never known what it was before, but he had met many boys and girls close to their age. Some were pretty. Most were not. But none of them had what Rygen did. It was not one feature, neither her gray eyes nor her blonde hair, but something about the way her whole face was put together that made Leo feel something whenever he looked closely at her.

Other children were...children, and Rygen was a child as well, Leo knew, but he didn't look at her that way. It was the same way he didn't think of himself to be as much of a child as the other boys and girls he had met on the farm or out in the city. He felt more like a young adult than a child, as if ready and eager to be fully grown, yet the years just hadn't caught up with him yet. Rygen was like...a woman, he was thinking as he watched her work. She was doing the work of a woman. She knew how to read like a woman. She was smart like a woman. Yet she was still a child. He was certain that if he asked her if she wished she were older, she would jump and agree as if her enthusiasm could make it so.

His thoughts became muddled after he switched places with her and started working again. She put her hands on his to help him imitate what she had just shown him, but he seemed to forget already. There was a moment when she did not take her hand off even when she'd finished her instructions. He didn't know why he chose to look so intensely into her eyes right then, but it seemed to make her freeze.

She was close to him, her arm pushed against his. He didn't want her to move. It felt as if he was doing something wrong. He looked away from her and spoke without thinking.

"I see it now." Which he realized was one of the stupidest things he could say.

"Oh," Rygen murmured. "Are you sure?"

Of course he wasn't sure. She hadn't even shown him how to correct his last error yet!

"Actually..." He laughed nervously. "Can you show me once more?"

She described how he should put his hand this time, not stepping in close, not touching him in any way. He had scared her.

He didn't know what came over him, but he could barely focus on what Rygen was trying to tell him. All he wanted was for her to be close again. She stepped toward him a few times, sending his heart aflutter, but she didn't demonstrate with her hands and arms anymore.

Eventually, he could focus on his work again and realized that it wasn't so hard to remember. If he was careful and worked slowly, he could sew the gatherings without issue.

Rygen watched him work for a while with neither of them speaking. When he finished another gathering, she set her hand on his arm. The hairs on his neck stood up the moment she touched him.

"That's good!" she said. "I think you know how without my help now."

Leo nodded. She let go of his arm, though he could still feel her touch. His whole body was so tense that he wasn't sure he could move.

"You're a good teacher," he said, gazing into her eyes again.

He pulled his gaze away before he became lost in hers again. He tried to get back to sewing, but he somehow pricked his other hand with the needle and dropped it as he let out a small yelp.

Rygen laughed. "I get the joke. I'm such a good teacher that you pricked yourself."

Leo played along with a smile.

*****

The rest of the day might've been dull if it wasn't for Leo trying to figure out these feelings sparked by Rygen. He had moved needle and thread in a repetitive cycle for another hour before they had started their walk home together. He found himself wishing she would touch his arm again, but even stronger was the urge to touch her. Butterflies flew around in his stomach every moment he thought of reaching out to take her hand. He could almost feel her reading his thoughts, but he just wasn't sure enough to take action. Or perhaps he was just scared of the shame he would feel if she jerked her hand back.

When Leo was home with the door closed, it took a moment for him to realize that his brother had said his name a few times.

"Leo, Leo. Leo!"

"What?" Leo regretted snapping at his brother when he noticed Andar's expression. His eyes were wide and red, a crease across his forehead. "What's wrong?"

"Do you know where Father is?"

"I never do. Why?"

"I don't think even he can help this time. Rhenol..." Andar put his hand over his eyes.

Leo hugged his brother. "It's all right," he said without feeling the words. It was the same thing their father would say anytime something was wrong.

Andar squeezed Leo, then pushed him back. "It's not this time, but I don't know what I could've done differently. I would've lost my hand."

"What happened?"

"He set up a trap today while I was gone. He paid an Ascendant to link a plate to a vase, then told me to wash all his dishes. I figured it out, Leo. When I moved the plate, the vase moved as well. And it felt different, like the plate was stuck in a spider's web. I noticed the link. Rhenol planned for me to break the vase. Then he would have cut off my hand."

Andar had spoken too quickly for Leo to feel anything but shock. "Are you sure about all of this?"

"Yes, and Rhenol even admitted it when I figured it out. He went for the plate himself and moved it so the vase would fall and break. I caught the vase. Then I caught the plate. He yelled that I was trying to steal them, but I left his mansion with nothing and made sure the other workers saw this. He couldn't claim anything except that I had tried to steal. He yelled that I was a thief."

Andar paused for a shaky breath. "He yelled it again and again."

"But no one believed him, right?"

"I don't think it matters. The guards will. Others did see me holding the vase and the plate."

"But they would cut off your hand for that?"

"No, because I did not actually take them. But they are expensive glass, painted in gold. I do think Rhenol will tell the farmers' guild master that I had tried to steal them, and it will be enough."

Leo's heart sank. He knew what his brother was saying, but he had to hear the words nonetheless.

"Enough for what?"

Andar buried his face in his hands again. "To forbid me and anyone in our family from working on a farm again."

Leo started to lose his balance. He fell into the nearby chair. He was certain Andar would be banned from the farm after this, but Leo and Darren couldn't work there, either? Or on *any* farm? Leo had already prepared himself to beg Rhenol for work so they wouldn't lose the house.

"Oh, gods."

"We have to get our belongings and go." Andar sniffled.

Leo couldn't look up from his lap. "What do we do?"

"Did you hear me? We have to go."

"*Where?*" Anger gave Leo the strength to stand again. "I don't know."

"Gartel warned me that there can be no other interruptions in my work. I will lose my position if there are *any* other interruptions. I just started binding today!"

"You can keep binding. We only need a place to sleep."

"Tonight? They're coming tonight?"

Leo didn't know who "they" would be—the men who forced his family out of their house—but they wouldn't be friendly, that was for sure. There would be no way to convince them not to do what they were paid to do. It was the same for everyone in this wretched city. Coin was more powerful than the human heart. It wasn't even a close competition.

That reminded Leo of something. "What about the money you've hidden?"

Andar turned partially away from Leo, as if guarding himself from an attack. "What about it?"

"Why don't you want father to know?"

"I've earned it so I can be responsible for this family as well. He needs help, don't you see that? He refuses to let us help, so we have to do so on our own."

"If all you want to do is help, then you should give it to him."

"I would if I trusted him, but he's never told us anything about how much coin he has or how much he needs for a house. He just tells us what to do, and we do it. I am tired of that. You will be, too, when you're older."

Leo hated being told how he would be when he was older, especially by Andar. The differences between the two of them had always been there. Andar had not changed as he'd gotten older, just as Leo would not, either. Andar would always talk back to powerful men, while Leo knew better. Andar would always be a...would always steal. Leo wouldn't.

Was this really something for Leo to be proud of? Why was Leo getting angry at his brother?

"How much coin do you have?" he asked.

"Do you promise not to tell Father?"

Leo shook his head. "I will tell him if you're never going to."

"Of course I will, but I have to trust him first. Perhaps you don't see him in the same way that I do. You're too young."

Leo stomped his foot. "Stop saying that!"

"You are! But if you're not going to agree with that, fine. At least you need to trust that I'm not going to let this coin go to waste." He stared at Leo.

"What do you want me to say?"

Andar made fists. "I want you to believe me! I'm tired of trying so hard for that to happen."

"I will trust you if you trust me." It was a line he'd heard both Father and Andar tell each other.

Andar showed a wry smile. "Smart argument."

"I've always thought so."

"Fine," Andar said. "I will tell you how much I have if you promise not to tell Father. I want to be the one to tell him when we are ready."

"I promise."

"I have two gold coins, thirty-seven silver coins, and one-hundred eighty coppers."

Leo cursed.

Andar laughed. "That's the first time I've heard you swear."

"That's so much! You have so much. That's..." Leo started to do the necessary math but gave up. He was too shocked to count. "That's so much!"

Andar smiled proudly.

But Leo was only scared for his brother. "That is more than enough for the guards to take both of your hands if you're caught."

"I only take from the rich dolts who probably won't even realize something's missing. It's easy. I won't be caught."

Leo remembered seeing his brother in the market when Leo was sent there to purchase the metal clasps. Andar had made no effort to disguise himself. He had always been sneaky. He was always quick and careful, able to protect himself or talk his way out should anything go wrong. Perhaps Leo shouldn't worry so much.

But he couldn't help it.

"All the coins together are worth seven and a half gold," Andar said.

"How much are houses?" Leo asked.

"More than that."

"More? How could anyone ever afford one, then?"

"Most people can't."

"They can't ever?"

Andar shook his head. "No, not ever. The only people who can are those who are fortunate enough to have a house built by their ancestors. Most of those houses need repairs, though. Some do collapse eventually, some even with people within them. We don't want another place like this." Andar lifted his hands and glanced at the walls and ceiling. "And we can't stay in the city, either."

"What?" No, Leo would not leave. There was no reason! Rygen was here. The Bookbinding Guild was here.

"We have to," Andar told Leo sadly.

"We don't!"

Andar frowned. "Right now, we just need to figure out where to sleep. We can speak about leaving later."

Leo didn't care what reasons Andar had. He wouldn't leave.

CHAPTER TWENTY-THREE

Darren had only a few brief moments to himself on the way back from the cavern before he was interrupted. He was in the midst of trying to figure out what to do about Erisena when he saw Raenik approach him.

The recent owner of DVend's identification papers said nothing as he stopped a few steps away from Darren. He motioned with a swing of his head for them to take one of the side streets. The two of them had argued many times. Raenik had either shown a smile when he thought himself to be victorious or a scowl when Darren spoke back to him. In this moment, though, Raenik looked like a different man. He appeared weak, showing a bit of a limp. He had clearly been beaten, a bruise darkening one of his cheeks.

Darren had not expected the "tailor" who falsified papers to be Erisena's messenger, but surely there was a reason for her to send him rather than someone loyal to her.

Darren asked himself how he could be sure Erisena was the one who had sent Raenik. *It's the only explanation that makes sense. Only an Ascendant could've broken the door to Raenik's shop off its hinges, and only a rebel Ascendant would leave city investigators confused about what had happened there. It might've even been Lane.*

"What did they do to you?" Darren asked.

"Why do you care?"

"I need to know how you're involved with them."

Raenik tossed his hand petulantly. Darren noticed another bruise across two of the man's knuckles. "Why would I be involved with rebels who destroyed my shop, took all my papers, and now hold me captive?"

"If that's true, then why don't you run right now?"

"They're everywhere, you fool." Raenik coughed violently, hacking up and spitting out some blood. He didn't appear surprised by the sight of it.

Erisena hadn't seemed like the violent type, but Raenik was. Perhaps the damage her followers had done to his body was in retaliation, but Darren didn't believe this looking at the defeated man. They'd wanted something from Raenik that he hadn't wanted to part with.

Could it be my papers? Do they have them now?

"Did they torture you?" Darren asked.

"Don't pretend to care."

Darren didn't. Raenik was the kind of man who deserved anything that came to him because of his practice. But Darren's children were involved in this now. He needed to figure out whatever he could about this group of rebels. Fortunately, Raenik's answer had already told Darren that yes, torture had been involved.

Even the king wasn't known for that.

Raenik hardly lifted his gaze from the ground, though he did make it to Darren's eyes eventually. "If you want your papers, you will meet with her. What is your answer?"

Darren was still nearly certain he would not join Erisena, but as soon as he told Raenik that, this conversation would be over. Darren needed to see what he could learn first.

"Did they want you to meet with Erisena and you refused?" It would be one reason they'd destroyed Raenik's door to get into his shop.

"They asked me nothing. They demanded, and I refused their demands. Now what is your answer?"

"What did they demand?"

"Papers!"

"Whose?"

"All of them."

"Why?"

Raenik took in a breath as if about to shout.

"And keep your voice down," Darren reminded him. It didn't seem likely that anyone loyal to the king would overhear them, but Erisena wouldn't have sent Raenik alone unless she was a fool. Someone had followed Raenik to watch this meeting. Darren didn't care who it was so long as they stayed far enough away not to hear anything.

He felt a chill as he thought of Lane spying on them. She already knew so much about his family, and his feelings for her made this dangerous. Hardly anyone took this connecting road between shops. He and Raenik were still near the outskirts of the city, where most businesses had trouble attracting enough patrons. The city extended outward—new houses were built on the edges, while old ones were left to rot. But not many people could afford a new house in Jatn, so hardly anyone lived around here.

Darren still couldn't determine whether his family would be safer having nothing to do with Erisena, or if he should at least agree to her requests until he had his papers in his own hands.

"They didn't tell me why they took all the papers I had, but they plan to use them for blackmail," Raenik said.

"How do you know?"

"It's the only reason someone would want original papers." Raenik clearly spoke for himself. He couldn't see that there were other benefits to knowing the true identities of so many people.

"Answer the damn question," Raenik said. "Am I taking you to this meeting or not?"

"I haven't decided yet."

"Decide," Raenik said with force. But Darren showed him a look that made Raenik take a step back.

"I will when you answer my questions," Darren informed him. "What will they have you do next?"

"They said they will pay me for the papers they took and for the damage they've done." It sounded as if Raenik didn't believe this would happen.

"And then what will they do with you?"

Raenik's head was lowered as he looked up at Darren. "I don't know," he answered softly.

At least Raenik was smart enough to know that a group of rebels to the king couldn't let someone like Raenik go. He knew too much, and he couldn't be trusted.

Darren didn't know why he worried about Raenik. He was not an innocent man.

The answer came quickly. Whatever happened to Raenik would likely happen to Darren and his family when he denied Erisena what she wanted.

Darren almost thought to tell Raenik to take him to the meeting, but he realized something then. This was the only time in which he had something over Raenik. Until he gave his answer, Raenik would have to stay here.

Darren could finally ask the question he had been holding within ever since Rygen brought the book of his family's history over to the house.

"Have you falsified papers for my sister?"

"Don't you think I would tell you?"

"Now why would you do that?"

"So I would have something more to use against you." Raenik spoke the words as if they were obvious.

"I don't think the same way as you do." He put himself in Raenik's face.

"There's no need for aggression, DVend."

"My name's Darren." He spoke the words with a threat behind them. "Now I believe my sister visited your shop one day for falsified papers, just as I did. Tell me what happened."

"You would strike me on an open street? I think not."

"What's the point of testing me?"

Raenik thought for a moment, scratching his cheek. "You know I must get your answer, and you're squeezing everything out of me. I don't like to be squeezed like a rag, DVend. I might have nothing right now, but I had nothing when I first came to Jatn. I will have wealth and power again. You'd better watch how you treat me in this moment, or I will be the only man to make DVend Quim cower."

"I see why you had me threaten people for you," Darren teased. "You are quite awful at it."

Rage flashed across Raenik's face. Darren had only seen this expression on a man about to attack. He readied himself for movement, but Raenik held back and grumbled an insult.

"There was a woman who came to my shop once. She was about two years younger than you, as your sister is said to be. She was tall and beautiful and desperate, exactly how I like them. But she was also indecisive and cowardly. She couldn't make the decision on whether to tell me who she was. She left angry, the same way you stomp out of my shop most of the time. She had black hair and dark eyes. Sound familiar?" Raenik gave a wicked grin.

"Where did she go?"

"Ah, but now you and I are in the same position. Why should I tell you anything more about her?"

"Because I will give you the answer to Erisena's question. I'm sure she told you not to return without it."

"Yes, but when you want to help your family, you will do anything."

"You don't actually know anything about Yune," Darren tested.

"I figured she was Yune Quim even before she spoke. Do you honestly believe I would let someone as valuable as her disappear?"

"What did you do to her?"

"You're going to do something for me first."

"I will give you the answer—"

"You will, but you will also get back the papers Erisena took from me."

"I couldn't do that even if I wanted to."

Raenik rolled his eyes. "Don't insult me with lies. You know what you're capable of."

"The stories of my swordsmanship are exaggerated," Darren told him flatly. "Besides, I would never kill for information, even if it is about my family."

"You actually believe that, don't you? I know you better than you know yourself!"

Darren checked his surroundings. No one was in sight. All the shops were closed. It would be night soon.

"I don't think you do." Darren grabbed Raenik by the neck and dragged him behind the nearest shop. Raenik struggled all the way there, trying to pry Darren's hands off his neck as he wheezed and gagged.

Darren already knew Raenik had no weapons, for Erisena's rebels would certainly have disarmed him. He tripped Raenik with his hands still on his neck, then pressed his knees onto Raenik's arms. Fear had taken over Raenik's face as he tried to say something. It would be so easy for Darren to keep squeezing until Raenik stopped moving.

Nothing within Darren told him to stop. Nothing made him want to preserve this man's life. The only reason he let go was because he knew killing Raenik to be wrong.

"Where did she go?" Darren asked the gasping "tailor."

"I don't know," he answered with a strained voice, then coughed up a storm. He turned and spat out more blood. He cursed. "You could've killed me! Get off."

"First, you will tell me everything you know about my sister."

"I know nothing! It was a bluff, all right?" Raenik coughed and spat out more blood, this time on Darren's shirt. Then he cursed again. "Get off!"

"Who might know where my sister is?"

"Erisena! Now get *off*!"

Darren believed him. He wiped the wet circle of blood off the best he could by rubbing it against Raenik's shirt, but it would still leave a stain. Darren got up as Raenik sat on the ground, blinking and shaking his head as if to regain his wits.

"Now," Darren said in a voice laced with steel, "tell me where to find her."

*****

It wasn't a far walk to Erisena's meeting place. She was already near the outskirts of the city, close to the cavern where Darren had spent the day before fetching his children. He wondered if she had predicted he would return to his work in the cavern or if Lane had gotten word to her so quickly. Or perhaps Darren wasn't as important as he thought he was, and it was just a coincidence that Erisena happened to be over here.

Darren climbed over the short fence that sectioned off the abandoned farm where he was told to meet Erisena. He had walked by this place many times over the years. It was always vacant. He'd imagined many scenarios to provide himself with a theory as to why no one worked here, the most obvious being that the soil was no good. But now as Darren made his way across the dirt—illegally, for the land was still owned by the Farmers' Guild—he had a closer look. Although the dark of night soon approached, he could still see that the dirt was dark and rich here. They should have no issues growing at least the more resilient crops.

He walked across the stretch of land as he looked for the well where he was supposed to find Erisena. The farm was not nearly as large as the one where Andar worked, but Darren couldn't make out much in front of him. He walked toward where he thought the center of the farm to be, in hopes the well would be placed strategically, but he found nothing but a barn without a roof. It was barren inside the walls. Looters had taken everything they could get away with easily enough.

Darren heard a growl behind him. It was wet and loud. If this was a dog, then this was the largest, nastiest dog Darren had the unfortunate luck of encountering. He was without a weapon.

He turned around and saw the silhouette of a four-legged beast in the dark, tall as the tallest of dogs. It let out a sound that terrified Darren, one of clear aggression. The beast opened its mouth and closed it with each intermittent roar, as if showing Darren how it would eat his flesh if he did not run.

"Erisena..." he called out. "Erisena!"

This had to be her beast, most likely the same one that had leapt up on his roof so long ago.

The silhouette of a woman appeared in the open doorway behind the creature. Darren recognized Erisena's firm tone.

"It's only Darren, Ravitch."

It came as a surprise when the beast let go of its aggression and walked to Erisena's side.

"Ravage?" Darren asked. "Not a very subtle name."

"It's Ra-*vitch*," Erisena corrected. "And he does more than just ravage, like help me find you on this dark night." She knelt near her beast and ran her hand down his back.

Darren approached for a better look at this summoned creature. He had seen a few during his time in Halin, but all had been small. Before he could get close enough to see anything, Erisena knelt and whispered something to the beast. It walked away from her as she lifted her arms, a stone in one hand. She gestured at the empty space nearby—what could only be the casting of a spell. A gust of wind hit Darren, an unfamiliar smell filling his nostrils that reminded him of desert air. He looked deeply into the darkness where Erisena seemed to be pointing her hands, but saw nothing. The beast jumped into the rift and disappeared.

"That was quite a show," Darren commented. "But I'm still not interested in joining your small group."

"It shows how much you still don't know that you call it small."

"Your enemy has fifty thousand men. If you don't have enough to stop that kind of army, then you have the same power as a small group. None. I apologize if I sound rude, but it's important that you know what kind of danger you're in."

She took a moment. "I cannot prove you wrong until I trust you, but you should know that you are."

"If you can beat that kind of army, then you don't need me."

"Neither of us need each other, DVend."

"Don't call me that."

"Fine. Be Darren the rest of your miserable life if you want. In fact, I can make it so no one will be able to prove otherwise." She produced a parchment. "I'm giving this to you now, whether you join us or not. You may destroy it if you wish."

He reached out for it, but she drew back. "Your past is so much more than just a secret that could get you killed!" She spoke as if irritated. "Tell me you have realized that by now? Part of who you are is who you used to be."

He thought on her words for a moment. "That's not true. The past doesn't matter. If a man is a farmer, a king, a philanthropist, or a murderer, then he is what he is. His past doesn't change anything."

"You of all people should know that a digger might always be a digger, no matter his past, but he is also much more than his profession. DVend still exists. Most people don't know the truth about him, but the truth doesn't matter because DVend *reminds* us of the king's injustice...and so much more that you don't yet know."

"Then tell me."

She did not speak for some time. Finally, she sighed and said, "You will not believe me until you see it for yourself."

That was probably true. "See what?"

"The Jaktius Perl."

"Pearl what?"

He thought he saw her shaking her head. "It's not common tongue," she said. "You will find out what it is in your lifetime, whether you join me or not." She finally handed him his papers.

Darren held the parchment close to his eyes, but he couldn't make out any of the writing in the dark. It could've been a blank page. He knew he should just tear it up and look at the pieces later, but something made him fold it and put it in his pocket instead.

"You need our help," she stated as if it were fact. "And we could use yours. I assume you found out by now that both your sons have an early connection to Artistry?"

They have more than you will ever know. "I found out."

"You know it can be dangerous for mages to grow up without training. If Andar's affinity started at Leo's age, then you will have two teenage Ascendants with no control over their ability. You might not remember what it's like to be a teenage boy, so let me remind you of how foolish you were when you first met the woman who would be your wife. You were seventeen. I'm sure you remember now."

Yes, he was a fool for many years. He had organized a tournament then with his father's permission for the sole purpose of impressing Farinda when she was sixteen. He had never seen anyone more beautiful. He had tried speaking with her, but each time he sounded more like a dolt. She would sometimes tease him, always showing off her quick tongue. He did better in writing, so they exchanged many letters, but every time she agreed to meet, he only made a fool of himself again. So he would fight in front of her instead, he figured. It had worked to attract many women, most of whom he had no interest in. And his skill with the sword was much better than his ability to speak with beautiful women.

He fought brutally, showing his dominance over the most skilled swordsmen, all of whom were older and had more years of training under their belts. He had injured more than half of them, most unnecessarily. At least he'd made sure not to cripple anyone, but his brutality had the opposite effect on Fari. She didn't speak to him for months afterward.

It was Darren's sister, Yune, who spoke to Fari eventually. Yune explained the truth about DVend. He was not a brute. He did not and never had enjoyed hurting the other duelists. He was just out of ideas on how to win Fari's heart because his words had failed him. He would do anything for her because he was in love.

"I agree," Darren told Erisena. "That tournament was foolish of me, but my sons are not like I was."

"Not yet. But every teenage boy makes one foolish decision that they regret. Now imagine that foolish choice was made with the kind of power that can end a life. I thought you knew about Artistry?" She paused for a moment. "Ah, I know what it is. You have only met trained mages, is that right?"

"What does it matter?"

"You never hear of the untrained ones. Most are dead or imprisoned because they have either killed themselves or someone else accidentally."

Her words seemed to stifle the cold breeze blowing through the open barn.

"You must've heard at least one story of a young man or woman who died suddenly with no explanation?"

"None of those stories are real."

"They are, Darren. My own sister was one of them. She died in an open field in Analyte land. I was right next to her the entire time. We were on our way to pick roses when she felt something strange, then concentrated on it. I had no idea what was happening, but suddenly she couldn't breathe. Her face turned blue. Her mouth was open, but she couldn't even gasp. She died right there at my feet while I screamed for help. The doctors thought it was something in the field that had caused her throat to close, but there was nothing but grass around us at the time. We hadn't even made it to the roses."

"And why couldn't the doctors have been right?"

"We had made that same walk many times. It was just outside our house." Erisena let out a sigh. "Neither humans nor Analytes can suffocate in the middle of a grass field."

Darren found himself to be nodding, for he couldn't disagree. "I'm sorry about your sister."

"She would've been a strong Ascendant had she or anyone in my family known she needed training. Instead, she made an accidental link to something that killed her."

"I have already vowed to keep my sons safe no matter what it takes, and joining a group of rebels to the king is not keeping my vow. I apologize, Erisena. I do believe in justice. I wish we could help each other, but my father chose to fight and now my whole family is dead or separated. The same—"

"Your whole family is not separated. I know where your sister is."

"Yes, she's in Jatn."

"I know *where* in Jatn."

He stepped close to Erisena, a reflex as he readied himself to threaten. Darren stopped leaning toward her, aware of his actions and sickened by how natural they'd become.

"Are you telling me the truth?" he asked.

"Yes. And I'm sorry to have to do this to you, but I will only tell you if you agree to join us."

He waited a moment to give her a chance to realize her mistake.

Without showing fear, she said, "You and your sons will be safer with me than your family will be on its own."

One of his options was surely obvious to both of them. He felt the need to state it aloud. "Why wouldn't I tell you now that I agree to join you just to find out where my sister is?"

"Because you are like me and my people. Trust is everything." Erisena let her words sit for a moment. "We have enough enemies. We wouldn't make more by lying."

This was the first time Darren's threat was not only ignored but returned in such a way that made his blood run cold with fear.

Nonetheless, nothing she had said was convincing enough for him to put Leo and Andar in certain danger. As it was now, there was a chance they would stay safe. A very good chance. That chance was gone as soon as Darren joined Erisena.

She let out a sigh as if she already knew his answer. "I can give you two more days to make a decision. It is the most I can afford. Meet here again when you are ready. I will have someone here each night if I cannot make it myself." She turned to leave.

"Why two?"

She did not answer. She wouldn't, he figured. So he asked something else that was beginning to bother him.

"What happened on this farm?"

"The workers rebelled," she said without turning around.

"And?"

She didn't answer at first, only sighed. "They were massacred, and there has been no justice for any of them."

It struck a nerve in Darren, his teeth grinding.

CHAPTER TWENTY-FOUR

King Mavrim Orello stood on the highest balcony in his castle. He never used to look down into the royal garden, usually opting for the view from the southern side where he could see the city—all the little houses and people that he had once thought of as fodder.

Peasants provided the food and services that the army required. The army protected the peasants. But what did they need protection from anymore? Raiders hadn't come north in decades. The Analytes to the east kept to themselves...for the most part. Rebels of the crown were the only threat, but the Orellos—and their enormous army of course—had squashed charismatic nobles like DFaren Quim for over a century. As king, Mavrim should continue to squash rebel pests until he passed the crown to his son. It was how his grandfather had taught his father to lead and how his father had taught him. Mavrim had long ago passed the lessons on to his son, who had turned thirty this year.

But the people were changing. The cities were evidence of this. Many farmers had come to realize the power they held over the kingdom. *They have already taken Jatn. The only reason the Farmers' Guild is safe for now is because it pays taxes.*

Taxes—the word had lost its meaning. *Blood coins,* Mavrim told himself, for that's what they were. *They pay for nothing but to keep one's blood in one's own body.* Mavrim had ordered the death of thousands, and for lesser crimes than refusing to pay taxes. Should the Farmers' Guild in Jatn one day decide that its army has grown powerful enough to beat Mavrim's army, then Mavrim was certain his family would condone the demolition of the entire city if that's what it took to kill every last one of them. Ten years ago, he would've condoned the action as well, but he had met some of the people whose lives had been destroyed along with each group of rebels.

His family had met the same people. His son had even married one of them. A forced marriage...and a forced pregnancy. The king gripped the banister in front of him with both hands, his knuckles white. Not only had he allowed it to happen, he had *ordered* it.

At least something beautiful had been brought into this castle because of it. There were many beautiful things to admire all around him, such as the paintings and banners, and even this garden before him. But there was only one beauty here that was pure and innocent. Everything else had come out of greed and destruction.

So has Fyra, Mavrim realized. The six-year-old girl might be the sweetest person with the warmest heart ever to step foot inside the castle, but she did not come from anything innocent. Her mother was once hailed as the most beautiful woman in the world. She had been married to DFaren Quim briefly before he was executed. Since then, her life had been nothing but misery. Imprisonment was a blessing to her, Mavrim had to assume. Everything was—so long as she was away from her husband, the prince. Mavrim had seen the way she averted her gaze from the man. *My son.*

Her name was once Karlinda Quim, but now she was an Orello. No one thought she would mourn for her late husband, DFaren, when he was executed. He was much older than her. She'd married him for his money. Everyone knew this. That was why it was so easy to trust her when she married Prince Gavval and showed loyalty to the Orellos immediately. She'd never cared about DFaren or the rest of the Quims.

But everyone was wrong about her, and Mavrim was glad they were. It took three years before she had the trust and the means to let DVend and Yune Quim free from their facing prison cells. Karlinda didn't waste another moment. Getting them out of their cells wasn't the hardest part. She had even gotten them out of the capital *and* provided them with horses. She'd known what kind of punishment would befall her, how her life would change. She'd lived a good life before that, an enjoyable one. But she had the unfortunate curse of having a caring heart. She would not ignore her guilt as Mavrim had for many years.

Mavrim was not a good king. He did not know how to improve the lives of the people in his kingdom. All he'd ever learned was how to keep the crown until it was time to pass it to his son. This he was good at. War he was good at. Trickery he knew well.

The garden was enormous and lush. At the center of its back wall was a tree that experts had told the king was the largest wisdom tree in the world. This they all agreed on, but what the tree could do was where their theories differed. It didn't matter to Mavrim. He no longer wondered about what mysteries a master Ascendant might uncover about the translucent, azure wood. Mavrim had long ago surpassed the skill over Artistry that his trainers had demonstrated. There were no secrets of Artistry to the wisdom tree. It was much like his family. The tree had been here so long that most everyone believed it had earned its place in this garden. But it belonged here as much as Mavrim did.

The only thing to note was how the Analyte king had looked at the wisdom tree when he'd crossed by a window that provided a view. There was no mistaking that he seemed surprised by the sight of it, but there was something more to his reaction as he stopped on the stairs and said nothing for a long moment. Finally, he had uttered in his odd accent, "What do you call that tree here?"

"A wisdom tree," Mavrim had answered. That was eleven years ago. The tree had not changed much since then, but everything else had. The Analyte king was an Ascendant like Mavrim. And just like Mavrim, his skill over Artistry was not publicly known.

There were other secrets Mavrim had learned that day. He had chosen to ignore them for the time being, for the Quims had gathered an army that needed to be squashed. But the Analyte king had reminded him later that there were worse threats than rebels and raiders.

King Mavrim had spent a small amount of time wondering what he could do to help the Analytes more than he already had, but he had himself to worry about now. People were conspiring. He could feel it. The citizens outside the castle were changing, moving away from feudalism. But everyone within the castle, especially those who worked closely with Mavrim's son and wife...they had changed as well. They held onto their power as if it was as valuable as life itself.

Mavrim heard footsteps behind him and turned to see a guard standing there. "Sire," the man asked. "Young Fyra wishes to look down on the garden. Her mother accompanies her."

"Allow them here, of course."

There were only a few times in the week when Mavrim smiled without forcing it. All were upon seeing Fyra.

Soon, he saw her running toward him. "Grandfather!" she squealed.

He knelt and opened his arms, letting her run to him. She nearly knocked him over.

"Careful, Fyra!" her mother said. "The balcony."

What a way for the king to finally fall. Thrown off the balcony by a six-year-old girl. Mavrim chuckled to himself. It was easy to play off his laughter as joy from seeing his granddaughter.

"Did the wise tree grow?" asked Fyra as she poked her head between the railings of the balcony.

"Yes, but not as much as you have in the past year." Knowing the girl was not only unafraid of high places but that she relished them, Mavrim surprised her by hoisting her up over the balcony. He dipped her over and let out an exclamation as if he might drop her. She squealed with delight.

But her mother gasped. Mavrim quickly put Fyra back on the floor where she was safe.

"Again, again!" called Fyra.

"I would," Mavrim said, eyeing a pale Karlinda. "But I think doing so might make your mother faint."

He could tell she wanted to scold him, but he was the king. Fyra was the last thing precious to Karlinda. She had honestly loved DFaren Quim. She had considered herself part of the Quim family, a rebel. An enemy to Mavrim and his family.

But she was no enemy anymore. No one was. The Analyte king had it right ten years ago when he gave Mavrim the advice to stop killing rebels. It was an odd thing to say after the Analyte king had brought an army of

Analytes here to help Mavrim do just that, betraying the Quims in the process. But there was a greater purpose behind it. The Analytes needed men and women...of any race. The kings had told the public that the humans who were branded and given to the Analytes would be farmers, but this was a lie.

Mavrim had not spoken to the Analyte king since the end of the last war, but he could tell that the humans sent to Analyte land had not been enough. There was still a great disruption to Artistry. The source of the disruption was still across the continent for all Mavrim knew, but he could feel it meddling with the otherwise common nature of the ground and air, the stability of the mountains, the flow of water. Something wasn't right. Enough Ascendants knew that now, but none of them had the solution.

Every day Mavrim considered traveling east, out of his kingdom, to see this disruption for himself. But he feared what would happen to his castle with his son in power. Prince Gavval had been taught how to keep power just like Mavrim had been taught by his father. Neither of them knew how to give their subjects what they wanted, only to take it away.

"Does the tree, um..." Fyra began. "Does it become wiser?"

She almost always found the right word if she didn't know it right away. It was her enthusiasm to learn. She was one of the few children who enjoyed the schooling on the castle grounds.

"Not as quickly as you are becoming wise," Mavrim told her honestly.

She smiled at that. "I want to teach when I'm older."

"That's a fine profession to choose, but you will have many options. You shouldn't set your heart on one too early."

He noticed Karlinda giving him a look as if reminding him that she was only six. Whatever she set her heart on now was likely to change anyway.

"What did you train as?" Fyra asked Mavrim.

"I was taught to be a king. To rule."

"Oh." She seemed to be in thought. "Can I learn to rule?"

Her mother laughed innocently, but Mavrim did not. He let her mother give her the news.

"Unfortunately, only men are allowed to be king."

"Why?" Fyra asked her.

It was questions like these over the last year that had ultimately changed Mavrim's way of thinking. He knew the world was not fair, but seeing it through a child's eyes made it even clearer. Fyra had asked many difficult questions about her family, especially about her mother and father. She had wondered why her mother must reside in a prison cell. When that became too hard to answer, Karlinda was let out. Fyra had seen her father a few times in the company of other women, drinking and laughing, sometimes even touching them affectionately. She wondered why she had never seen him act this way with her mother. Mavrim had scolded his son after that and demanded that he be more careful.

But the hardest questions to answer were the ones about Mavrim's tasks as king. He had never realized just how much time he spent worrying about power being taken away until he was asked to talk about his day—his strategies and orders.

Mavrim's wife had told him not to spend so much time with his granddaughter. *The queen senses me changing. My son does as well.* Mavrim wished he could take a side, a stand against oppression, but no opportunities had presented themselves. So now he waited, removing himself from the game of power, for it disgusted him. But this meant that many decisions fell to the prince. A shift had taken place in the castle. Some messengers and nobles no longer went to Mavrim first. They went straight to their future king.

"Can I read to you?" Fyra asked.

"She has a new favorite book," Karlinda said. "But Grandfather needs to be asked in advance, remember Fyra? He's very busy."

"I remember. Can I read to you, later?" the child asked Mavrim.

"I would love that," he said.

She brightened and tried to tell Mavrim about the book, but her sentences went in a few different directions at once. Rather than interrupt, he let her gather herself and try again.

Mavrim smiled as he pretended to pay attention, but his mind was elsewhere. He focused on the sound of someone calling for the king, most likely a messenger. The voice sounded urgent.

"Excuse me," he told Fyra as he left the balcony and descended the stairs. He didn't need to explain further. As king, he had many luxuries that even a child understood. It was only when he'd started perceiving himself through her eyes that he once again began to appreciate these privileges. He was in no hurry to rid himself of power, but if that's what it took to please the people, then he would do so. He was done living with regret.

The messenger ran up the stairs to meet the king. Out of breath, the man said, "Your son needs you in the meeting hall as soon as you can get there."

"Is it only my son?" the king asked.

"It's my understanding that your wife and council also join him."

The king hurried. Something must be wrong.

Or perhaps something was right, finally.

He promptly made it to the meeting hall to find that everyone with any say was already there. It was customary for the king to be summoned last so that he would not have to wait, but this discussion seemed to have begun without him. Mavrim figured there had been other discussions to which he had not been invited.

The first to greet him was his wife, who lowered her head in deference as she had been taught to do when she was just a child. She stood close, with an open seat next to her. The table before Mavrim was long, with a map spread across it and held down at the corners by miniature statues of swordsmen and mages. Their poses of aggression set the theme of this room. Swords and shields were mounted to the walls decoratively. The banner of the Orellos sat above the fireplace.

This was a place where the first planning of battles had begun, where plots of how to best control the people were set. Mavrim remembered making some of his most difficult decisions here, but his motives were always clear. Power must be retained.

When Mavrim had ordered the kidnapping of a small boy—the grandson and supposed reincarnation of KRenn Trange—there was no question in Mavrim's mind whether it was morally right or wrong. The only debate between him and his council was how the thousands of religious folk would react. This grandson was still in the castle, a prisoner just like Karlinda and her daughter. But this man was a Trange, not an Orello. He had been allowed to study and pray, but he would not be released no matter how many religious folk or holymen came to the castle doors and spouted nonsense about the gods' wrath if the reincarnate of KRenn was not released. Mavrim would find a use for him when an opportunity presented itself.

Mavrim's council was a group of men he had once trusted with his life. Now they were grandfathers both of their families and of the castle, clinging to their old habits. All rebels must die. Power had to remain in the hands of those who already had it. The land was theirs. It didn't matter that none of them actually worked it. They'd earned it and knew how to keep it.

Mavrim's son was at the other end of the table. He was the only one left standing after everyone had bowed to the king.

"News, Father, from Jatn," said the prince, a man all too eager to wear the crown. The Orellos weren't known for their beauty. Long noses ran in their family, as well as puffed up cheeks to match the air they often held in their lungs. Mavrim's hair had gone gray, but his son's was still brown. It wasn't any of the fancy browns that a poet might choose, like hazel or chestnut. It was brown like Mavrim's hair used to be. Brown like the dusty old fur of a bear. Gavval looked younger than he was, as did his father. Each of them would likely live to be one hundred so long as nobody interfered.

News from Jatn—this was probably nothing. *The farmers control the city and pay taxes. They are too strong a force for anyone to break the cycle there.*

"What news?" Mavrim asked.

"A Tisary," said his son, but there was none of the same excitement in his voice that Mavrim had heard the last time, when a Tisary was discovered in Halin. It had led to the brief yet brutal war in which the Analytes had betrayed the Quims and sided with Mavrim. The celebrations in the castle afterward had been more epic in nature than the battle itself, which could only be called a slaughter. In the years that followed, the Orellos had created many gems out of the Artistry in the Tisary. Now they were rich beyond measure.

"And what else?" Mavrim asked.

"How did you know there's something else?" asked Richan, the youngest of the old men who provided counsel. Mavrim suspected it was Richan who first noticed the king changing. He was perceptive yet skeptical. He did not appear a day younger than fifty, nor was he. The question he posed to Mavrim sounded like a test. Perhaps there had been discussions among the council about whether Mavrim had some way to receive news of the happenings of the land.

Unfortunately, this was not the case. Mavrim had been undecided about going forward with a betrayal. Now it was too late. His son and the rest of the council were more involved in the affairs of his kingdom than he was. Mavrim was slowly becoming invisible to everyone but Karlinda and Fyra. Those two were prisoners, though, even if Fyra didn't know it. There was nothing they could do to help Mavrim change anything.

Mavrim stared at Richan, forcing him to remember his place. He was not to question the king in such a manner.

"I only ask so that we do not waste time," Richan said nervously. "If you already know the news, there's no reason to hear it again."

"So all of you here already know?" Mavrim took his seat at the end of the table opposite his son.

They looked to one another rather than answer. Eventually their gazes settled on Gavval.

"Yes, we know, Father."

"Then have you already discussed what you wish to do about it?" Mavrim showed his anger through his tone. He had no idea what the news was besides the Tisary, but he still had too much pride to admit it. Besides, it was better that they thought he still had allies in this castle of rats.

"We wanted to wait for you," Gavval said, his tone now respectful. "What are your thoughts?"

Was that a lie? It seemed to be—they had probably already agreed upon something. What could the issue be besides the Tisary? The answer seemed obvious based on history. Someone had already taken control just as the Quims had the last time a Tisary had been discovered. It was probably the Farmers' Guild this time. Perhaps they had already begun amassing an army in preparation to fight back the army of the king.

No, they couldn't be that stupid. The Quims had been just as powerful—no, *more* powerful—because they had the support of the people of their city. And they were still killed.

But the Analytes supported us then.

Mavrim thought for a moment. *They might again. They always need more men of any race.*

This meant there could be another battle. A pang of disappointment made Mavrim scowl before he could hide it.

"What's wrong?" Richan asked.

Rather than answer, Mavrim wanted to ask this lot of greedy men and his overindulged, overfed wife two questions. Weren't they sick of taking? Weren't they sick of all the death? But questions like these could be the beginning of his demise.

Was this the opportunity he had been waiting for to make a change? Could it be the only opportunity he'd have before he was poisoned or stabbed in his sleep? But supporting the Farmers' Guild in Jatn would do no good. They were more like the royal family than they were like the Quims. They would take whatever power they could and hold onto it no matter what it cost the citizens of their city. Supporting them would not change a thing.

"You are a wise man, Richan," Mavrim said. "I want to hear what you propose."

For once, Richan stared back at Mavrim as if he didn't want to say a word. He set his gaze on Gavval.

"What is it?" the prince asked.

But Richan remained coy and did not answer. "Sire, I think it would be best if you spoke first," he told Mavrim.

The king stood with his palms on the table. "Enough. This is the king's council, not a game. Now we must discuss a course of action. Richan, you will begin by telling us everything you know and offering a suggestion."

Richan looked as if he wouldn't speak, even after the king had given the order, but he took a deep breath, then stood and cleared his throat. "As all of us know, a Tisary has been discovered by the Diggers' Guild in Jatn. They are owned by the Farmers' Guild, which means the Tisary is under their control." He shot a look toward Gavval before returning his gaze to Mavrim. "But that is not the worst news. It's this: An army of rebels has gathered in Jatn."

"An army?" exclaimed the queen. Apparently she had been left in the dark as well. Her eyes widening in alarm, she looked toward her husband. "We have to do something."

This must've been why Gavval had begun inviting his mother into these meetings. Gavval still lacked the confidence he needed to disagree openly with Mavrim. But whatever Gavval couldn't do on his own, his mother would gladly help.

"We will," Mavrim answered his wife. She was right, something must be done.

This was his opportunity after all! Rebels, finally. An army of them. If only he could speak with them, find out what they wanted. Perhaps arrangements could be made and the land could finally change for the better.

"You knew about them already, Father?" Gavval asked.

"No, I haven't heard of rebels in Jatn." He stared at Richan to remind him of the previous order. *Everything you know, now.*

"They did not come from Jatn," Richan explained. "In fact, their leader is an Analyte."

"What?" the queen shouted. "Have we been betrayed?"

Mavrim shot his son a look, blaming him for bringing her in here so now they had to deal with her outbursts.

"I don't know her allegiance yet," Richan said.

"Her?" the queen asked.

"Yes, she's a woman."

It was the queen who seemed the most surprised by this. Mavrim had met plenty of women with the intelligence and confidence required of a leader, but none of them had the opportunity to lead even if some possessed the will. He had hoped for more from his daughter when she was younger, but it was only Gavval who sought power.

Mavrim didn't suppose these rebels were announcing their motives publicly. Even in a city like Jatn, all citizens should fear the wrath of the king's army. Especially an Analyte. Their punishment would be more severe. Why? Because they were different, simple as that.

What in KRenn's mind would possess an Analyte woman to lead a rebellion against me?

"How did you find out about these rebels?" Mavrim asked Richan.

"They believe they have turned someone who is secretly still loyal to you, sire."

Loyal to me, or to you, Richan?

"Who is it?"

"You have never met."

Obviously. "And have you?"

"A long time ago, but we've remained in contact because it was important to both of us."

Mavrim thought for a moment about this "loyal" person. There was no telling who it could be. Some or even all of Richan's statements could be lies, though Mavrim doubted it. What would the point be?

"Speak only in facts now, Richan. What do you *know* about these rebels?"

"They plan to take Jatn and the Tisary."

The queen gasped. "They must be stopped."

Mavrim ignored her theatrics. "How many support this Analyte woman?"

"If I'm to speak only in facts, then I can't say. But our loyalist believes she has over a thousand followers dedicated to her."

"A thousand?" asked Gavval. "Is that all?"

"These are not ordinary soldiers," Richan explained. "They are Ascendants, summoners, and swordsmen of exceptional skill. It is not an army of numbers that Erisena, the Analyte, has gathered. Her intention is not to march upon our army."

"Then what does she hope to accomplish after taking Jatn and the Tisary with only a thousand troops?" Gavval asked.

"We don't know."

"They must be stopped," repeated the queen.

"She's right," the prince agreed.

"Richan just admitted that we don't even know what they want yet," Mavrim told them.

"They plan to take Jatn and the Tisary!" said the queen.

"From the Farmers' Guild," Mavrim told her pointedly. "They have enough wealth and troops to fend off a thousand rebels even if these men and women are elite. We shouldn't get involved at this juncture except to speak to...Erisena, did you call her?"

Richan seemed too stunned to even nod.

Gavval looked more concerned than confused. "You wish to speak to the *leader* of the *rebels*?"

"We don't even know they are rebels to the throne yet, only to those who control Jatn and the Tisary there."

Everyone looked toward one another as if hoping someone else would speak their thoughts.

"I am tired of fighting and killing!" Mavrim announced. He knew it was a mistake as soon as he saw Richan give Gavval a look as if he had predicted this, but Mavrim couldn't stop now. "Battle must be reserved as a last resort when it is against our *own* citizens. Their complaints deserve to at least be heard before we send an army there to slaughter them."

"Sire, I respectfully disagree," Richan said all too proudly. "They aren't aware that we know of their plans. The advantage we have over them is surprise."

"The advantage we have over them is an army with over fifty times their numbers!" The king paused to survey their expressions. "I can see you all disagree, but I will not condone the death of more humans. So many already died in the battle against the Quims, and that doesn't include all those taken to Analyte land...as farmers," he added. They didn't know the truth, and that was not a discussion for this time.

"Father," his son began, but Mavrim interrupted.

"I have decided what we will do, and it is no longer up for debate." He divulged his plan, knowing full well it would be disobeyed: "We will send a messenger to find Erisena and inform her that we are aware of her rebellion and wish to speak so that we can resolve this without bloodshed. We will allow her to decide when and where I am to meet her."

"Are you serious?" the queen asked, though she appeared to regret her question when Mavrim shot her a look.

It was a terrible plan, the king knew. But he still wore the crown. No one could openly disagree with him without facing punishment.

But that didn't mean that they would follow his orders. He would be betrayed by his own family. He was not only certain, he wanted it to be the case. His real plan was the only way he could give these rebels a chance, for they truly were the one opportunity he had been waiting for all these years.

"This is to be settled without war," Mavrim announced to closed ears. "And on the subject of rebels, I also decree that the search for DVend and Yune Quim is to cease."

The king's suspicions of betrayal were confirmed, for no one even pretended to appear surprised. They had already figured Mavrim had changed; they had already planned to remove him. This would set their plans in motion.

Mavrim held in a smile. He gladly let them think he was an old man who had given up on holding onto his power. His family and councilmen would meet secretly later today. They would soon send an army after these rebels and force Mavrim to accept the outcome when it was over, or die.

What they didn't know was that the cunning strategist still existed within the king. He would keep his true plan hidden from everyone, especially from the one man who would unwittingly save the rebels from complete obliteration.

The army of the king would arrive first, unfortunately. Mavrim could do nothing about that. There would be bloodshed. Jatn was about to become a battlefield. But what Mavrim could do was give the rebels a way to regain their strength after their losses.

He left the meeting hall and waited until he was alone in his quarters before he let his smile show in the mirror. It had been years since he'd gotten a good look at himself. He appeared to be a different man than he remembered. He was older, his wrinkles deeper, his teeth yellow. He was not a beautiful man, but he was a talented one with an ever-growing heart.

All he had to do now was make sure that his plan worked. His smile faded. The hard part had yet to begin.

CHAPTER TWENTY-FIVE

Everyone figured Mavrim would never let the boy go. The child was just seven at the time Mavrim took him as a prisoner. The boy had done nothing wrong then, and even during all these years in captivity, he'd never misbehaved. When the boy became fourteen, the age of manhood, he had stopped asking Mavrim when he would see his father again. Never had Mavrim seen such a transformation from boy to man. All requests for anything stopped. If the young man couldn't do it on his own, then he wouldn't do it at all. He was nineteen now.

He had an unfortunate name: FLip Trange, pronounced Fa-*lip*, with emphasis on "lip." His father just *had* to follow the honorific use of double capital letters. It was the father's right, Mavrim supposed. Any father with an honorific name could impart one upon his son. But the fact that he chose the name FLip showed his inability to make difficult decisions. Philip would've been better, stronger. The boy was supposed to be KRenn reincarnated! How could he have such a weak name as Fa-*lip*?

It was the father's inability to make decisions that led to his son's imprisonment in the first place. The father's name was HSon Trange, pronounced Ha-*sawn*. He was the son of KRenn himself, which used to mean something to Mavrim but didn't anymore. When Mavrim had taken FLip prisoner, he had issued a challenge to HSon that the gods must've overheard as well. Yet the gods had never taken up this challenge, and neither had HSon or his many followers.

Mavrim no longer believed in the gods, though he still thought there were other forces that dictated the rules of the world, such as Artistry and rifts. One such force might be KRenn himself, if he was still alive.

One thing was for certain. KRenn had not been not reincarnated into FLip. Mavrim didn't care that the nineteen-year-old supposedly had the same birthmark on his arm as KRenn. There was nothing else magical or godly about the young man. He had no power over Artistry, while KRenn was the renowned master Ascendant of the world. FLip was no summoner, either. He had no connection to the other dimensions, like his grandfather had. And FLip was certainly no gemcrafter. One had to have some control over Artistry to imbue precious stones.

All FLip did was pray and study. He read everything he could, including philosophical and scientific texts that directly contradicted many religious allegories written by FLip's father.

Mavrim hadn't spoken to FLip much over the years. The king didn't enjoy dealing with people who held grudges against him, but it wasn't right to say that Mavrim ever had to *deal* with FLip. The young man was a pacifist. That would have to change for Mavrim's plan to work.

FLip wasn't required to stay in a prison cell. Just like Karlinda, it eventually seemed pointless to keep him behind bars. He was removed after the first year of imprisonment. He had his own room in the castle, but never was he treated as a guest. Mavrim, along with the rest of his family and council, were too worried that someone with hidden ambitions would get him out of the castle one day.

That day would be today. No one would suspect that it was Mavrim who'd let him out. If done right, even FLip himself would believe that it was the gods who'd lifted him out of the castle.

Mavrim visited the young man in his quarters. FLip was on his knees in front of the altar he'd made himself, a holy book on a tray before some candles. Many of the holy texts in this room had been rewritten by his father, the originals burned whenever HSon got his hands on them. It was obvious that HSon had tried to make himself a god in the eyes of men the same way KRenn had done. But KRenn was at least an exceptional man. HSon was not.

"I must interrupt for a moment," Mavrim told FLip as he entered his quarters.

The young man finished his prayer by speedily whispering to himself before he stood and faced his king. He wore a robe of light purple over a thin frame that even the robe could not mask completely. He had a sheen of blond hair combed neatly and was always cleanly shaven. His eyes never appeared tired or red no matter how much FLip buried his nose in texts.

"Yes, sire?" FLip asked. There was a hint of disdain in his tone.

Good, this will not work if he is indifferent to me.

"How are you feeling?" Mavrim teased. Even as a boy, FLip had never gotten ill.

"Fine. Is there something I can do for you?"

The answer to that would require some questioning.

"Do you know what I would do if you escaped from the castle?" the king asked.

"I suppose order some heinous punishment like cutting off one of my hands."

"I'm asking you what I would do the moment you escaped, not after you were caught."

"You would order my recapture."

"Yes, and where would my men look?"

FLip stared into Mavrim's eyes. As a boy, he had never shown any fear of the king, nor any respect. Indifference was his attitude. But this had changed.

"They would search the land and church owned by my father."

"Yes, and if they did not find you there, where would they look?"

"I assume they would search the cities, as they have done to look for the remaining Quims."

"Yes."

A puzzled look came across FLip's face. "Why question me about this? I have no plans of escaping."

"And why is that?"

"Because I barely know my father," the young man answered without hesitation. "I feel no need to reunite with him, and I assume you have plans for me. You will marry me to someone eventually. I know there must be requests."

"Yes, there have been many, but none of the proposals are worth losing you."

"What would you lose by getting rid of me?"

Mavrim walked over and picked up the holy script at the altar. "*KRenn Trange: His Birth and Death*," he read the title aloud. "You claim not to care about reuniting with your father, yet you worship his holy book about your grandfather."

"I only worship the gods."

"And the statue on the first floor," Mavrim pointed out.

"It represents the gods." FLip's puzzled look returned. "I don't understand the point of this conversation."

"I like that you have always been blunt, even with me."

"There's little reason to be anything else."

"For now," Mavrim hinted. "The reason I have not allowed you to be married yet is because I believe you might be what your father claims you to be."

FLip's blond eyebrows lifted. "If you believe I'm my grandfather reincarnated, then aren't you worried about the wrath of the gods?"

"No. Let the gods do what they want with me, and I will deal with them as I have dealt with so many others."

"That's a haughty attitude, even for a king."

Mavrim paced, holding his chin as if in thought even though he had every line planned. FLip was just like many of the other holymen Mavrim had dealt with. They were all predictable.

"If you prove to be blessed, as your grandfather was, then you will be of far more use to me than any marriage proposal I could ever be offered. I will use you to amass an even greater army, recruiting all the religious folk who blindly follow your father."

"Those are the same people who refused to fight for you against the Quims," FLip said.

"You don't need to remind me. I will always remember why you are here."

Before agreeing to the Analytes' demand for their aid, Mavrim had chosen to use his alliance with HSon Trange instead. However, HSon broke his promise. It was the reason FLip was in this castle.

HSon Trange was the most powerful of any lord, noble, or holyman. He did not possess a castle, however, only a church. But this church was different than the rest of the churches in the human kingdom. It was the church where KRenn Trange was born, the same church where he prayed. Even men like Mavrim, who did not believe in the gods anymore, still believed that KRenn was something more than a mere man. There was no other explanation for his power.

The Analytes looked at him in a different way. He was the one responsible for what they called in their language *Jaktius Perl*. As far as Mavrim knew, no humans were aware of the trouble in Analyte land except those sent as "farmers," who were really to be used as fodder. None would be returning here to tell the truth.

KRenn was a priest as well as an Ascendant. He passed the church to his son when it was time for KRenn to leave. HSon still controlled the church and had gained many more followers since KRenn disappeared. Even eleven years ago, before the battle against the Quims, HSon Trange had an army of religious folk at his disposal. Many would fight for him so long as it was the will of the gods.

When the Quims took control of Halin and the Tisary nearby, Mavrim needed more troops to ensure victory. A marriage had already been arranged between Mavrim's daughter and FLip, but the children were too young. The battle was going to begin before the marriage. The alliance had not yet begun between the families, but Mavrim didn't think that should matter. He requested troops from HSon.

His request was denied.

He vowed to punish HSon. As soon as Mavrim made it through the brief yet brutal war, he rode into HSon's land with his army behind him. The priest did not run. He did not hide. At least he had courage. The same could be said about his son.

FLip, a young boy at the time, had watched from the upper window of the church as his father came forward to meet the king. Many of the religious folk had taken up arms and gathered around the church, but HSon commanded that they drop their weapons. It would be a slaughter if they fought, just as the battle against the Quims had been.

Mavrim had challenged everyone who could hear him near the church, including the gods. "All of you refuse to fight for your king. Let's see what you will actually fight for."

He had ordered HSon to bring his son out of the church. HSon had refused. It had looked as if another battle would begin until FLip came out by his own volition. He had given his father one last look before getting in a carriage and being taken to the castle, where he'd stayed for more than eleven years now.

Many religious folk and holymen had come to the castle over the years to plead for FLip's release. All would leave yelling out the same phrases: They would pray for Mavrim to make the right decision. They would pray for FLip's release.

All these years had gone by, and their prayers had done nothing. There was no way to prove that the gods did not exist, but this was close enough to proof for Mavrim. He had taken FLip out of anger, kept him out of pride, then waited out of curiosity. The king's family had grown even more powerful during this time. None had fallen ill. They'd seen only good fortune.

He explained this to FLip. "You might be the very reason that my family will remain in power for centuries. If you are godly, then you'll continue to bless this castle with your presence. I will never let you leave. You will not marry. You will die here. And you will see my grandson crowned to rule his empire."

Mavrim had no grandson yet, but it was only a matter of time. Karlinda was still taken into Gavval's quarters frequently. She no longer put up a fight.

Mavrim felt a heavy heart for the woman who was once hailed as the most beautiful in the world but now appeared much older than her actual years. The beginning of his plan was almost set, but no part of it involved her and her innocent daughter. Their rescue would have to come later.

FLip's mouth twisted in a way Mavrim had yet to see before. It was anger, no doubt. The young man's face went red.

"I'm moving the statue of the gods," Mavrim told him. "It will be on the top floor of the castle from now on."

FLip's mouth dropped open. "I don't have access to that floor."

"So you will pray in the garden until something is figured out. Go there now."

"Why do this?" FLip asked as Mavrim was leaving.

"You will find out later. I will meet you in the garden. Wait there until I arrive."

CHAPTER TWENTY-SIX

It had been Mavrim's father's idea to keep Mavrim's skill with Artistry a secret. When Mavrim showed promise as a boy, his father made the Ascendant who came to train Mavrim swear an oath not to tell another person. Mavrim was horrified years later to find out that his instructor, a kind woman who had taught him everything he knew, had been beheaded. His father had ordered such a drastic measure as punishment after rumors came out about Mavrim's talent. The most bitter part in Mavrim's memory was how his father used the gruesome incident as a lesson.

"Kings have to be drastic," he had told Mavrim sternly. "Do you understand?"

As a mere teenage boy, Mavrim did not, and he told his father this along with a few choice words. He went to bed hungry that night and was not permitted to speak to his father until he could explain why kings must be drastic.

Mavrim didn't speak to his father for weeks, if his memory was correct. His father punished him in every way imaginable. He was to eat a disgusting dinner every night. The chicken liver stood out the most in his memory. It made him relieved to see mush the other nights. He was to do nothing but study with his tutor during the day, but just like Mavrim, she was not herself since the execution of the other "tutor." She had been told that the other tutor, who was strictly teaching Mavrim the subjects that were not in any books, had betrayed the king and that's why she was executed. But even if the tutor believed this, it did nothing to relax her. Her lessons were boring and ineffective because she was too worried she might teach something the king did not approve of and lose her own head.

During the night, Mavrim was to remain in his room and think about his father's lesson. Why do kings have to be drastic? He didn't care. His father was drastic, and he didn't want to be anything like his father.

What had happened to that goal? How had he forgotten it even though he had never forgiven his father? It seemed to happen all of a sudden—he had realized one day that he had done many drastic things. He had slaughtered thousands to gain control of the Tisary in Halin. He had stolen a young boy prophet who many saw as a god. He had killed so many people based on simple rumors that rebels were gathering.

He really was his father.

And now his family would send an army to destroy a group of people in Jatn because of another rumor. Not one person in his family or on his council cared about the inevitable damage to the city.

At least Mavrim did. He cared about many things now. It was only recently that he could feel proud of himself, for even a king must care about someone other than himself to feel pride. Otherwise, it could only be called arrogance.

He met FLip Trange in the garden after making sure everything else was ready. No one had questioned the king's command to move the statue of the gods to the highest floor in the castle. They had only asked how it was to be done. They would hoist it, of course, he'd told them. Some of the men had expressed concerns that the hoist itself might not hold. It was a risk the king was going to have to take.

The troop of religious folk should be at the gate soon. The king had sent a messenger for them. He would have to come up with a lie later to tell his council as to why he had summoned them, but that would be easy. Lying always was.

The most difficult part of his plan was using Artistry when it was time to begin. He couldn't help but think that all of his training had led to this moment. Even after his father had taken his Artistry tutor away from him, he had refused to give up. Much of the time he'd spent alone. When he was supposed to be learning how to be king, he was really learning how to be a mage. But no mage had been known to create a link strong enough to accomplish something like this.

Unless someone was an Ascendant, they didn't know that the most important part to forming a link was the initial bond. There was simply no way to create a strong link out of a weak bond. Fortunately, the religious boy had created quite a bond with the statue of the gods—the two gods sculpted into poses of peace. The god of life stood on the left, one palm turned up and extending out, the other hand resting at his side. The god of afterlife, to the right, mirrored the other's position. Both appeared purely focused, beckoning for something.

How FLip could bond with a statue was a mystery to Mavrim. It was made of stone. It was inanimate. It should bond better with another statue, or even with the walls of the castle around it. But the bond between it and young Trange was as solid as any bond Mavrim had ever felt. It even made him wonder at times if there was something more to the statue or to the prophet that Mavrim couldn't sense. He once thought the same about the wisdom tree, for it had bonded to all sorts of lifeforms over the years.

The bond between FLip and the statue of the gods was the only thing that Mavrim could use to get FLip out of the castle, for even Mavrim could not arrange an escape in which the teen would evade recapture. Besides, if Mavrim let the young man go, Mavrim's council would likely use FLip's release as the evidence they needed to finally unmake the king.

"What are we doing here?" FLip asked when Mavrim met him in the garden. He clearly knew that something was amiss, staying an extra step back from the king.

"Something is different about today," Mavrim mused. "Can you feel it?"

FLip glanced at the translucent bark of the wisdom tree. Nothing seemed to catch his attention, so he looked across the garden to the wall of the castle keep. Did he want to go back inside? Could he possibly want to remain here even after Mavrim's threats?

He didn't have that choice.

"It feels like any other day," said the so-called prophet.

"It isn't," Mavrim informed him. "There are plans in motion."

FLip raised an eyebrow.

"Not only mine," Mavrim said. "Everything will be different soon."

"Better or worse?"

"That depends on who you ask."

FLip made the same expression of confusion that was beginning to bother Mavrim. "Sire, I don't understand my role in this."

"You are to do nothing. That is your role! You will continue to do nothing. You were born into destiny, and I took that destiny for myself. I will now see it fulfilled, and so will you."

FLip's mouth twisted. "You play games with my emotions."

That was true, though it was not Mavrim's intent.

"Will there be more murder?"

"Murder?" Mavrim asked, surprised. "Such an accusation..."

"I meant killing. Death."

"I'm sure you did," Mavrim said sarcastically. "Yes, there will be death until everyone without power accepts their role, and those with power do not lust for more."

"There has not been such a day in history."

"No, and there never will be unless the gods themselves finally take action." Mavrim raised his voice so that his nearby guards could hear him. "This will be the last chance in my lifetime for the gods to prove themselves. What are they waiting for?"

"The gods do not wait, they test."

"A quote from one of your father's books, no doubt. Let me ask you this, then. What kind of test are they giving you?"

"A difficult one," the teen muttered.

"That's me testing you, FLip. You're mistaking the gods for your king."

He shook his head.

"You defy me?" Mavrim tested.

FLip's expression hardened. "I will not disagree with my beliefs. The gods test all of us, even kings."

"And I suppose you believe that I am failing their tests?"

It was a surprise to see FLip pause to think about this, just when Mavrim figured the young man's anger had gotten the better of him.

"I do not have the wisdom to answer that, but I believe that one day I will."

The statue began to lift. The king could feel the bond bending between it and the holyman. He poured his focus into the Artistry that made up this invisible link, wrapping his mind's hand around it like a casing.

FLip's eyes widened as he started to lift off the ground. "What?" he muttered.

Mavrim gritted his teeth, unable to speak as he put his strength into keeping the link strong. FLip jerked higher, then stopped midair. He flailed his feet as if expecting to land at any moment, but he did not come down.

"Holy spell!" FLip's legs relaxed. He looked down, then up. Then he stretched out his arms and set his gaze at the top of the wall in front of him. *Good, he's already embraced it.*

Mavrim could hear his armored guards running in from behind him. They blurted out comments of confusion about the flying holyman. FLip lifted higher, smoothly now. The men hoisting up the statue in the keep seemed to have found their rhythm.

Mavrim's legs shook. Keeping a link together was a balancing act of strength and precision. The statue was just inside the keep, but there was a wall between it and FLip. The link not only had to extend to make up the distance between them, it had to bend sharper through the doorway and windows because it would not go through stone.

Mavrim drew Artistry from the air, the ground, and even trace amounts from the people in his vicinity. He pushed the Artistry into every inch of the link, feeding it the power it needed so that it would not break. But this was still not enough. Mavrim held an extra layer of Artistry around the entire link. This exhausted him instantly.

He could feel the link bending drastically where it came out of a second-story window, so he patched it there with his mind as best he could. But he slipped up where the link was strongest, at the base of the keep where the door was open. It nearly broke before he swept his mind down and across the link, feeding more Artistry all around it.

"Archers are here, sire!" said one of the guards.

"Do not shoot!" Sweat burned Mavrim's eyes, but he had to look up. FLip was almost over the wall. The young holyman retained his godly pose, his arms out, his body relaxed.

The hardest part was now. Mavrim was too old to accomplish this. What was he thinking? He was an overconfident idiot. He always had been.

"Shoot him!" yelled the prince from one of the balconies behind Mavrim.

"Do not shoot!" Mavrim screamed, his voice hoarse from the strain.

"We need a healer for the king!" yelled someone else.

Mavrim was on his knees. He didn't remember falling. People began to mutter something around him as they put their hands on him. His vision was blurred. Everything was white.

He gave up trying to watch and just hoped FLip was high enough. The statue was only to be lifted, not to be moved horizontal in any way. That had to be all Mavrim.

The link shook violently as the king stretched it, pushing it against FLip's back in the air. Mavrim had to feed more Artistry into it to keep it together, but more broke off as the link threatened to shatter. Mavrim guided the breaking Artistry back into the link, repairing it almost as quickly as it was being destroyed.

He pushed FLip forward hard, for Mavrim was losing himself to fatigue and could not go much longer.

"He's over the wall!" the prince yelled. "Go after him!"

The link stretched so far, bending every which way. It came out of the castle keep like tendrils, arcing and twisting yet still attached. Letting FLip down would be easy if Mavrim could just get some air, a moment of strength. He gasped and panted as he let the natural pull of the earth stretch the link to its limit.

Suddenly it broke.

*****

Mavrim came to on the ground, his back on the cold grass. He felt hot and feverish, ready to slip back into whatever state of mind he'd just came from. He barely had the strength to open his eyes. His son looked down on him. The prince did not appear concerned.

"What are your orders?" he asked.

"What happened?" Mavrim replied weakly.

"I don't know how, but FLip flew over—"

Karlinda interrupted him. "We don't know what happened, sire. You seem to have fallen ill. We'd better get you in bed."

Was she the only one in this castle who still cared about him? And her daughter, Fyra, of course.

"I sent a hundred men after FLip," said Gavval. "But he has quite the start on them because a retinue of holy folk was outside the wall with horses ready. It's almost as if they knew what was going to happen."

So FLip got away, at least for now. "Bring him back here," Mavrim commanded, though his voice was only a whisper. "Send as many as it takes."

"But…" Gavval stopped himself.

But you already sent almost all the men we had available to Jatn, to destroy the rebels. You will need to gather the others from around the land. FLip will have enough time to reunite briefly with his father and recruit all the religious folk. But HSon will want to hide FLip somewhere and keep all the religious folk for himself.

All Mavrim could hope for was that FLip was not the same kind of man as his father. He had better not want to hide, or this was all for nothing. He should have a brief struggle for power with his father and soon win over the religious folk. Then he should take them to Jatn to meet the surviving rebels who would've surely fled the city by then.

Mavrim's robes were drenched with sweat. Blood streamed from his nose and reached his lips, where its metallic taste found its way to the tip of his tongue.

"You must take him to a healer," Karlinda said.

Mavrim could no longer keep his eyes open.

CHAPTER TWENTY-SEVEN

It was late by the time Darren arrived home after his meeting with Erisena. He had hoped his boys had eaten and gone to bed, but they were both in the kitchen with a lamp burning. They did not stand as Darren shut the door behind him. Even Leo showed no intention of giving him a hug.

There was something on the table, a scroll rolled out with the lamp on top. Darren had one just like it, from Erisena, rolled up in his pocket. He had been eager to read it to ensure it really was his identification papers, but there had been no light on the way back from the abandoned farm. He felt chills thinking back to how he'd stood before her growling beast in that dark barn, but these chills did not compare to the horrific feeling his children were giving him as they stared at him with deep sadness.

"What's this?" Darren asked and sat in the last empty chair. Neither boy answered. He took the lamp off the scroll and read aloud.

"By the law of the Farmers' Guild, the possession of this home will return to us in one week's time. Any belongings left..." Darren stopped himself. "What happened?" he asked Andar.

"Rhenol tried to set me up...so he could take my hand."

Andar spoke the words so calmly that Darren thought he had misunderstood at first. It had been a long night, Darren reminded himself. His boys had waited a while to speak with him. They had likely discussed the situation many times without him. It was the only reason they were calm.

"How did he set you up?" Darren asked.

"When you came to take me away from work earlier, Rhenol paid a mage to make a link between his gold vase and his gold plate, then he told me to wash his dishes."

"How did you know there was a link?"

"I could tell he wanted me to fail somehow, so I was on my guard. I felt something strange when I touched the gold plate. He showed up. I told him I knew what he was doing. I would not break it. But he tried to break it himself. He planned to claim that I did it and have my hand for it."

Darren knew that Andar would never have convinced Rhenol to change his mind once the plan was in place, so something else had happened.

He wants my boy's hand, but I shall take his before I leave.

Darren stood and put his hand on Andar's shoulder. "You did well to get out of there."

"Don't say that before you find out what happened. I had to carry the vase and plate with me toward the door to keep Rhenol from breaking them. He yelled that I was stealing, so I set them down and made a commotion for everyone to see. He couldn't claim I broke anything after that, and he couldn't claim I stole anything."

"But he claimed anyway that you were trying."

Andar seemed surprised. "How did you know?"

Darren sighed. "I know men like him. They all think the same way. Stand up."

Andar stood, and Darren wrapped his arms around his son. "You were on that farm far too long anyway."

Relief washed over Darren as Andar returned his embrace. He couldn't remember the last time his eldest had hugged him.

"But what will we do now?" Andar asked.

Leo stood and hugged Darren. "Andar says we have to leave."

Darren stepped away to look at the older boy. How did he know already that they would be leaving? Perhaps there was something more that he had yet to tell Darren.

"Don't tell me that you took revenge already, Andar."

"No, but I did...I have been...taking coin."

"Coin? How much? Were you caught?"

"I will tell you everything, Father, but I want to know everything as well."

"We both do," Leo added.

"Where were you tonight?" Andar asked, catching Darren off guard.

Darren looked at his two boys. Their world was so small. Here the three of them were, in this wretched house, in this corrupt city, soon to be without walls or roof. They were miserable. Darren had known this for a long time, but at least he could keep them alive and fed even if he did not know how to bring them happiness. Joining Erisena might give them joy and excitement, but it would also mean an early death for all three of them.

At least they had time to change cities and get to somewhere safe. Perhaps one day they could be happy.

The move had to happen now. They would be removed from their home anyway. Besides, Erisena had hinted that something would occur here soon. It was probably a battle for the Tisary.

Not just the Tisary, Darren realized. *It could be for all of Jatn.*

But were his boys really ready for the truth? Leo had just turned ten. Andar was thirteen. They were so young. Their lives had been so difficult compared to Darren's when he was their age.

But they were old enough to have secrets of their own, secrets they'd kept from their father. He couldn't expect them to trust him anymore if he did not give them the same courtesy.

"I was meeting with a woman named Erisena," he told them and motioned for them to sit. They obeyed silently. Darren took a breath. "She's an Analyte with a grudge against the king."

Andar seemed to know what this meant more than Leo, putting his palms on the table and leaning forward. "Why would you meet with someone like her?"

Leo showed his understanding then with a lean to mimic his brother. "And why does she have a grudge against the king?" he asked nervously.

The story they had read of Darren's family was certainly not lost on them. All this time he figured they would argue against him if he told them the truth, that they would opt to join Erisena's rebellion if it meant a different life than this one. Darren had figured they could not understand real danger, but perhaps they weren't as young and naive as he thought.

"Everything I'm going to tell you must not be spoken to anyone," Darren told them. "Not even Rygen. No one."

"What would happen if we did?" Leo asked.

"If the wrong person found out, all of us could be killed."

"Killed?" Leo repeated. "Just for talking?"

"The king has killed many people just for talking." Darren sat at the table with them and took each boy's hand. "But we are a family. We must trust each other with everything now." He looked straight at Andar. "Everything."

"Father, what are you getting involved in?"

"Nothing. Erisena has two things that belong to me. I have been trying to recover them without getting myself involved in her plans against the king. I have been successful in getting one so far."

"What things could she have taken from you?" Andar asked.

"It isn't quite like that." Darren removed the folded scroll from his pocket. "Remember that everything I'm telling you is not to be spoken to anyone."

He could see something in the eyes of both his sons. It was the same look they often had when speaking about the book that retold the story of their grandfather's strife with the king. They had known that book was special somehow, just as they knew this one scroll had something written on it that would change their lives.

Darren still hadn't looked at his identification papers, but he trusted Erisena. She'd been right when she told him that trust was all they had.

He unfolded it. His sons stared with wide eyes. Darren didn't know what to say, so he just watched the boys read his true name, DVend Quim, his true birthplace, the City of Halin, and his true father, DFaren Quim. They had seen Darren's false papers before and had asked to look again a few times throughout the years, obviously suspecting something. But Raenik had created the false papers to look identical to those that were authentic, even with a wax seal of the king at the bottom.

When Andar and Leo were done reading, they looked at Darren again. He couldn't tell what they were thinking behind their wide eyes, though they didn't seem shocked.

"Father?" Leo asked fearfully, as if the man in front of him might not be his flesh and blood anymore.

"Of course he is," Andar answered. "This doesn't change who *he* is to us. It changes who *we* are!" His eyes glistened as he stood. "I knew there was something more to our family! I knew it! All your secrets over the years, and it was this!" He began to weep, though Darren couldn't tell why. Andar didn't bother to hide his tears, but he did have trouble continuing. "You...you..."

"I'm sorry," Darren said. "I wanted to tell the two of you the truth, but you were too young. If anyone found out, you both would be imprisoned and I would be killed."

"And now?" Leo asked with a shaky voice, a tear falling down his cheek.

"Now no one will find out because we can trust each other to make sure of it." Darren ripped the paper into quarters, then held the pieces together over the lamp's flame.

Andar quickly fetched a metal bowl so Darren could drop the burning pieces into it. They watched his papers disintegrate, the only sound the soft crackle of the dying fire.

"So we are the Quims?" Andar asked, though it didn't quite sound like a question.

"Are you all right?" was all Darren could think to ask.

Andar nodded and smiled. He and Leo kept their thoughts to themselves as they stared at the ashes in the bowl.

"I knew there was something," Andar muttered again.

"Aye," Darren said. "I'm glad to finally get it out."

He expected hugs but both his boys stared at the ashes of his papers without moving.

Eventually Darren asked, "Andar, how much coin do you have?"

"About seven and five," Andar answered nonchalantly.

Seven and five? No, that was too much for a thirteen-year-old to have stolen, even for Andar.

"Do you know what you're saying?" Darren asked.

"I do," Andar said with a grin. "I know that's how men of business speak."

"You're saying you have seven gold coins and five silver ones," Darren informed him.

"Yes, I know. I have about that."

"Andar..." But he didn't know what else to say to his proud son. Obviously he had not been caught yet, or he would be missing his hands. He also clearly knew how dangerous this city could be. It was the only way he'd escaped from Rhenol this evening losing only their house.

"I suppose I'd better start trusting that you know what you're doing," Darren said, "but that doesn't mean I'm going to stop worrying."

Andar frowned. "You're not pleased with all the coin I've gained?"

"That depends on who you got it from."

"I would never steal from anyone who needs it. The rich don't know what it's like to be poor. I do. I don't care if I'm starving; I would never take anything from another family like ours."

He spoke of the poor and the rich as if they were at war. It was not a war, though. It was more that there was an absence of pity on both sides, yet it only mattered to one.

"The rich think they all deserve their good fortune." Andar clenched his hand into a tight fist. "Rhenol is no better or smarter than I am. He doesn't work harder than I do. The rich I stole from are just like him. They have time and coin that we don't have. I've watched them for years.

They enjoy wasting their coin! They spend it on clothing they don't need. They purchase sweets and toys!"

"Not all the rich are the same," Darren had to inform his child. "You are right about many of them, especially in this city. Your grandfather, however, was not at all like those men. He was born into wealth, but he understood what it was like to be poor because of his education. He helped those in need so long as he believed they deserved it. You must remember that not all the poor are like us, either. Good fortune or not, there are all kinds of people on both sides. If you have been thieving, then you may have seen other thieves. Many of them do not have your kind heart. They will steal from anyone. Some would even kill for a few copper if they knew they could get away with it. You can't expect the rich to understand all poor when there are men like that out there. If you're caught, you will be labeled as one of them—a thieving, potential murderer who needs to be behanded before he does more harm. There's nothing I can do to save you from that." Darren paused to let his words sink in. "Do you understand?"

Andar nodded.

"Good, then we can move on to our plan."

"You have one already?" Leo asked. "But you just found out about Andar's coin."

"Can we hear more about grandfather one day?" Andar asked.

"Yes, there will be time to answer all your questions about our history on the way to our new home. That is the plan, Leo. We are to leave Jatn."

"Isn't there some other way?" Leo asked, though he already sounded defeated, as if Andar must've helped him realize the truth earlier. There was nothing for them in this city anymore.

No, that wasn't true. Leo still had a life here. He had Rygen and the Bookbinding Guild. But Darren and Andar had nothing, and the three of them would soon have no home.

Darren could see Leo hurting and hoping at the same time, looking up with his large eyes. Darren thought through his options one last time. Besides leaving Leo here, alone, there was nothing, and Darren would never do that.

"Jatn will soon be a battlefield," Darren explained. "It's dangerous for us to stay here and wait for the battle, and there is no future for me or your brother afterward." He put his hand on Leo's shoulder. "We will find you work that you enjoy just as much as the Bookbinding Guild."

Leo looked down at his feet for a while before glancing up again. "Can Rygen and her mother come with us?"

"I was planning on speaking to Verona about that. I will have to lie about the reason we are moving. We are not supposed to know about rebels or a battle." Darren thought for a moment. "I will tell her that I think the city is dangerous because of the Tisary, which is true. But Leo, I doubt she and Rygen will come with us. We don't have the means for a horse and carriage for them, and neither do they."

"Are we spending all my coin on the trip?" Andar asked.

"Even all of that on its own won't be enough for the trip," Darren said. "But I have accumulated gold myself. I should've been paid more, but I had to take what I could get. We have enough for the trip to a new city, but the nights will be difficult once we get there. We don't have enough for a home. We'll have to figure out something, but we can do that after we arrive."

He waited to see what his boys thought of this news. They looked back at him as if ready for orders. It brought him pride.

"Now it's quite late," he said, "and there's much to do tomorrow. We should all be in bed already. I know the two of you must have many questions, but there will be plenty of time to talk during our travel." He gestured toward their room.

Neither Andar nor Leo moved. They looked to one another.

"What about this Analyte woman?" Andar asked Darren. "You haven't told us anything besides that she's…" He lowered his voice to a whisper. "A rebel of the king. How did she get your papers, and how did you get them back?"

"That is a long conversation."

"Please," Leo said. "We won't be able to sleep unless we find out."

If he told them the truth right now, they certainly wouldn't sleep a wink. But Darren doubted they would get much sleep tonight anyway, with how their curious minds worked. He had already decided to trust them with everything. They deserved to know what he had discovered when he'd tested them earlier today.

He let out a sigh, for he was so very tired. Hungry as well, his stomach grumbling. Andar surprised him by taking a large loaf of bread out from one of the cupboards. He set it on the table. Darren's guilt kept him from eating for a moment, even as he began to salivate.

"We know you have been working hard, Father," Andar said as he ripped the bread in half. "You haven't taken a moment for yourself for years. It's all been for us. But now I want to do the same."

Darren had to hold back a tear. No thirteen-year-old boy should have to take on such a responsibility.

"You are too young for that," he said. But Darren had to be honest. Where would they be right now without Andar's help? Even with it, they would soon be without a home and with just enough money for the trip, nothing more. Darren was certain his children would be stick-thin if Andar had never contributed to their meals. At least now they had their health as well as a chance for a decent life in another city.

"I know," Andar agreed. "But it can't be helped." He regained his proud smile, biting into the half of bread he looked ready to share with Leo.

But Leo was staring down at the table as if looking hard enough could make him turn invisible.

"Leo," Darren said, and waited for his youngest to look up. Darren put on a smile. "You have done more than any boy should have to. The two of you are much stronger than I was at your age."

"Stronger than you?" Leo asked in disbelief.

"In more ways than you know." Darren took a breath. "Which Erisena figured out before I did. I confirmed it with the test earlier today. The two of you have a connection to Artistry." He stopped. He wanted to tell them of the link developing between them, but he didn't know enough about links between children to know if it might be dangerous to let them know. Being young mages made them a danger to themselves already. To be linked to another mage at this age was not something Darren had heard of.

His sister surely knew more than he did. She was the last thing he needed from the city before he left, the last facet of how Erisena could help him.

"I knew it was Artistry!" Andar said triumphantly.

"But remember, this ability doesn't make you better than any other hard-working man or child," Darren reminded them. "In fact, you and Leo will face more challenges because of it, at least while you're young."

He wasn't sure Andar heard him by the way he was smiling. "Will you train us how to use Artistry?"

"I will tell you what I know, but I have no skill myself."

"What about the sword?" Leo asked. "Are you as good as they say?"

Darren raised an eyebrow. "Are you more interested in the sword than you are Artistry?"

Leo perked up. "Do I have a choice?"

"I hope so. I vow to do everything I can to give both of you every option available, but I'm going to need help. My sister—your aunt—is somewhere in the city. I have to find her before we leave."

"How do you know she's here?" Andar asked.

"She authored the book you read on our family history. She used an anagram, which I believe she did so I might figure out she was here. I've looked for her ever since, but I haven't been able to locate her. Erisena claims to know exactly where she is. Tomorrow I will find out."

"What's an anagram?" Leo asked.

"It's a phrase made from rearranging letters," Darren explained. "Your aunt's name is Yune Quim, although I don't know what she goes by in the city. Do you remember the name of the author?"

"Miqu Yenu," Leo said. His eyes lifted to the corner of the room. "Quim...Yune. I get it."

Andar jumped up and shoved out his arm. "Look, my hairs are standing! This is all incredible. What did Mother think of all of this?"

Darren did not share the same excitement. "She and I agreed on hiding all of this from the two of you until you were older." *I hope she would say I'm making the right choice now by telling them.*

Darren still wasn't sure, for Andar had shown a level of enthusiasm that Darren had not predicted. It was not concerning on its own, but enthusiasm tended to cloud one's judgement, especially when it competed with caution.

"So Mother is not Larena Litxer?" Andar asked.

"That's not her birth name, no."

"She's Farinda Quim, from the story," Andar realized.

"Yes, but her name or history does not change how much she cared for you and Leo, and it does not change what happened to her in this wretched city." Darren's emotions were getting the better of him, so he took a breath to stifle them. "She still became ill, and there were plenty of doctors who had the medicine she needed to live. But none of them would help us. I begged all of them, including everyone who had a coin to spare. She died needlessly. Had I come into contact with a man like my father, I'm sure she would still be alive today. But not a single person in this city would help."

The three of them shared a moment of silence.

Andar had a dark look about him as he glanced up. "I want to take revenge against the evil in this city. There must be something we can do before we leave."

"What about the rebels?" Leo asked. "Did you call their leader Erisena?"

"Yes, that is her name."

"She wants all of us to join her, doesn't she?" Leo asked. "It's why Andar and I were followed."

Shock came across Andar's face. "You're right!" he said too loudly. "She doesn't just want you, Father. She knows—"

Darren gestured for him to keep his voice down.

"She knows Leo and I will be strong one day," Andar continued in a whisper. "We should join her. It's the only way to really fight."

Darren shook his head. "Let me explain why that is a bad decision. We expect right to win over wrong. We expect goodhearted leaders to beat those with greed. We expect our family to overcome illness. But the two of you are old enough now to hear the truth. I hope you never have to learn this through experience, for it takes being beaten down again and again before many realize it, which is why you must believe me now: The only person that you can trust is yourself and your family." He could see that he was scaring his children, but it was important that he make his point. "We have to be there for each other, just as we have to be there for ourselves at times. If we stay here and join Erisena, we will die with them."

"How do you know?" Andar asked fearfully.

"The king kills rebels. It's how such a heartless man like him is still king. If I know Mavrim as well as I think I do, then there's already an army on the way here. The king does not care about the destruction that such a battle will cause to the city. He would destroy all of us and our homes just to kill some rebels." *And to obtain the Tisary.* But that was another conversation, and it was far too late.

Darren stood. "There's no reason to be afraid. You two will be safe with me, but we must leave the city. Do you understand that now, Leo?"

He nodded. "I hope Rygen can come."

"I will do everything I can." Darren really would, but he was nearly certain that the five of them leaving together would not be in anyone's best interest, except the two youngest.

"When do we leave?" Andar asked.

"Hopefully everything will be ready by tomorrow evening. I will be up early. The two of you can stay here and sleep until you've rested enough. Andar, will you trust me with your coin now?" Darren let out his palm.

Andar didn't hesitate as he drew a coin purse from his pocket and handed it to Darren.

Darren closed his hand around the full purse. He gave his son a proud smile.

Andar stepped in and swung his arms around his father. "Thank you."

Darren didn't know what he was being thanked for, but he patted his son's head. "Of course." They separated so Darren could take out a silver coin. He gave it to Andar. "When you wake up, buy something to eat for you and Leo, whatever you'd like. I will be out looking for a horse and carriage to purchase at a good price. Then I will find out from Erisena where my sister is."

"What do you have to give her for that information?" Andar asked.

"My final answer."

"That's it? That doesn't seem like a fair trade for her."

"People like Erisena aren't concerned about fair in circumstances like these. They take what they can get."

"But what have you even given her?" Andar asked.

"Nothing, because there's nothing I can give her."

There was a long silence. Darren could feel his children's empathy for this Analyte woman, but nothing could be done to help her without putting them all in danger.

"Get to bed," Darren said. "Try not to let your thoughts distract you tonight. You can give them their due time tomorrow." He escorted his children to their bedroom. They were too old to be tucked in, but he didn't trust them to fall asleep anytime soon after everything they'd learned. So he stayed and straightened out their one cover each, ensuring both boys were as comfortable as they could be. Neither of them spoke until Darren had started to close their door behind him.

"I know what we can give Erisena," Leo called out.

Darren stepped back into the room. "What's that?"

"A promise."

"What kind of promise?"

"That we will join her one day."

"I agree," Andar said. "We will be ready one day, Father."

Darren put up his hands. "Just wait a moment. We have not decided as a family that we will be joining rebels, even if we wait years to do so. That is not a decision any of us are capable of making right now. And promises like that are currency between people like us and Erisena. You would not promise coin that you might never pay, so you shouldn't make such a claim that you might never keep."

"But I want to keep that promise," Leo said. "And I know Andar does as well."

Andar sat up. "I do. How else are we supposed to change anything in this world without someone like Erisena?"

"We will find our own way," Darren said, but his children didn't seem to accept it. Leo sat up as well. It was too dark to make out anything but their silhouettes.

Darren sighed. He could trust his children with information, but they were still too young to understand that many good-natured wishes were only fantasies. There was no way in this moment that he could make them see that. So he supposed he had to indulge them, at least slightly.

"One day we might find another group who— depending on the circumstances—might share the same goals that we do...at the time. But I'm not promising anything in this moment to you or to Erisena, except that I'm going to keep us safe. All right?"

"Agreed," Andar said, lying back down.

Leo took an extra moment. "Agreed," he eventually said.

Finally they were both in their beds and Darren had the door closed. He stayed there for a moment, his ear to the door.

He could hear both boys getting out of bed, whispering and laughing. They sounded excited, their feet pattering as if they might even be dancing.

Darren walked away and let out his breath. He supposed they could stay up as long as they wanted tonight after all. There was nothing they needed to do in the morning. The responsibility was all on him to get them out of the city, so he'd better get some rest.

CHAPTER TWENTY-EIGHT

Leo hoped his brother had not awoken yet. It was early in the morning, no sunlight coming through the slit in their window. Leo tried to sit up quietly, but he must've made a sound, for Andar awoke immediately and sat up.

"You're getting up already?"

"I want to go to the Bookbinding Guild, for work, in case we don't leave after all."

"You mean you want to see Rygen."

There was no point in lying. "That, too."

"Are you going to tell her even though Father told you not to?" Leo didn't detect any judgment in his brother's voice.

"I don't think so."

"Let Father speak with her mother later." Andar stared across the small room as he waited for Leo to answer. He spoke again. "Everything we do now could be dangerous."

"I know."

"So you won't say anything about us leaving?"

"I won't." Leo tossed off his covers and started to get dressed.

Andar hopped out of bed. "I'll get us some breakfast." He threw on some pants and a coat, and was headed out before Leo had even finished getting his clothes on completely.

"Wait, I'll go with you."

"But then..." Andar thought for a moment. "I plan to take some food and belongings."

"We have coin."

"Yes, but we need to save all that we can. We'll be leaving the city soon, so now is the best time to steal from the rich."

It sounded to Leo as if there was something in particular Andar had in mind, but he knew better than to ask. He would rather not know what Andar had planned because he wouldn't be able to convince his brother to change his mind. All finding out would do would make Leo nervous, and he already had enough to worry about with the possibility of leaving Rygen behind.

"I'll be back soon with food," Andar said as he left. "Don't figure out too much about Artistry without me!" he teased.

Leo grinned. He looked forward to a time when he and his brother could focus on what they could do with Artistry, but they had already tried last night when they were supposed to be sleeping. Nothing had come out of it, and Leo was too exhausted to try again. Now was not the time anyway. He made his bed, then he lay on top of it and shut his eyes.

Just as he was starting to fall asleep, he realized something that caused him to bolt upright. Andar was probably truthful in that he had his eye on many things he wanted to take before leaving the city, but there was something obvious to Leo that Andar wanted more than anything. He waited nervously for his brother to return.

As soon as Andar opened the door, Leo told him, "Promise me that you are not going to try to take revenge before we leave."

Andar seemed indifferent to the request as he looked at Leo for a long while. "Of course not," he said. "My revenge will come, but it will not be soon."

Leo worked beside Rygen all morning after breakfast, but he wasn't himself. There was nothing he could concentrate on beside Rygen. She had to repeat herself many times as she instructed him, all the while Leo noticing things about her face he hadn't taken the time to realize in the past. If he'd been asked to describe Rygen, he might've said she had a small nose. She didn't, in fact. It wasn't large, but it certainly wasn't small. If Leo was asked to draw a nose, he would ask to look at Rygen's. It seemed as if everything about it was exactly as a normal nose should be.

Her eyes were certainly large, though. No one could argue against that. There was always a lot of light in the Bookbinding Guild, her gray eyes seeming to capture it and shimmer. She glanced around as she spoke, but she stared at Leo when it was time for him to mimic what he had seen. Her gaze seemed weighted, pressing down upon him so hard he could barely act. He was incredibly aware of every motion he made. He tried to move smoothly so as to impress her, but he seemed to be more stiff and clumsy as the day went on.

Her lips were the most distracting. They looked so soft—the way they moved as she spoke, or when she frowned at his mistakes.

Gartel gave them a break for a midday meal. Leo was happy to be fed with the rest of the workers now that he had progressed past parchment making. He ate silently beside Rygen at their table, just the two of them. He didn't know how he was going to make it the rest of the day without telling her that he was leaving, the guilt eating him away.

"Did I do something to upset you?" Rygen asked quite suddenly after they had resumed their work.

"No. I just didn't get much sleep."

"Why not?"

Because my family is leaving tomorrow, and we will probably never see each other again. "I don't know."

"Leo," she said. "I know when something is wrong. Is it your father or brother?"

He took a moment. There really was no chance of making it through the day with his secret intact. He might as well just get it out.

He whispered, "My father says we need to leave Jatn. There is danger coming to the city."

Rygen took a moment to glance around. Her lifted eyebrows made her appear more confused than anything else as she glanced back. "Why are you whispering about this? If there's danger, shouldn't everyone know?"

Leo shouldn't have opened his mouth. To know about rebels without telling the guards could mean a trip to the dungeons. He shouldn't put Rygen in that same jeopardy. He would have to think of something else to say.

"My father won't say more yet, I think because it's dangerous to even speak about it. That's why I'm whispering. He's going to stop by your house tonight to speak with your mother about coming with us." Leo looked deep into his friend's eyes. "I don't want to go, especially if you can't come with us, but I have to."

Rygen appeared too shocked to reply. She didn't take her eyes off Leo, the color draining from her face.

"This is one of those times we read about, isn't it?" she asked. "A time when everything could change."

"I think the change is already happening." He stopped even pretending to work, setting down the thread in his hand. "It's up to us to decide our path."

Rygen took a long while to think, while Leo's own thoughts distracted him. He remembered just a short time ago when becoming a bookbinder had been everything to him. Now it seemed mundane. Sure it was better than the backbreaking work on the farm, but there was so much more to life. One day he might be an Ascendant. Or perhaps a swordsman, like his father. Maybe even both? He certainly wouldn't be stuck in a wretched city like this one. He would be a hero on a mountaintop, looking down at a city like Jatn and plotting how he would fix the problems of the deserving. He was young still, but he would grow up fast. His father and brother would help him.

Leo remembered his promise to Rygen that felt as if he'd made so long ago. He had been too afraid to help her when Erisena's beast had been rummaging around outside her home. He was already much stronger now than he'd been then, even skilled with a blade, which his father had confirmed. Leaving Rygen behind would mean never fulfilling that promise to protect her the next time she was in danger, and danger was coming now.

Leo felt a cold sweat on his forehead. He looked around the Bookbinding Guild, at all the workers. He was wasting himself here. If it wasn't for Rygen, he would've left this place in that instant to be with his brother.

"How does your father know of the danger?" Rygen asked. "He must've at least told you something."

Leo had had enough time during her silence to prepare an answer for that. "The discovery of the Tisary. Remember what happened in Halin?"

"But that is unlikely to endanger people like us, who stay away from the Tisary. It's on the outskirts of the city."

"I can't answer that myself, but I do trust my father. He knows these types of things well."

"Perhaps, or perhaps it's just his protective nature that makes him overly cautious."

"Rygen, there is something coming. I can feel it."

Leo worried for a moment that she would brush it off, but she didn't divert from his gaze.

She took a slow breath. "I think I feel it also. But my mother and I don't have the means to leave. We don't have any coin to spare."

"My family might have enough for all of us to make it to another city."

"How is that possible?"

"Through great difficulty," was all Leo could say.

He was glad when she didn't pry.

"Then I guess all we can do is wait for your father to speak to my mother tonight?"

Leo nodded. "We'd better get back to our task."

They worked for a little while, Rygen halfheartedly showing Leo what to do. Neither of them seemed to have any interest anymore.

Eventually she asked, "Are you completely certain your family is leaving?"

He supposed there was the tiniest chance that something drastic could happen to change Darren's mind, but it didn't seem likely. His father was not a capricious man.

Just then, he noticed his father enter the Bookbinding Guild. Darren made a straight line for Leo, his gaze diverting briefly to Rygen for a quick nod when he was close.

"I need to borrow my son for a moment," Darren told Rygen.

She nodded stiffly.

Gartel came running down the stairs as Leo started to follow his father toward the door. "Leo, if you leave with him again today—"

"We're only going to be speaking right here," Darren interrupted. His deep voice held great power. Leo immediately felt safe near his father, only then realizing how scared he was with everything happening. "We just need a moment, Gartel."

Darren stared at Gartel until the bookbinding guild master turned away with a bit of a huff.

Leo's father crouched down to meet Leo's eye level. "I have secured everything we need for the trip. Our horse and carriage will stay safe with the seller until tomorrow morning. That's when we leave. That way we won't have to start our journey during the night."

"All right," Leo said with forced courage. He looked over at Rygen to find her staring back at them. "I couldn't help but tell her that we're leaving."

"Leo..."

"I'm sorry." He recited what he had revealed, hoping he hadn't said too much. He knew it was better to tell his father, though.

When Leo had finished, his father didn't seem too displeased, glancing over at Rygen.

Nonetheless, Leo apologized again.

"It's fine," Darren said. "I will speak with her mother tonight. It will be a long and uncomfortable ride with all of us in the carriage, but I did purchase one large enough to fit us all. I believe I might be able to convince Verona after all."

Leo hopped with joy. "Thank you!"

His father did not smile. "There will be tough times ahead of us. It will be even harder with Rygen and her mother coming, but having people we can trust will one day prove more valuable than any amount of coin." He took a breath, then mumbled, "At least I hope so."

"It will, Father." Leo hugged him.

During their embrace, Darren said, "Now I have to speak to Erisena so I can find your aunt. She'll be coming with us as well. Is Andar at home?"

"He was when I left this morning, but I don't know what he's doing now."

Darren frowned. "I think we both know what he's doing."

Leo nodded. "Should I try to find him?"

"No, just be home in the evening and try to have supper ready. Can you do that?" He gave Leo a silver coin.

"I can."

"Good. I might be very late."

"All right, Father."

Darren stood and walked out the door. Leo almost called out to him. He wanted to tell his father that he loved him, perhaps share one more embrace.

He felt empty when he was standing there alone, having not done either. Why? What was he afraid was going to happen?

Leo ignored the feeling as he returned to Rygen and told her the good news.

CHAPTER TWENTY-NINE

The moment Darren stepped foot on the deserted farm, he was reminded of the unforgiving destruction of those who held power. So many workers had died here, when all they'd wanted was fair pay for their labor. If Darren was right, the king's army was already on its way. Another blemish in history, a red scar across the timeline of the kingdom. And it wouldn't be the last.

He went to the rundown barn where he had encountered Erisena's beast of a pet the last time. He was surprised to find her already there.

She showed him a smile. "I thought you would come." She wore a hood that hid the violet tint of her hair, though a loose silvery strand blew around her neck in the wind. She moved it behind her ear.

"I would've expected you to have sent someone else here in your stead," Darren told her. "Don't you have better things to do than meet with me?"

"That depends on the news you're about to tell me."

He showed her his answer with a look. Her face fell.

"I'm sorry," he said. "It's just too dangerous for my family. But I must thank you for giving me my papers. With them now destroyed, I can leave the city without fear of my identity catching up with me. I was even able to tell my sons everything. We will be leaving Jatn soon, and I think you should as well. Take your rebels elsewhere. This is not the place to be right now with the discovery of the Tisary."

She had folded her arms and appeared impatient for him to finish, so he stopped himself from saying more.

"The king is not my priority," she informed Darren. "Although he needs to be replaced in the near future, the issue I intend to resolve is not even in his kingdom. Not yet, at least." She dropped her folded arms. "Let me explain something to you. Your children have an ability you might not have picked up on yet." Erisena paused and stared for several heartbeats.

She knows about the link? He made sure his unchanging expression would not reveal his thoughts.

"Do you know already?" Erisena asked.

If he couldn't trust this woman, who seemed to know everything that could put his family in prison, he supposed he couldn't trust anyone. In fact, she was probably the only person he knew of who might be able to provide some guidance about his sons' abilities.

"I know of their link, yes."

"Then you know how dangerous it can become."

"I do, but the dangers of Artistry are what I think of as 'future' dangers for them. There are more immediate risks I'm concerned about."

"Your children will be taken care of if you allow them to join us. They will be safe, Darren, at least until they are grown enough to make their own decisions on how to use their power."

"Yes, because I will make sure of that."

She turned her head and looked at him sideways, as if she couldn't stand to meet his gaze anymore. "You have such little confidence in me."

"Because I don't know you, Erisena. But I do know myself. I won't let any harm come to them."

"You are not *equipped* to protect them from every danger. They will be mages one day, and you are not one. Remember my sister? Had she had any training, she would not have died. I don't want to see the same thing happen to your children. All it takes is one wrong link with no other mage there to break it."

"I know you speak the truth about that future danger, but it doesn't change the fact that my family must leave this city now. Perhaps if you were planning to leave as well, I could reconsider your offer. But it sounds to me that you plan to stay here and fight for the Tisary. That is not a battle my family is ready for."

"Your children are not ready for that, I agree. But *you* will be as soon as the rest of us are. Let me keep the three of you where you will be safe. I have the means to do so. When it is time to fight, only you will join us. Your children will remain safe as they grow and train."

Darren took a moment to choose his words, for he didn't have the time to keep bickering. "I want to care about replacing the king as much as you do. I want to care about this issue in the Analyte kingdom as much as you do. I want to care about the lives of your rebels. But none of those issues are nearly as important to me as my children. I don't trust anyone else right now to take care of them as well as I can, so I cannot risk my life to fight for you, even if they will be safe." He took a breath to collect himself. "Besides, we both know that anyone who joins the rebels is not safe, no matter where they hide. History has proven that." He didn't pause to let her reply. "I came here for only one thing, Erisena. I need to know where my sister is. Where is Yune?"

Erisena let out a sigh. "I want to tell you, but you have offered me nothing."

Darren's voice was tinged with guilt. "I wish I could give you more."

"You can. All you have to do is stand with us. You alone, Darren. If everything goes according to plan, there will be very little fighting. No death on either side. My plan is not one of war. It's of peace. There will be destruction in our lifetime unless we do something about it."

You are the one starting a chain of events that will lead to destruction. "What kind of destruction are you speaking of?"

"Of everything."

Erisena did not specify, only stared back at him.

"Everything?" Darren repeated.

"Yes. KRenn Trange did not die. He disappeared after he made a terrible mistake in the land where I come from. He caused something...an unbalance. It's growing. My king does everything he can to slow it, but it's not working. Your king knows of this."

"Don't call him my king."

"*Mavrim* knows of this," she corrected herself. "But he doesn't take action. The humans need a king who will. Your father would've been that man. He's gone, but you can still do something."

He ignored her implication that he would lead even a single man.

"What kind of unbalance?" Darren asked.

"That's what the master Ascendants there are trying to figure out. There is still time, but everyone who can help must do so. I would not spend this much time recruiting anyone else but you and your family because I know that all of you are the key to this."

"You can't possibly know that." It sounded like a speech she gave to anyone with a hint of power. The men and women she recruited were all made to believe that they were necessary to the success of the rebels. That's the only way some of them would risk their lives to join, for they believed everyone would die without them. The rest had joined simply because they were out of options, but Darren still had one for his family. He would take his sons and get out of Jatn.

"All the mages we have are much older than your boys," Erisena continued. "They've already learned how to control Artistry. But these mages have habits in Artistry manipulation that will not change. Andar and Leo are different. They are young, malleable, and they have something the other Ascendants don't. This link. They are key," she repeated. "Key."

Darren wouldn't let himself be convinced no matter how hard Erisena tried, but he did wonder something. How had she found out about the link between them? Had she or any of her rebels spent time close to Leo and Andar?

Her continued speech distracted him. "They will be taught to control not just Artistry but how to open and close rifts. One of them may even step into another realm one day and find the solution all of us are waiting for. And you, DVend, will be at their side defending them with your sword and your wisdom. You were beside your father throughout everything that happened in Halin. I know you learned much from the right choices he made and even more from his wrong ones. You will be invaluable to us."

Darren put up his hands. "I've already made up my mind. I'm sorry, Erisena. I truly am. But I don't have much time left. Please tell me where my sister is."

Erisena gave a great sigh. "Fine. She will be visiting your home tonight. I was going to have her do that no matter how you answered."

"Has she joined you?"

"Not exactly. I don't have much time left, either, and I'm sure she'll tell you everything." Erisena put her hand on his shoulder. "It would be a waste for me to tell you now to take care of your family, so all I'm going to say is that you should consider, as your father would have, that there is more in this realm than just the Quims."

"My father had the means to consider such things. I do not."

She still would not take her hand off him. "You will one day."

He removed her hand for her. "If so, then that is when I will find you."

She nodded and even showed a half smile. "Good."

Darren's keen sense of hearing picked up a woman shouting. Her words were yelled from too far away to understand, but there was no mistaking the tone. Darren took note of Erisena's position near the backside of the barn. She was vulnerable with her back to the opening.

He ran toward the opening behind Erisena. Two archers, arrows loaded, stepped into the walkway. There was no way to stop both of them.

The gaze of one archer didn't stray from Darren, so he went for the other, who had his sights on Erisena. Darren jumped and kicked the bow as the man shot at her. The arrow broke against the wall. Darren grabbed the man by his shoulders as he dropped his bow and tried to reach for the dagger on his belt. Darren drove him stumbling backward toward the other archer, who was trying to line up a shot around his comrade.

To Darren's surprise, the archer released. The arrow broke through the other man's shoulder as he screamed. He fell forward too strongly for Darren to keep hold. Darren ran for the archer trying to load another arrow, who quickly gave up and turned to flee, but Darren dove on top of him.

Other details had only now come to register in Darren's mind. These men had the sigil of the Orello family on their armor: a complex series of diamonds that Darren could draw from memory, for he had seen it too many times in his nightmares.

The king would never have sent only two soldiers. There were always hundreds, if not thousands, to follow.

"Someone betrayed me!" Erisena called out from just behind Darren. He looked over his shoulder at her as he pinned one man beneath him. She was pulling her dagger out of the other archer's chest, completely unaffected by his gurgling scream.

There was no time to question the archer beneath Darren as to who'd betrayed Erisena. A line of thirty archers had appeared over one hill. Their commanding officer ordered them to fire.

Erisena had the same idea as Darren, the two of them running back into the barn. Arrows pattered against the ceiling, many bringing down chunks of its rotten wood around their feet. The two soldiers who had attempted to assassinate Erisena by surprise hollered as the blanket of arrows fell upon them. Darren took Erisena to the ground and bent over her head. He protected his own with his hands as best he could, but something struck him in the back. He took the blow with stiffened muscles and felt nothing for the moment.

The rain of arrows came to a stop. Darren pulled Erisena to her feet and ran with her out the other side of the barn. The soldiers had come from the northwest, from outside the city. There was no way they had already captured Jatn. Darren should be able to get to his boys before anyone else saw him with the leader of the rebels.

Arrows fell down around them as they exited the barn. A quick look back showed archers rushing over the hills of the farm.

"This way," Darren said as he turned to lead Erisena to a rundown stable for cover. One wall was missing a few planks as if someone had come to loot some of the wood.

This was the only wall they could hide behind where no archers seemed to have a clear shot, but there was nowhere to go from here.

"Where are your guards who I heard shout—?"

Darren's question was answered by an explosion. There was an Ascendant among Erisena's guards.

"Only one guard," Erisena told Darren. "I did not think I would need more."

"Where is she?" Darren asked, knowing exactly who was out there somewhere.

A patter of arrows fell around them.

"Get down," Darren said as he resumed the same position over Erisena as in the barn.

The swarm of arrows cracked against the stable as Lane Writhe crashed into Darren in her wild attempt to take cover.

"There's too many," she said, out of breath. "We have to run for the city."

"There's no path," Darren told her. "Where are the reinforcements?"

"We have none here...at the moment." Lane gave a knowing look at Erisena that was lost on Darren.

"No," Erisena told Lane. "It would be a waste."

"They have almost closed us in!" Lane said through gritted teeth. This was not the same woman who Darren had seen in the caverns. Panic had taken over. It was the most dangerous emotion in battle, worse than fear. Nothing spread faster.

"No!" Erisena told Lane again, a tremor in her voice.

They have not seen battle before, Darren realized. *They have not held their own survival in their hands, until now.*

"We are going to die here," Lane seemed to be telling Erisena, though Darren wasn't paying attention to their conversation. He went around the stables for a look from the other side as arrows beat against the roof while more arrows buried themselves into the grass.

He took a risk poking his head out, but he had to see who would soon be behind them. He lost his breath for a moment. It could've been half of the entire army of the king marching over the northwestern hills. Knowing Mavrim, the other half was already moving through the city to cut off all routes of escape. Rebels like Erisena had to be killed as soon as they were found. None could escape.

Darren went back to the other side of the stable where the two women were quiet as they watched him.

"There is no safe route into the city from here," Darren said. "So we'll just have to run, and run fast." He kicked into the broken wall of the stable several times until he loosened a plank of wood he could rip off. He gave it to Erisena.

"They're coming for us now," Lane told him as he worked on freeing another plank for her.

"There's time," he said, remembering how far the approaching army was from them. *And the closer the soldiers are, the fewer arrows will be shot at us.*

He gave Lane her makeshift shield, then kicked and ripped away the tallest plank for himself.

Normally he would tell his fellow soldiers to keep him between them and the archers as they ran, but these were not his fellow soldiers. They were two women who had gotten themselves into this mess, and Darren as well.

He had his children to look after, which he couldn't do if he was dead.

"Keep up!" he said as he sprinted out from the stables. The city wasn't far from here, but hundreds of soldiers knew it was Darren's destination. They had already begun the race there. The rest of the army made a beeline for Darren and the two women. There were easily over a thousand, all in stiff armor of leather with swords in hand. They would be slower, at least.

Darren looked over his shoulder to find with dismay that Erisena and Lane were not as quick as he was. "Straighten your shields!" he commanded, for both were letting the planks of wood tilt too far forward. Two arrows nearly missed Erisena in just the short time that Darren watched her. She was their target. Perhaps a little distance from her was prudent.

He heard a crack and a scream. He slid to a stop and turned around. Lane was already getting back on her feet, picking up her shoddy shield that now had an arrow stuck through it.

Darren knew he shouldn't wait for her or even Erisena to catch up, but he couldn't leave them, at least not yet. He ran back and gave Lane cover until she was ready to move. An arrow flew over their heads. Others landed short. One struck Darren's makeshift shield but did not stick.

The race to the city was back on. Soldiers closed in. Soon the fence that marked the end of the abandoned farm was just ahead, but they might not make it without an engagement.

They needed another fireball from Lane, but there was no fire for her to use close by. She must've come from the city, for there was a roaring blaze atop a pile of wood she must've set. The soldiers were closer to it than

Darren's small party was, but using it was the only way they could get the lead they needed to escape this pursuit.

"How close do you need to be to the fire to use it?" Darren asked Lane, already veering toward the flames.

"Very," she yelled from behind him.

Darren examined the lead soldiers. A dozen or so had pulled ahead of the rest, these men with no armor to slow them down. They only seemed to have daggers. A commander behind them was now close enough for Darren to hear his shouts.

"Cut them off! The Analyte is not to reach the city!"

Many of the men sneered as they saw Darren head straight for them. He tilted the plank of wood that was his shield, shifting his hold so he could throw it like a spear. It bounced off the chest of the foremost soldier and flew into the air. Darren got low and hoisted up the next charging man, throwing him backward, then he took a moment to look for the plank. He sprinted for it as it came down, jumping to kick both boot heels into another soldier trying to stab him.

He caught the plank from the ground and used it to block a downward thrusting dagger. He swept the legs out from his attacker and finally had a weapon, ripping the dagger out of the weaker man's hold.

He figured he had given Lane enough time. "Now!" he yelled to her as he ran away from the battle.

An enormous fist, hot as coal, punched him in the lower back and lifted him into the air. His limbs flailed out of control for just a moment until he composed himself. He would not lose this dagger, keeping a firm hold as he came down to the ground fast and hard.

He rolled and sprang back to his feet. He found the two women to be near him again as the three of them sprinted toward the city, a fire raging behind them.

A look over Darren's shoulder showed that there was some distance now between them and the rest of the soldiers, many of whom lay on the ground defeated by Lane's blast, a large patch of scorched grass beneath them. There was no way to know whether they stayed down because of injury or death, but that did not matter anymore. Whether Darren turned around and surrendered or killed a dozen more, he would still be hung if caught.

"I need to go south for my boys," he told Erisena when the outer homes of Jatn were behind them. "What is your evacuation plan?"

"Are you coming with us?" Erisena asked.

"It depends on your plan." He didn't yet trust Erisena to lead anyone to safety, let alone him and his boys.

"The rest should already be grouped," she said. "They'll move toward the edge of the city that's least protected and wait for us. That should be the east."

"Mavrim will have the city surrounded already. Think of a better plan."

She huffed for breath and did not answer. They hustled through the crowded streets. Every man and woman sprinted in the same direction as them, away from the soldiers. *We might be able to lose the soldiers among the citizens.* Darren could remain in the city another day if none of the soldiers had gotten a close enough look at him.

No, he was too large, his chiseled face too unique. Someone would recognize him, perhaps even a soldier from the previous war.

"We're going to have to fight through wherever the line is weakest," he said. "You could be right that it's the east. Where are the rest of your rebels now?"

"The center of the city."

"The market?" Darren hoped to be wrong.

"Yes."

"There are too many citizens there! It would be easier to get through a bog."

"That's where they are!" Erisena snapped.

This woman may know how to recruit, but she doesn't know how to prepare.

"I will meet you—"

Darren stopped as he noticed a woman looking back into an alley she had just passed. She seemed confused for a moment. It was just enough to tip Darren off.

"Stay behind me," he told his comrades as they neared the side opening in the street.

Two soldiers with swords but no armor stepped out in front of an archer with an arrow nocked. Darren threw his dagger into the chest of the archer as the man released his arrow. It went high.

He could not charge the swordsmen head on without a weapon, so Darren slowed and waited to counterattack.

He heard a rift open to his side. The cracking sound came with a taste in the back of his throat of something thick and fiery.

Erisena's beast, Ravitch, galloped ahead of Darren and leapt shoulder height. Its victim was too slow to get his sword up, taken backward from the creature's weight and momentum. Startled, the other swordsmen gave Darren his chance to charge.

Darren grabbed the hilt of the soldier's sword as he swung at Darren. He shouldered the man, knocking him away from his weapon.

Darren now had a sword. He felt safe, if just for a moment.

Ravitch made quick work of the screaming soldier as all three of the king's men lay on the ground. With two quick swipes, Darren cut deeply into both legs of the only one who could still get up.

With the beast now beside them, they ran deeper into the city.

A group of soldiers was close behind. Darren was still faster than his two female comrades, even with sword in hand. They would not make it through the city without another fight.

That did not matter to him now. The only hope Darren had of reuniting with his boys was to lose his pursuers. He turned to head toward the most crowded street. Of the denizens who ran the opposite way, they seemed to have a destination in mind. Many climbed through windows to remove themselves from view. But every house would be searched, Darren knew. Everyone's papers would be demanded. If he led Erisena and Lane into a home or a shop, they would be trapped there.

My sons will be questioned soon enough. It's not safe for me to be there. But reaching them was the only way he could get them out of the city.

Darren's party followed the crowded streets, attempting to lose the soldiers in the chaos. All citizens appeared too afraid to think of anyone but themselves. They crashed into each other, ripped belongings out of each other's hands, and even tried to break down doors so they could be hidden away when the soldiers came.

Darren, Erisena, and Lane weren't too far from the market in the center of the city when they made a turn and came face to face with a horde of soldiers. There was no reason to go back, for an even larger brigade trailed close behind.

"That's Erisena!" yelled the commander at the front line. His men ran for the Analyte as if her death would bring them riches. She had kept her hood on for the most part, but it didn't seem to matter.

Darren could easily kill a few of the overeager young men if he stood his ground, but he would fall soon after.

"Up onto the wall!" Darren ordered the women behind him.

The wall protected a mansion on the other side, no doubt belonging to a rich family Darren hadn't had the pleasure of meeting during all his hardships in this wretched city. He would not die here no matter what it took to save himself, and he couldn't care less about any damage that his escape route caused to the wealthy.

The wall was not only thick, it was tall. Darren would barely be able to get himself up with a jump, while most other men could not. That would be to his advantage if he could just get his comrades up there.

He bent down and grabbed Erisena by her legs and practically threw her high enough for her to grab hold. He lifted Lane up next, then he used a hand beneath each foot to give her the boost she needed to wiggle and crawl the rest of the way up.

"Take my sword," Darren told them as he held it up hilt first.

Erisena was ready first, grabbing it as Lane turned on her knees atop the wall and stupidly offered Darren a hand. He would pull her right off if he took it.

Ignoring her, Darren jumped and grabbed hold of the top of the wall. He pulled himself up with some help from his feet finding the grooves between bricks. He had to leave Erisena's beast behind, for there just wasn't enough time to help the creature up.

But to Darren's surprise, Ravitch was already there, swiping at one man jumping just high enough to take hold. A small nip was all it took for the man to scream and let go. The beast looked for another. It had round eyes with slits for pupils, akin to cat eyes. Now in the light Darren could see that the creature reminded him more of a mountain lion than a dog. It had a dense, dark coat of fur, with long claws on its feet. Its head and face appeared more like that of a bear than any other animal, with sharp fangs at the end of its snout.

The commander below ordered his men to help each other up. Darren batted away any who tried climbing up as he also looked for archers who would be the death of him and the two women. Finding none in view, he then tried to figure out the next part of their plan. There were too many tall buildings in the north for him to see over, and the streets were already overrun with soldiers. There was no point in going that way. Before he could check south, Lane was already pointing in that direction.

"Look," she said.

There were at least a thousand troops still marching into the city. A line of horsemen waited behind the foot soldiers. They would run down Erisena if she escaped, able to catch up to her no matter which direction she took.

Darren's throat closed around his next breath. Erisena would die today, and so would he and Lane unless he thought of something.

He checked to the east, where he had first assumed the majority of the army to be marching in. The hills were clear, but moving troops filled the abandoned farm.

Must you send so many, Mavrim? Is it not enough to outnumber the rebels? You must instead massacre them while the rest of your land remains unprotected?

Perhaps Erisena was right. This king did need to be removed, and soon. He cared about nothing but keeping power.

And all the men like him should be removed as well.

Darren took out his anger as he booted a soldier in the face who was about to stab Erisena in the ankle. The man fell and took down the two soldiers who had been holding his legs, but there were so many more of them that it did not seem to matter. Erisena's beast clawed anyone who got close, but it was bleeding from its furry side. A soldier must have stabbed it during the brief moment Darren took to survey the land.

"I need to go for my boys," he warned Erisena and Lane. He would have to abandon the women soon.

"If you leave us now, we will die!" Erisena cried.

"Your boys are safer without you there anyway," added Lane.

They were both right, Darren knew, but he couldn't abandon his children. They might never see him again if he left with the rebels. They could assume him to be dead.

There was some solace knowing that Rygen's mother would do her best to take care of all of them, but could she really handle three children without help?

Darren felt his energy draining. The bitter taste of defeat found the back of his throat. Here he was worried about his boys and he wouldn't even make it off this wall alive.

There was nothing he could do but keep trying to fend off the enemy. No ideas came to mind except the possibility of surrendering.

Why was it up to Darren to save these two rebels? They had gotten themselves in this mess.

"I see no way off this wall," he told them hopelessly. Perhaps Erisena would realize it was over and give herself up. Darren couldn't bring himself to suggest it, though, at least not until death was imminent...which would be as soon as archers arrived.

He and the women fought without speaking for what felt to be a long while.

"Let one of them up," Lane suddenly said with a strong tone.

Darren only had to stop slashing at heads and fingers for a moment, and suddenly two men were on the wall in front of him. They seemed almost surprised to be up there, one looking back down as if he'd forgotten something. *A plan, perhaps.* These men were driven by greed, Darren reminded himself. A bounty for Erisena's head.

The two soldiers appeared afraid to face Darren. There was just enough room for them to stand abreast, both inching forward.

"Get one of them off," Lane told him.

One soldier stopped to let the other go first as Darren approached. It was easy to duck under the wild swing of his sword. Darren didn't even need to touch the man. His own momentum took him off.

"Archers are here, sir!" someone was yelling above the clamor.

Darren had no idea what Lane had planned, but it had better be now.

The last soldier on the wall seemed more interested in finding a way down than in engaging with Darren. This gave Darren time to look over his shoulder to see Lane with her head down and her hands up, as if pushing against an invisible wall.

"Kill him, you coward!" yelled the soldiers below.

The man lifted his leg as if to walk forward but seemed to be stuck. He appeared surprised as he strained yet couldn't move against some invisible force.

"Knock him down as hard as you can!" she said.

Darren charged and slammed his shoulder against the light leather armor protecting the man's chest.

For a moment, Darren thought he had misjudged leather for steel, for it felt as if he had run into a solid wall, the force of it nearly separating Darren's shoulder from its socket. The man did not fly backward as Darren had expected but only staggered back, eventually stumbling off the wall.

However, there was a commotion below as dozens of soldiers fell, taking many others down with them.

She made a link from the similarity of their bodies and armor, Darren realized. Many others were unaffected, but enough had fallen to at least make it impossible for anyone to climb up in that moment. It gave Darren's party just enough time.

Without swords swiping at their ankles, they sprinted across the wall with Erisena's beast. They ran the entire length of the wall until it ended in front of a small smoke shop. Darren jumped onto its roof with the two women following suit. He hurried to the other side and glanced down. No soldiers yet. Many buildings along the wall blocked the soldiers from taking a direct route. He swung himself over and dropped, his comrades close behind.

Now perhaps Darren could separate, but he hadn't had time yet to figure out whether his boys were better off alone for now. He continued toward the market with the women as he thought of the best possible scenario should he leave them.

The only way Darren and his boys would be safe is if he made it to them and got them out of the city without a soldier recognizing him as a rebel. If that failed, all three of them could be imprisoned or even hung, for the family members of rebels often received the same fate, especially the males. It was possible to get them out of the city, he supposed, but incredibly dangerous and difficult. Soldiers from the last war might recognize him as DVend Quim even if he was no longer running with rebels, and it was unlikely that the soldiers were letting anyone flee the city, no matter what their papers said.

Andar and Leo would not be safe with him, yet they should at least be safe from arrest or harm if he was not seen with them.

Was this really what Darren must accept? Was he to abandon them?

Just temporarily, he told himself. He would find a way to come back as soon as the soldiers cleared enough for a path. All he could do in this moment was to keep himself and these women alive.

He was still wondering whether he had made the right decision when they arrived at the market and joined what had to be at least five hundred rebels, all with weapons ready.

"You should've led them out already!" Erisena yelled at a man Darren had not met before.

"We wouldn't leave without you. East has the clearest path, but we still have to fight through them. We must rush now so that we do not become surrounded. If we are, then we're going to need your cre—"

"Not in the city," she interrupted. "I told you I would not summon him in the city no matter what."

"All of us could be killed here, Erisena!"

"Not in the city!" she repeated. "Too many innocents will be killed."

He let out a quick grumble before turning to address the waiting army. "We run east!" he commanded. "Protect each other, but do not stop no matter what."

An arrow zipped past Darren's eyes and went through the commander's chest. He collapsed with teeth gritted. Erisena grabbed his hand and tried to pull him up, but he snatched it out of her hold.

"Run, you fool," he managed to get out.

Erisena bolted. "Get out of the city!" she yelled to her rebels.

Darren could hear from the panic in her voice just how good their chances were of making it.

He abandoned the rebels, turning south toward his sons without a look back.

Atop the wall around the mansion, he had seen glimpses of soldiers entering shops and homes. They would question everyone in the city as well as ask for their papers. If the soldiers had any suspicion they were speaking to rebels, they would imprison or torture them right there. The soldiers would steal, and even rape and kill the rest of the people if they wanted to so long as they figured they could get away with it.

Darren could not reach his house before the soldiers had surpassed it during their march through the city, but it was better this way. With his children having already been questioned and their papers inspected, their house would no longer be a target.

Never had Darren wished to be smaller until that moment. He was too large to go unnoticed in a crowd. Some of the enemy soldiers or commanders had probably already recognized him. Word was no doubt spreading that DVend Quim was here along with Erisena. He was certain another bounty was out not just for his capture, but for his head.

He skulked through the streets, most of which were nearly empty now. Everyone had found shelter somewhere, but that didn't stop the screaming. Darren heard doors breaking and shrieks of fear. How could he forget what kind of king Mavrim was? Erisena was right about the need to replace him. The importance of Darren's children had masked everything else that used to be important. They were his world. But so was this, the city where his boys had to work and suffer. And now they had to witness the wrath of a tyrant. Perhaps the best way to help them after all was to change the world, and with their help.

Darren was getting too confident. He had walked through many streets without encountering a soldier, and he was already thinking of his family's future. First, he had to get his sons out of the city.

But the closer he got to his house, the more soldiers he found. Eventually, every street was filled with men of the same leather armor as those who had tried to kill him on the wall, swords as well. Darren would be able to fight through more than a few of them, but there was no point in trying if he couldn't kill them all, for that would be the only way he made it.

There wasn't one street south that he could take to get closer to his house now. He would have to take a longer route and circle around, but the soldiers had come through every street, forcing him back north just to avoid being seen. He supposed he could drop his sword and hope to walk past them. He would give them his false papers if they asked. There was a small chance they might let him go. A very small chance, for all it took was one man to recognize him.

And when that happened, all of this was over.

He tried to think of another way. What about using the roofs? No, they were spaced too far apart, and he wasn't exactly inconspicuous jumping from building to building. The noise alone would be enough for him to be noticed.

As he tried to think of something, he saw many soldiers grab women. They ripped off the women's hoods to check their hair, no doubt looking for the Analyte. They questioned everyone about an Analyte woman, but no one seemed to know anything.

The more time Darren wasted, the harder it would be to rejoin Erisena. He cursed under his breath. That really was the only choice, at least for now.

He ran east.

CHAPTER THIRTY

Leo had been headed home with Rygen when they'd heard the start of the battle. His first instinct had been to run, but then he'd found his courage. He would protect Rygen this time. He would not be a coward.

They had made it to their homes before the soldiers had crossed by. Rygen had separated to check if her mother was already there. When she didn't come back, Leo figured that Verona was there and had told Rygen not to leave the house. Otherwise, Rygen would've stayed with Leo and Andar.

Leo's brother had climbed atop their roof during the first signs of battle. He'd told Leo that soldiers were coming into the city from every direction.

But now an hour had passed. Andar had returned to wait with Leo in a place that wouldn't be their home much longer. They could do little else but sit and hope that nothing would happen to them, or to Rygen and her mother. But it was their father they most worried about.

There was only one answer as to why he wasn't here yet. Something bad had to have happened to him.

Andar had insisted that Father wasn't dead. Leo didn't know how his brother could be sure of this, but he felt the same way and was glad to hear Andar say it. Leo trusted his brother more than himself right now. He would do whatever Andar said.

There was little conversation in the time they waited. The soldiers had to be here for the rebels, they agreed, just as Father said they would. And just as Father had said, there were so many that it didn't seem that any number of rebels Erisena could have gathered could fight them off.

So many people would be killed today, but Leo didn't think his father would be one of them.

"He would only lose against a hundred soldiers, all surrounding him," Leo told Andar. "And he wouldn't let himself be put in that situation."

"It could just be one archer," Andar said darkly.

"Father wouldn't give them a good shot."

Andar thought for a moment before nodding.

The conversation repeated itself many times in Leo's head as they waited. He wondered if Andar really believed him or had only agreed to make him feel better, but Leo was too afraid to ask.

As the door opened, hope brimmed. It fell as two soldiers walked brazenly into the kitchen as if this was their own home. One passed between Leo and his brother without more than a glance at each of them and went into Father's bedroom. The other spoke.

"Papers, and hurry up."

Leo and Andar already had their papers in their pockets and handed them over.

The mustached man's eyes told Leo this soldier didn't care about finding good, only wrong. He stared at Leo first, then at Andar. He seemed uninterested until someone shouting made him turn his head. A reflex told Leo that now would be the only time to get away. He could grab the knife from the table and stab the man in the neck before he and Andar fled.

Leo's breath caught. He could do it—he could. But there was no reason to. Not yet.

The other soldier came out of Darren's room and went straight into the boys' room. Both men wore leather to protect themselves, but Leo wasn't sure it was strong enough to stop a knife. He knew they didn't have plated armor because it was expensive. There were so many of them. Not all could be completely protected. These men probably weren't of high rank. They probably weren't wealthy, either.

The other isn't looking only for Father. He's looking for anything to steal.

As if sensing Leo's discomfort, Andar put his hand on his brother's shoulder.

"Everything's by the law," Andar told the solider.

The man's moustache twitched as the solider glanced up from their papers. He stared as if contemplating something, then handed them back rather roughly, crinkling Leo's. Leo quickly began to straighten it, but a question interrupted him.

"Where is your mother and father?"

Where are, Leo corrected in his mind.

"Our mother's dead," Andar answered. "Our father should've been home by now. We are worried. He works with the Digging Guild. Do you think you could look for him? Something might've happened."

"Come on," the soldier called to the other.

The second soldier walked between them again, showing Andar a mean look as if annoyed there had been nothing to take. When they left, Andar quickly closed the door after them.

Leo and Andar went back to waiting quietly. It would be dark soon. Father certainly wouldn't be at the mines anymore. Andar had only attempted to bother the soldiers into leaving. Leo had feared his brother's temper might get them in trouble, but Leo had been wrong to worry. So long as Father came home, all three of them should be safe.

It wasn't long before shouting could be heard, this time close enough for Leo to understand the words. "Rebels here!"

"I told you we're not. You're making a mistake!" a man replied. The terror in his voice scared Leo. He had never heard a grown man speak like that before. He and Andar ran to their window and opened it for a look.

The soldier shouting about rebels had his sword drawn, but he still seemed surprised by the rather thin man coming out of his house with his own blade, about to strike.

Two more citizens, equipped with swords, came around the outer walls. They swarmed the lone soldier, each getting a clean stab in where his armor did not cover his flesh. He screamed, "Rebels!" again, attempting to flee rather than fight.

Leo knew he shouldn't watch as the man was cut down, but he couldn't take his eyes away.

The three rebels darted off when they were done, disappearing around the small homes. The sounds of their next bout rang out, and the distant screams Leo had become accustomed to were drowned out.

Through Leo's fear, he had a single curiosity. "Why are there rebels here and not with Erisena?"

"They must've hoped they wouldn't be found. Now that they have been, they will fight to their death," Andar replied.

Leo hoped Andar wasn't predicting the same outcome for them. Leo was too small to fight.

But he remembered his promise to Rygen and decided to search for courage within himself. He went to his bedroom to look out the window. No soldiers seemed to be entering her house. Perhaps they had already come and gone, like they had at Leo's.

He rejoined his brother in hopes of another glimpse of the rebels. He could still hear them fighting. Perhaps they would make it to Erisena, wherever she was. Father was probably with her now, for he said he would be meeting with her to find out where his sister was.

Another group of rebels with swords hurried down the street. They were probably on their way to join the others. Leo noticed flashes of red blood upon their weapons. He couldn't tell how much of it was theirs and how much was their enemies'. That made five of them altogether. Did such a small group have any hope?

"Stand back," said a woman. "Let my beast make pieces out of these rebels." Her voice was too calm for the situation. It irked Leo, like watching a guard standing still in a rowdy tavern. This woman's confidence of the rebels' destruction was an insult to their capability. Leo wanted her to pay even before glimpsing her. He ran with his brother into their father's room to look out the window.

She was tall, with broad shoulders that made her as large as the male soldier at her side. She wore leather armor just like the men, a sheathed sword on her belt. Her hair was black and short. If it wasn't for the feminine features of her face, Leo would've thought her to be a man.

The soldier to her side seemed to be hesitating as he stared at her.

"Go!" she demanded.

At that, he ran as a man does without pride, only fear.

Leo was glad when the woman ran toward the sounds of battle, for it took her away from them and Rygen.

Leo and his brother were completely silent as they waited for the sound of the summoner to call her beast here from the other realm. Leo was unsure if it had happened yet, as he heard nothing but the repetitive clash of steel and the screams that followed. But then there was a silence unlike any since this had begun. Leo could feel terror in the air akin to when someone drops and breaks something expensive. A fierce roar broke out.

"I told you not to summon an incenfiend!" yelled a man.

The street before Leo was empty, and yet he could still feel the presence of the creature. He did not know how.

"You'd rather your troops be killed?" the summoner retorted.

"It's just as likely to kill innocents as it is our enemies. It could even kill our own."

"Then you'd better flee. I want to see how it fights."

A silence followed that confused Leo. No one screamed. No one seemed to be fighting any longer. Perhaps his brother knew why.

"What's happening?"

"I think everyone's running from it."

The silence drew on, until finally Leo heard a woman shriek far away. There was a terrible sound of gore that Leo tried to not listen to, but the woman's screams were piercing. Then, just as suddenly, they stopped. The next thing Leo heard was a group of people yelling to run.

The sound of a heavy patter followed that shamed the power of a galloping horse. Suddenly, he caught a glimpse of the beast, a quick view between houses in the distance. It was long and thick, dark in color, flesh not fur.

Soldiers flew down the very street that was once empty. A few cursed a name.

"Celia!"

The incenfiend chased a lone soldier the other way, right toward Rygen's house.

Keep going, Leo willed it. *Do not stop.*

But something seemed to catch its attention as it halted suddenly, Leo's heart as well. Then it turned around to head back toward the shoddy walls of Rygen's home.

It had a face with more teeth than any beast should need, with one short pair of horns curving down from its temples and another rising up from its jaw. It looked mean, as if destruction was all it knew. It was thick with muscle, yet flesh-covered bones still jutted out around each curve of its leg and spine.

It put its massive legs up against Rygen's wall, nearly reaching her roof, then turned up its head as if looking for a scent. It let itself down with no small crash, then came around the corner. It stopped to roar as if angered. There was no doubt in Leo's mind anymore. It wanted a way in, and it would find one soon enough. Even the wooden plank across the door wouldn't be enough to stop it.

Leo grabbed the knife from the table. His legs were shaking. He couldn't move. Where had his courage gone? He heard Andar ask what he was doing, but Leo was too afraid to even make use of his voice.

She's going to die if you do nothing.

He finally found his courage again and was surprised at just how much strength it gave him. Suddenly, he felt capable of handling whatever would happen. He would not die today. Nor would Rygen. He ran from his house as the incenfiend came around the side of Rygen's home, no doubt finding the door on the other side. Leo heard a crack of wood. Rygen and her mother screamed.

There was a small voice in Leo's head telling him that this was what he had trained for. He must remember what his father had said. *Do not succumb to your* emotions. *Do not fight wildly. Your mind is the best weapon of all.*

He blocked out the sounds of Rygen's mother screaming. By the time he had made it to the doorway, Verona had stopped. She was spread across the kitchen floor, her body and face torn to pieces. She still seemed to be alive, but there was so much blood. She would be gone in a moment.

The incenfiend had left her behind it as it now approached Rygen with a strange caution to each step. It stopped growling, making Leo pause. It didn't seem as if it would ravage Rygen as it did her mother, nor did it seem to hear Leo creeping closer behind it. The beast was too focused on Rygen, who had backed into the wall and shrunk down into a ball.

The incenfiend edged closer, sniffing around her face. Rygen half stifled a cry, whimpering. She looked like a toddler in front of the giant animal, her eyes as wide as they could be.

Leo was almost close enough to stab his knife into the back leg of the beast, but what good would that do? He had only one strike. He had to kill with it.

A floorboard creaked underneath Leo's step. The beast turned and lunged at him so quickly that Leo didn't remember getting the knife up in time, but there it was between him and the incenfiend. He had a strong hold of it even after it had bounced against the beast's teeth.

The incenfiend reeled back and swiped one of its massive claws at Leo, but Darren had swung at him many times just like that during practice. Leo ducked and saw an opportunity.

He jumped forward and plunged the blade into the side of the beast's neck. He felt flesh break under the dagger's point and expected the beast to fall, but another claw came up from the other side too fast for Leo to dodge.

He was thrown across the kitchen, rolling until a wall stopped him. Leo didn't check whether he was injured. He could get up, so he did and looked for something else he could use to defend himself as the incenfiend came at him. The blunt end of the knife stuck from its neck. The beast was huge, making the knife seem insignificant. What could stop it?

Leo dove out of the way to roll toward the only other weapon he could identify, one of two chairs that had been knocked away from an upturned table.

He grabbed the chair, turned, and just got it up in time, legs held outward, as the beast pounced. The force seemed to go right through the chair. Leo lost his grip as he slammed into another wall. He couldn't tell what had happened to the chair.

The beast came at him again. Blood poured out of its mouth and neck, its roar wet. Leo had nothing left to defend himself. The incenfiend jumped. Leo shrunk as low as he could at the last moment. He felt heat above him as he heard the beast crash into the wall.

Leo rolled away in fear of being crushed, but his leg got caught—his pant leg under one of the beast's claws. He tried to pry it loose with a panicked turn, noticing his brother charging the beast out of the corner of his eye.

The incenfiend, too, had begun to turn, but it didn't seem to see Andar jumping and bringing down the chair over the side of its melon head. One of its horns took the brunt of it, the chair shattering. The beast lost its footing, allowing Leo to slip out and move away as it stumbled and fell.

Andar seemed to be going for the knife when the beast thrashed at Andar from the floor. He leaned back to avoid it, then rushed close to the beast to pull out the knife from its neck.

Andar slammed the blade down into the creature's head, between its top two horns. It thrashed wildly as it roared and slipped, flinging Andar into the wall. The incenfiend tried to get up but fell. It tried again, only to fall harder this time. Finally, the beast's eyes closed as it gave a last twitch.

Leo turned to check on Rygen, but it only took a moment to see she was unscathed. She was walking toward her mother, horror in her eyes. There was no doubt that Verona was already gone. The sight of it turned Leo's stomach upside down.

He wanted to get Rygen away from the terrible image, but he could do nothing but retch. Fortunately, Andar was holding Rygen and turning her away from her mother by the time Leo was done. She wept into his chest.

"We're going to our house," Andar announced as he steered Rygen toward the door.

"I need to stay here!" she said as she fought him.

"She's gone, Rygen." Andar overpowered her. "There's no reason for you to look." Soon he had her out of her house. "Come on, Leo," he called back.

Leo had forgotten himself for a moment, feeling everything through Rygen. He didn't know what to do, though he knew Andar to be right. There was no reason to stay, except for one thing.

He went over and pulled the knife out of the incenfiend's head to take back with him. They might need it again.

*****

The fight through the city was bloody, but Darren had made it out alive. Night had fallen upon them. Many of the rebels fighting alongside him had been struck down. The soldiers had shown no interest in capturing them. Darren had watched one rebel, with a deep cut that prevented him from running, flipped over onto his back and stabbed through his heart.

Darren had the blood of many soldiers on his sword. It had once belonged to a soldier. Therefore, it had belonged to the king. Now it was Darren's.

DVend. His name was DVend again. Enough soldiers had recognized him from the war for word to have spread among his enemies. There was no hiding his identity anymore. He would come to terms later with what that meant for him and his children, for he was not safe yet even if he and the rebels were out of the city.

He had, however, made the right decision to leave. Some rebels had joined them late in the escape. During the fight against the king's army, these men and women had spread word about many rebels still in Jatn, safe, their identities still hidden. The soldiers were not killing those they believed to be innocent.

That meant Leo and Andar should be safe, though Darren did fear for Rygen and her mother. It wasn't a question of innocence that put them at risk; it was the female parts on their bodies. The soldiers of the king were known for more than pillaging, yet Mavrim had never seemed to care.

Hopefully, there were enough moral soldiers in the army to stop the others, for there was nothing Darren could do now but stay alive.

"Charging horsemen!" someone called out.

Panic spread across the rebels who separated and screamed as a thick line of horsemen rushed over the nearby hill. These were no doubt the prized cavaliers of King Orello's army that Darren had seen earlier while atop the wall around the mansion. Stories said that this was the trained brigade who had chased down thousands of rebels over the last century.

They gained on Erisena's troops quickly. Darren could only be safe if the rest of the rebels were as well, and it was only the mountains a mile ahead that would provide the cover they needed to lose their pursuers.

There was no hope of making it now with horsemen behind them.

"We have to turn and fight," Darren told Erisena so she could give the command. Every other command had been done in the same fashion, and it was the only way the lot of them had made it out of the city. Erisena had no mind for tactics. It was no wonder she had put so much effort into recruiting DVend Quim.

Darren knew this was not a fight they could win, but dying while fighting was better than being run down while fleeing and stabbed in the back.

"Take them to the mountain," Erisena told Darren as she stopped.

"What are you doing?" Darren stopped with Erisena, but Lane grabbed his arm and tried to pull him with her.

"Trust her," Lane implored.

Darren made the decision to do as the women told him, picking up speed once again. He was about to order the rest of the tired rebels, who he had expected to slow when their leader had, to keep going. But to his surprise, half of them showed no signs of stopping. The others appeared aware of Erisena as they glanced back at her with what seemed to be gratitude. Surely they didn't think she could stop all the cavaliers on her own. But perhaps they knew something Darren didn't.

He left Erisena behind, though that didn't stop him from watching over his shoulder.

She made a wide arc with her arm. Dark edges formed in the air, trailing her hand. The black lines widened. White and gray cracks formed. All the floating strokes of color seemed to waver unsteadily as Erisena made a new black line along the ground. Then she pushed out her hands and a dark rift burst open between the borders.

It was the largest rift Darren had seen, and yet it grew even larger until it was the size of his house. A massive creature bounded out, its head tucked low to clear the rift.

Darren did not know the name for such a creature. He had never seen a beast so large. The behemoth straightened its neck and head, growing taller still. It made the approaching horsemen look like little toys.

The creature looked around and found Erisena behind it. She pointed at the cavaliers and shouted something Darren couldn't make out but was clearly a command to fight. The beast obeyed with an agile turn and an earthshaking stomp.

Erisena fled. Darren and Lane waited for her to catch up. He noticed tears in Erisena's eyes as she neared.

"It had to be done," Lane told her.

The sight of the beast had stopped the cavaliers, at least for the moment. There were so many that not even a creature of this size could fight them all back, but it would allow everyone to make it to the mountains.

"All those years gaining his loyalty," Erisena said as she fled with them. "Just to be sacrificed. I had hoped for so much more out of him."

It was finally sinking in—Darren was going to live, and so were so many others. He didn't know how he was going to get back to his children. The soldiers would take control of the city and the Tisary soon. They knew who he was. They would kill him the moment they saw him again.

He cursed loudly as he realized that he still had all his family's coin. All of it! Not only was he abandoning his children, he was leaving them with absolutely nothing. He stopped, unable to help it. He couldn't go on.

Lane was grabbing him again. Erisena was yelling at him. He hardly noticed either of them as he tried to think of something.

Eventually, both women were pulling him too hard to ignore. He shed a few tears himself as he fled.

He looked at the people he would have to call allies. There were no animals with them, no bags of food or supplies. All of them would make it through the day, but many would die in the week to come.

He would live, however. He would find water and food even if he had to trek through the entire mountain range to reach it. He would find a way back to his children.

*****

The three children waited for Darren to return. Andar knew that's what the three of them were—children. He couldn't keep the thought out of his head, but it was better than the other thought that made his legs feel weak, the fear that his father would not come back.

Rygen seemed unable to speak or hear anything, so Andar and Leo had stopped trying to comfort her. The three of them waited in silence, each in their own chair in the kitchen of Andar and Leo's house.

They waited through the night. Andar had fallen asleep and awoken many times. He noticed Rygen and Leo dozing off as well. No one seemed to want to stay awake, but no one was able to remain asleep, either. They didn't share a single word.

Andar dreaded the coming morning, but eventually there was no denying that it was upon them, light filtering in through the window shutters. He was the oldest here. It was his responsibility to decide what to do.

He stood up and found Leo's and Rygen's eyes on him instantly.

"Father was either killed with the rebels or escaped with them," Andar said. "I believe he escaped, but we don't know when he's coming back. We can't sit here any longer waiting for him."

"What do we do?" Leo asked.

"The two of you should go to the Bookbinding Guild. Hopefully, it hasn't been destroyed. I'm going to see just how much coin the soldiers carry on them."

"They'll kill you if you're caught."

"We'll starve as homeless orphans if I don't."

There was indifference to both their tones. It almost felt to Andar as if they were reading a script. Andar had said what he needed to say, and Leo had done the same. They both knew what would happen now, and there was no point to argue about it.

There was one concern, though. Where would they live? A man or woman fourteen or older had to reside in the house provided by the Farmers' Guild for the family to stay there. Rygen's father died when she was a baby, and her mother was now gone. She would be recorded as an orphan soon, so Rygen had one week to leave her home.

She could stay with Andar and Leo. Hopefully they could keep up the facade for a little while that Darren Litxer still resided there. But then what? They surely couldn't pretend Darren was there long enough for Andar to turn fourteen and be deemed a man.

That still meant someone had to work on a farm so the Farmers' Guild wouldn't take away their permission. However, Andar had gotten his family banned from all farm work in the city.

He looked at Rygen. She had her gaze on Leo until he looked over at her, then it darted down to the ground. Andar couldn't ask her to do farm work. She had just lost her mother in such a gruesome way.

Rygen glanced up at him with a sparkle in her eyes. She stood up.

"Someone needs to work for the Farmers' Guild so we have a house to live in," she said in the same tone of indifference. "I will do it before a week is up. It's the least I can do to thank the two of you for saving my life."

"Thank you," Andar said before Leo could object.

But Rygen sat back down and gave an exhausted sigh.

It was silent for a moment. Andar realized that it was still up to him to get them out of those chairs.

"Let's all meet back here in the evening," Andar said, feeling sorry for the day Leo and especially Rygen would have now. He figured she would continue working at the Bookbinding Guild for much of the week. She should ask Gartel to keep up the funding for her to live in her home.

Andar wondered if he should suggest it. If it worked, then he and Leo could stay there without anyone needing to work on the farm.

Give her time to reach the right decisions on her own.

Rygen looked toward her house. "My mother…"

"I will make sure the soldiers give her a proper burial," Andar told her. "It might take some time. Don't go back in there until I know it's been done. I will get your belongings for you now."

He waited for her to show she understood with a nod. Then he left.

The door to Rygen's house was broken off its hinges. Andar was surprised that no one had come to loot at least the kitchen table, but then he saw Verona's mauled body again. The sight of it was bad enough to scare off even the most hardened thieves. She was strewn across the floor, a pool of her blood reaching almost from wall-to-wall. Andar didn't know how he was going to walk across without it getting on his boots.

Then there was the dead beast in the other corner. It almost seemed capable of returning to live, sparking fear in Andar's chest.

He heard cries of anguish and weeping all around. This wasn't the only death, and he had a feeling there would be more. He knew his father to still be alive, but would he be able to return to the city...ever? He had taken their coin with them. All their coin.

How were they going to make it without any coin and without Father? Andar became too weak in his knees to walk another step. He collapsed there and cried, letting out all his fears and worries with sobs that he tried to keep quiet, but soon he gave up.

He cried out in anguish like so many others around him, thankful for their noise. He hoped Rygen and Leo couldn't hear him, for there was nothing he could do to stop himself now as he wailed.

He didn't know how he was going to go on. What could he do? His father had struggled so much to take care of him and Leo, and Father was unmeasurably stronger than Andar.

He cried until even shedding tears was too tiresome to continue. Then he lay on the cold wood of Rygen's kitchen, wishing he had perished instead of her mother. Let this responsibility fall upon her, not him.

But it hadn't.

Out of tears, he had nothing left to do but stand up and go fetch Rygen's belongings. He would see them through this, even if it killed him.

END OF BOOK 1

Reviews

Thank you for reading. Please consider leaving a review. They are very important to the life of a book, especially for a self-published author like myself.

New Releases

To receive an automatic email when I release a new book, go here and enter your email:
http://eepurl.com/Aletn

Your email address will never be shared, and you can unsubscribe at any time.

Author and Series Information

If you want to discuss the book with me or just want to say hello, email me at btnarro@gmail.com or look up my Facebook page (B.T. Narro) and add me. You can also visit my website at www.btnarro.com.

If you enjoyed the book and are looking for something else to read as you wait for the sequel, I recommend taking a look at my other 4 series. There are 17 books throughout those series, all taking place in the same world as each other, which is a different world than Aathon from this book. The first novel in this other world is Bastial Energy. Here is a timeline of all the other books, each series related to the last and completed.

THE RHYTHM OF RIVALRY SERIES
Book 1: Bastial Energy
Book 1.5: The Sartious Mage
Book 2: Bastial Steel
Book 3: Bastial Explosion
Book 4: Bastial Frenzy
Book 5: Bastial Sentinels

THE PYFORIAL MAGE SERIES
Book 1: Fire Games
Book 2: Wrath Games
Book 3: Pyforial Games

THE KIN OF KINGS SERIES
Book 1: Kin of Kings
Book 2: Rise of Legends
Book 3: Shadows of Kings
Book 4: A Crumble of Walls

Book 5: The Edge of Shadow

THE MORTAL MAGE SERIES
Book 1: Awaken
Book 2: Akorell Break
Book 3: The Mortal Mage

Thank you for supporting me by purchasing my book. I'm so lucky to be able to write for a living. I will do my best to finish the sequel to Echoes of a Fallen Kingdom as fast as I can. I hope you enjoyed the story.

Made in the USA
Middletown, DE
26 February 2020